# TARGETING THE DEPUTY

## DELORES FOSSEN

# CONARD COUNTY: CHRISTMAS BODYGUARD

## RACHEL LEE

MILLS & BOON

First Published in Great Britain 2021
by Mills & Boon, an imprint of HarperCollins*Publishers* Ltd
1 London Bridge Street, London, SE1 9GF

www.harpercollins.co.uk

HarperCollins*Publishers*
1st Floor, Watermarque Building,
Ringsend Road, Dublin 4, Ireland

*Targeting the Deputy* © 2021 Delores Fossen
*Conard County: Christmas Bodyguard* © 2021 Susan Civil-Brown

ISBN: 978-0-263-28360-0

1121

MIX
Paper from
responsible sources
FSC® C007454

This book is produced from independently certified FSC™ paper to ensure responsible forest management.

For more information visit: www.harpercollins.co.uk/green

Printed and Bound in Spain using 100% Renewable electricity at CPI Black Print, Barcelona

# TARGETING
# THE DEPUTY

**DELORES FOSSEN**

# Chapter One

Deputy Leo Logan heard the movement behind him a split second too late. He whirled around, automatically reaching for his gun. But before he could draw it, he felt the pain slice over his arm.

He caught a glimpse of the knife. Another glimpse of the guy holding it. The man was wearing all black and had on a ski mask—also black. He was lunging with the knife to try to cut Leo again.

That gave Leo a major surge of adrenaline. And a hit of raw anger. He didn't know who the hell this idiot was, but Leo had no intention of just standing there while he stabbed him.

Leo ducked, avoiding the next slice, and in the same motion lowered his head and rammed right into the guy's gut. His attacker made a strangled sound, like a balloon dteflating. Leo had obviously knocked the breath out of him, but he took it one step further. He stood upright and plowed his fist into his attacker's face. The guy didn't fall but only staggered back, so Leo punched him again.

The man dropped to his knees on the ground, the knife clattering on the concrete next to him.

Leo heard another sound. Running footsteps behind him. He pivoted in that direction, this time managing to draw his gun. However, it wasn't the threat his body had geared up for. It was his brother.

Sheriff Barrett Logan.

It wasn't a surprise to see Barrett since this was the parking lot of the Mercy Ridge Sheriff's Office, but it was the last place Leo had expected to be attacked. It took a lot of guts, or stupidity, to come after a lawman on his own turf.

"What the hell happened?" Barrett snapped. He didn't wait for a response before he added, "Your arm's bleeding. Are you okay?"

Leo gathered his breath and tried to figure out the answer to his brother's question. He didn't think the wound was that deep, but it was already throbbing like a bad tooth. The knife had cut through his shirt, making a gash on his forearm. And there was blood. Thankfully, the wound wasn't gushing, but it was enough that he'd need it cleaned and bandaged.

"This moron attacked me," Leo growled.

As if he'd declared war on it, Leo kicked the knife away from the man, reached down and yanked off the ski mask. It was almost 6:00 p.m. but there was still plenty of light, so he had no trouble seeing the guy. Brown hair, brown eyes. Bulky build.

He was a stranger.

"Who are you?" Leo demanded, and that was just the first of many questions he had for this goon.

Barrett moved in to frisk him.

"I want a lawyer," the guy yelled.

Leo groaned. He didn't mind people exercising their civil rights, but this jerk hadn't minded violating Leo's rights by knifing him.

Barrett cuffed the man, dragging him to his feet. His

brother took a wallet from the guy's pocket and handed it to Leo.

"Milton Hough," Leo relayed to Barrett. "He's got a San Antonio address."

Leo had known the guy wasn't local. Mercy Ridge was a small ranching town, and Leo had lived here his entire life. He knew every resident and vice versa, and he was certain he'd never laid eyes on Milton.

"I want a lawyer," Milton repeated, shouting now. "Call Olivia Nash, and she'll get one for me."

Despite his throbbing arm, that got Leo's full attention, and everything inside him went still. Unlike Milton Hough, that name was *very* familiar to Leo. In fact, Olivia was the mother of his one-year-old son, Cameron, and Leo and she were in the middle of a nasty custody battle.

One that Leo didn't want to believe had just gotten a whole lot nastier.

"Olivia?" Barrett questioned, his eyes meeting Leo's.

"Yeah," the thug verified. "Just get my phone out of my jacket pocket. The last call I got was from her, so her number's on top."

"Right," Leo snarled. "And I'm to believe some idiot who'd attack a cop."

"Check the phone for yourself," Milton offered.

Leo debated it for a few seconds before he reached into Milton's jacket pocket and took out his cell. It felt as if he'd been clubbed again when he saw Olivia's name and number there.

*Hell.*

"Told you she called me," Milton said, and while his tone wasn't exactly a gloat, it was close.

Barrett certainly wasn't gloating. He was cursing and

looking at Leo with a mountain of concern. "I'll book this guy. Go to the hospital, get your arm checked and then you can go see Olivia. You sure you're okay to drive? I can have the ambulance pick you up."

"I'm fine," Leo snapped.

He ignored the pain in his arm, got in his truck and drove away once Barrett had Milton inside the police station. There was a deputy and a dispatcher working this shift, so Barrett would have help if he needed it. Maybe Barrett would be able to find some answers, too, but Leo hoped to get a jump-start on that by seeing Olivia.

Olivia didn't live far, only a couple of miles away in the nearby town of Culver Crossing, so it only took Leo a few minutes before he pulled into the driveway of the Craftsman-style house. It was small and modest, not exactly the kind of place most folks would believe an *heiress* should live, but Olivia had bought it so that Cameron would be closer to Leo. The For Sale sign in front of it reminded him, though, of the rift between them.

Had that rift caused Olivia to go off the deep end and hire someone to hurt him? Or even kill him?

Leo didn't want to believe it. After all, he and Olivia had once been lovers. But they hadn't been in love. Not the kind of love that lasted anyway.

That was one of those "fine line" distinctions.

What they'd had was a short affair that had ended in her sudden breakup with him. When Leo had found out she was pregnant, Olivia hadn't denied it was his child, but she certainly hadn't done anything to remedy their breakup. And now she was challenging their agreement so she could move Cameron out of state.

Since his arm was still bleeding, Leo tore off his shirt-sleeve and tied it around the gash like a makeshift bandage. That way, Cameron wouldn't see any blood. His little boy wasn't old enough to understand what'd happened, but he might be alarmed if he realized his dad had been injured.

Leo got out of his truck, went straight to Olivia's door and knocked. Impatience caused him to knock again just a few seconds later. He finally heard the locks being disengaged. The front door opened.

Olivia.

She clearly hadn't been expecting company because she was wearing jeans and a baggy T-shirt, and her dark brown hair was scooped up in a messy ponytail. Cameron wasn't with her. Under normal circumstances, Leo would have wanted to see his son, but he was thankful for some privacy. Privacy that he ensured by stepping inside and shutting the door behind him. Olivia didn't have any close neighbors on either side of her house, but there was one across the street.

"Oh my God, you're bleeding." Olivia's normally cool green eyes widened.

He ignored her and glanced around. "Where's Cameron? Is he with the nanny?"

She shook her head, her attention still on his arm. "He's asleep. He missed his afternoon nap and was so cranky that I went ahead and put him to bed early. I sent Izzie home."

Izzie Landon was the nanny, and while Leo liked the woman, he was glad she wasn't there, either.

"What happened?" Olivia asked.

"You tell me. Milton Hough." He threw the name out there and watched for any signs of recognition.

Leo didn't see any.

He wished he could say that he knew her well enough

to know if she was hiding the truth, but he obviously wasn't a good judge when it came to Olivia. He definitely wouldn't have had an affair with her if he'd thought she was capable of sending a thug after him. And if she'd truly done that, there was no way in hell he was going to let his son stay another moment with her.

"Milton Hough?" she repeated, seeming genuinely confused. "Who is he?"

Leo continued to stare at her. "About ten minutes ago, he came after me in the parking lot of the sheriff's office. He had a knife and did this to me." He tipped his head to his injured arm.

Olivia opened her mouth. Closed it. Then she gasped. "This man tried to kill you?"

"Yeah." Leo dragged in a breath before he continued. "Then, as Barrett was arresting him, he cried for a lawyer and said I was to call you."

"Me?" she blurted out. "Why would he say that?"

"You tell me. I checked his phone, and you called him about a half hour ago."

"No." Olivia frantically shook her head. "I didn't."

"I saw your number in his phone," Leo argued, and had to tamp down the anger. However, he didn't tamp down his own confusion and his cop's instincts. Now that he was thinking straight, he had to ask himself why Olivia would have left any record of her contact with Milton if she'd hired the man to do him harm.

And the answer was—she wouldn't have.

"Show me your phone," he insisted.

Some of the color drained from her face. "I can't. I lost it. I don't know where, but I was going to drive into San Antonio in the morning and get a new one."

"You lost it," he mumbled and then silently cursed.

Before Cameron had been born, that was profanity Leo would have said aloud, but he'd learned to tamp that down, too.

"Yes." Her breath swooshed out, and Olivia looked as if she might stagger back. Or even collapse. She didn't. She steeled herself and met him eye to eye. "Someone must have used my phone to call that man."

Leo could see that happening. Of course, that led him to the next question. Or rather, to a comment.

"Your father," was all he said.

Samuel Nash. He was a rich cattle broker, and he hated Leo for getting involved with Olivia, his precious daughter.

She shook her head again, denial all over her face. "You can't think my father's responsible," Olivia insisted.

Samuel had never had a friendly word for Leo, had always treated Leo like dirt, but it was still a stretch to believe the man was capable of something like this.

"When and where is the last place you saw your phone?" Leo persisted.

More of that color left her face and she hesitated for a long time. "I was at work in my office...at my father's."

It didn't surprise Leo that's where she'd last used her phone. Olivia was often at her family's estate just outside San Antonio, and she did, indeed, have an office there where she ran her late mother's charity foundation.

"I didn't notice it was missing until I got home," she went on. "The pharmacy here had some of those no-contract phones and I bought one so I could call Bernice and have her look for mine."

Bernice Saylor, the household manager for the Nash estate, would have been a good person to contact. Well, good for Olivia anyway. Bernice had made it clear to Leo that she hated him as much as Samuel did. Apparently, Bernice didn't think her boss's daughter should have been slumming around with a small-town cop.

"Bernice couldn't find my phone," Olivia added. "But it's possible I dropped it somewhere. Maybe even here when I was getting out of my car."

Yeah, that was possible. But if that'd happened, it meant the person who'd found it had used it to set up Olivia, to make her look guilty of orchestrating the attack against him.

To the best of Leo's knowledge, there was no one in Mercy Ridge who had that kind of grudge against Olivia. But Milton might know for certain who'd hired him. Leo figured he was more likely to get a truthful answer from him than he would from Samuel or Bernice. Still, both of them would have to be questioned.

"You really need to have someone take a look at that arm," Olivia murmured.

When he glanced down at the makeshift bandage, Leo saw the fresh blood seeping through the cloth. Mercy. He might need stitches, after all. But there was an even bigger concern here.

"Look, I don't know what's going on," he admitted, "but if someone is setting you up, Cameron and you could be in danger."

That grabbed her attention. On a muffled gasp, Olivia pressed her hand to her throat. "You really believe that?"

"It's a possibility." He wouldn't sugarcoat this. "I don't want you two alone here tonight." Then he added what he knew Olivia wasn't going to like. "I'll stay with you."

He waited for her to object, and he could tell that's exactly what she wanted to do. Her father would give her all kinds of grief if he found out Leo had spent the night.

But Leo didn't care a rat about that. He only needed to make sure his little boy stayed safe.

"You shouldn't be out driving anywhere tonight, either," Leo continued. That would nix any idea she got about going to her father's. "I also don't intend to get another deputy to do this. Cameron's my son, and I'm the one who should protect him."

Olivia finally nodded. "You can stay tonight."

Maybe it wouldn't take longer than that because Barrett would get the answers they needed from Milton. If someone had actually hired Milton to attack Leo, he might give them the name if he were offered some kind of plea deal. Then Barrett could make an arrest and there wouldn't be any sort of threat to Olivia or Cameron.

"You still need someone to check your arm," Olivia reminded him.

Leo huffed, knowing she was right. He took out his phone and called the Culver Crossing Hospital. He requested an EMT come to Olivia's house. That way, he wouldn't have to leave her alone.

"How good is your security system?" Leo asked, putting his phone away.

"It's very good. My father had it set up for me when I moved here."

Of course, he had. Samuel was overly protective of Olivia in every possible way. Not just her safety but her personal life, too. Leo supposed that might have had something to do with Samuel losing his wife in a car accident when Olivia had only been ten. But the man crossed too many lines as far as Leo was concerned.

"Your father's got to be upset about me challenging you for custody." Leo threw the words out there, already knowing the answer. Yeah, Samuel would be upset. Olivia was, too.

"He is," she admitted, dodging his gaze now. "He doesn't want me to move to Oklahoma."

That was probably the only thing that Leo and Samuel agreed on. Well, that and their love for Cameron. Even though Samuel could be a hardnosed SOB, Leo didn't doubt that the man loved his grandson.

"I'm not going to rehash all of this tonight," Olivia said, sounding a whole lot stronger than she had just seconds earlier. Leo could practically feel her digging in her heels.

They had indeed gone through all of this. Many times.

Olivia wanted to relocate to Tulsa to take over a nonprofit home and counseling center for troubled teens. She had an emotional connection to the center since it was something her mother had started twenty years ago, just months before her death. Leo couldn't dispute that it was a worthwhile cause, but he knew Olivia could run it from Culver Crossing, as she'd been doing for the past decade. Then, she wouldn't have to take Cameron out of state and to a place where Leo wouldn't be able to see him as often as he did now.

As much as Leo wanted to accommodate her on the no-rehashing, he had to know something. "Would Samuel do something to try to discredit you? Is he so pissed off at you over this move that he would try to take both of us out of the custody picture?"

There it was. All laid out for her.

"My father wouldn't do this," Olivia murmured, her voice shaky now.

Hell. There was enough doubt in her tone to confirm

that her father was truly a suspect in this attack. He would need to pay Samuel a visit first thing in the morning.

Leo turned away from Olivia when he heard the vehicle come to stop outside her house. "It's probably the EMT. Stay back until I make sure."

That put a fresh round of alarm in her eyes, but Leo wasn't taking any chances. That's why he waited until Olivia had left the foyer and gone into the living room. He also put his hand over his weapon when he opened the door. The moment Leo did that, however, he heard a sound that he definitely didn't want to hear.

A gunshot.

# Chapter Two

The terror shot through Olivia, causing her heart to jump straight to her throat as she ran back to the foyer. Because she knew what she'd just heard. Knew what it meant.

Someone had just fired a shot at Leo.

Oh mercy. Someone was trying to kill him.

She latched onto his arm, yanking him deeper inside the house, but Leo was already moving in that direction. He slammed the door, locked it and then raced to the window in the living room that faced the front yard. Obviously, he had already geared up for a fight.

"Cameron," Olivia said, her son's name gusting out with her breath.

Leo didn't try to stop her when she started running to the rear of the house. Even if he had, she would have fought him off. She had to get to her son. She had to make sure he was okay, protect him.

She heard another shot just as she reached the nursery, but she didn't look back. Olivia rushed to the crib and, thanks to the night-lights in the room, she saw her baby. Asleep. Unharmed.

Safe.

The relief came like a flood, and she scooped him into her arms, brushing kisses on his cheeks and head. Cameron woke and made a fussy sound of protest at being disturbed. Olivia ignored that, too, and raced into the bathroom with him. She stepped into the shower stall where she hoped the tiles would stop any bullets from reaching them.

But the shots could definitely reach Leo.

That brought on a fresh round of terror. It didn't matter that he despised her. Didn't matter that they were at odds over this custody issue and her intended move. He was still Cameron's father, and she didn't want him hurt.

However, she did want to know why this was happening.

First, the knife attack by a man who claimed she'd called him. Now this. Olivia prayed they'd find out soon what was going on so they could put a stop to it.

When her lungs began to ache, she released the breath she'd been holding and continued to listen. No more gunshots, thank goodness, but she did hear Leo talking to someone. Maybe to someone on the phone.

"Olivia, are you and Cameron all right?" Leo called out to her several moments later.

"Yes," she managed to say. "I have him in the bathroom."

The sound of her voice caused Cameron to start fussing again. Olivia tried to rock him so that he'd go back to sleep. If he was awake, he might pick up on her tense muscles and therefore her fears.

Olivia heard the footsteps and, even though she knew it was probably Leo, she turned Cameron away from the door, putting her body between him and anyone who might enter. But the person who came in was Leo.

He looked like a fierce warrior with his black hair and stone-gray eyes. Tall, rangy and ready for battle.

The anger was coming off him in thick waves that she could practically see. But for once that particular emotion wasn't aimed at her.

"The shooter sped off. I couldn't go after him," he said, though she wasn't sure how he could speak with his jaw muscles set so hard.

"No," she quickly agreed. Because that would have meant leaving Cameron and her alone. Olivia didn't have a gun and wouldn't have wanted to face down an armed man when she had Cameron to protect. "Did you see who it was?"

He shook his head and moved closer, his attention on Cameron. Thankfully, the baby had gone back to sleep on Olivia's shoulder. Leo leaned in—so close that she caught his scent—and brushed a kiss on top of the boy's head.

Olivia looked away, unable to make herself resistant to Leo. She'd never managed to do that. But she had plenty of reasons why she couldn't give in to the flickers of heat he caused in her body.

"I locked the front door and then called the Culver Crossing PD," Leo said, gently brushing his fingers over Cameron's hair. Hair that was identical in color to Leo's. Ditto for her son's eyes. "Sheriff Jace Castillo will be here in a few minutes. It's his jurisdiction," he reminded her, not sounding very happy about that.

Olivia knew the reason for that unhappiness. There was bad blood between the Castillos and the Nashes because, several decades ago, Leo's mother had had an affair with Jace's father, and it had ripped both families apart. Olivia was well aware of how some events from the past could affect the present.

Not in a good way, either.

"I'm surprised you didn't call Della instead," she murmured. Since Della was a Culver Crossing deputy sheriff and also his soon-to-be sister-in-law, Leo would have no doubt found her easier to deal with.

"I heard my brother mention that Della had just finished a long shift. Besides, Jace would have had to come in on something like this anyway."

Yes, because what had happened was so serious—the attempted murder of a police officer. And not the first attempt tonight, either.

Sweet heaven, what was going on?

"We'll wait in here until Jace arrives." Leo moved in front of her then, taking up the stance to protect them both if someone made it into the house and came through the bathroom door.

"All the windows and the back door are locked," she told him.

Olivia was certain of that because it was something she did even in the daytime. Cameron was walking now, and he was fast. She hadn't wanted to risk him getting outside the house. But she'd never thought it was something she'd need to do to keep out a would-be killer.

"I locked the front door," he added. Leo paused, the muscles stirring in his jaw again. "The shooter fired at the house." There was fresh anger in his voice now and in his eyes. "I don't think the bullets got through the walls, but they could have. *They could have*," he repeated in a hoarse mumble.

Olivia also felt plenty of anger, but it was beneath the fear and the question. "Did that man, Milton Hough, escape and do this?"

"No. I called Barrett, too, and he still has Milton in custody."

Normally, she would have considered that a good

thing, but in this case it meant there were two attackers. At least. It also meant whoever had done this had no regard for the safety of a child.

"Who would have done this?" Olivia came out and asked. When he didn't give her an immediate answer, she added. "And it wasn't me."

"I know it wasn't you. No way would you have put Cameron at risk."

That stung. Because while it was true about Cameron, she wouldn't have put Leo in harm's way, either. In fact... well, she didn't want to go there. Not when she had other questions and concerns.

"Is this maybe connected to one of your investigations?" she suggested.

He opened his mouth but didn't get a chance to say anything because there was a knock at the door.

"It's me, Sheriff Castillo," Jace called out.

"Wait here," Leo instructed her, his weapon drawn as he left the bathroom and closed the door behind him.

Olivia held her breath again. She didn't suspect Jace of being behind the shooting, but the gunman could still be outside somewhere, waiting for Leo to answer the door so he could fire more shots at him.

Thankfully, she didn't hear any gunfire. Just the murmurs of a conversation between Jace and Leo, followed by footsteps. Several moments later, Leo opened the bathroom door. He came in, but Jace stayed in the doorway.

Even though the men weren't saying anything to each other, Olivia could feel the tension. She hoped that wouldn't stop them from working together on this because she was going to need all the help she could get.

"Are you okay?" Jace asked her.

Olivia nodded, but it was a lie. She was far from being okay. "Did you see the man who shot into the house?"

"No," Jace answered. "But I'm going outside now to have a look around. I want Leo to stay in here with the baby and you, if that's all right."

Jace obviously knew about the custody battle. Heck, everyone in Mercy Ridge and Culver Crossing did. And Jace was clearly concerned that she wouldn't be comfortable with Leo being around her. She was uncomfortable, but that would skyrocket if she had to stay inside alone with Cameron.

"Leo should stay," she agreed.

Jace gave her a nod and shifted his attention to Leo. "You said the shooter's vehicle was a late-model pickup truck, either dark blue or black?"

"That's right. He was behind the wheel when he fired the shots, and he sped off after firing two rounds. I couldn't make out the license plate."

"And you're sure it was a man?" Jace pressed.

"Yeah. He had wide shoulders and beefy arms, and he was wearing a ski mask, just like the guy who attacked me earlier in Mercy Ridge."

That tightened Olivia's stomach even more. Someone had sent two men after Leo tonight, and both had used what could have been deadly force.

"After I've had a look around, I'll need to talk to both of you again," Jace said, sounding all cop. "I'll need statements. I'll also want you to tell me who you believe would do something like this, so be thinking about that while I'm gone."

Leo made a sound of agreement but, judging from his stony expression, it was a hard pill for him to swallow to be taking orders from a fellow cop. One he didn't especially like.

When Jace left, Leo stood in the bathroom doorway so he could look out into the hall. Keeping watch. Olivia tried to help by focusing on what Jace had told her to do—think about who had done this. She wished she could draw a blank, but she couldn't.

"Bernice." She hadn't intended to say that aloud, yet it was the first name that came to mind.

Leo looked back at her. "You think your father's household manager could have done this?"

"No. Not really." Flustered, she shook her head and wished she'd kept her mouth shut. "But she's upset about our custody fight. Upset with *you*," Olivia amended.

Leo certainly couldn't dismiss the possibility of Bernice's involvement. The woman could be overbearing, and she was fiercely loyal to Olivia's father. That meant Bernice was also upset with Olivia's move to Oklahoma.

"Bernice wouldn't have put Cameron in danger," Olivia stated. She would have added more to try to convince him about that, but his phone rang.

"It's Barrett," he relayed and, much to Olivia's surprise, put the call on speaker.

"How are things there?" Barrett immediately asked.

Leo took a deep breath before he answered. "No sign of the shooter. And Sheriff Castillo is on scene."

The sound that Barrett made conveyed both his sympathy and concern. Yes, there was definitely still bad blood between Jace and the Logan brothers.

"Milton clammed up," Barrett said a moment later. "He's waiting for a lawyer to drive over from San Antonio. Probably waiting for the DA to offer him some kind of plea deal, too."

"Hell," Leo muttered after he glanced at Cameron. No doubt to make sure he was still asleep. He was. "The shooter could have hurt my son." There was plenty of raw emotion in his voice.

"Cameron's okay?" Barrett asked.

"Yeah. It needs to stay that way. That's why I want to know if someone hired Milton and this other thug who fired into Olivia's house. I'll need the person's name, and if the two weren't hired, I have to know why they took it upon themselves to try to kill me."

"I want that, too," Barrett verified. "We might not need to deal with Milton, though. I'm getting a warrant to go over his financials to see if I can find a money trail. Then I might be able to figure out who paid him to do this. I'll also try to get his medical records."

That got Olivia's attention.

Obviously, it got Leo's, too. "Medical records?" he questioned.

Barrett paused again. "I found a bottle of prescription meds in Milton's pocket, and I looked it up. It's something that's given to patients with severe psychological disorders."

Olivia tried to process that. Maybe there'd been no hired guns. Just a mentally ill man who'd attacked Leo. Of course, that didn't explain the person who'd fired the shots outside her house, but it was a start.

"Where's my daughter?" someone shouted. "I want to see Olivia now!"

She groaned because she easily recognized that voice. Her father. And his being here definitely wasn't going to make things better.

"I need to make sure Cameron and Olivia are all

right," her father went on. "If somebody shot at her, I want to see for myself that they weren't hurt."

"I have to go," Leo said to Barrett. Obviously, he also knew her father was there, and he ended the call.

"I told you that Olivia and your grandson are fine," she heard Jace say. The sheriff sounded just as annoyed as Leo looked.

But Olivia was past the mere annoyed stage. Why had her father come? Better yet, how had he known about the shooting? Her neighbors didn't know her dad well enough to have his phone number.

Moments later, Samuel stepped into the doorway of the bathroom. He was tall, bulky and imposing, a bouncer's build. And somehow his iron-gray hair didn't make him look old, only more formidable.

As usual, her father was wearing a suit, a dark gray one this time, and he had a gold sycamore leaf pin on his classic red tie. The pin was the symbol of his estate, Sycamore Grove, and he didn't just wear the emblem, it was also on the iron gates that fronted the house, on the vehicles' license plates. Even on the front door.

Jace was right behind Samuel, and Leo didn't budge to let her father come any closer to her. However, Olivia stepped closer because she wanted to see her father's expression when she asked him the questions that were causing the anger to ripple through her.

"Were you having me watched?" Olivia demanded. Cameron stirred and she patted his back to try to soothe him. She definitely didn't want her son to hear any part of this conversation. "Is that how you found out about the shooting?"

Maybe it was her steely tone, but her father flinched as if she'd slapped him. Of course, he could have reacted that way to make her feel sorry for what she'd just said. But Olivia didn't feel sorry for him.

"No, I'm not having you watched." Her father's voice was tight now, and his eyes were slightly narrowed. "I got an anonymous text, saying that Cameron and you had been attacked. I tried to call you several times. When I didn't get an answer, I drove straight here."

Since Olivia's replacement phone was in the kitchen and set to vibrate, she wouldn't have heard the calls, but the other part of his explanation didn't make sense.

"An anonymous text?" She sounded skeptical because she was. Olivia huffed. "Look, if you had someone spying on me, then that person saw the shooter. You need to give your watchdog's name to Sheriff Castillo and Leo so he can help them find this gunman."

At the mention of Leo's name, her father slanted him a glare. Leo glared right back.

"Do you have a watchdog around here?" Leo demanded.

Her father's glower got significantly worse. "No. I got a text, like I said. And you have no right to question me."

"I have the right." Jace jumped in. "If you know anything about the shooting, I want to hear it."

Samuel ignored Jace and stared at her.

"Leo." Her father spat the name out like venom. "He's the one you should be doubting and questioning. Go ahead—ask him. Have him tell you what this is all about."

Everything inside Olivia went still. "What do you mean?"

Her father didn't actually smile, but it was close. "Leo's the reason Cameron and you could have been killed. This is all his fault."

# Chapter Three

After dealing with Samuel for the past two years, Leo knew he shouldn't be surprised by the accusation. But there was something in Samuel's expression that had Leo wondering if there was any truth to it.

Olivia was already moving forward, but Leo motioned for her to stay back. It was somewhat of a miracle that Cameron was still asleep, and Leo didn't want him closer in case this *conversation* got loud. That was always a possibility when dealing with Samuel Nash.

"You actually believe these two attacks were my fault?" Leo questioned.

Samuel jabbed his index finger at Leo. "You bet they were. Because of your botched investigation, Randall Arnett is a free man and now he wants to get back at you."

Leo had wondered how long it was going to take for Randall's name to come up. He'd already considered it. But what Samuel had just said was a mix of truth and lies. Randall wasn't behind bars, but Leo hadn't botched the investigation into the man's missing girlfriend. Simply put, there hadn't been enough evidence to charge Randall.

"Randall threatened you," Samuel reminded him.

"Yeah, over a year ago," Leo verified. What he wouldn't say was that he'd been keeping close tabs on Randall, looking for anything he could use to prove the man's wrong-doing. "It'd be stupid for Randall to come after me like this," Leo added.

Samuel shrugged. "That doesn't mean he didn't. The person who texted me said Randall was responsible for the shooting. I can show you. It's right here." He took out his phone, holding up the screen for Leo to see.

"'Get to your daughter's place now,'" Leo read aloud. "'There's been a shooting. Dig into Deputy Leo Logan's case files if you want to know who pulled the trigger.'"

So, the person who'd sent that text hadn't specifically mentioned Randall. Interesting. Interesting, too, that Samuel had jumped to that conclusion.

"How exactly did you know about Randall Arnett?" Leo asked.

Samuel blinked, maybe surprised by the question. But he shouldn't have been. He should have known that was something Leo would press, especially since the man didn't live in Mercy Ridge and wouldn't necessarily be privy to the town talk about Randall.

"I make it a point to know what you're doing because it affects my daughter and grandson," Samuel insisted.

Olivia huffed. "You've been digging into Leo's investigations. You're looking for something you can use against him in the custody case."

Bingo. Leo was glad Olivia had realized her father would do something like this. The man fought dirty. Maybe dirty enough to stir up Randall to get him to launch an attack?

Maybe.

It was definitely something Leo would look into.

Samuel shifted his attention to Olivia. "You know I only want what's best for Cameron and you. I have to keep you safe. That's why you'll need to come home with me. Look at Leo's arm, at his gunshot injury. Something worse could happen to Cameron and you if you stay around him."

And there was another *bingo*. Samuel would use this shooting and anything else he could come up with to get Olivia and Cameron under his roof.

Exactly where Samuel wanted them.

"No," Olivia said before Leo could tell her that he thought it was a bad idea. The shooter could follow Olivia there, and while her father likely knew how to use a gun, he wasn't trained in law enforcement.

Samuel sighed. "I know you're upset. And scared. But you can't stay here. The man who fired those shots could come back."

Now, Leo did manage to speak first. "Olivia and Cameron won't be staying here. But they'll be placed in protective custody until I can figure out what's going on."

Leo was surprised that lightning didn't bolt from Samuel's eyes. "Your protective custody?" he questioned as if that were a stupid idea.

"Either mine or Sheriff Castillo's." Leo hoped that, despite their differences, Jace would back him up.

He did. "Olivia and Cameron definitely won't be staying here," Jace agreed. "This is now a crime scene, and the grounds need to be processed. I've already called in a CSI team to look for tracks and spent shell casings. While that's going on, Olivia needs to be in a safe place, and Leo should be the one to decide where that safe place will be."

"Leo and Jace are right," Olivia said.

Her voice sounded strong but was edged with nerves. That was expected, Leo supposed, though he thought he detected something else beneath the surface. Maybe her father and she had had some kind of disagreement. If so, it probably had something to do with the move she wanted to make to Oklahoma. Samuel wouldn't want Olivia that far away from under his thumb.

"You'll go with Leo?" her father snarled.

She nodded, swallowed hard. "And before you tell me all the reasons why that shouldn't happen, remember this. Leo is Cameron's father and he'll do anything to protect his son."

"So will I," Samuel howled.

This time Cameron didn't just stir. The boy let out a loud wail, the sound tugging at Leo's heart. Samuel's shout had scared him.

Shooting a scowl at Samuel, Leo went to Olivia, who was trying her best to soothe the baby. However, the moment that Cameron spotted Leo, he reached out for him and babbled, "Dada." That tugged at Leo's heart, too, and he took Cameron into his arms.

"It's all right, buddy," Leo whispered to him and brushed a kiss on the top of his head.

Jace's phone buzzed. The sheriff gave each of them a long look, as if deciding whether or not he should leave them alone while he took the call. He must have decided a fight wouldn't break out because he stepped into the hall.

"You're a fool to trust him," Samuel immediately said to Olivia.

Leo didn't have to guess that Samuel was talking about him. Definitely no trust between them. But what did surprise Leo was his glimpse of a flicker of distrust in Olivia's eyes.

"I'd be a fool not to do what it takes to keep my son safe," Olivia countered.

Samuel huffed, and Leo decided if the man raised his

voice this time, he would give him the boot. Cameron had been upset enough without adding more shouting to the mix.

"You can be safe with me," Samuel said, staring at Olivia. No shouting. In fact, his voice leveled and took on a pleading tone. "I need you home. I'll be sick with worry over Cameron and you."

Olivia's expression and posture stayed stiff as she moved closer to Leo and stroked her hand down Cameron's back. That put Leo arm to arm with Olivia. A sort of united front against her father.

Something that wouldn't last.

Olivia always caved to Samuel.

"You know this is already a tough time for me," Samuel added a moment later.

"Because of Mom," she muttered.

Leo knew it was a tough time for Olivia, too. The anniversary of her mother's death was in a couple of days, and it would no doubt stir up some bad memories. Olivia had been just ten when her mom, Simone, had been killed in a car accident. Olivia had been in the car with her, trapped inside, while she watched her mother die.

Yeah, it would be bad.

And now it'd be worse because of this attack tonight. No way to push aside the sounds of those shots that'd been fired into the house.

Leo wanted to put his arm around Olivia, to try to comfort her. That was his kneejerk reaction anyway. Not only wouldn't she welcome that, it also wasn't smart. After all, they weren't exactly friends right now.

"You shouldn't have been in the car with Simone that night," Samuel muttered, and it seemed as if he was lost in the grief. "You shouldn't have had to go through that."

Olivia cleared her throat, her gaze shifting to meet Leo's. She was certainly a puzzle tonight because he wasn't sure what he was seeing there. Maybe, though, it was just the start of an inevitable adrenaline crash.

"Come home with me," Samuel insisted. The plea was gone, probably because he didn't like all the eye and arm contact she was making with Leo.

"No," she said, and repeated it when she turned back to her father. "No. And I need you to leave now."

The muscles tightened in Samuel's jaw, and Leo didn't think he was mistaken that the look the man gave his daughter was a borderline glare. A glare that Samuel would have likely added some venomous words to if Jace hadn't come back into the room.

Jace stopped, eyeing them all again. "A problem?" Jace asked.

"No," Olivia quickly answered. She began to stuff some diapers, clothes and toys into a large diaper bag. "I've already explained to my father that I'll be taking Cameron to Leo's."

Jace nodded, though he didn't seem convinced about Olivia's denial.

Neither was Leo. Something other than the obvious was wrong here.

"I need to go by the sheriff's office in Mercy Ridge," Jace told Leo. "I have to see Milton. But I'm in my cruiser, so I can take Olivia and you to your place first. I can go through it, too, just to make sure no one had tried to break in. Once you're there, the EMTs can have a look at that arm."

It was a generous offer, and it would free up Barrett from having to send out a deputy for backup duty.

"Cameron has a car seat in my truck," Leo explained.

"I'll need to drive that, but I'd appreciate it if you'd make sure we get safely back to my ranch." He paused. "I'll want to question Milton, too, but I don't want to take Cameron there."

"I'll let your brother know what's going on," Jace assured him.

"Olivia," Samuel said, "reconsider this."

"No." She didn't hesitate, either. "Give me a minute to pack a bag," she added to no one in particular and hurried out of the room.

Samuel immediately turned to Leo. "You can convince her not to go to your house."

Leo gave him what he was certain was the flattest look in the history of flat looks. "Leave, Samuel," Leo insisted, making sure it sounded like an order from a cop. He'd had enough tonight and didn't want to deal another second with this man who'd tried to make his life a living hell.

Samuel shifted as if he might make that plea to Jace, but Jace managed a darn good flat look of his own. Leo didn't know how well the two men knew each other, but there didn't seem to be any tinge of friendliness.

"You're not going to take my daughter and grandson away from me," Samuel snarled to Leo, and with that, he finally headed out of the house.

"I'll lock the door behind him," Jace offered.

"Thanks," Leo muttered. He didn't want to take Cameron near an unlocked door until it was time to leave.

Leo fired off a quick text to his head ranch hand, Wally Myers, to alert him to be on the lookout for the shooter and to also patrol the grounds. Wally lived in the bunkhouse, along with two other hands, and Leo knew he could count on them to make sure the place was as safe as it could be.

Maybe that would be enough.

Olivia was true to her word about only taking a minute to pack a bag. She hurried back into the room, glanced around and seemed to take a breath of relief when she saw that her father wasn't there.

She hoisted her bag over one shoulder and put the filled diaper bag over the other. What she was also doing was avoiding eye contact with him. He would have called her on that, but Jace returned.

"There's no sign of the shooter," Jace said, "but I'd like to get Olivia and the baby inside the vehicle as fast as we can."

Olivia made a sound of agreement, and Leo handed Cameron back to Olivia. He also took her bag. As she'd done, he looped it over his shoulder to free up his shooting hand. He prayed it wouldn't be necessary, though, to do any firing. Not with his baby so close that he could be hurt.

"I want to see Milton, too," Olivia said as they made their way to the door. "I want to see if I recognize him."

There were safer ways for her to take that look. Leo fired off a quick text to Barrett to let him know they were leaving and to ask him to send a photo of Milton.

"Stay close to me," Leo instructed her, using his key fob to unlock his truck.

And he sucked in his breath, holding it.

Praying.

He fired glances all around but didn't see a gunman. Of course, the guy probably wouldn't just stand out in the open, not with two lawmen around. Still, the guy had been gutsy enough to launch an attack.

Jace moved when they did, and Leo and the sheriff kept Olivia and Cameron between them as they hurried outside and got into the truck. The moment Jace shut the passenger's-side door, he hurried over to his cruiser. Leo only waited long enough for Olivia to strap Cameron into his seat before he took off.

"Keep watch," Leo told her. He also wanted to tell her to get down on the seat so that she'd be out of harm's way, but he needed her eyes. If she could spot any signs of trouble, it could help him avoid being the target of more gunfire.

He hoped.

Right now, Leo was hoping a lot of things. He needed to catch the idiot who'd put Cameron and Olivia in danger, but he didn't want that to happen with his little boy around.

"Later," he said, giving her a heads-up, "I'll want to know what's going on between you and your father."

He'd figured Olivia would dole out a quick denial that anything was going on. But she stayed silent.

Hell.

Whatever this was, it had to be bad. Then again, things were rarely good when it came to Samuel. Leo wanted to know if her move to Oklahoma had anything to do with this father-daughter rift or whatever the heck it was.

His phone dinged. Rather than take his eyes off the road, he passed it to Olivia.

"It's from Barrett," she said. "It's a picture of Milton."

Thinking Barrett had gotten that photo rather fast, Leo made a quick glance at the screen. It was Milton's DMV photo.

"I don't recognize him," Olivia muttered. "I swear, I didn't hire him to kill you."

Leo had thought they'd already hashed this out. Apparently not. "Yeah, I got that."

And he left it at that. Because a conversation about a would-be killer could be a huge distraction, too.

Cameron made a fussy sound that caught Leo's attention. He never wanted to hear his boy cry, but such a sound now could drown out other things that he needed to be hearing. But the one fuss was it. While Leo drove on, the baby thankfully drifted back to sleep.

He heard Olivia make what he realized was a sigh of relief and, like him, she continued to keep watch as he drove. It wasn't a long trip, less than twenty minutes, but each mile felt as if it took an eternity. Leo didn't relax, however, when he pulled into his driveway. He did more glancing around, making sure there were no signs of an attacker. Nothing. And he hoped it stayed that way.

He spotted Wally at the side of the house. The ranch hand was carrying a rifle, but he gave Leo a welcoming nod, an assurance that all was well. Good. Leo pulled into his garage, but he didn't get out. He waited for Jace to join them and then shut the garage door to give them some extra cover.

"I can pause my security system with my phone," Leo explained as he pulled up the app.

No sensors had been triggered. That was the good news. The bad news was that no security system was foolproof.

"Wait here with Olivia," Leo instructed Jace once they were inside the mudroom. "I can go through the place faster than you can."

And *fast* would be key. Leo didn't want to be away from Olivia and Cameron any longer than necessary. That's why he drew his gun and started hurrying through the rooms—all twelve of them—checking each window, door and closet. He even looked under the beds and turned on all the lights as he went. That would help to illuminate the grounds, but it would also prevent a potential attacker from knowing which room they were in.

Leo had been raised in this house. The home that had once belonged to his parents before things had fallen apart. Before his mother had left them and his father had committed suicide. There were plenty of bad memories here. Plenty of really good ones, though, too. Right now, he needed to make sure nothing else bad happened to add to what had already taken place tonight.

While he made his way downstairs, he texted Wally again to instruct him to continue to keep watch. It'd be a long night for all of them, but any and all precautions were necessary.

"It's okay," Leo immediately told Jace and Olivia when he joined them in the mudroom. He looked at Jace. "Thanks."

Jace nodded. "I'll let you know if I find out anything about Milton."

Leo muttered another thanks and locked the front door when Jace left. He also reset the security system.

"We're staying in the nursery tonight," Leo insisted. "All three of us. You can take the sleep chair." It was an oversize recliner that Leo had used plenty of times himself when Cameron had stayed nights with him.

Olivia didn't object to them all sharing the nursery. She followed him upstairs to the room he'd set up for Cameron. Leo had purposely made it as identical as possible to the one at Olivia's so the boy would have some continuity.

Cameron didn't stir when Olivia put him in the crib,

but neither Leo nor Olivia moved away despite the baby being sound asleep. They stood there several long moments, watching him, and Leo was pretty sure that, like him, Olivia was silently uttering some prayers of thanks that their little boy hadn't been hurt.

"We need to find out who's behind the attack," she whispered.

Yeah, they did, and Leo intended to get started on that tonight. First, though, there was another matter they had to discuss. He took Olivia by the hand and led her to the other side of the room. Far enough for them to keep an eye on the baby but not so close to the crib as to wake him.

"Okay..." Leo started, "want to tell me what's going on between you and your father?"

She dragged in a long breath, opened her mouth then closed it as if she'd changed her mind about what she was going to say. A few seconds crawled by before she finally spoke.

"I think my father might be a killer."

# Chapter Four

*I think my father might be a killer.*

The moment Olivia heard what she'd said, she wished she could take it back. This was definitely not something she should have brought up tonight, not when Leo and she were still recovering from the shock of the attack. In fact, she shouldn't have dropped the bombshell at all unless she had some proof to back it up.

She didn't.

But what she did have was a tightness in her chest and stomach. An unsettling feeling that what she'd said was the cold, hard truth.

Leo's eyes narrowed and he gave her a cop's stare. "You're going to need to explain that," he demanded.

Since there was no way Olivia would be able to dodge answering him, she gathered her breath and hoped this didn't blow up in her face. After all, Leo and she were in a custody battle, and he might be willing to use this against her.

"I got the police report of my mother's car accident," Olivia explained. "I read it, and I couldn't stop thinking about it."

Dreaming about it, too. The nightmares hadn't been as bad as actually witnessing her mother die. Nothing could have been that bad. But the nightmares had definitely shaken her.

"You hadn't read the report before?" Leo asked, no doubt hoping to spur her into continuing with her explanation.

"No. I didn't think reading it would help. It didn't," she added in a murmur. "There were drugs in my mom's tox screen. A combination of sleeping pills and amphetamines. I don't remember my mother ever taking either of those. Just the opposite. She was sort of a health nut and didn't even take over-the-counter pain meds when she had a headache."

Leo stayed quiet a moment, obviously processing that. "You think your father gave her those drugs?"

Olivia met his gaze. She wanted to shake her head again, wanted to erase all the doubts and worries about her dad having some part in this. But she couldn't.

"They were arguing a lot, and I heard my mom tell him that she wanted a divorce," she went on. "My dad might have drugged her out of anger. *Might*." She gave emphasis to the word, then groaned. "He wouldn't have done that, though, if he'd known I was going to be in the car."

"You sneaked into the car," Leo stated when she stopped. "Neither your mom nor your dad knew you were in the back seat. Isn't that right?"

Even though it was a question, Leo knew the answer. When they'd been lovers, she'd poured out her heart to him. No. Her parents hadn't known she'd been in the vehicle. After yet another argument, she'd heard her mother tell her father that she was packing her things and leaving. She hadn't heard her mom say anything about taking her along, though, so Olivia had hurried to the garage and gotten down on the floor behind the driver's seat. Her mother had only discovered her seconds before the crash.

"Right," she verified. "The drugs definitely affected my mother's driving. I remember her weaving on the road, and that's when I lifted my head and asked her if everything was okay."

It hadn't been okay at all and, within minutes, her mother was dead. The crash had injured Olivia, too, but in the grand scheme of things, a broken arm and bruises had been minor, especially considering she hadn't been wearing a seat belt.

"Where was your mom going that night?" he asked. "Did she say?"

"She didn't say specifically, only that she needed some fresh air and was going for a drive to try to clear her head. But I remember her telling my dad that she'd be filing for a divorce, that she'd had enough."

Leo continued to study her as if trying to pick apart every nuance of her expression. She didn't dare do the same to him. Best to avoid eye contact. Other kinds of contact, as well. Olivia didn't consider herself stupid; she'd felt the old attraction still simmering between them. An attraction that even an unplanned pregnancy and a custody battle couldn't cool. She couldn't play with that kind of fire again. It was too dangerous.

"You said your father could have drugged your mother out of anger," Leo said. "Had he done anything like that before?"

"Not that I know of. I don't remember him ever hitting her, either. They just argued a lot."

Leo touched his fingers to her chin, turning her head and forcing the very eye contact she was trying to avoid. And there it was. More than just a flutter of heat. The flash of it through her body. Leo had always been able to do that to her. Still could.

Olivia stepped back, away from his touch. But it didn't stop the need he'd stirred inside her. However, his expression helped with that. Obviously, he wasn't thinking about sex tonight. Nope. She was certain his expression was the same one he used when interrogating suspects.

"Why do you think your father might have had some part in the car accident?" he asked.

She seriously doubted the answer she'd give him would convince him that her father was guilty. Or that she was telling Leo the whole truth—which she wasn't. But she tried anyway.

"Because my father keeps bringing it up," she said. "For the past couple of weeks, he keeps telling me how sorry he was that I was in the car. Maybe it's just because of the anniversary of mom's death, but there seems to be more."

"*More?* You mean like guilt?" he pressed.

"Exactly like guilt," she confirmed. So, maybe Leo would understand her gut feeling, after all. "When I ask for more details of that night, he dodges the questions. Not hard questions, either. I asked him why they were arguing and wanted to know if Mom had threatened to leave him before."

Leo mumbled some profanity under his breath. "I'm betting he didn't like that."

"No." In fact, her father had stormed off during one of those conversations. The man definitely had a temper, and that hadn't been the first time she'd seen flashes of it. Many times, he'd aimed his temper at Leo.

"I also talked to Bernice," Olivia continued. "I asked

her point-blank if my father could have had any part in that car accident, and she said absolutely not."

"Did she have an explanation for your mother's tox screen results?" Leo asked.

"None other than she was positive my father wasn't responsible. Of course, the woman idolizes him, so she probably wouldn't rat him out. The only reason I brought up the subject to her was that I thought I'd be able to read her expression if she thought there was any hint of wrongdoing on his part."

Again, Leo went quiet for several moments. "Is all of this why you want to move to Oklahoma?"

And here was the leverage this discussion could give him. Leo would use whatever info he could to keep her from taking Cameron out of state.

"It's part of it," she admitted.

But only part.

Leo wouldn't like to know that he was the main reason for her intended move.

He was obviously waiting for her to finish her explanation, but Olivia didn't get a chance to say anything else because his phone dinged. When he pulled it from his pocket, she saw Barrett's name on the screen.

"I need to take this call," Leo grumbled. "We'll finish our conversation when I'm done."

That last part sounded a little like a threat, and he hit the answer button while he went across the room and into the hall. No doubt so that he wouldn't wake Cameron. But Olivia followed him. This was likely an update about the investigation. Or more. It could be a warning that another attack was on the way. That possibility had her leaving the nursery door open in case she had to hurry in and scoop up the baby.

"Please give me good news," Leo said to his brother, and he surprised her by putting the call on speaker. Olivia had thought Leo would want to process any bad news before passing it along to her.

"Sorry, but I don't have any," Barrett quickly answered. "I just got a preliminary report on Milton. He's been in and out of mental health facilities for years. I can't get access to his medical records, but I've arranged for him to have a psychiatric eval. Unfortunately, that won't happen until morning when the doctor from San Antonio can get here."

"The doctor might be able to convince you that Milton is a liar," Olivia insisted.

There was silence, both from Barrett and Leo. Barrett might not have known she was listening, so perhaps he was rethinking the conversation he'd intended to have with his brother.

"Leo, are you okay with Olivia being there?" Barrett came out and asked after several long moments.

Leo paused again, just a heartbeat this time, but Olivia already knew the answer. No, he wasn't *okay* staying under the same roof with her. That wouldn't improve once they finished the talk they'd started before this phone call.

"I want to keep Cameron and Olivia safe," Leo finally said. "I stand a better chance of doing that with them here."

This time Barrett's response wasn't silence but a slight sound that could have meant anything. However, Olivia was pretty sure it was the concern that he hadn't been able to tamp down. Barrett was no doubt worried she'd hurt his little brother all over again.

And she could.

No matter what she did, Leo could end up getting hurt.

Or worse. She needed to do whatever it took to make sure *or worse* didn't happen.

"Since Olivia can hear this, I just got an interesting call from Rena Oldham," Barrett threw out there.

Olivia pulled back her shoulders. Rena was her dad's girlfriend. Or rather his on-again, off-again girlfriend. Rena had held that particular status for years. Their pattern was for them to be together for a couple of months, break up and see other people, only to start up their relationship again.

"What'd Rena want?" Olivia asked.

"Info about Samuel and you. Info I didn't give her," Barrett quickly added. "Apparently, she'd heard about the attack and said she was worried, that Samuel hadn't answered his phone when she'd tried to call him."

"My dad often doesn't take her calls. And Rena can be…clingy," she settled for saying.

"She can apparently also be opinionated, and she doesn't appear to have a high opinion of you. She wanted to know if you had anything to do with the attack tonight."

Olivia groaned. "Even if Rena thought I was capable of something like that, she knows that I'd never put my child in danger."

"I mentioned that to her," Barrett assured her, "and then I ended the call because I had better things to do. She did say, though, that she was out looking for your dad, so she might try to get onto Leo's ranch. Just a heads-up."

The ranch hands wouldn't allow that. Well, hopefully they wouldn't because Olivia didn't want to deal with Rena and her drama tonight.

"What about the second attacker? Any sign of him?" Leo asked.

"No, but Milton said that Olivia hired him and a couple of other attackers to go after you."

"She didn't."

Barrett made a sound, as if reserving judgment about that.

"She didn't," Leo repeated, sounding much more adamant this time.

That helped with the tightness in Olivia's chest. Having Leo believe her was a start because she was going to need him on her side. She had to convince him to do some things that would keep him safe.

"If Milton was right about someone hiring other thugs," Barrett went on, "then I need to find them so I can question them. Maybe then, we can figure out what the heck is going on. What's your theory as to who's behind this?"

"Randall is my top pick," Leo answered without hesitation.

"I figured you'd say that, and that's why I called him. Or rather, I tried to call him. He didn't answer his cell, so I called his house. His sister, Kristin, answered. She said Randall was staying overnight with a friend in San Antonio. She didn't have the friend's name or contact info."

Leo groaned softly and rubbed his free hand over his face. "Kristin would lie for him."

"Oh yeah," Barrett agreed.

Olivia was right there with his agreement. She didn't actually know Randall's sister, but from what she'd heard, the siblings were very close. And both bitter that Leo was trying to put Randall behind bars for murder.

"I'm also trying to find out if Randall actually sent that text to Olivia's father," Barrett went on. "My guess is that he didn't. Randall wouldn't be that stupid."

"No," Leo quietly answered, glancing back at the crib when Cameron stirred a little.

Olivia did the same and moved a little closer to the baby but not so close that she wouldn't be able to hear the rest of Leo and Barrett's conversation.

"But maybe Randall did it using a burner cell," Leo continued. "One that couldn't be traced back to him. Then, it'd be sort of a reverse psychology. His lawyers could argue that he's innocent because he wouldn't implicate himself."

It sickened Olivia to consider that Randall's hatred of Leo was at the core of the attacks. A man who hated that much wouldn't care if an innocent child got hurt during his quest for revenge.

"I'll see what I can learn about Randall's whereabouts," Barrett assured his brother. "In the meantime, try to get some rest. If you get any kind of signal that something's wrong, just call me. I'll be working from home."

That was good because Barrett lived only a couple of minutes from Leo. The ranch hands were decent backup, but if there was another attempt on their lives, she wanted Barrett there.

Leo ended the call and stared at the phone a moment as if to process his thoughts. When he turned toward her, Olivia knew what he wanted. And it didn't have anything to do with this heat zinging back and forth between them.

"Cut to the chase," Leo said, his voice low but with an edge. "Tell me about your father and this move you want to make to Oklahoma."

Olivia mentally tried to go through her answer and decided there was no way she could sugarcoat this. No way to stop Leo from doing something—maybe something bad—about this gut feeling she had.

She gathered her breath before she spoke. "First of all, I don't have any actual proof, but this isn't something I can keep to myself." Olivia had to pause again. "I believe my father could have been the one who hired Milton to kill you."

# Chapter Five

Olivia's words played through Leo's head for most of the night and had cost him some sleep. Of course, he probably wouldn't have actually gotten any sleep what with a would-be killer after him, but Olivia's accusation had only added more fuel to his mountain of worry. Not for himself but for Cameron.

And for Olivia, too, he reluctantly admitted.

Leo knew it had cost her to tell him about her fear that her father had possibly hired Milton. She'd always been protective of Samuel. Or so he'd thought. But in hindsight, he had to wonder if it was something else that'd kept her from straying too far from her father's side.

Fear.

That was something he'd pressed her about last night, but after dropping her bombshell, she'd dodged giving him any real answers to his questions and had insisted on going to bed. Her bottom line was that she didn't have any proof her father was guilty of hiring Milton or of killing her mother. Only the feeling in the pit of her stomach that something wasn't right.

He believed in those kinds of feelings. As a cop, trusting his gut had even saved his butt a time or two. That's why Leo had already started digging into not only her mother's car accident but also looking for a money trail that would lead from Milton right back to Samuel.

Leo poured himself another cup of coffee, already his fourth of the morning, and it was barely 7:00 a.m. He doubted it'd be his last because he'd need the caffeine to keep him alert and focused. He used some of that focus now to go through the reports and the latest emails on the investigation.

He turned when he heard the footsteps and spotted Olivia making her way into the kitchen. The diaper bag looped over her shoulder, she was carrying a squirming Cameron. She looked harried, and Leo immediately figured out why. Cameron's clothes were a little askew and, along with those wiggles and squirms, he was making fussing sounds. No doubt because he hadn't wanted to be dressed. The boy preferred stripping down to his diaper.

"You should have come and gotten me when he woke up," Leo said, setting his coffee aside so he could take the baby. Despite all the bad stuff going on, he gave Cameron a smile and a kiss. "I would have helped."

"I didn't want to pull you away from your work." Olivia's gaze drifted to his laptop open on the kitchen table. "Anything?"

He debated what to say and just went with the truth. "I've uncovered nothing that links your father to Milton. Not yet anyway." He would have continued, but Olivia interrupted him.

"How's your arm?" she asked.

Leo scowled when he glanced down at the bandage, one that an EMT had put on him after he'd cleaned the wound. It still throbbed, but he was hoping the over-the-counter pain meds would soon kick in and give him some relief.

"It's fine," he lied. "Are you ready to continue that discussion we started last night?"

However, the moment he asked it, he knew it'd have to wait a little longer. Cameron pointed to the high chair and kicked his legs to let Leo know he was ready for his breakfast. Olivia moved closer to help with that. As Leo strapped the baby into the chair, she took the makings for oatmeal from the diaper bag.

Olivia didn't look at Leo while she began to prepare the oatmeal, and she didn't object when he took the bag of cut-up fruit that he kept on hand for Cameron's visits. Leo put out some bits of peaches and pears that Cameron could manage to eat on his own. That kept him occupied while Leo turned to Olivia.

*"'I believe my father could have been the one who hired Milton to kill you,'"* Leo repeated to her to refresh her memory, though he was dead certain no refreshing was necessary.

She still didn't look at him, but Leo saw her hand tremble a little as she stirred the oatmeal. He finally took hold of her hand and turned her to face him. He saw it then. The fear. And he didn't think it was all related to the attack. It made Leo take a step back, but almost immediately Olivia stopped him by catching the sleeve of his shirt. It was the first time in ages that Leo remembered her actually touching him.

And he reacted.

Hell. His stupid body didn't seem to get it—that Olivia was off-limits. Not just because of the custody battle, either, but because it was obvious she was keeping things from him.

"Are you afraid of your father?" he came out and asked.

She opened her mouth, closed it and then squeezed her eyes shut a moment. "My father threatened you."

That was no big surprise. Samuel was always slinging barbs at him. But this seemed different. "Threatened me how?"

Olivia drew in a breath, moistened her lips. "He said if I stayed with you, that he'd figure out a way to ruin you. I was furious and told him to back off, but he said it'd be a shame if something happened to Cameron's father. Something that would take you out of the picture completely."

Okay, so her father had never actually made comments like that to Leo's face. With reason. Samuel probably hadn't wanted to risk arrest or to have Leo kick his butt. There was only so much he could take from the likes of Samuel Nash.

"You believed him?" Leo prodded.

He could tell the answer was yes even before Olivia nodded. And Leo didn't have any trouble filling in some very important blanks.

"Your father's threats are the reason you want to move to Oklahoma," he stated. It wasn't a question. "You want to put some distance between him and you."

She didn't nod. Didn't have to. He could see the confirmation in her eyes.

Leo felt the slam of anger that Samuel would try to manipulate Olivia this way. "Why the heck didn't you tell me?" But again, he knew the answer. "You knew I'd confront him."

"Yes," she admitted. "And I figured one of two things would happen. He'd hurt you, or you'd hurt him. Or kill him," Olivia added in a mumble. "That would have likely sent you to jail."

"Maybe, but it would have been worth it." Of course, that was the anger talking. Leo didn't want to go to jail and be separated from his son. Especially if Samuel would still be around to bully and threaten Olivia so he could try to bend her to his will. And that made him wonder something else.

Just how long had this bullying been going on?

Since it wouldn't necessarily be easy for her to answer, Leo checked on Cameron first. The boy was still chowing down on the fruit, but Leo added more to the tray to keep him occupied a couple of minutes longer.

He then turned back to Olivia. Leo had geared up to verbally blast her for not telling him all of this sooner, but she hadn't shut down her feelings fast enough. And he saw it.

The toll this had taken on her.

He wasn't immune to the emotion on her face. Leo didn't know everything about what she'd been through, but obviously it'd been plenty.

Before he could think, or stop himself, he reached out to pull her into his arms. He assured himself it was something he would do for plenty of people. But Olivia wasn't just anybody. She had been his lover, and this kind of contact was at best ill-advised and at worst, just plain stupid.

She made a small sound, a moan that sounded as if it was from both relief and pleasure. It confirmed the "just plain stupid" part. No way should they be playing with fire like this. Of course, if they gave in to the heat, it would fix some things. At least it would get them on the same side again.

Olivia didn't stay in his arms, though. She pulled back, moving several inches away, and he could practically feel her putting up barriers between them. "It was my decision," she blurted out.

Leo considered that a moment and bit off saying the profanity that nearly made its way to his mouth. "Exactly what decision are you talking about?" He was pretty sure he knew, but he wanted to hear it. And when he did, he figured he'd be doing plenty more mental cursing.

Olivia swallowed hard, but he had to hand it to her. She steeled herself, squaring her shoulders and looking him straight in the eyes. "To end things with you. If I hadn't," she quickly added in a whisper, "my father would have made our lives a living hell."

This time, the slam of anger was stronger. A hot smash of heat that hit him in the gut and spread. "You broke up with me to keep things smooth with Samuel." He'd had to speak through clenched teeth.

She didn't break eye contact with him. "Our relationship had run its course. I didn't see any reason to keep hanging on to it when it could have caused both of us so much trouble."

*Our relationship had run its course.* Well, that was news to him, but it explained why she'd given in to her father. If she'd loved Leo—hell, if she'd just cared enough about him—she would have stood with him so they could handle the *trouble* together.

"Besides," she went on a moment later, "this made things more peaceful for Cameron. I didn't want him to be around all the negativity."

He gave her a flat look to remind her that there was plenty of negativity over their custody fight and her plans to move to Oklahoma. He would have told her that verbally if Cameron hadn't started to fuss. Both Olivia and he turned toward the boy, but before Leo could go to him, his phone rang.

"It's Barrett," he relayed to Olivia after glancing at the screen. It was a call he had to take.

Leo went to the other side of the room, taking up position by the sink so he could keep watch out the back window. Olivia got started feeding Cameron his oatmeal, but Leo had no doubt she'd want to hear what his brother had to say. That's why he put the call on speaker.

"Olivia's listening," Leo told Barrett right off. "She and Cameron are in the kitchen with me." That would cue his brother to tone down whatever he had to say. "Is everything okay?"

"I was going to ask you that," Barrett countered. "Things are fine here. No signs of any other attackers."

"Same here. You got my email about Samuel? I'm running a financial check on your father," Leo added to Olivia when she looked at him.

"I got it, and I'll help you with that when I clear up some things."

"One of those things is Milton," Leo supplied.

Barrett made a sound of agreement. "The psychiatrist will be here any minute. I'll let you know as soon as she's done with her eval. In the meantime, I managed to get access to sealed juvie records for Milton."

It didn't surprise Leo that there was a juvie record since Milton had also been arrested as an adult for larceny, assault and public intoxication. He'd had no cage time though, only parole.

"Milton's pretty much been in trouble since he was old enough to sneak out of his house at night," Barrett continued. "And he has a history of violence. I'll send you the records to read for yourself, but Milton has a bad habit of being an accessory, situations where he was talked into doing something illegal or just plain stupid."

Leo would indeed read the reports, but he trusted Barrett's interpretation. It meant that Milton had possibly been coerced this time. Hell. More than possibly. Highly likely. Because, as Olivia had pointed out, her father could be behind this. Except that left Leo with one Texas-sized inconsistency. Even with all his faults, Samuel wouldn't have endangered Cameron.

"I'll need Olivia's official statement on the attack," Barrett went on. "And you can't be the one to take it."

No, because there were already enough conflicts of interest without adding that to the mix. "I'm keeping Cameron and Olivia in protective custody," Leo stated, though he was certain his brother already knew that.

"I've got no problem with that, but it means you'll either have to bring her here or else I'll need to go out to your place. I'm short-handed right now, but I should be able to get there by early afternoon."

Leo knew his brother was in a bind when it came to manpower, especially since Leo himself wouldn't be able to do his regular shift, but he wouldn't take Olivia outside unless he was certain it was safe.

"I'll let you know," he told Barrett. "Call me if you get any updates."

He'd just ended the call when he heard the sound of a car engine. Every muscle in his body went on alert, and in the same moment, a text flashed on his screen. It was from Wally.

Cameron's nanny just arrived, Wally had texted. Is it okay to let her in?

"What's wrong?" Olivia immediately asked. "Who's here?"

"Izzie," Leo quickly assured her, some of his own tension easing because Wally would have recognized the nanny on site. So, this wasn't a situation of someone trying to sneak onto the ranch.

Olivia released a breath that she'd obviously been holding. "I called Izzie last night and told her what was going on. I'm sorry I forgot to tell you that she'd insisted on coming in case we needed help."

Leo thought they might indeed need help with the baby, but he didn't like that Izzie was out and about and could therefore get caught up in another attack.

"Wait here," he told Olivia. "And stay away from the windows."

That last part was something he should have already warned Olivia about, but he'd let their conversation— and her—distract him. Not good. Right now a distraction could be fatal.

Leo went to the front of the house and disengaged the security system only long enough to open the front door and motion for the nanny to hurry inside. Izzie did. She raced across the yard and onto the porch.

As usual, the woman was wearing jeans and a plain cotton shirt, and she had her hair scooped up in a pony-tail. Leo had run a background check on the nanny when Olivia had first hired her, and he knew Izzie was forty-nine and had a twenty-three-year-old son. She'd been a nanny for the past fifteen years. Plenty of experience and no smudges.

"Are all of you okay?" she immediately asked.

Izzie looked exactly as he'd expected. Worried.

*Welcome to the club.*

"We're okay for now. I want to keep it that way." He shut the door, locked it and rearmed the security system. Leo also glanced out the front windows to make sure no one had followed Izzie. He didn't see anyone and was certain that if Wally spotted an intruder, he'd call ASAP.

"Olivia and Cameron are in the kitchen," Leo told the woman.

He motioned for her to follow him even though Izzie knew the layout of his house. She'd been there several times since Olivia had had the nanny drop off Cameron for his visits when Olivia hadn't been able to do it herself.

Izzie greeted Olivia with a hug and murmured some reassurances that all would be well before she went to Cameron to greet him. Leo reached for his laptop, intending to take it into the living room so he could read Milton's juvie records, but he stopped when his phone rang again. He didn't recognize the number on the screen, and he got an immediate jolt of concern. It was too early for a telemarketer, but this could be connected to the investigation. Sometimes, would-be killers liked to taunt and gloat.

"Deputy Logan," he answered, ready to hit the record function on his phone. But it wasn't a stranger's voice he heard.

"It's me, Bernice Saylor," the caller said.

Since Bernice made a habit of giving him the cold shoulder whenever he ran into her, he couldn't imagine why she'd want to talk to him. Then he remembered that Olivia didn't have her phone and Bernice might not know the number of her prepaid cell.

"I'm sorry for calling at such an early hour," Bernice said.

"Did you want to speak to Olivia?" he asked.

"No. I need to talk to you. It's important. It's about the attack."

That got his attention. "What about it?"

"I need to talk to you in person," Bernice insisted. "I have information you need to hear. I believe I know who's trying to kill you."

# Chapter Six

Olivia wasn't certain what Bernice had just told Leo, but whatever it was, he abruptly stepped out of the kitchen and motioned for her to join him. Olivia did, handing off the oatmeal to Izzie so that the nanny could finish feeding Cameron.

"Bernice, I need you to repeat what you just said," Leo instructed.

Even though he didn't put the call on speaker, Olivia moved close enough so she could listen. She figured this would be some kind of ploy to get her to mend fences with her father. Bernice was not objective when it came to Samuel. In fact, Olivia believed the woman was in love with him. Not that her father would return that love. No. Her dad relied on Bernice, but the woman fell very much into the close employee category.

"I told you that I believe I know who's trying to kill you," Bernice said.

Everything inside Olivia went still. She'd never known Bernice to say a negative thing about her father, but maybe the woman had seen or heard something to change her mind.

"Who?" Olivia blurted. "My father?"

She had no idea if Leo wanted her to make her presence known, but Olivia wanted to hear every word of this conversation. That included Bernice's answer to her question.

Bernice made a sharp sound of surprise. "No, not your father. Of course not him. Samuel would never do anything like that."

As far as Olivia was concerned, that was to be determined. Leo apparently felt the same way. "You're sure about that?" he fired back at Bernice.

"Positive. Samuel is a good man who loves his daughter and grandson. He wouldn't hurt you because it'd hurt them."

Again, that was to be determined. "Then who tried to kill Leo?" Olivia prompted, not waiting for the woman to respond before she added, "And you'd better not accuse me of it."

There was a long moment of silence before Bernice spoke. "Not you. But Samuel told me what happened with someone using your phone, and I think I know who's responsible. Rena Oldham."

"Samuel's girlfriend," Leo supplied.

"Ex-girlfriend," Bernice corrected. "Samuel broke things off with her a few days ago. She was pressuring him for marriage, again, and he got fed up with it."

Olivia didn't bother asking Bernice how she became privy to such private information because it was possible she'd learned it from the source—Samuel. If not, Bernice would have made it her business to find out what'd happened. Olivia suspected there was very little that went on at the family estate that Bernice didn't know about.

Well, very little except for the real reason that Olivia had planned to move to Oklahoma. Bernice hadn't seemed to latch onto the fact that Olivia had been planning to protect Leo.

For all the good it'd done.

It certainly hadn't stopped someone from trying to kill him.

"Are you saying that you think Rena Oldham conspired to commit murder?" Leo bluntly challenged.

More silence. "Yes," Bernice finally answered. "And I have some things I think will convince you to arrest her."

"What things?" Leo snapped.

"I'm not getting into this over the phone. I'll meet you at the sheriff's office, but I want you to bring in Rena, too. I want you to question her after you see what I have."

Leo groaned. "You can take whatever you think you've got to my brother, Sheriff Barrett Logan. I'll call him to let him know to expect you."

"No." Bernice definitely didn't pause this time. "I'll only talk to you, so if you want to see what I have, you'll meet me at the sheriff's office. I'm sure Olivia will be very interested in what I have, too."

Olivia was close enough to Leo to see his eyes go cop flat. "If you're withholding evidence pertinent to an investigation, that's a crime. A felony. You want to be arrested Bernice?"

"No." Again, no pause, and there was a bitter edge to her voice. "If you won't meet me at the sheriff's office, then come here to Samuel's estate, or I can go to your place."

"You're not coming here," he snapped but then paused when he got an incoming call.

Olivia saw that it was from Barrett.

"I'll have to call you back," Leo told Bernice. Without

waiting for her response, he switched over to his brother's call. "Is something wrong?" he asked Barrett.

"I'm not sure."

And just those three words put Olivia on full alert. Leo, too, and they both turned toward the kitchen to make sure Cameron was okay. He was. Izzie had moved him away from the window and was feeding him the rest of his breakfast. Thankfully, their son was oblivious to any bad news they were about to hear.

"Milton's psychiatrist isn't here yet, but he's insisting on talking to Olivia," Barrett explained. "In fact, he says he'll make a full confession to her."

"A confession," Leo repeated, and she heard the skepticism in Leo's tone. "Has he made any calls, ones where he could have arranged another attack?"

"No. But I think he's coming down from whatever high he was on. He's been pacing his cell and mumbling about this all being a mistake. I pressed him on exactly what mistake he meant, but he insisted he'd only talk to Olivia."

"It could still be a trap," Leo muttered moments later.

"Could be," Barrett agreed. "But if so, he would have had to set up an attack before his arrest. He was allowed one call, and he didn't use it, not even to contact a lawyer."

Interesting, but that didn't mean the man didn't have something up his sleeve. Still, Olivia would like to hear what Milton had to say.

"I wouldn't want to take Cameron to the sheriff's office," Olivia insisted. "But if you could arrange for a deputy to be here with him, maybe Leo and I can come in. My father's household manager, Bernice Saylor, wants

Leo to meet her there, so we could kill two birds with one stone."

"Why does the household manager want to meet you?" Barrett immediately asked.

It was Leo who answered. "She claims that Samuel's ex-girlfriend is the person responsible for the attack and says she has proof. In fact, Bernice wants the ex brought in for questioning, which might not be a bad idea. Her name is Rena Oldham."

"She's Samuel's ex, you said?" Barrett questioned.

"According to Bernice, she is," Olivia explained. "She's been my father's longtime girlfriend, and they've broken up before. I didn't know about this particular breakup, though."

Barrett stayed silent a few long moments, obviously processing that. "You think Rena's capable of setting up a murder?"

Olivia hadn't had much time to consider the possibility, but she gave it some thought now. "Maybe. She's been on and off with my father for years, and she has a temper. She also claims she's in love with him, so I'm not sure how she'd react if he truly did end things with her for good."

"I'll bring her in for questioning," Barrett assured them. "Where does she live?"

"Culver Crossing." That wasn't far at all and was in the same town where Olivia lived. If Barrett could get in touch with Rena, he might have the woman in his office in under a half hour.

"What about Bernice?" Barrett asked. "Want me to bring her in, as well?"

"Sure. But I can text her," Leo said. "Can you spare a deputy to be with Cameron and his nanny?"

"I'll do better than that. I'm texting Daniel as we speak. He can be at your place in just a few minutes, and he can stay with Izzie and the baby."

Olivia released the breath she'd been holding. Along with being a deputy, Daniel was Leo's brother. He'd do everything within his power to protect Cameron.

"Keep your ranch hands on alert," Barrett advised. "And I'm sending Scottie out to your place for backup. He'll arrive in the cruiser, and Olivia and you can ride with him to town. He won't be able to stay once he's dropped you off because he's not on duty, but I'll get you back home after we're done here."

Again, Olivia was relieved. Scottie Bronson was yet another deputy, one that she knew Leo trusted. Plus, a police cruiser would be a lot safer than a regular vehicle. Still, it would mean leaving Cameron, and Olivia knew that wouldn't be easy, not even for a short time. But if they could get answers to help the investigation, it would ultimately make things safer for her little boy.

"I say we go ahead and bring in Randall," Barrett added. "And Samuel. That way I can ask about alibis and maybe rile at least one of them enough to spill something."

Her father would indeed be riled at being treated as a suspect, but Barrett was right. Sometimes, pushing the right buttons led to answers, and they very much needed answers right now.

Leo ended the call with his brother and immediately texted Bernice to let her know they would meet her at the sheriff's office. Bernice responded with I'm already on the way there.

Good. Olivia didn't exactly relish the idea of dealing with Bernice, but at least this way they wouldn't have to wait long for her to arrive. Besides, if Bernice actually had proof about Rena being involved in this, then maybe Barrett would be able to make an arrest today.

Olivia went back in the kitchen to tell Izzie their plans and to finish feeding Cameron, but only a couple of minutes had passed before she heard the sound of a car engine. Leo's phone also dinged with a text.

"It's Daniel," he relayed. "He's here." And he headed to the door to let his brother in.

Olivia filled in Izzie while Leo and Daniel made their way to the kitchen. Daniel's eyes met hers, and she felt the chill. No doubt because Daniel didn't care much for the custody fight she was giving Leo.

Correction—the fight she *had given* Leo.

Once the danger had passed, she really did need to figure out what to do. If her father was behind the attacks, then her leaving could end up only making things worse.

"Olivia," Daniel greeted, his voice as cool as his eyes. Ironic since they were a genetic copy of Leo's and Cameron's. Thankfully, though, there was no chill when Daniel went to Cameron and brushed a kiss on the top of his head.

Cameron babbled a greeting, grinned and offered Daniel a piece of peach. Obviously, her son was very comfortable around Leo's brother.

"I didn't see anything unusual on the drive over," Daniel explained. "But keep watch. I'll do the same."

Leo nodded in thanks. "I'll text Wally and explain to him what's happening." He shifted his attention to Izzie. "Daniel and some of my hands will be on guard while Olivia and I are out."

"We won't be gone long," Olivia assured the woman. She hoped that was true.

She could tell that Izzie was trying to put on a brave face. Olivia was doing the same thing, and she tried to keep up the pretense that this was just a normal breakfast while they waited for Scottie. However, the moment Leo got the text that the deputy was in front of the house, her nerves and fears returned. Not fear for herself but for Cameron.

"He'll be fine," Daniel said as if reading her mind. He ruffled Cameron's hair, grinned at him.

Olivia wanted to rattle off some instructions, repeating for them to stay away from the windows and reminding them to lock the doors. But Daniel would know to do those things. Once Scottie arrived, Olivia had to force herself out of the kitchen, but she didn't do that until she'd given Cameron several kisses.

When Leo led her out the front door, she saw that Scottie had parked the cruiser directly in front of the house. She also spotted the ranch hands that were standing guard.

As soon as Leo and she were in the back seat, Scottie took off. He didn't offer any greetings, instead keeping his attention on their surroundings. Leo and she did the same. She doubted a gunman would come after them in broad daylight, but she couldn't be sure since she didn't know who or what they were dealing with.

Soon, she hoped, that would change.

"I'm sorry," she muttered to Leo.

His gaze practically snapped toward her. He didn't ask "what for," but she could see the question in his eyes.

"I'm sorry for…everything," she settled for saying. "But especially for not telling you sooner about my father."

A muscle flickered in his jaw before he made a sound of agreement. Maybe he was accepting her apology, or it could be this was simply a discussion he didn't want to have in front of Scottie. Either way, it was her signal to table the subject. That was probably a good thing. It was best to have everything worked out in her mind before she had to hash things out with Leo.

Leo's phone rang, and he snatched it from his jeans' pocket. It was an understatement that they were both on edge, and Olivia immediately began to consider all the worst-cast scenarios.

"It's Randall," he told her.

That certainly didn't make her relax. After all, it was possible that Randall had been the one to hire Milton.

Leo hit the answer button and, like before, Olivia was close enough to hear when Randall snarled, "Deputy Logan, are you trying to get your butt sued?" The man didn't wait for an answer. "Because you and your sheriff brother are harassing me by dragging me in for an interrogation this morning, and that's grounds for a lawsuit."

"The sheriff and I want you in for questioning," Leo stated. "You have means, motive and opportunity for attempted murder of a law enforcement officer. Me," Leo clarified just in case Randall had any doubts.

"I have an alibi," Randall wailed. "My sister told you where I was when you got knifed. I wasn't anywhere near Mercy Ridge or you."

Leo fired right back. "You know that doesn't get you off the hook. Someone hired the idiot who came after me, and you're a person of interest."

Randall spewed a string of raw profanity. "You're just pissed off because you couldn't pin murder on me, and you can't pin this one on me, either." He did more cursing. "I'll bring my lawyer for this witch hunt of an interrogation. Then I'll be filing that lawsuit right after.

You'd better be prepared to pony up lots of cash because I'll sue you for every penny the Logans have." With that, Randall ended the call.

If Leo was concerned about the threat of a possible lawsuit, he didn't show it. He just dragged in a weary breath and continued to keep watch.

It took Scottie less than fifteen minutes to reach the sheriff's office, but every mile felt like an eternity to Olivia. So did the mere seconds it took to get out of the cruiser and inside. She immediately tried to steel herself up for Bernice, but the woman wasn't there. There was only a female deputy at the dispatch/reception desk and Barrett, who was making his way from his office toward them.

"The psychiatrist has been delayed, Bernice and Rena should be here any minute," Barrett told them. "Randall is due in an hour, and Samuel will be in this afternoon."

"Randall called me a couple of minutes ago," Leo informed him. "He wanted to express his disapproval at being called in." He dragged his hand over his face. "This smacks of something Randall could have done, and he's at the top of my suspect list."

"Mine, too," Barrett agreed. "What better way to get back at you than to have you murdered and to set up the mother of your child to take the blame?"

That put a huge knot in Olivia's stomach. Because it could be true. All of this could be about revenge, and Randall probably wouldn't care if Cameron became collateral damage.

"I'll go ahead and move Milton to an interview room so he can get started with that confession he says he wants to give you," Barrett added to Olivia. "Leo and I will be in there with you, and I'll also be recording everything that's said."

She nodded and had fully expected the recording. What Olivia hadn't expected was to be in the same room with Milton. She had thought she'd be speaking to him while he was behind bars. In hindsight, she should have realized that Barrett would need to make this an official interrogation.

"Wait here, and I'll get Milton," Barrett said, heading in the direction of where Olivia figured the holding cells were.

"Want some coffee?" Leo asked, going to the small serving area on the far side of the room.

However, he stopped when a bell rang to indicate the front door had just opened. The adrenaline shot through her when she saw Leo place his hand over his weapon, and she whirled around to see what had caused that reaction.

Rena Oldham walked in.

She wasn't what anyone would call willowy. In fact, she had what Olivia thought of as an Amazon warrior's build on a sturdy five-foot, ten-inch frame. Rena obviously worked out a lot, too, because her arms and legs were well toned.

Despite the somewhat early hour, the woman looked well put together in her red summer pants, white top and sandals. There wasn't a strand of her shoulder-length honey-blond hair out of place. Ditto for her perfectly applied makeup, but then again Olivia had never seen her look any other way. Bernice had mentioned something about Rena being in her fifties, but she looked much younger than that.

"Where's Bernice?" Rena snarled, and her tone gave

Olivia a taste of the temper that she'd mentioned to Leo. "I want to confront that busybody witch for lying about me."

Leo skipped getting any coffee and went to Olivia's side. "How'd you know Bernice is lying?"

"Because she called me and told me she was coming here, and that she had so-called proof that I'm the one responsible for you and Olivia nearly being killed." Rena turned her cool blue eyes on Olivia then. "I didn't have anything to do with that."

"So, why does Bernice think you did?" Leo challenged.

"Because she's a jealous, vindictive witch," Rena readily supplied. "She doesn't want anyone near her precious Samuel except her. Well, she can have him. I'm done with Samuel."

So, it was true that her father and Rena had broken up. Not really a surprise. Olivia had been down this path with them before.

"What exactly does Bernice have that she's calling proof of your guilt?" Leo asked.

Rena threw her hands in the air. "Your guess is as good as mine. But whatever it is, it doesn't point to me as a would-be killer because I'm not one. You put that on whatever official record you need."

Leo nodded. "Let's move this conversation to an interview room." He motioned for them to follow him, but they hadn't even reached the hall when Barrett came out with Milton.

Everyone froze.

Milton's gaze zoomed right to Olivia, and he smiled. She felt the flash of disgust followed by the rage. This SOB had tried to kill Leo and had tried to pin that on her.

Olivia glared at him and had to rein in that rage to keep from going to him and slapping him. But Milton's attention was no longer on her. He looked at Rena.

And smiled again.

This was a different kind of smile, though. Not a taunt like the one he'd doled out to her. This one had a glimmer of recognition, and his eyes practically lit up. Rena, however, didn't have that reaction. She squared her shoulders and groaned softly.

"You two know each other?" Leo asked, clearly picking up on their body language.

"No," Rena said at the same moment that Milton answered. "Yeah, we do."

Leo aimed a scowl at Rena. "Do you know this man?" he pressed.

Rena huffed. "He knew my brother, Brett. They were drug users, so I distanced myself from both of them."

"Then, you do know Milton," Leo stated, his voice flat. Obviously, he didn't care for the lie that Rena had told with her previous response.

Annoyance and anger sparked through Rena's eyes. "If you're trying to connect me to this piece of scum, then you'd better stop right there. I haven't seen or spoken to Milton in years, not since my brother died of an overdose from drugs that this snake gave him." She tipped her head at Milton to indicate *he* was that *snake*.

Milton tried to shrug despite the fact that he was cuffed and Barrett had his arm in a grip. "Brett supplied me with plenty of stuff, too. I just got lucky and he didn't."

Rena took a step toward him as if she might launch herself at him. Since Olivia had wanted to do the same thing just minutes earlier, she totally understood the woman's reaction. But Leo stepped in front of Rena to stop her. No way did he want a brawl when they hadn't even had a chance to deal with Milton.

"Wait here," Leo ordered Rena, and he glanced at the deputy at the desk. According to her name tag, she was Cybil Cassidy. "Stay with Miss Oldham while Olivia and I have a chat with Milton."

"I've changed my mind," Milton blurted when they started for the interview room. He smiled at Olivia again. "I've decided I don't want to make a confession, after all."

Olivia muttered some profanity before she could stop herself, and she got a second slam of anger. "Why not?" she demanded.

With a ghost of that sly smile still on his mouth, he shook his head. "I'm not feeling well. I should probably talk to the psychiatrist first. Then, if I'm feeling better, you and I can have a heart to heart."

Coming from Milton, that last part sounded like a threat. Felt like one, too.

"What kind of sick game are you playing?" Leo demanded, going closer to Milton.

Milton looked Leo straight in the eye. "I'm a sick man, didn't you know? And it's my right not to say anything that could incriminate me."

"Was this a ploy to get us off the ranch so someone else can try to kill us?" Olivia quickly asked.

Leo had already gone there, and he fired off a text to Daniel to make sure everything was okay. Daniel gave him an equally quick response to let him know that it was. Leo then warned his brother to be extra cautious, though he figured Daniel was already doing just that.

Leo shifted his attention back to Milton and didn't break the intense stare he had with the man until the door opened again. This time there were two visitors, both women. The first to walk in was a tall, slim woman with auburn hair that fell right at her chin. Leo didn't know her, but he figured she was the psychiatrist. Leo had no trouble recognizing the second one.

Bernice.

Like Rena, she was tall, but that's where the similarities ended. Bernice had a stocky build with wide shoulders, and her dark brown hair was threaded with gray. No makeup, and her clothes didn't look as if they'd have a designer label. She wore a fitted gray dress that wouldn't have looked out of place on a hotel maid.

Bernice and Rena started a glaring match of their own, but Barrett handed off Milton to Deputy Cassidy with instructions to take him to the interview room.

"Dr. Kirkpatrick?" Barrett asked, and the woman nodded. Once he'd checked her ID, he motioned for her to follow Deputy Cassidy and Milton. "I want a copy of your eval as soon as you have it."

"I'll give you any information that I can," the doctor countered.

That meant she likely wouldn't tell Barrett everything that went on in the eval. She followed Milton and the deputy, leaving Olivia with Barrett, Leo, Rena and Bernice. The air was practically crackling with tension, and most of it was coming from Rena.

"How dare you accuse me of trying to kill someone," Rena said through clenched teeth. "You're vindictive and jealous, and you have nothing connecting me to any of this mess."

Bernice's glare softened when she turned to Leo. She took a large manila envelope from her purse and handed it to him.

"I think once you read everything in there, you'll see what I mean about Rena being the one who hired Milton," Bernice calmly stated.

"I didn't hire him," Rena practically shouted, and she tried to snatch the envelope from Leo. He shot her a look that could have frozen the deepest level of hell.

"What's in here?" Leo asked Bernice.

The woman took a deep breath before she answered. "Copies of emails that Rena sent Samuel after he broke up with her this last time. She threatened to get back at him."

Rena rolled her eyes, obviously dismissing that, but the anger stayed on her face. "I was furious and hurt. Those emails meant nothing. And you had no right to read them," she added to Bernice. "Those were private emails I sent to Samuel."

"I run the estate," Bernice pointed out. "That includes going through correspondence and emails. You threatened to get back at Samuel, and you said it'd be awful if something bad happened to someone he loved."

"I was angry," Rena argued. "I didn't mean it. I didn't mean it," she repeated, aiming her plea at Olivia.

Olivia had no idea if Rena had meant it or not. Maybe her temper had just gotten the best of her. Maybe not. She could be looking into the face of the person who'd set up the attack.

"Rena broke into the estate just yesterday," Bernice added. "I found her trying to go through Samuel's office when he wasn't there."

"I didn't break in." Rena's voice held as much of a snarl as Bernice's. "Samuel gave me a key and the security codes—"

Bernice just talked right over Rena. "I had the locks

and security system changed last night after I insisted she leave the premises. She wouldn't tell me what she was looking for in Samuel's office, but I suspect she was there to steal something."

Rena gave the woman a much cooler look, her mouth curved into a sly smile. "I was looking for my earring that fell off when Samuel and I had sex on his desk. Did you listen in on that, too, Bernice? Did you get an eyeful of your *employer* getting down and dirty with me?"

Olivia groaned. That was so not an image she wanted in her head. Apparently, neither did Bernice because she gave Rena a cold stare.

"Samuel's with so many women that I don't notice such things," Bernice said, her voice as icy as the look. "You are one of dozens. *Dozens*," she stressed. "And none of them, including you, lasted."

That clearly rattled Rena. She opened her mouth, closed it and then narrowed her eyes. "Samuel still has feelings for me," Rena insisted. "You just wait and see. He'll come back to me. He always does."

"Keep thinking that," Bernice grumbled and turned to Leo. "I hired a PI to do a thorough background check on Rena, and I learned that she has criminal contacts. Your suspect, Milton Hough, for one. She knows him."

"So I just found out." Leo lifted the envelope and ignored the sound of outrage that Rena made. "I'll read what's in here, but I want to know if any of the emails mentioned Milton?"

"No. But there is something you might find interesting." Bernice tipped her head to the envelope. "Read the PI's report, and you'll see that Rena has another connection to you. Or rather, a connection to someone who wants you dead." She gave a satisfied nod. "Rena's been bedmates with none other than the man who'd do any-thing to ruin you."

"And who would that be?" Leo asked.

Bernice lifted her chin. "Randall Arnett."

# Chapter Seven

Randall Arnett.

Leo wasn't surprised to hear that particular name come up in this investigation, but he hadn't expected this kind of connection. He stared at Rena, waiting for an explanation. Olivia and Barrett were doing the same thing. However, it seemed to take Rena a couple of long moments just to compose herself.

Rena made a throaty sound and whipped out her phone. "I'm calling my lawyer."

"Good," Barrett advised her. "Because you're going to need one." He glanced at Leo. "You want to take her in for questioning, or should I do it?"

Leo stared at the envelope a moment. "I want to go through this envelope first. That'll give her lawyer a chance to get here."

Rena was already speaking to someone on the phone, presumably her attorney, and it made Leo wonder just how often the woman required legal services that she would be able to make contact this quickly. But that was a question for another time, another place. For now, he wanted to get a look at what Bernice had put in the envelope.

"You can have a seat out here," Barrett told Bernice.

"I'll need to take your statement, too, but you'll have to wait your turn."

"Oh, I'll wait," Bernice assured him. "I'll do whatever it takes to get that piece of temperamental fluff out of Samuel's life."

Beside him, Leo saw Olivia go a little stiff. "You do this sort of thing often for my father?" she asked.

Bernice's chin came up. "I take care of him. Which is more than you do," she snapped. "He's worried sick about Cameron and you."

There it was again. The territorial attitude that Bernice had always had for Samuel. Normally, Leo didn't see anything especially sinister about it, but this felt... well, different.

Bernice had obviously gone to some expense and trouble to dig up dirt on Rena, but he knew from experience that a person doing the digging could be selective about what they found. In other words, Bernice could have looked solely for info to discredit a woman she saw as competition for Samuel's attention. Or a woman Bernice wanted to punish because she had not gone quietly after this latest breakup with Samuel.

Since he wanted to get Olivia away from Bernice—and away from the windows—he motioned for her to follow him. He didn't have an office of his own, none of the deputies did, so they went into Barrett's and he shut the door. He'd still be able to hear if anyone came in because the bell on the door would alert him, but this way he and Olivia would have some privacy to go through the envelope. Plus, there was no worry about Bernice not staying put. It was crystal-clear that the woman intended to put the screws to Rena.

Leo took a moment once they were alone to try to absorb all the information he'd just gotten from Rena and Bernice. Apparently, Olivia was doing the same because she didn't say anything, and he heard her draw in a long, deep breath and then slowly expel it.

"If there's anything in the emails, can you actually use it to arrest Rena?" she finally asked as she sank into the chair next to the desk.

Leo shrugged and sat, too. Opening the envelope, he took out the papers. "Maybe. There could be a chain of custody issue, though. Bernice could have altered the emails she's printed out, so we'd have to see the originals and verify that Rena did, indeed, send them."

Of course, Rena hadn't denied the sending part, only the intent. And intent in an email was hard to prove. Even if she'd threatened Samuel to hell and back, it didn't mean the woman had actually gone through on the threats. Then again, she did have those criminal contacts.

Including Randall.

Leo pondered that a moment while he glanced through the first email. Yeah, it was a threat, all right. One peppered with a lot of profanity, capital letters and exclamation marks. What he didn't see were any details of how Rena would carry through with getting back at her lover for dumping her. There were no specifics, no time and place references, just the "something awful" that might happen to someone Samuel loved.

But it wasn't as black and white as Bernice had painted it.

I was in love with you, Rena had written. Just imagine something awful happening to someone you love, and that's how I feel right now. You've crushed my heart, Samuel, and I hope that one day you'll hurt as much as I'm hurting now.

Definitely no "I'm going to kill someone you love" as Bernice had made it seem. Still, there was a lot of emotion in that handful of sentences, and sometimes emotion could cause people to do all sorts of bad things.

He handed the email to Olivia so she could read it for herself and then went onto the next one. There were five total, all where Rena had vented and spewed some venom. He passed those to Olivia, as well, and studied the next page. It was an account of what Bernice had overheard when Rena and Samuel had argued about the breakup. It was clearly hearsay, but if Samuel verified it, then it could be used to show that Rena had had motive to set up the attack.

"Did your father say anything to you about his breakup with Rena?" Leo asked Olivia.

"Nothing specific, but they've broken up so many times that it's not something he'd talk to me about." She looked up from the paper and their gazes met. "It doesn't feel as if Rena would try to get back at my father through you. With her hot temper, it seems as if she'd just go directly after him."

"That'd be what everyone would expect. But maybe Rena reined in her temper long enough to figure that out. After all, if someone tried to kill Samuel, she'd be a prime suspect. This way, he's still punished because you were set up to take the blame for the attack."

She nodded, took another of those long breaths. "So, Rena could have hired her late brother's friend." Olivia paused. "Or hired Randall."

"Yeah," Leo agreed as he put aside the rest of Bernice's account of the breakup so he could look through the PI's report.

It was thorough. That was Leo's first impression. The

PI had basically provided details of the last twenty years of Rena's life. He'd used social media posts and info that he'd garnered from her friends to detail a pattern of being with Samuel, followed by a breakup, followed by short romantic relationships with other men. Short career ventures, too. Rena came from money and had a trust fund, one that she'd practically drained to set up one failed business after the other.

"If this report is accurate," Leo remarked to Olivia, "then Rena is hurting financially. In fact, she's flat broke and financing her lifestyle off credit cards. Maybe that's one of the reasons she was pressing your father for marriage."

"Maybe," Olivia agreed. "But if she's broke, then she wouldn't have been able to pay Milton for the attack."

"No, but it could be she didn't need cash for that. Perhaps she just stirred him up enough. Or he could have done this as a favor since he knew her brother."

"Maybe," Olivia repeated, not sounding convinced.

Leo was on the same page with her. He wasn't convinced, either.

Olivia stood so she could read the report from over his shoulder. Of course, that meant her face ended up very close to his.

He caught her scent.

When she'd showered that morning, she'd obviously used the same brand of soap that he had. That's what would have been in the guest bath. It was pretty basic soap, but it managed to smell damn special on her since it mingled with her own unique scent. One that he remembered all too well. And one that stirred him in the wrong places.

"Rena was with Randall for about two and a half

months," Olivia said, going through the report. She was totally unaware of the effect she was having on him. "Do I have the timing right? Rena was with Randall shortly after he was with the girlfriend who went missing?"

"Jessa McCade," Leo provided. Yes, the timing was right for that. "I'll want to question Rena to find out if Randall said anything to her about Jessa. Or if Randall was ever violent with her—as I suspect he had been with Jessa."

In fact, Leo figured the violence had maybe started as an argument and had escalated when Randall had killed Jessa in a fit of temper. Then Randall had disposed of the body and it hadn't been found. It was the only thing that made sense to Leo since he wasn't buying that Jessa had just run off, leaving her family and five-year-old son. No. All the indications were that Jessa loved her little boy and had just gotten mixed up with the wrong man—Randall.

He felt Olivia brush her hand over his shoulder, but it took him a moment to realize she'd done that as a gesture of comfort. Apparently, she'd picked up on the vibes he was giving off. Regret over not being able to bring Randall to justice.

"Randall killed Jessa," Leo stated. "There's plenty of circumstantial evidence, but I wasn't able to do what I needed to do to find something more concrete." Maybe Rena could provide that missing piece.

He glanced over to where Olivia still had her hand on his shoulder. But it was bad timing on his part. Because he did that at the exact moment she looked down. His mouth grazed her cheek. And he felt that slight touch in every inch of his body.

Every inch.

Hell. He still wanted her. Bad.

She didn't pull away from him. Instead, Olivia shifted her gaze so they were staring directly into each other's eyes. Leo could have sworn that the temperature in the room heated up a full twenty degrees, and he fought not to latch onto her and kiss her. It was a battle that he thought he was winning.

When Olivia kissed him.

She made a small sound, a mix of surprise and pleasure. Not good. Because that pleasure kicked his need for her into overdrive. Now, he did latch onto her, turning in the chair so that he could take her mouth the way he wanted. He made the kiss long and deep, more than enough to qualify as foreplay. Foreplay that shouldn't be happening. No way should he be muddying the waters like this with her.

Olivia seemed to agree with him on that last part because she pulled away. Her breathing was way too heavy. Her face flushed. She took several steps back to put some distance between them.

"We should be talking about Randall," Olivia muttered, still fighting to level her breathing. "And about Milton. We shouldn't be kissing."

Leo couldn't argue with any of that. Of course, at the moment, he couldn't speak to argue about anything. It took him several moments to shake off the heat and gather some common sense. The investigation. That should be their focus because the only way to stop the danger was to find the person responsible.

Olivia cleared her throat and sat back down. "Did Randall's alibi check out for the attack?" she asked.

Since she'd managed to get past the kiss, Leo made sure he did, as well. "On the surface." He'd gone through Barrett's report first thing this morning. "His current girlfriend said he was with her, but that doesn't mean he's innocent."

It also didn't mean the girlfriend was telling the truth. Lovers lied for each other all the time. Heck, Olivia had lied to him when she'd ended their relationship. Lied because she hadn't wanted him to incur her father's wrath. Later, it was a discussion that Olivia and he needed to have, but for now he went back to the PI's report on Rena. He'd barely finished the next page before the landline phone rang on Barrett's desk.

"Deputy Logan," Leo answered.

"Deputy Logan," the caller repeated. "Good. I would have called you next. I'm Deputy Chief Trey Mercer from the Culver Crossing Fire Department. I'm trying to reach Olivia Nash."

Leo immediately felt the punch of dread. "She's here. What's wrong?" he demanded, and he put the call on speaker.

"I've got a crew on the way out to her place now," Trey said. "A call came in from an anonymous source about twenty minutes ago, and the person said he'd set fire to her house."

Olivia practically leaped to her feet. "You've verified there really is a fire?" she asked. And Leo knew what she was thinking—that it could be a lure to draw them out.

"Not yet. But the caller said there was a second fire. This one is out of my jurisdiction, though. He claims it's in Mercy Ridge, so I've alerted the fire chief there."

Leo got to his feet, too, just as his own phone rang. "Where in Mercy Ridge?" he snapped.

"According to the call," the deputy chief answered, "there's an incendiary device on a timer, and it's set to go off at your house in ten minutes."

# Chapter Eight

The fear cut through Olivia like a switchblade and, for a second, the air vanished from her lungs. She couldn't catch her breath, but she turned and started out of the office. Leo, right behind her, took hold of her arm before she could bolt out the front door.

"Wait," Leo insisted over the sound of his still ringing phone. "This could be a trap."

Olivia hadn't even thought of that and didn't want to think of it now. She only wanted to get to Cameron and to make sure he was okay.

"What's wrong?" Bernice asked. "Is there trouble?"

Leo didn't respond to the woman, but he did answer his phone. Olivia saw Mercy Ridge Fire Department on his screen. "Are you on your way out to my place?" Leo demanded the moment he had someone on the line.

"Yes," the caller assured him. "Our ETA is about ten minutes."

That felt like an eternity. Way too long to make sure Cameron was safe.

"Get there as fast as you can," Leo insisted.

He ended the call and immediately made another one. This time to Daniel. And he did all that while hanging on to Olivia's hand, probably to ensure that she didn't run outside.

"Daniel," he said when his brother answered. "Culver Crossing PD got an anonymous tip that there could be a device rigged to set a fire at my house. Any signs of trouble?"

"None," Daniel said without hesitation. "We've all been keeping watch, and no one has gotten near the house."

That didn't cause Olivia to breathe any easier because, if there truly was a device, it might not have gone off yet.

"Go get Barrett," Leo told Olivia.

She wanted to leave, to get into the cruiser and head straight to Leo's, but she did as Leo asked and hurried to the hall where there were two interview rooms. Deputy Cassidy was standing guard outside one of them, no doubt where Milton was having his eval with the psychiatrist.

"What's wrong?" the deputy asked.

"There's a problem!" Olivia exclaimed as she threw open the second door where Barrett was questioning Rena.

Barrett clearly saw the alarm on Olivia's face because he was already on his feet. "Wait here," he told Rena before rushing out into the hall with Olivia. "Keep an eye on both Milton and Miss Oldham," he directed the deputy.

Olivia didn't waste any time running back toward Leo. He was still on the phone, but he tossed Barrett a set of keys that he took from the dispatcher's desk. "Let's go," Leo demanded. "I'll fill you in on the way."

Barrett didn't question his brother. He snatched the keys out of the air, and the three of them raced to the cruiser that was still parked directly in front of the station. As they'd done on the drive to the sheriff's office, Leo and she jumped in the back, but this time it was Barrett who got in behind the wheel.

Olivia's pulse was thick and throbbing, making it hard for her to hear, but she caught bits and pieces of the instructions that Leo rattled off to Daniel. *Truck. Car seat. Road.*

"Someone might have put a firebomb at Leo's house," she explained to Barrett when his eyes met hers in the rearview mirror.

That was all the info Barrett needed to hit the siren and the accelerator. They sped away from the sheriff's office. Judging from the way Barrett started firing glances all around them, he must have thought this could be some kind of ruse, as well. If so, it had worked because it'd gotten her and Leo out of the building and on the road where they'd be easier targets.

"Daniel and the hands haven't seen anything suspicious," Leo relayed to them the moment he'd finished his call. "But we're taking precautions anyway since it's possible that someone planted a device days or even weeks ago before we were on watch."

Oh mercy. She hadn't even considered that, but Olivia certainly considered it now. "Cameron," was all she managed to say.

"He'll be fine," Leo quickly told her, but she saw that the assurance didn't make it to his eyes. He was just as terrified for their baby as she was. "Daniel's moving my truck into the garage, and Izzie will get Cameron into his car seat before they drive out. They won't go far, just about twenty yards from the house, and the hands will guard the truck to make sure no one tries to sneak up on them."

Those were good security measures, and it would prevent Cameron from being in the house in case it did catch fire. But Olivia wasn't sure those measures would be enough.

"Someone could fire shots into the truck," she reminded him.

"No. Because no one will get close enough to do that. The hands are armed with rifles, and they're all good shots. No one will get in position to try to hurt Cameron."

Olivia wanted to latch onto that. Wanted it to be the gospel truth. But there were thick trees along Leo's property line, and a sniper could climb one of those and start firing. Of course, if that happened, Daniel would almost certainly protect Cameron with his life, but it might not be enough.

*It might not be enough.*

She had to choke back the sob that tried to make its way out of her throat, and she forced herself to keep it together. If she gave in to the fear and panic now, it wouldn't help and in fact could hurt. After all, they needed to be focused on any possible threats waiting for them between here and Leo's place.

Leo's phone rang again, the sound shooting through the cruiser. Shooting through her, as well. Olivia's gaze automatically flew to the cell's screen where she expected to see Daniel's name. But it wasn't. It was the Culver Crossing Fire Department again. Leo answered the call right away and put it on speaker.

"It's Deputy Chief Trey Mercer," the caller said. "I've got some bad news."

Olivia could have sworn her heart stopped. Just stopped. A thousand thoughts went through her head, none good.

"We're out at Olivia Nash's place," the fireman continued, "and we're not going to be able to save it. The roof's already collapsed, and the fire's spread into the yard. My men are working to contain it now."

Under most circumstances, Olivia would have found that new devasting, but it was a relief because the *bad news* didn't involve Cameron. She was finally able to release the breath that was now burning in her chest.

"Are you on your way out here?" the fireman asked.

It was Leo who answered. "No. I'm not sure when Olivia will be able to get there. Days, maybe. She's in protective custody."

"Oh." Judging from his surprised tone, the deputy chief hadn't expected that. "All right, then. I'll send you my preliminary report when I can get it done. It'll take a while, though, because this is definitely an arson investigation. There's a strong smell of accelerant."

She hadn't doubted that the fire had been intentionally set. But why? Was it just another distraction, or had their attackers thought she was there? Obviously, someone had wanted to set her up to take the blame for Leo's murder, but maybe she was now the primary target. Or else someone wanted them to believe that.

Leo's phone dinged again with a text message. "It's from Daniel," he said to Barrett and her. "The fire department is at the house, and there are still no signs of a device. The bomb squad's on the way."

Olivia grasped the part about there being *no signs of a device*. The seconds ticked by slowly, and she moved to the edge of her seat as Barrett took the turn to Leo's ranch. It wouldn't be long now before she could see Cameron and, better yet, get him in the cruiser so he'd be better protected. However, the house was still out of view when Barrett slammed on his brakes, sending the tires screeching on the asphalt.

Olivia immediately saw why Barrett had done that. There was a man in the middle of the road, and he was waving his hands around as if trying to flag them down. There was a truck behind him, from which he'd likely made a quick exit because the driver's door was still open.

"Randall," Leo snarled. "What the hell does he want?"

That revved her heartbeat up again. Olivia hadn't recognized the man, though she'd seen his photo in the news during the investigation of his missing girlfriend. Unlike the picture that'd been taken at a party where he'd been dressed in a suit, today he was in jeans and had an unbuttoned denim shirt over a white tee.

Randall was also armed with a rifle.

Barrett didn't lower the window but instead spoke to Randall through the microphone that he unclipped from the siren. "Stop where you are and put down your weapon," he ordered when Randall came closer.

Randall didn't stop. Just the opposite. With both hands gripped on the rifle, he began to run toward the cruiser.

"Get down," Leo told her. He drew his gun. Barrett did the same.

Olivia didn't want to get down. She wanted to hurry to the ranch to check on Cameron, especially since Randall could be there to set off the timer on any firebomb he might have planted. But there was no way they could ignore this threat that was coming right at them.

Barrett got out and, using the cruiser door for cover, took aim. Leo did the same on the other side of the vehicle.

"Stop," Barrett shouted out again.

However, the moment Barrett gave that command, the blast tore through the air. Not a gunshot. No. This was an explosion, and Randall's truck became a fireball.

THE BLAST CAUSED the cruiser doors to slam into Leo and Barrett. Leo cursed and nearly dropped from the pain when the door caught his injured arm. But he forced himself to stay on his feet. to focus. And to assess what the hell was going on.

Barrett was cursing in pain, too, because his door had rammed into his shoulder. Randall was on the ground where he'd landed face-first. His rifle was no longer in his hands, probably because it'd been thrown clear from him in the fall. That was the good news, that Randall was no longer armed. Good, too, that Olivia wasn't hurt— Leo glanced at her to see that she was shaken up, but she hadn't been injured.

The bad news was that pieces of Randall's truck were raining down around them. Fiery bits of metal and rubber that could be just as deadly as bullets.

"Get back in the cruiser," Leo told his brother, and he did the same. He got another jolt of pain from his arm when he had to use his hand to slam the door shut.

In the front, Barrett did the same, and he grabbed the microphone again. "Randall, if you can move, take cover under the cruiser. There could be a secondary explosion from the gas tank."

Randall lifted his head, shook it as if to clear it and, with plenty of effort, got to a crouching position. He was bleeding. Leo couldn't tell how badly he was hurt because the black smoke billowing off what was left of his truck immediately engulfed him.

"You tried to kill me!" Randall shouted. "So help you, you Logans will pay for this."

Obviously, Randall thought they were responsible for whatever had caused his truck to explode. It was possible, though, that this was some kind of sick plan to make himself look innocent. If so, the ploy had clearly gotten out of hand. He could have been killed.

Randall came out of the smoke, walking now. Or rather, stumbling and limping. But he didn't move toward the cruiser. Instead, he made his way to the side of the road, dropped down into the ditch and headed for a cluster of trees. What he hadn't done was pick up his rifle. It was still on the ground.

"I'll call for assistance," Barrett said, using the phone on the dash as he put the cruiser in Reverse. "I can't get past the fire, so I'll have to use the ranch trail."

The trail would indeed get them to the house, but it would take longer than the road. Plus, there was the huge concern that someone might be lying in wait along the route since his ranch hands weren't patrolling that particular area of his property.

Leo took out his phone to call Daniel, but it rang in his hand and he saw his brother's name on the screen.

"We heard a blast," Daniel said the moment Leo answered. "Are you all okay?"

"Yeah. What about Cameron, Izzie and you?" Leo countered.

"Fine. What blew up?"

"Randall's truck. He wasn't in it at the time, so he's still alive," Leo added, and he glanced in the direction where he'd last seen the man. He was no longer in sight. "The road isn't passable right now, so we'll use the west trail. Our ETA is about ten minutes. Eight," he amended when Barrett hit the accelerator and got them speeding out of there.

"Any idea who blew up Randall's truck?" Daniel asked.

"Not yet. Maybe Randall himself. Possibly the person who hired Milton. Just keep Cameron safe," Leo stressed.

"Will do. See you in a few."

Leo ended the call and turned to Olivia to do another check on her. She was way paler than usual, but she looked a lot steadier than he'd thought she would be.

"You're hurt," she muttered, reaching for his sleeve that now had some blood on it. The impact of the cruiser door had obviously reopened the wound.

"I'll clean it when I get home," he assured her, hoping there'd be a home for him to go back to.

Until he'd seen Randall's truck get blown to bits, Leo hadn't been sure there truly was a device rigged with an explosive. Obviously, there had been, and now he could only pray there wasn't a second device. Especially one anywhere near Cameron that someone else could set off.

Olivia didn't listen to his comment about taking care of the wound when he got home. She eased up his sleeve and had a look for herself. Leo didn't glance down when she started to dab away the blood. He kept his attention on the turn that Barrett made onto the trail.

Unlike the main road, the west trail was narrow, only wide enough for one vehicle. Along with plenty of potholes in the gravel surface, it was lined on both sides with trees and thick underbrush. Plenty of places for someone to hide, though Leo didn't think they had to worry about Randall. Even if the man had managed to run at full speed, he wouldn't have been able to get here and set up position for an attack.

Going as fast as he safely could, Barrett sped down the trail, hitting his breaks to take a deep curve. The moment he did, Leo heard a sound he definitely didn't want to hear.

A gunshot.

Hell. This was exactly what Leo had feared would happen. And what he'd hoped they could avoid.

The first bullet didn't hit the cruiser, but the second one did. It slammed into the front of the vehicle, and Leo immediately pushed Olivia down onto the seat. He also glanced around, looking for the shooter.

And he soon found him.

There was a man just ahead, leaning out from a spindly tree. He wasn't wearing a mask, so Leo saw his face but didn't recognize him. A stranger. That meant this was likely a hired gun.

"Hold on," Barrett warned a split second before he aimed the cruiser in the direction of the shooter.

Obviously, the guy hadn't been expecting that because he scrambled out of the way before he could get off another shot. Barrett slammed on his brakes, the side of the cruiser scraping against the tree.

Leo already had his weapon ready. So did Barrett. They fired glances around, looking to see if this idiot was alone or if he'd brought backup. Leo didn't see anyone else.

The moment the cruiser stopped, Leo and Barrett threw open their doors, both taking aim at the gunman who was still trying to get his balance.

"I'm Sheriff Logan," Barrett called out. "Drop your weapon and put up your hands or I'll shoot."

The man whirled around and in the same motion, brought up his gun. Definitely not a move to drop the weapon as Barrett had ordered. And Leo got confirmation of that when the man fired a shot at them. Leo had no doubts that this idiot would kill all of them if he got the chance. And that's why Leo pulled the trigger. He aimed for the guy's chest and sent two rounds into him.

That stopped him.

The man froze, the look of shock washing over his face. He dropped his gun so he could clasp his hands to his chest. Not that it would do any good. No. Leo could see that the guy was bleeding out fast.

"Call an ambulance," Leo told Olivia, tossing her his phone.

Maybe, just maybe, they could keep this SOB alive so he could tell them what the hell was going on.

*Chapter Nine*

Olivia made the call for the EMTs to come to the ranch trail to try to save the man who'd just tried to kill them. Maybe the same man who'd also blown up Randall's truck. If they got lucky, he'd be able to tell them for himself.

"Take the cruiser and get Olivia out of here so you can check on Cameron," Barrett instructed Leo. "I'll wait here until the ambulance arrives."

Leo shook his head and glanced around. "I don't want to leave you alone because this guy could have a partner or two."

Barrett made a sound of agreement. "And if he does, he'll be going after Olivia and you. Take her to your house, and move Cameron and the nanny into the cruiser where they'll be safer. Then, all of you can go back to the sheriff's office until we get the all-clear on your place."

Olivia also had worries about leaving Barrett, but she was desperate to see her son and to make sure he was okay.

"All of you can bunk in the breakroom until we figure out a better place," Barrett added and then motioned for Leo to move. "Go ahead. Get Olivia away from this."

Leo nodded, but there was a lot of hesitancy in his expression. However, he finally got behind the wheel and took off. He also called Daniel and gave him a brief explanation as to what was going on and asked that Daniel come to assist Barrett as soon as Olivia and he were back at the ranch. It wasn't a great plan because any or all of them could be in danger from a sniper, but at the moment he had no great plan other than to make things as safe for Cameron as he could.

Olivia dug her fingers into the seat as Leo maneuvered the cruiser through the snaking trail. She also kept watch, praying that there wasn't a second gunman. Thankfully, she didn't see anyone until they reached the edge of the ranch, and she recognized the man as one of Leo's hands. He gave Leo a nod of greeting and continued to stand guard.

"Don't get out until I'm right next to the truck," Leo told her, figuring that she would indeed scramble to see Cameron.

Olivia obeyed, but she put her hand on the door, ready to open it, and waited for Leo to park side by side with his truck. Daniel must have been ready, too, because Leo and he moved as if they'd rehearsed it. Within seconds, both Izzie and Cameron were in the back seat of the cruiser with Olivia.

She immediately took her son from his seat and into her arms.

Cameron was smiling and babbled some happy sounds, so he obviously wasn't aware of what was going on. Good. She wanted to shelter him as much as she could. For now, Olivia showered him with kisses and lifted him when Leo looked back at the boy. Cameron had a big smile for him, too, and reached out for his dad to take him, but Leo just gave him a kiss and ruffled his hair.

"He needs to go back in his seat," Leo instructed. "I don't want to stay here in case the place explodes."

Izzie didn't gasp, but Olivia saw the nanny's bottom lip trembling. "Daniel told you what's going on?" Olivia asked and got a nod. "We'll be okay," Olivia tried to reassure her.

While Olivia strapped Cameron back in, Daniel hurried over to the truck, no doubt to go to Barrett. Leo also made a call and, within just a couple of minutes, two of his hands drove up in a dark blue truck.

"They'll follow us back to the sheriff's office," Leo advised, driving away the moment she and Izzie had on their seat belts. "We can't go out the main road because of Randall's truck, and we can't use the west trail since Daniel and the ambulance will have that way blocked. We'll have to go through the trail that leads off the back pasture."

Olivia was grateful for the backup and hoped it would be enough. She didn't want the reassurance she'd just given Izzie to be lip service.

Leo's gaze met hers in the mirror for a split second. Maybe he was trying to dole out some encouragement, too, but Olivia also took it as a signal to keep watch. After all, there could also be another sniper on this trail.

And that caused her to consider something.

Even if the person behind these attacks hadn't actually paid Milton, he or she would have likely had to pay the wounded man on the trail. Perhaps had to pay others, as well. She doubted payments like that would be cheap.

That brought her back to Randall and her father.

They had the kind of money to order a hit and to create this kind of chaos. Rena did not. Olivia didn't know if Bernice did, either, but if money was a factor here, it'd rule out Rena. Then again, money could be borrowed or stolen, and services could be bartered or coerced. In other words, any one of their suspects could have pulled this off.

Olivia pushed all of that aside and continued to keep watch. Every few seconds, she also checked on Cameron. It was still too early for his morning nap, but his eyelids were getting droopy. so it was possible he'd sleep through the rest of this horrible ordeal.

It took nearly twenty minutes for Leo to thread his way through the rough trail and back to the road, and he did so by using his hands-free set on the cruiser to make some calls. One was to the dispatcher to report that Randall had been injured and had run from the scene. He asked that an APB be put out on the man.

When they passed by what was left of Randall's truck, she spotted the fire department and the bomb squad. Good. Once they finished with the burned-out vehicle, then they could check Leo's place.

"Daniel said your house burned," she heard Izzie say. "I'm so sorry."

Olivia wasn't surprised she'd actually forgotten about that. It was a loss, not the house itself, but the things she had in it. Her photos, Cameron's favorite toys, and the cedar chest filled with things that had once belonged to her mother—jewelry, photos and even her journals. She was certain that later she'd feel the sting of losing those things, but it was hard to feel loss when her son's safety was her priority. Thankfully, it was Leo's priority, as well.

"Thank you," Olivia murmured to Izzie just as Leo pulled to a stop in front of the sheriff's office.

Deputy Cassidy was in the doorway, clearly waiting for them, which meant Barrett had likely alerted her. "This way," she said once Olivia had Cameron out of the cruiser. She kept him in his car seat since he was not only sound asleep now but because the seat would also better protect him if someone fired shots at them.

But no shots came.

Olivia said a quick prayer of thanks for that and was also relieved that neither Rena nor Bernice was in the large front office space. It was empty except for another deputy, a lanky built man, who was now at the dispatch desk.

"Where are Milton, Rena and Bernice?" Leo asked, glancing around but aiming his question at Deputy Cassidy.

"Milton's back in his cell. The psychiatrist finished with him and left about twenty minutes ago. Barrett told Rena and Bernice to leave after the trouble at your place. He said he'd reschedule their interviews."

Olivia wasn't sure when Barrett would find time to squeeze that in since he now had a new facet of the investigation. One that involved a firebomb that'd destroyed Randall's truck. That reminder that her wondering where the man was.

Even though it was maybe too early for the APB to have gone into effect, Olivia turned to the deputy. "Any sign of Randall?"

Deputy Cassidy shook her head. "Nothing yet. And call me Cybil. I've tried to call Randall twice, but it goes straight to voice mail. Could be he's just trying to avoid being brought in for questioning."

True, but the man had been hurt. "I'm guessing you checked the hospital?"

Cybil nodded. "The one here and the one in Culver Crossing. He hasn't gone to either." She led them through the hall and toward the back of the building. "Barrett asked me to fix up the breakroom as best I could."

Even though she'd visited Leo several times at work when they'd still been together, Olivia had never been to this part of the sheriff's office, and it wasn't as bad as she'd expected. It was actually two spacious rooms, one with bunkbeds, probably for anyone who got stuck pulling long shifts. The main room had a well-worn brown-leather sofa, a TV, some lockers and even a small kitchenette. It smelled like coffee and the cinnamon ba gels that were in a plastic bag on the counter.

The place looked safe enough what with the wired-glass window, but it gave Olivia an uneasy feeling to know that they were now under the same roof as Milton.

"I changed the sheets on the beds," the deputy told Leo, and he muttered a thanks. "Wasn't sure how long you'd have to be here, but I thought you'd need a place to sleep," she added, shifting her attention to Olivia. "The sheriff said you might need someone to get baby supplies."

Olivia had no idea and had to look at Izzie for the answer. The nanny had brought the diaper bag, but Olivia didn't know what she'd managed to stuff in there before they'd had to evacuate the house.

"We're okay for now," Izzie replied. "But if we're still here tomorrow, we'll need extra diapers, wipes and some baby food."

"Just give me a list and I'll get whatever you need," the deputy assured her. She pointed to the door on the left side of the sofa. "That's a small bathroom with a shower.

Maybe you'll want to get that blood off you. You, too," she added to Leo.

Olivia glanced down at her top and saw there was indeed blood. She'd probably gotten it when she'd examined the wound on Leo's arm. There was blood on his shirt, as well.

"You need an EMT to take a look at that?" Cybil asked him.

"No." He answered fast while taking the infant seat with Cameron from Olivia. "I've got a first-aid kit and a change of clothes in my locker. There's also an extra shirt in there for Olivia."

Olivia nearly asked if someone could go by her place to pick up some of her own clothes, but then she remembered that the only clothing she owned was what she was wearing.

"Why don't I take Cameron into the bunkroom so he can finish his nap?" Izzie suggested when Cybil left. "That'll give you two a chance to change and redress that wound."

Neither Leo nor Olivia objected. If Cameron woke up, she didn't want him to see the bloody clothes. Plus, Olivia needed some time to steady herself. She wasn't sure that was actually possible, not with the adrenaline still pumping through her, but she had to try.

Once Izzie and Cameron were in the bunkroom, the nanny eased the door shut. Leo must have taken that as his cue to get started with their "chores" because he went to his locker and took out a small first-aid kit along with two shirts, one a black tee and the other a pale blue button-up. He tossed the blue one to her and shucked off his bloody shirt.

He also winced.

Leo had probably hoped to cover that up, but Olivia saw it, all right. On a heavy sigh, she went to him. "Let me clean that wound before you put on the T-shirt."

That would make it easier to deal with the gash, but of course, it also meant she'd have her hands on a bare-chested Leo. Considering their earlier kiss and the steamy attraction that was always there between them, that probably wasn't a bright idea, but his injury needed some tending.

"I need to text Barrett first to make sure he's okay," Leo muttered.

She waited for him to do that, waited some more for a response from Barrett, who confirmed all was well and that the signs were that the gunman had been working alone. Barrett added that he'd call as soon as he had more info.

With that weight off Leo's mind, Olivia had him sit on the sofa as she looked through the kit to find some fresh bandages, antiseptic cream and gauze pads. She wet a couple of the pads in the sink in the bathroom so she could wash away some of the blood. The wound had, indeed, reopened, and it was red. It had to be hurting him.

"You really should see an EMT again," she said, frowning when she saw him grimace in pain.

"It'll be fine. It's not that deep of a cut."

It really wasn't, and it would almost certainly heal on its own if he kept it clean and didn't flex the muscles beneath it. She could make sure the first happened but not the second. If they came under attack again, she knew that Leo would definitely do some *flexing* to protect Cameron and her.

She sank next to him on the sofa to apply the fresh bandage and felt him shudder when the back of her hand brushed against his chest. Olivia lifted her gaze to apologize for hurting him, but then she realized Leo's wince wasn't from pain.

No.

There was some heat in his eyes. Heat spurred by her touch. Maybe other things were playing into this, too. After all, they'd just survived nearly being killed, which had almost certainly left them as raw as the cut on his arm.

"You keep saving me," she said, her voice thick.

She hadn't intended for it to sound like a whispery come-on, but it did. No doubt because she had been affected by that touch, as well. And just by being this close to Leo. His scent was like foreplay to her. Ditto for his incredible face. It didn't help when the corner of his equally incredible mouth lifted into a near smile.

"At least this gets your mind off the fire and the attack," he drawled. That voice was like foreplay, as well.

"It gets your mind off things, too," she countered, figuring that would jar him back into remembering that the last thing they should be doing was looking at each other like this.

Olivia had no trouble remembering that. Still, she stayed put and didn't take her eyes off him. She didn't move, either, when he leaned in and brushed his mouth over hers. It seemed to be some kind of test to see how she'd react. Or maybe how *he* would react. Apparently, not good, because he squeezed his eyes shut a moment and ground out some profanity.

That's why she was shocked when his mouth came back to hers.

This time, it wasn't just a touch. It was a scalding kiss that sent a wave of fiery need straight to the center of her body. That was the problem with kissing a former lover, one she was still seriously attracted to—the heat instantly skyrocketed and made her want to do a whole lot more than just kiss him.

Leo accommodated her on the *more*. He hooked his uninjured arm around her and pulled her to him. Olivia landed against his bare chest. That definitely didn't help cool things down any.

Her pulse kicked up a notch, and she couldn't stop herself from sliding deeper into the kiss. Or stop herself from touching him. She slid her hands around his back and gave herself the thrill of feeling all those taut, toned muscles respond to her touch. Then again, Leo had always responded to her.

And was responding now.

The sound he made was one of pure need. An ache so strong that it seemed to come off him in thick, hot waves and wash over her. She fought to get closer to him, adjusting her position so that her breasts moved over his chest. Another thrill. More fuel for this blistering heat that'd make her crazy if it didn't stop.

Leo must have remembered where they were and that anyone could come walking in at any second because he broke the kiss. He didn't move back, though. He sat there, his breath gusting, his forehead pressed against hers.

The air was so still, it felt as if everything was on hold, waiting. Olivia was certainly waiting for his reaction, to see if he would be disgusted with himself. However, it wasn't disgust on his face when he finally pulled back and locked eyes with her. The heat and need were still there, still eating away at him as it did her.

"Well, at least you have a foolproof way of making

me forget about the fires and danger for a couple of seconds," she murmured.

He smiled. And, mercy, it was good to see it. It'd been so long since she'd seen Leo happy. Even though she doubted he was actually happy right now. He'd just grabbed on to something to anchor himself and create a distraction. She understood that because the kiss had shaken her to the core.

"When I kiss you like that," he said, his voice husky, "I have a hard time remembering that we're not together. And an equally hard time remembering why we broke up."

She had the same problem. But she didn't get a chance to tell him that because his phone rang and she saw Barrett's name on the screen. That got Leo moving away from her. He hit the button to put the call on speaker and set down his phone long enough to slip on the black T-shirt.

"Everything okay there?" Barrett asked.

"Yeah," Leo answered and then quickly followed with a question of his own. "Did they find a firebomb at my house?"

"No. Not yet anyway. That's the good news. The bad news is that the shooter died before the EMTs arrived. He never regained consciousness, so I couldn't question him. His wallet was in his pocket, though, so I got his driver's license. His name was Lowell Jensen."

Leo's forehead bunched. "That sounds familiar."

It rang a bell for Olivia, too, but it took her a moment to figure out where she'd heard it. Or rather, had seen it. "I'm pretty sure a Lowell Jansen was in the PI report that Bernice gave us. Lowell was one of Rena's ex-lovers and he has—*had*—" she amended, "a police record."

"That report is in your office," Leo interjected. "I'll go get it."

"That can wait a couple of minutes. What I'll need you to do is arrange to have Rena brought back in. I'd let her go when all hell broke loose out at your place, but I want to ask her about this."

"I'll also look for any money trail," Leo noted. "But if he's her ex, then maybe she didn't pay him with money. It could be she used sex, or maybe he was just doing a favor for her."

The anger rolled over Olivia again and she hoped that this time when they questioned Rena, the woman broke down and confessed. If she were guilty, that was. Since someone had used her own phone to set her up, Olivia knew that things weren't often as they seemed on the surface.

"There's more," Barrett went on. "We found Lowell's Jeep just off the trail, and there were some things in it that might have been taken from Olivia's house. It was a bag with her mother's journals."

Olivia drew in a sharp breath. "Yes, they were at my house." But she had to mentally shake her head. "Why'd he take those?"

"I was hoping you'd have the answer to that. And, no, I'm not accusing you of anything," Barrett quickly added. "I just wondered if you had any ideas as to why someone would want to steal them and only them. There was nothing else of yours in the Jeep."

Olivia forced away the fog from the spent adrenaline and the kiss, and tried to make sense of it. She couldn't. "The journals, all thirteen of them, were right next to some of my mother's jewelry. Some of the pieces were worth a lot of money and looked it, too. By that I mean anyone who saw them would know they were valuable."

Barrett didn't ask her why such pieces weren't in a safe or a safe-deposit box, and Olivia was thankful for it. She didn't want to explain that she'd needed to keep close what few things she had of her mother's. It was a way of remembering her and not just the car wreck that'd claimed her life. However, there was something about the journals she thought he should know.

"I made digital copies of the journals," she told him. "Just in case something happened and they were damaged or destroyed. I knew that wouldn't be the same thing as having the originals in her own handwriting, but it was a way to preserve her memories."

Especially since those journals were something Simone had devoted plenty of time to keeping up. Her mother hadn't written in them daily, not even weekly, but there were at least a couple of entries every month.

"Any chance there's something in the journals that could connect to what's going on now with the attacks?" Barrett prompted.

She opened her mouth to say an automatic no but then rethought that. "I don't think so. I mean... I've read every entry multiple times." Some, like the ones her mother had written days following Olivia's birth, she'd read hundreds of times. "They have great sentimental value to me, of course, but my mother didn't say anything in them that would hint of a crime or such."

At least, she didn't think Simone had, but once she got her hands on them again, Olivia wouldn't mind taking another look. It'd been years since she'd actually looked through any of the entries.

"All right," Barrett said a moment later. "I'll have to

take the journals into custody as evidence for a while, but I'll see that you get them back."

She muttered a heartfelt thanks just as an incoming call flashed on Leo's screen. It was from her father.

Olivia could see the hesitation pass through Leo's eyes. He was likely considering if he should just let the call go to voice mail. However, he must have decided against that.

"Samuel's calling," Leo explained to his brother. "Let me see what he wants and I'll get back to you."

Leo switched over to her father, but he took a deep breath before he said anything. "I'm busy," Leo snapped. "Make it quick."

"Where are Cameron and Olivia?" Samuel fired back.

"They're safe," Leo assured him while also dodging the question. "And if that's why you called, this conversation is over—"

"It's not the only reason I called." Her father was talking quickly, his words running together, probably because he thought Leo might just hang up on him. "I'm at Olivia's house now, and it's been burned to the ground. I heard the firemen talking, and they said it was arson. What they wouldn't tell me was if Olivia and Cameron were inside when the place caught fire."

Leo sighed. "They weren't in the house. They're okay."

"I need to see them," he insisted. "I need to see you."

"Me?" Leo snarled. "Why?"

"I take it you haven't gotten a call about it yet?"

Her father's question had Leo glancing at her to see if she knew what he was talking about. She didn't.

"Explain that," Leo ordered. "And just know, if this is some kind of scheme so you can try to see Olivia and Cameron, then I'll arrest you for impeding an investigation."

"It's not a scheme," her father insisted. He muttered a curse. "Someone just called me from an unknown number. I didn't recognize the voice, but the person said I was to go to Olivia's house and look for...something."

"Something?" Leo questioned.

"A body," Samuel said after a long pause. "The caller said that someone had been murdered."

# Chapter Ten

"A body," Olivia murmured.

Even though her voice was barely audible, Leo could hear the fresh worry. And the fear.

Hell. Would this never end?

Leo was about to tell Samuel—and maybe reassure Olivia in the process—that the anonymous call to report a murder could be bogus. A foolish prank by someone who'd heard the news reports of the attack and just wanted to stir up trouble. But his phone dinged with another incoming call and his gut tightened when he saw the name on the screen.

Sheriff Jace Castillo.

Without saying anything else to Samuel, Jace hung up on him and switched over to Jace. He also slid his arm around Olivia. Coming on the heels of that kiss, touching her probably wasn't a good thing, but he hated the look this had put back in her eyes. She was having too much dumped on her too fast, and he didn't want her caving into the fear.

"Let me guess," Leo greeted when Jace was on the line. "You got a report about a body being out at Olivia's?"

"I did," Jace verified. "I'm on my way there now. Do you have ESP or did you get a call, too?"

"Not me, but Samuel did. Any chance the caller told you specifically where to look for this body?" Leo prompted.

"No. I guess he or she didn't want to make it too easy for me. And I didn't have any luck tracing the call, either. The person was using a burner cell."

That didn't surprise Leo. But the first part of what Jace had said did catch his attention. *"He or she?"*

Jace made a sound of agreement. "The caller's voice was muffled. Not like through a scrambler. It was much more low-tech than that. Probably a cloth or hand held over the mouthpiece."

"Samuel didn't say anything about that, but if he's still at Olivia's place when you get there, you'll want to ask him about it."

"Oh, believe me, I will. If I miss him, I'll bring him in for questioning. And won't that be fun?" Jace added in a grumble.

Leo nearly smiled. Nearly. Jace and he didn't have much in common, but apparently they both had an extreme dislike for Olivia's father.

There was a sound from the bunkroom—one that Leo quickly recognized. Cameron was fussing about something. Olivia untangled herself from his arms and hurried in that direction. Leo looked in, as well, but Cameron was just having a finicky spell after waking from his short nap.

"Any chance this caller mentioned to Samuel the identity of this DB I'm supposed to be looking for?" Jace asked.

"He didn't say, but it could be someone connected to the arsonist." Since Leo didn't want Cameron to hear any part of this, he stepped back into the breakroom.

"Or maybe he was the arsonist." This could all be tied together with the other attacks. "You've heard about the dead gunman near my place?"

"I did," Jace confirmed. "Also heard that someone rigged it so that your house would go up in flames, too."

"Nothing so far," Leo assured him, and hoped it stayed that way. Not just because the ranch was his and Cameron's home but also because it'd been in his family for several generations. Still, the house was something he could rebuild if it came down to it. The important thing was to keep Cameron safe.

And Olivia.

Somehow, she had become as important as Cameron in that "keep safe" equation. It was because of the kisses and the damn heat that just wouldn't go away. But it was more than that, too. It wasn't just his body that was revving up for her again. No. The rest of him had gotten in on it, as well, and he knew without a doubt that he was falling hard for her again.

That meant Olivia would have a second chance to crush his heart.

It was really bad timing for that thought to pop into his head, so he forced it aside. Not just for the moment, either, but he told his body to knock it off, to stop thinking about anything but the investigation that would hopefully lead to them all being safe. Because right now, the danger wasn't just limited to Olivia, Cameron and him. Anyone caught in the crosshairs of these attacks could be hurt or worse.

"I'll let you know if I find anything at Olivia's," he heard Jace say, and that helped snap Leo the rest of the way back.

Leo thanked him, ended the call and just stared at his

phone for several more seconds. His "knock it off" lec-
ture to himself had apparently paid up because he started
mentally ticking off things he should be doing. And none
of those things involved kissing Olivia or thinking about
kissing her.

"Are you okay?" Olivia asked, touching his arm to get
his attention. He'd been so lost in thought that he hadn't
heard her come back into the room.

Leo nodded and put his phone away. "How's Cameron?"

"Cranky. Izzie's taking out the toys from the diaper
bag. That should distract him."

Maybe, but Leo couldn't imagine there were a lot of
things for the boy to play with in that bag. If he couldn't
take Cameron home to his place soon, then he'd need to
have some brought here.

"I'm going to Barrett's office to get the envelope Bernice gave us, a laptop and any other files that I think will
help me start sorting out some details of this case," Leo
explained, tipping his head to the table where many of
the deputies often ate lunch. "I can work there."

She glanced in at Cameron, who was indeed occupied,
for the moment anyway, with a book. "I'll go with you
and help you bring back the stuff." She relayed that to
Izzie and followed Leo down the hall to Barrett's office.

Cybil was back at the dispatch desk, and she looked
up when they came in. "Everything okay?" It was obvious she was on full alert because she shifted as if she
might have to spring to action.

Leo shook his head. "Just need some things." He went
into the office, handed the envelope and some other files
to Olivia, and grabbed two laptops. One he took from
Barrett's desk and the other from his own. "You can read

through some reports," he said to Olivia. "It wouldn't hurt to have a fresh eye on them. Plus, there'll be reports coming in from Culver Crossing."

Reports on the fire that had destroyed her house. Maybe even one on the "body" that Jace was looking for. She welcomed the task because it would make her feel as if she were actually doing something to help. However, they hadn't even started back to the breakroom when the front door opened and Barrett walked in.

The brothers' gazes met and held for a few seconds, and she thought that maybe they were assessing to make sure each was okay. Barrett frowned when he saw the fresh bandage on Leo's arm.

"Olivia couldn't talk you into having an EMT check that out?" Barrett asked.

"No," she answered on a sigh just as Leo said, "It's fine."

Leo tipped his head to the evidence bags in Barrett's hand. "Is that what you got from the dead gunman?"

Barrett nodded, but he sighed, too, probably because he knew that Leo had just shut him down on the possibility of getting medical treatment. "I have his phone. A burner," Barrett added, "so I don't expect we'll get much." He shifted to show the other bag, a much larger one with a form attached to it. Since it was clear plastic, Olivia could see what was inside.

Her mother's journals.

No mistaking those distinct Tiffany-blue covers or the size. Not large notebook journals but rather more the dimensions of slim diaries. Each of the thirteen had only fifty pages, and her mother had filled those pages front and back.

She automatically moved to take them but then remembered they were now evidence. Evidence that might somehow help them unravel this case. Well, it would if they got lucky and figured out why a now-dead arsonist/ would-be killer would have taken them in the first place. Olivia was giving that more thought when she saw someone approaching the sheriff's office. And she groaned.

"My dad's here," she warned Leo and Barrett. Obviously, he'd driven straight over from her place after he'd called Leo.

Both Leo and Barrett adjusted their positions, stepping so that they were like a shield in front of her. Leo took it one step further. He put the laptops on the nearest desk to free up his hands. One of those hands he slid over the weapon in his holster.

Olivia wanted to think that wasn't necessary, that her father wouldn't harm her, but with the memories of the latest attack still right at the front of her mind, she didn't have a lot of trust for him right now.

"I figured you'd be here," Samuel said and, as usual, he threw a glare at Leo. One at Barrett, too.

Maybe Leo was also feeling distrustful of her father because he slipped his free arm around her, easing her behind him. It wasn't a gesture that her father missed. She hadn't thought it possible for him to narrow his eyes even more, but that did it.

"Olivia, please tell me you're not thinking about getting back together with him," her father snarled, adding some extra venom when he said the word *him*.

She thought of the kisses. The heat. The intimacy that was now between them because they were working to solve this case and to keep Cameron safe.

But it was more than just the investigation.

Her feelings for Leo were as strong as ever, and she

wasn't sure there was a reason to continue putting up barriers to keep them apart. Her father had created those barriers by threatening to ruin Leo, and maybe he would follow through with those threats. Or perhaps he'd try to do worse if he was the one behind the attacks. But she still couldn't see that as a reason to shut Leo out. It was past time that she dealt with her father head-on.

"It's none of your business whether I'm with Leo or not," she said. Olivia made sure it sounded like the warning it was. "In fact, nothing I do is any concern of yours."

He flinched, as if she'd actually slapped him. Her father stayed quiet a moment, but she could see the anger simmering. Anger that he might have intended to aim at Leo. However, his attention landed on Barrett. Specifically, on the large evidence bag that Barrett was still holding. He flinched again, but this seemed different than his reaction to what she'd said.

"Those are your mother's diaries," Samuel murmured, glancing at her before turning back to Barrett. "What are you doing with those?" he demanded.

"They're potential evidence," Barrett said. His voice was calm, but after one glance, Olivia could see that he was studying her father. Leo was, too. "The man who tried to kill Olivia, Leo and me apparently stole them from Olivia's house. Would you happen to know anything about that?"

Her father's shoulders went back, and it seemed to her that he changed his mind as to what he'd been about to say. "You kept them?" he demanded from her.

Of all the questions she'd thought he might ask, that wasn't one of them. She nodded. "After she died, I went into her office and got them. She used to let me read some of the entries she'd made when she was pregnant with me, so I knew where she kept them."

They'd been in a small wooden storage box on her bookshelf. It had looked like part of the rest of the decor in her office except this particular box had a false bottom. Her mom had called it her private place to keep her secrets. Others had known about the journals, of course, since they'd seen her mom writing in them from time to time. Obviously, her father had known for him to have instantly recognized them.

"Why would someone steal them?" Samuel asked, and his confusion seemed genuine.

*Seemed.*

"You shouldn't have kept them," he continued without waiting for an answer. "All they can do is stir up old, bad memories."

Well, that seemed to be what they were doing for him. And that brought Olivia right back to the doubts and suspicions she'd been having about him.

"Did you drug my mother the night of her car accident?" Olivia came out and asked. "Are you the reason she's dead?"

Clearly, she'd shocked Barrett because he glanced at her and then, obviously wanting to hear the answer, turned his cop's stare on Samuel. But her father was well beyond being stunned. His jaw went slack, and she didn't think it was her imagination that he lost some color. Or stopped breathing. Her breath had even seemed to have stalled in her chest.

"You think I killed Simone?" he finally managed to say. There was no anger in his voice. Hurt maybe. But oh, the anger came. Olivia saw it flare in his eyes. "You think I risked your life by drugging her?"

"I don't believe you thought I'd be in the car," she countered and then repeated a variation of her question. "Did you drug Mom because you wanted to get her out of your life?"

The anger in his eyes went up a huge notch. "No," he answered despite his jaw being set as hard as stone. "I've never killed anyone, and I never gave your mother any drugs."

"Her tox screen proved she had drugs in her blood," Leo quickly pointed out.

Samuel shifted that stony look to Leo. "Well, she didn't get them from me. Is this some kind of witch hunt?" Samuel volleyed glances at all of them before he settled on staring at her.

Leo shook his head. "No. We're just after the truth, and that's the reason I'm planning to ask the Texas Rangers to reopen the investigation into Simone's death. Who knows—maybe there's something in those journals that'll help them find out what really happened that night."

The anger was a raging storm inside her father now, practically coming off him in thick, hot waves. This was a man who could kill, she realized. This was a man who could have drugged his wife and gotten away with murder.

"If there's anything in Simone's journals that points to me, then she had it wrong," Samuel decreed.

"She wanted a divorce," Olivia said. She'd heard enough of their argument that night to know that.

Her father certainly didn't jump to deny it. In fact, he lifted his shoulder in what he probably thought was a casual dismissal, but his muscles were too tense to dismiss anything.

"There's no reason to hash all of this out now," Samuel concluded.

Leo disagreed. "Yeah, there is. There's no statute of limitations on murder, and if you drugged your wife, then it's murder."

Samuel froze. For a moment anyway. And he turned for the door. "If you have anything else to say to me, go through my lawyer."

"You're not leaving," Barrett warned him, stopping her father in his tracks. He glanced at Cybil. "Deputy Cassidy, why don't you wait here with Mr. Nash until his lawyer arrives? Then I'll start an interview."

Since Barrett had planned to interrogate him anyway, it didn't surprise Olivia that he'd want to go ahead and do that. But it clearly didn't please her father. Neither did the rest of what Barrett said.

"Leo, go ahead and contact the Texas Rangers about reopening the investigation into Simone's death. I'd like for them to get started on that ASAP in case it connects to what's going on now."

Her father stayed quiet for several moments, but he conveyed a lot with his glare, which had intensified. "You'll be sorry you ever started this," he said like a warning. A warning that he aimed at Olivia.

She didn't respond. Didn't have to. Leo saw to that. He picked up the laptops and motioned for her to follow him. She did. Not only because she wanted to put some distance between her father and herself but also because they were heading for the breakroom where she could check on Cameron. Olivia didn't even cast a glance at her dad, though she could practically feel him staring holes in her back.

"You okay?" Leo asked her.

No, she wasn't. She was shaken up by what'd just happened, but she wasn't going to dump that on him, too.

He was already dealing with enough. Besides, he knew how hard that had been for her to face down a man who'd made an art form of bullying her.

And maybe an art form of murder, as well.

After all, it'd been years since her mother had died, and if he'd been responsible, then he'd been a free man all this time. Unpunished. But that could change. If that happened, if he did end up in jail for it, then she was just going to have to cope with the fact that she hadn't tried sooner to get justice for her mother.

Leo and she had just made it to the breakroom door when his phone rang again. He shifted the laptops in his arms so he could take it from his pocket. He hit the answer button and put the call on speaker.

"Well, I wish it'd been a hoax," Jace started the moment he was on the line, "but it wasn't. I found the body just up the road from Olivia's house. And yeah, the guy is definitely dead."

# Chapter Eleven

Leo had hoped that Jace was calling to tell them that all was well, but that hope vanished when he heard Jace's words.

A dead body.

Two in one day, and Leo figured it wasn't a coincidence that Jace had found it so close to Olivia's house. No. This was connected to the attacks and the fires. Maybe even connected to her mother's death. Hell. It could be all one tangled mess with her father at the center.

"Who's dead?" Leo asked Jace.

"Not sure yet. That's because he's been shot in the face, and there's not much left of it."

Leo saw Olivia flinch, and he figured that had turned her stomach. It wasn't an easy image to have in your head.

"I've got my CSIs on the way out here," Jace went on, "and once they arrive and the scene is secured, I'll have a look around. There's no vehicle, no sign of a struggle in the immediate area. It looks like a body dump to me."

A body dump that was probably meant to be some kind of message to Olivia. A warning maybe or perhaps just a tool to torment her. But who was he and why had he been used as that warning/torment? Had he been a hired gun who'd screwed up enough that it'd cost him his life?

If so, then Leo sure as hell wouldn't feel any sympathy for him. His only regret was that he wasn't alive so they could possibly get answers from him.

"I'll let you know when I've got an ID on the body," Jace said and ended the call.

Leo took a moment to gather his thoughts, looked at Olivia and figured she was going to need more than moment. He carried the laptops into the breakroom and put them on the table. Did the same to the files she was carrying. Then he turned to her.

Yeah, she needed some time.

She certainly wouldn't want to go check on Cameron while her nerves were this frayed. Of course, there wasn't much he could do to help with that, but Leo still pulled her to him. Olivia came into his arms as if she belonged there. Leo didn't miss that, and apparently neither did she because the sound she made was part relief, part moan.

"I'm sorry," he told her because he didn't know what else to say.

It'd been a helluva morning what with being shot at, her house burned down, confronting her father and now this. Her life as she'd known it had vanished in a matter of a few hours. Added to that, they were about to take a step that could end up with Samuel being charged with murdering her mother. That would also mean he'd come darn close to getting Olivia killed, too.

"I'm trying to make sense of it," she said, her voice barely a whisper.

He was doing the same thing, but it wasn't adding up the way Leo wanted. He preferred it when all the pieces fit, and that wasn't happening.

Unless…

If Samuel had truly felt he was losing Olivia, he could

have maybe set up her to take the fall for hiring Milton to kill Leo. Then Samuel could have petitioned for custody of Cameron, which Leo and Olivia had already considered. Considered, too, that everything after that could have been part of a plan that had just gotten away from him. Because, as much of a bullying snake as Samuel could be, Leo just couldn't see him endangering Cameron. It could be that this latest DB was a way of wrapping up a scheme that Samuel was trying to ditch.

"The danger could be over," Leo said, which had Olivia easing her head back to meet his eyes.

He saw her latch onto that hope, and it was a hope that he wished he could give her. Give *them*, he mentally corrected. But it was just a theory and they'd have to wait to see how it played out.

"Milton's in custody," he explained. "The second gunman's dead, and since he had your mother's journals, it points to him being the one who set fire to your house. Maybe to Randall's truck, too."

Yet that was one of the puzzle pieces that didn't fit. Why Randall? Unless the person behind the attacks wanted to make Randall riled enough to come after Leo and kill him. Considering that possibility, Leo made a mental note to check on the man since Randall was scheduled to come in for an interview.

"You're thinking our attacker might just give up?" she asked.

*"Might,"* he said emphatically. "I still want us to take precautions, and I want this investigation to play out." He started to launch into some questions, but that could wait a couple more minutes. "Let's check on Cameron. If he's settled, then we can do some work."

She nodded but didn't move away. Leo didn't loosen

his grip, either. They just stood there, both wearing their emotions on their sleeves. Not just the emotions of the dangers and threats but also the personal stuff.

He cursed. Groaned. "I don't know what the hell I'm going to do with you," he grumbled.

The corner of her mouth lifted into a half smile. "I feel the same way about you. We've been on opposites sides for so long that this feels wrong." She tipped her head into his arm that was around her. "And it feels right, too."

Leo totally got them. They couldn't just go back and erase the nasty breakup or the way she'd shut him out of her life. But apparently the breakup and fallout afterward hadn't soured him on the notion that—yeah, it did feel right.

"Check on Cameron," he reminded her. Reminded himself, as well. And even then it still took several seconds for them to peel themselves away from each other and head to the bunkroom.

Izzie had put a quilt on the floor where both Cameron and she were sitting, his toys scattered around him. He was eating a snack, but he didn't seem especially happy about it.

"He's still so tired that I'm going to try to get him to finish out his nap after he eats," Izzie explained.

"You need me to help?" Olivia asked.

Izzie shook her head. "I can manage." She paused. "How's everything going?"

Leo didn't want to fill her in on the dead bodies with Cameron around so he settled for saying, "There have been some new developments in the case. As soon as the bomb squad's done at my house, though, we should be able to go back."

The nanny seemed to understand that "going back"

might not happen for a while. "All right. Then, let me get this boy to sleep."

Olivia and Leo gave Cameron a quick kiss and left them to go back to the breakroom. The first thing Leo did was point to the fridge. "There'll be Cokes, water and maybe even some snacks in there. Help yourself."

Leo settled for a cup of coffee. While he was pouring it, he called a friend, Texas Ranger Griff Morris. The call went to voice mail so Leo left him a message, explaining that some new concerns and questions had resurfaced in the fatal car accident of Simone Nash and that he wanted Griff to use some leverage to have the case reopened. Leo had no doubts that Griff would make it happen.

When he turned back around, he saw that Olivia was staring at him. "A problem?" he asked.

She quickly shook her head. "I, uh, it's hard to explain." She paused and eased into the chair as if her legs had given way. "It's just…if my father is guilty, then it'll be hard. In some way, it'll be like losing her all over again."

He understood that and hated this was something Olivia would have to go through. "Do you still have nightmares about the accident?" Because he recalled her having a bad one when they'd been lovers and she'd stay the night at his place.

"Sometimes." She shook her head again, but this time he thought she was trying to push aside the images. Ones that didn't wait until nightmares to surface. "That's why the reopened investigation will be hard. The Rangers will have to question me, and I'll have to go through it in detail."

Leo frowned. "You'd rather keep this as is?"

"No," Olivia quickly answered. "No," she repeated on

a heavy sigh. "If my father killed her, then he needs to answer for that. And my reliving it will be just a price I have to pay for making sure he doesn't get away with it."

Reliving it wouldn't be easy, and Leo wasn't sure he could help her with that. He'd try, though. Especially since it was his attack that had brought all of this back to the surface.

He slid his hand over hers and cursed himself because he was going to have to bring even more to the surface. "I know Barrett asked you if there was anything in the journals that connect to the attacks..." he reminded her. "You said no, but is there a chance there's really something in your mother's journals to incriminate your father?"

Olivia drew in a long breath and then released it before she spoke. "Nothing that I can think of. I've read every entry multiple times," she added.

"What about your father?" Leo asked. "Has he read them?"

"I'm not positive, but I don't think he did. My mother didn't keep them in plain sight, and I'd never heard my father mention them before today."

Leo gave that some thought. "She didn't keep them in plain sight, but Bernice could have snooped around, found them and showed them to your father. Any reason she'd do something like that?"

"Oh, Bernice would do it. She's always been fiercely loyal to my dad. I knew that even when I was ten years old. So, yes, Bernice could have found them and showed them to him if she thought my dad would *appreciate* her doing it."

"'Appreciate'?" Leo repeated. "Nothing sexual between them, though?"

"No. I'm sure of that. There's a different vibe when

he's with Bernice than there is when he brings his other women around. Like with Rena, for instance."

Leo paused again. "Could Rena have known about the journals? How soon did she start seeing your dad after your mom's death."

Her mouth tightened. "Rena's been around a long time, and yes, maybe he was with her while my mom was still alive. Rena and he used to do charity fundraiser stuff together. As for the journals, maybe Rena would know, but if she did, she wouldn't have learned about it from my mother."

"Your mom didn't like Rena?" he asked, obviously considering that.

"I don't think so. I remember Rena's name coming up in a couple of their arguments."

Interesting. So, maybe Rena could have egged Samuel on to kill his wife. Then again, Rena could have done it.

"Do you remember if Rena was around the estate about the time of your mother's car accident?" he asked.

"No." She stopped, her eyes widening. "Oh, I see. You believe Rena could have given my mom those drugs?"

"Do you believe it?" he countered.

She took another of those deep breaths, but this one had a weariness to it. And Leo knew why. Her mother's case hadn't even been officially reopened, and here Olivia was having to pull all these memories back to the surface. To the surface where they could take little bites out of her all over again.

"I don't know if Rena could have done it," she finally answered. "Sometimes, I think she's as obsessed with my father as Bernice, just in a different kind of way."

Yeah, Leo was coming to the same conclusion. Both women had their own way of being toxic. Then again,

Samuel was a toxic kind of guy himself, so he deserved them both.

He hated to keep digging at Olivia, but Leo couldn't get past the look on Samuel's face when he'd seen the journals in the evidence bag. "Your father didn't know you'd kept the journals. I'm guessing that means you didn't show them to him over the years?"

"No," she readily answered. "My mom always said they were secrets that she shared only with me. So, a couple of weeks after her death, after I got out of the hospital, I went into her office and got them because I heard Bernice say they were going to clean out the room. I didn't want them getting tossed. Or read," she added. "I wanted to keep her secrets."

"So you hid them," Leo concluded, and he waited for her to confirm that with a nod. "But your father did recognize them, so he must have seen them at one point?"

Again, she gave him a confirming nod. "I can't say, though, when that happened. My mother wrote in them for years, so there would have been countless opportunities for him to see them."

Definitely. And countless opportunities for Samuel to object to what his wife had put in those entries. "Your mother wrote about the arguments and such that she had with your dad?"

"She did a couple of times. You can read the entries for yourself," Olivia offered. "When I was in high school, I scanned the pages and put them in an online storage cloud. That way, if anything happened to the journals, I'd still have what my mother had written."

Though Leo figured it'd take more time than he had to go through years of her mom's journal entries, he knew it was something that had to be done. He'd need to read them with an objective eye, a cop's eye, to see if there was anything that Olivia had missed. Of course, that likely meant Olivia would be rereading them, which wouldn't help her tamp down those memories that still gave her nightmares.

"Download them," he instructed and gave her hand a gentle squeeze. He knew it was a lame gesture considering what this would end up costing her. But apparently Olivia didn't consider it so lame because she smiled at him.

Oh man.

A smile wasn't good. Not now anyway. It made him want to taste that smile. Taste the rest of her, too. Thankfully, he didn't have to dig up enough willpower to resist her because his phone rang and he saw a familiar name on the screen. Morgan Strait, the head of the bomb squad unit that'd been at his place.

"Morgan," Leo greeted when he answered the call. "You have good news for me?"

"I do," the man assured him. "We've gone through every inch of your house and the grounds surrounding it, and we haven't found a thing."

Leo felt some of the tightness in his chest ease up a little.

"I still have men working their way through your barns and outbuildings," Morgan went on, "but none of those are close enough to your house to do any damage if there happened to be an incendiary device in any of them. I've instructed your hands to stay away from them just in case."

"That is good news," Leo told him.

"The bad news is that I don't have the manpower to go through every acre of your ranch, so someone could have rigged something on the trails or the pastures. Heck, even in the shrubs or trees. My advice would be to have your hands be on the lookout for anything suspicious."

"Thanks. I will."

"No problem," Morgan said. "We'll be wrapping up here in about an hour if you want to come back."

Leo very much wanted to do that. The sheriff's office was safe, but Cameron, Izzie and Olivia would be much more comfortable at his place than here. Of course, that'd mean not having the hands check the pastures since Leo would want them close to the house.

"What about Randall's truck?" Leo asked. "Have you had a chance to look at it?"

"I did, and there was definitely something used to trigger the explosion. Not sure what yet. The lab will need to look at it, but they should be able to tell us something. In the meantime, I'm having what's left of the truck towed to a large evidence holding facility in San Antonio. Have the owner contact me if he has any questions about when and if he can get back his property."

"I will." Though so far Leo hadn't had any luck getting in touch with Randall. Still, when the man surfaced, he'd probably want answers, not only about the truck but maybe about everything else, as well.

Leo thanked Morgan again and turned back to relay what he'd just learned to Olivia.

"You can go home," she said, letting him know that she'd gotten the gist of the conversation.

He nodded, would have added more, but he heard a loud voice coming from the front of the building. Leo couldn't make out the exact words, but the tone was definitely one of anger. And that anger was coming from none other than Samuel.

Olivia sighed, got to her feet. "I can see what he's yelling about," she offered.

But Leo had no intention of sending her out. Not when Samuel was at the top of their suspect list. With Olivia right on his heels, he hurried from the breakroom to see if Barrett or Cybil needed any assistance.

"I didn't try to kill anyone," Samuel was shouting. "Not my wife. Not your brother." He'd added his usual venom to the *your brother*, and Leo knew that part was for him.

Rena was there, as well. She was behind Samuel, had hold of both of his arms and was a doing a fairly decent job of keeping him from charging at Barrett and Cybil. That would have been a Texas-sized mistake because not only were Barrett and the deputy armed, Barrett could have taken down the man with a single punch.

Samuel immediately shifted his attention to Leo and Olivia, and Leo hadn't thought it possible, but the man's scowl was even worse than what it had been earlier.

"The sheriff just read me my rights," Samuel roared. He stopped struggling, but Rena kept her arms wrapped tightly around him.

"Because he wouldn't shut up," Barrett explained. "I figured if he kept yakking, he might blurt something out, something I couldn't use against him if I didn't Mirandize him first."

So, apparently Samuel hadn't waited for his attorney, and it was also obvious that he wasn't going to heed his right to remain silent.

"I won't be treated like this," Samuel snarled. "I won't let my daughter taint my name with nonsense allegations that I killed her mother. Those journals mean nothing. Nothing! And they shouldn't have any part in this."

He hadn't said *my daughter* with any affection whatsoever. Just the opposite. Olivia was his enemy now, too. Apparently, so were those journals.

"Calm down, Samuel," Rena insisted, her voice a lot calmer and softer than his. The woman was practically cooing to him. "Your blood pressure's probably through the roof right now. Come with me and let's talk. I can get you some water."

Samuel put up some resistance. At first. But after a couple of seconds where he glared at Olivia, the man allowed Rena to lead him to the other side of the room where there was a water cooler. She did, indeed, get him a drink and then practically sandwiched him against the wall while she continued to talk to him in a murmur.

Cybil waited for the nod from Barrett. When she got it, the deputy went back to the dispatch desk. Barrett stayed next to Olivia and Leo, not exactly in a huddle but close, and all three of them cast wary glances at Samuel.

"Olivia's downloading the pages of her mother's journal." Leo kept his voice low when he spoke to his brother. "After hearing Samuel's latest outburst, I'm even more interested in reading them."

Barrett made a sound of agreement. "Samuel's definitely worried about them."

As if to prove that, Leo saw Samuel's eyes drift into Barrett's office. He was pretty sure the man was looking at the evidence bag of journals on Barrett's desk. Rena followed his gaze and then saw, too, that Barrett, Olivia and Leo were watching them. She caught Samuel's chin, turning him back to face her. Leo couldn't hear what the woman said to him, but Samuel seemed to be listening.

Leo thought about Rena's claim that Samuel and she

would get back together. It certainly seemed as if that was exactly what was happening.

Olivia sighed, causing Leo to turn to her. He was pretty sure they were on the same page of thought when it came to Rena and Samuel. The easy intimacy between them had Leo considering if maybe they had worked together to stage the attacks and set up Simone's car accident. But that didn't feel right because, if that's what had indeed happened, then Leo couldn't see Rena keeping that to herself when Samuel and she were on the outs. A woman capable of writing those threatening emails didn't stay silent about much.

"I told Leo that I thought my father was more agitated than usual about my mother because the anniversary of her death is coming up," Olivia explained. She stopped and shook her head. "But maybe it's more than that. Maybe it's guilt."

Neither Barrett nor Leo disputed that, and Leo watched again as Samuel glanced over at the journals.

"He thinks Simone wrote something incriminating," Leo concluded. "He's worried about what we'll find when we read them."

Barrett made a sound of agreement.

"I wish there was something incriminating to find," Olivia said, punctuated with another of those sighs. "I wish there was something in them that would make him come clean about what happened, because I believe there could be more to it than what he's admitted."

Leo thought that, as well. That's why he considered something. It was a long shot. More of a weak bluff. But sometimes all it took was a nudge, and maybe this would be the right one.

"What if you tell your father that there is something?"

Leo suggested, still whispering. "What if you lie and say that your mother wrote that someone was trying to kill her?"

Leo figured it would take Olivia a couple of minutes to mull that over. She didn't. She nodded and immediately moved away from Barrett and him. Walking closer to her father, she pointed to the journals.

"You're worried about what's in those," Olivia said, her voice surprisingly strong. "Well, you should be."

It wasn't anger now that flashed in Samuel's eyes but rather concern. Maybe even fear. Rena didn't have as extreme of a reaction, but she definitely quit cooing and soothing.

"What do you mean?" Rena asked. "Did Simone say something...bad?"

"Yes," Olivia said, adding to the lie. "She said someone was trying to kill her." And with that, she stared directly at her father.

Leo steeled himself for the burst of outrage he figured they were about to get from Samuel. But no outburst. The man just wearily shook his head and squeezed his eyes shut. Then he said a single word that Leo definitely hadn't been expecting.

"Bernice," Samuel muttered, still shaking his head. "Bernice wanted Simone dead."

# Chapter Twelve

When Olivia had decided to go with the impromptu ruse to get her father to say something incriminating, she hadn't actually expected it to work. Nor had she thought that name would come out of his mouth.

"Bernice?" Olivia repeated.

Both Barrett and Leo moved closer, flanking her, while the three of them faced down her father. Their stares were definitely demands for him to explain why he'd just blurted out Bernice's name.

Samuel cursed, pushed the cup of water away that Rena was offering him, and he began to pace. "I shouldn't have said that," he grumbled. "I don't have any proof that Bernice did anything wrong."

He was backpedaling, which wouldn't help them get to the truth.

"But you must suspect her," Olivia quickly pointed out. "Did Bernice give my mother those drugs the night of the car wreck? Did she?" Olivia pressed when her father didn't answer. She finally stepped in front of him, stopping him and facing him down. "Did she?"

Her father looked at the spot just above her shoulder. Definitely avoiding eye contact. "Maybe," he finally said.

"She's certainly capable of that," Rena insisted. "The

woman is a control freak. She probably wanted your mother out of the way so she'd have a better shot at getting more of Samuel's attention."

Samuel sniped Rena a scowl. "If Bernice did it, it wasn't because she wanted Simone out of the way," he snapped.

"Then why?" Olivia demanded.

Her father groaned and tried to pace again, but Olivia did another block, pinning him between Rena on one side and Barrett and Leo on the other.

"Bernice thought Simone was no longer thinking clearly," her father said, and it sounded to Olivia as if he were carefully choosing his words. "Bernice believed, wrongfully so, that Simone would leave—disappear," he amended, "and that Simone would take you with her so I'd never be able to see you again. Bernice knew that'd crush me."

Olivia tried to pick through that to see if she could tell if he was lying. She just didn't know. But it didn't surprise her that Bernice would have such a strong opinion of her mother or that her father's household manager would be privy to her parents' marital problems. The truth was Simone had spoken of a divorce, so it wouldn't be much of a stretch for Bernice to believe that Simone would take her daughter with her when she left the estate.

"I want you to go through every detail of what happened that night," Barrett told her father as he took out his phone. "I'll call Bernice and get her back in here. I'll need to hear what she has to say about all this."

Her father cursed again, and Olivia could see that he regretted opening the subject. But it could lead to something. A confession, maybe. Then again, even if Bernice had had something to do with her mother's death, it wouldn't clear up the recent attacks and fires.

Barrett stepped into his office to make the call, and Olivia continued to stare at her father. "Why didn't you say anything about Bernice before now?" she demanded when he didn't continue.

"Because I don't know if my suspicions are right." He dragged his hand over his face. "What I do know is your mother didn't use drugs, period. So, either she dosed herself up that night for the first time, or someone else did it. I didn't do it, so that leaves Bernice."

Maybe, but Olivia shifted her attention to the woman who was now patting her father's arm. "Were you at the estate that night?" Olivia asked her.

Rena's eyes widened and her mouth dropped open. "You're accusing me now?" she shrieked.

"*Asking* you," Leo clarified. "But I'm going to insist that you answer the question."

Rena's indignance meshed with the anger. "No, I wasn't there. If I remember correctly, your father and I had some business a week or so before that, but I wasn't in the house when Simone died."

Both Leo and Olivia looked to her father to confirm what Rena had just said, but he only shrugged. "I don't remember a lot about that night," he admitted. "Simone and I argued, and she stormed out. She said she was going out for a drive. After she left, I had a few drinks. Maybe more than a few," he added in a mumble.

"Was Simone acting as if she'd been drugged while you two were arguing?" Leo pressed.

Her father stayed quiet a moment and his forehead bunched up as if he were trying hard to pull out the memories. Or else that's what he wanted them to think. But it could be an act. All of this could be an act.

"No," her father finally said. "Not drunk or high. She was just pissed off." He paused again. "But she didn't leave right away after she stormed out. I think it was at least a half hour before she left."

"At least a half hour," Olivia agreed.

And here it came. Her own flood of memories. She didn't know how they could manage to stay so fresh, so raw, after all this time. Her father's recollections didn't include the wreck itself. Nor had he heard the sound of her mother's dying breath.

Leo turned to her. "Are you okay?" he whispered.

Olivia nodded and, even though the nod was a lie, she pushed the images and the sounds aside so she could explain her version of the timing of that night.

"I heard the argument between my parents," she said. "I heard my mom say she was going to leave, so I sneaked into the garage and got into her car. I didn't have a watch, but I know she didn't come out in only a few minutes. It was much longer than that. In fact, I'd fallen asleep."

Olivia had no idea how long it'd been before the drugs in her mother's system had taken effect, but that was something she intended to find out.

"Bernice will be here in a couple of minutes," Barrett announced when he returned from making his call. "She's at the diner just up the street."

It surprised Olivia that Bernice hadn't gone back to the estate. Then again, the woman might not have wanted to make that trip since Barrett had made it clear earlier that he wanted to interview her. Now, he'd have something else to question her about.

Her possible involvement in Simone's death.

Olivia didn't have to guess how Bernice would react to that. She would be many steps past being enraged, and the woman was likely to aim that rage at Samuel. After all, he'd been the one to throw Bernice's name into the mix of suspects.

Leo's phone rang, and he showed her the screen after he checked it. Jace. That meant this could be important.

"We can take this in Barrett's office," Leo told her, and Olivia headed there with him.

Obviously, Leo hadn't wanted to have this conversation in front of her father and Rena, and he shut the door before he put the call on speaker.

"I got an ID on the body," Jace said, not starting with a greeting. "And it's someone you know. Randall Arnett."

Leo jerked back his head. No doubt in surprise. Olivia was having a similar reaction and because her legs suddenly felt a little unsteady, she caught onto the edge of Barrett's desk.

"You're sure it's Randall?" Leo asked, taking the question right out of her mouth. After all, the body that Jace had found had been shot in the face, which would make it hard to ID him. Olivia couldn't help but wonder if Randall had set up his own death.

"Yeah," Jace verified. "I did a quick fingerprint check and I got a hit. It's Randall, all right."

So, not a faked death. Probably not suicide, either, because she remembered Jace saying it'd looked like a body dump.

"He can't have been dead for long," Leo said. "His truck blew up at my place just a couple of hours ago. He was injured, but he was still able to run off."

"Why'd he run?" Jace wanted to know.

"He said something about me trying to kill him. I

guess he thought I'd put the firebomb in his truck." Leo stopped. "But I don't know why he drove to my place to tell me that. And I sure as hell don't know how he got from my ranch to Olivia's."

She was trying to figure out the same thing. Her house wasn't far from Leo's, but it would have taken Randall hours and hours had he been traveling on foot. Plus, on foot wouldn't mesh with Jace's body dump theory.

"So someone gave Randall a ride," Olivia concluded.

"Or else he went back to his ranch and got another vehicle," Leo suggested.

True. A trip like that wouldn't have taken nearly as long as getting to her place. "Did you find another vehicle near Randall's body?" she asked.

"No. But I did find a phone, and I'm taking it into evidence. Maybe it belongs to the killer. Or if it's Randall's, he could have called the person who ended up killing him." Jace muttered some profanity that had a frustrated edge to it. "Or the phone could belong to one of the responders to the fire. I'll let you know when I figure it out."

Leo thanked him, ended the call and glanced back toward the squad room where they'd left her father and Rena. He dragged in a deep breath as if steeling himself for another round, but he didn't move. Neither did she because she, too, needed a moment to compose herself.

"Since I believe Randall got away with murdering his girlfriend," she said, "it's hard for me to feel sympathy for him. Still…" She left it at that.

Leo's nod let her know that his feelings were leaning the same way. Randall's murder now made him a victim. A victim almost certainly connected to the attacks on Leo and her. Why else would his body have been left so close to her house? Even if the reason was just to muddy the investigation, it was still another body to add to the death toll.

A toll that the killer would no doubt like to add to by murdering both Leo and Olivia.

"This takes Randall off the suspect list," she muttered, talking more to herself than to Leo.

But Leo made a sound of agreement. "That doesn't mean, though, that he didn't set up the attacks."

Her mind took a mental stutter and she shook her head. Olivia was about to say that didn't seem possible, but then she considered it from a different angle.

"You think Randall's own hired gun could have killed him?" she asked.

"It's possible. Maybe the hired gun got spooked when his comrade, Lowell, was killed. Or Randall could have reneged on payment or done something else to make this guy off him. Killers aren't known for playing by the rules."

No, they weren't, and this could certainly have been a plan that'd backfired on Randall.

"Milton," Leo added a moment later. "He might be willing to talk now when we tell him about Lowell's and Randall's murders. It could make him scared enough to finally rat on who hired him."

Yes, Olivia could see that happening and, if so, Leo might have been right about the danger finally being over.

Leo ran his hand down her arm. "I have to go out there and help Barrett deal with this mess. You can go back to the breakroom if you want."

It was tempting. Mercy, was it. She was drained and shaky, and Olivia doubted being around her father and Rena would improve that. Still, she couldn't just put her head in the sand, especially since one of them might say something that would help shed some light on her mother's fatal car wreck and the current investigation.

The sound of a bell ringing had them both moving. Because it was the bell on the front door and it meant someone had come in. Olivia didn't have to guess who that someone was because she immediately heard Rena say Bernice's name.

Leo and Olivia entered the squad room, but before they dealt with Bernice, Leo pulled his brother aside and whispered, "The DB at Olivia's is Randall's."

Barrett got the same shocked expression that Leo and she had had. "I'll want details about that later," he said on a sigh just as Rena blurted something to Bernice.

"Samuel thinks you killed Simone."

Olivia turned in time to catch Bernice's reaction. If looks could kill, Bernice would have certainly accomplished it with the stony glare she aimed at Rena.

"What are you blathering about now?" Bernice asked.

"Rena," her father warned, taking hold of her arm.

But Rena just shook off his grip and went closer to Bernice. "Samuel thinks you might have killed Simone," Rena repeated. There was a smugness to her tone and expression, probably because she'd waited for years to have Samuel put Bernice in her place.

But this was more than "her place." This was an accusation that could land Bernice in jail for the rest of her life.

Bernice shifted her attention to Samuel. "What's she talking about?"

His head dropped down for a moment and then, on a heavy sigh, he stepped closer to Bernice. "I know you didn't like Simone," he said.

That was it. Apparently, the full explanation he intended to give her. But it was enough. Olivia saw the verbal blow land on Bernice as effectively as a heavyweight's fist. The woman flinched, and there was no longer anger in her eyes. Just the unbearable hurt of betrayal by someone she almost certainly loved.

The shock didn't last long, though. She pressed her lips together for a moment, cleared her throat and turned to Olivia.

"You told your father that I might have killed your mother?" Bernice asked. There was a coldness now; a thick layer of ice far more formidable than anger.

Olivia ignored the question and went with one of her own. "Did you kill her?"

Bernice looked her straight in the eyes. "No. It's true that I didn't like her, but I didn't have anything to do with her death." She turned, aiming that cold at Samuel now. "But you believe I did?"

He didn't break eye contact with Bernice, either. "I believe it's possible that you could have been trying to protect me by getting Simone out of the way."

Again, that was a blow, and this time Bernice's icy facade shattered a little. The sound she made was a hollow laugh. This time, it took several more moments for her to compose herself. And just like that, the anger was back. Anger she aimed not at Samuel but at Rena.

"I don't have to guess that you put all of this nonsense into Samuel's head," Bernice said, not waiting for the woman to respond. "Did you also remind him that you had a much stronger motive than I did for *getting Simone out of the way*?" She added some extra bite to those last words.

In contrast, Rena looked completely unruffled. "I had

no motive. Simone and Samuel's marriage was falling apart. It was only a matter of time before they got a divorce. There was no reason for me to hurry that along."

"No reason other than the biggest one of all," Bernice argued. "You could have killed her so you could get your claws into Samuel sooner. No waiting for a divorce. But that didn't work, did it? Here it is, all these years later, and you still don't have Samuel."

That caused Rena's *unruffled* to shatter and she hooked her arm possessively through Samuel's. "You jealous witch. You're the one who's tried to get her claws into him—"

"Stop!" Barrett snapped, issuing his cop's glare at Rena, Bernice and her father before looking at his deputy. "Go ahead, Deputy Cassidy, and take Bernice to an interview room so we can get her statement on record. I'll need the same from both of you," he added to Samuel and Rena.

That didn't please any of the three. They turned their displeasured looks to Barrett, which he ignored. He motioned for Cybil to go ahead and take Bernice out of there.

But Bernice held her ground. "Did Rena tell you that she was at the estate a lot in those days before Simone's death?"

"I wasn't," Rena insisted. "It'd been at least a week."

"I keep very good records," Bernice said, and it sounded like a threat. "You were there nearly every day the week she died. And I suspect you're the one who drugged her."

"What!" Rena howled in outrage.

"I think you put the drugs in Simone's tea or maybe that energy juice she was always drinking. Maybe you got lucky with the timing of her getting behind the wheel, or maybe you just thought she'd die of a drug overdose. Either way, I'm sure the sheriff will take a hard look at you."

"Oh, I will," Barrett assured her and gestured again for Cybil to take Bernice away. This time, Bernice cooperated but not before she shot Samuel one final glare.

Her father muttered some curse words that seemed to be aimed at himself. Perhaps because he hadn't wanted things to play out like this.

That seemed to be Rena's take on things anyway.

"Don't you dare feel sorry for that woman," Rena snapped. "You should have fired her years ago. She's done nothing but run your life, and she's done that by trying to shut me out."

That put some strength in her father's spine and he pulled back his shoulders while staring at Rena. "Don't you dare try to make this about you." He turned to Barrett. "I'd like to wait in an interview room, too, while I call my lawyer."

Barrett nodded and motioned to the hall. "Just go that way and take the room that isn't occupied by Bernice."

"It is about me," Rena called out to him. "It's about Bernice turning you against me any chance she gets."

Apparently, Rena couldn't see that she was trying to do the same thing to Bernice. Olivia found the two exhausting and wasn't surprised when her father walked away, turning his back on Rena.

Tears filled Rena's eyes, but that didn't stop her from giving one of the desk chairs an angry kick.

"You wait there," Barrett warned her and motioned toward the chairs in front of the dispatch desk. "If you leave, I'll charge you with obstruction."

That didn't improve Rena's mood, and she whipped

out her phone, saying she was calling her lawyer. Barrett left her to that and tipped his head for Leo and Olivia to follow him into his office.

"Tell me what happened to Randall," Barrett said the moment he had his office door closed.

"Jace and I both got a call about an hour ago to tell us about a body near Olivia's," Leo explained. "Jace checked it out and found Randall. He'd been shot in the face, but Jace ID'd him through fingerprints."

Obviously processing the information, Barrett sat on the edge of his desk. "About an hour ago," he repeated. "Shortly after the time Olivia and you got back here to the sheriff's office."

"Yeah," Leo said, and it seemed to Olivia as if he was also agreeing with something else his brother hadn't spelled out. "It means Rena, Samuel or Bernice could have gotten to Randall, killed him and dumped the body."

"The question is—why?" Barrett continued. "Other than to distract us or to throw a wrench in the investigation, I can't see why. Unless—"

"Randall's connected to the attacks or the hired thugs used in the attacks," Leo finished for him.

Barrett nodded and took out his phone. "I'll text Cybil and have her ask Samuel about an alibi. He probably won't want to say anything without his lawyer, but he might slip up. I also need to call the diner. I want to see how long Bernice was there before I had her come back here."

Olivia considered herself a step behind the two lawmen when it came to following the threads of this investigation, but she latched onto this angle right away. The person who'd killed Randall had called both Leo and Jace. Had maybe even personally done the body dump.

Bernice couldn't have managed that if she'd been sitting in the town's diner for the past couple of hours.

While Barrett made the call, Olivia glanced out at Rena, to make sure she was still there. She was. And the woman was still on the phone, maybe griping to her lawyer.

Or plotting another attack.

"Don't worry," Leo said. "We'll check her alibi, too."

Rena would probably claim she wasn't capable of killing Randall and shoving him out of a vehicle. And maybe she wasn't. But Rena worked out a lot. In fact, of their three remaining suspects—Rena, Bernice and Olivia's father—Olivia thought Rena might be the strongest of them physically. Of course, it wouldn't have taken strength had the person responsible hired some muscle to do their dirty work.

"Bernice had only been at the diner for about ten minutes when I called her," Barrett relayed when he got off the phone.

So, no alibi. Well, not one in the diner anyway. That didn't mean the woman couldn't account for where she was and what she was doing. Barrett would certainly try to get the info out of her.

"I have another possible angle," Leo said, making his own call. He held up a finger in a wait-a-second gesture when Barrett questioned him. The person he'd called had obviously answered. "Jace," Leo greeted, putting the call on speaker. "Anything on that phone you found near Randall's body?"

"No. I haven't gotten into it yet. It's got a passcode, so I'll have to see if the lab can do anything with it."

Leo groaned. "That could take days," he mumbled to her. "Weeks even."

Olivia wanted to groan, too. They didn't have that kind of time. Heck, they might not even have hours before someone tried to attack them again.

"But I was about to call you about something else," Jace continued a moment later. "I've got an eyewitness in Olivia's neighborhood who saw a black SUV around the time the body would have been dumped. It's a woman who lives across the street, and she said she's seen that vehicle or one like it many times before. She said she couldn't see inside because the windows are tinted."

That got Olivia's attention. "What vehicle?" she asked.

"One with a logo on the driver's-side door."

And suddenly Olivia knew exactly what logo Jace meant. "A sycamore leaf?" she managed to ask.

"Yeah," Jace verified. "I was just checking, and the only vehicles anyone around here has seen like that all belong to your father."

# Chapter Thirteen

What he was doing was a risk, but Leo knew anything he did at this point would be. Still, it'd bring some normalcy back to Cameron's life. Or at least it would if Leo could get his son, Olivia and Izzie safely back to the ranch.

The fire department and bomb squad had given Leo the all-clear to return, so at least he didn't have to worry about the specific threat of the place going up in flames. And he'd added even more security, bringing over some ranch hands from Barrett's place to patrol the grounds and prevent someone from sneaking onto the property and putting some sniper skills to bad use.

Still…

Yeah, that *still* was going to haunt him until he had everyone tucked safely inside the house.

Izzie was treating the ride in the cruiser as a fun adventure for Cameron by reading to him from a book that made animal sounds whenever Cameron touched one of the pages. His son was giggling, definitely not showing any signs of worry or fear. Unlike Olivia and Leo.

Olivia was keeping watch as he drove to the ranch. Leo was, as well, and so were Cybil and Daniel, who were in the cruiser behind them. Unfortunately, his fellow deputy and brother wouldn't be able to stay at the ranch. There was just too much going on at the sheriff's office, and that's where Leo needed them to be. Their best chance at ending the danger was to get answers from their now three suspects and to follow the new lead they'd gotten from Jace.

Someone had used one of the vehicles from the Sycamore Grove estate, and Leo wanted to know which who. If Barrett couldn't pull that info out of Rena, Bernice and Samuel, then maybe he'd be able to hold them for at least a couple of hours.

Until Leo could make this drive and get off the roads.

As long as they were out in the open, the risks skyrocketed. It would have been worse, though, to make the trip at night. That's why Leo had timed it so that it was still a while before sunset.

He held his breath when he took the turn to his ranch and then released that breath when he realized someone had already removed Randall's truck from the road. Good. That was one of the reasons Leo hadn't left the sheriff's office any sooner and had in fact stayed nearly eight hours after getting the call from Jace.

Along with setting up those extra security measures, Leo had wanted to give the bomb squad time to deal with the truck. If not, he would have had to use the trails to get to his house, and he hadn't wanted to risk driving them since they would be prime areas for another sniper to lay in wait.

He drove past the burned-out area left by Randall's truck and spotted the first of the hands. There were others, all armed and clearly on guard, just as Leo had instructed. Another was on the porch where he would stay until Leo had Olivia, Izzie and Cameron inside. Then he would join the other hands to patrol the ranch. If a gunman managed to get past the ranch hands, then Leo would have the security system turned on to alert them if anyone tried to break in.

Leo parked the cruiser in the garage and quickly got Cameron into the house. Olivia and Izzie were right on his heels, and the moment he'd reset the security system, he fired off a quick text to Daniel and Cybil to let them know it was okay for them to go back to town.

"I can take Cameron to the nursery," Izzie volunteered, easing Cameron into her arms and looping the diaper bag over her shoulder. "I'm sure he needs to be changed. Then I'll bathe him and get him ready for bed. I'll let you know before I put him down so you can say good-night to him."

Leo was thankful the nanny was there to keep Cameron on schedule. Doing that was huge, and it freed him up to try to make some headway on the investigation.

"I can sleep in the nursery with Cameron, if that's okay," Izzie offered.

Leo thought that staying with his son was something he'd like to do. The trouble was, he wasn't sure when Olivia and he would be turning in for the night, and Izzie probably didn't want to stay in limbo, waiting for them to decide. He nodded, thanked her, but knew that he'd be sleeping very close to his boy. No way did he want to be too far away from Cameron in case something went wrong.

When Izzie left with Cameron, Leo turned to Olivia to see how she was holding up. As if she knew he was checking for that, she lifted her chin and put on what he thought was a decent attempt at a strong expression. But he knew beneath the surface that she was just as rattled as he was. Heck, they were all rattled, including his brothers, which was a reminder for him to get in touch with Barrett to let him know that they'd arrived safely.

He took out his phone and pressed Barrett's number. He answered on the first ring. "We're home," Leo told him. "We're okay."

"Good. I didn't want to call you while you were on the road. Didn't figure you'd want the distraction."

"If it's good news, it's not a distraction," Leo quickly assured him.

"Sorry. It's not good. Bernice, Rena and Samuel have all lawyered up. The three of them did insist, though, that they're innocent, but since none of them is spouting proof of an alibi, I'm guessing they don't have any."

So, they wouldn't be able to eliminate any one of them. Not yet. But now that Bernice wasn't so chummy with Samuel, the woman might be willing to spill some secrets about him. Samuel might be willing to do the same.

Leo ended the call with Barrett and turned back to Olivia. Even though he hadn't put the call on speaker, she'd obviously heard, and she sighed.

"Hiding behind their lawyers," she muttered. "I guess it was too much to expect for one of them to confess."

Yes, it was. A confession now would result in charges for first-degree murder, attempted murder, assault with a deadly weapon, and conspiracy. If convicted, the death penalty would be on the table. Plus, Leo doubted that any of the three had their consciences troubling them enough to come clean.

"I'm sure you didn't get much sleep last night," he said after she made another weary sigh. She looked exhausted and no doubt felt it, too. "You should probably try to rest at least for a little while. There's a bed in the guest room or you could go into my room."

Olivia lifted an eyebrow, and he realized that his suggestion had sounded a little like a come-on. Probably because they'd had sex in his room and it'd been damn amazing.

"You're too tired for sex," he added.

He'd tried to go for light, but he'd failed big-time. Her eyebrow quirked again, and she stepped into his arms, sliding her hands around him until they were body to body. Until breath met breath.

Suddenly, he didn't feel too tired or too busy for sex. But it couldn't happen. Not when their little boy could still be in danger.

Leo settled for brushing his mouth over her cheek. It was the kind of kiss meant to soothe. And maybe it had. But the rest of his stupid body reminded him that it was only a short distance from her cheek to her mouth. Of course, a real kiss would break some rules and only make him want more. *More* couldn't happen. Not right now anyway. But it would be night soon, and eventually they'd have to go to bed.

Maybe even go to bed together.

Sex did seem inevitable between them. It didn't seem to matter how much they fought it, how much they knew it shouldn't happen.

And that's why Leo broke one of those rules and kissed her.

Since the kiss was a huge mistake and couldn't last long, he made it count. He deepened it, letting the taste of Olivia slide right through him. The heat was right behind the taste. Then the need. Of course, the need had never been far from the surface when it came to the two of them.

As the heat urged him to kick things up even more,

Leo pulled away from her. Her breath was gusting. Her face flushed. And her mouth looked as if it'd just been thoroughly kissed.

"I'm glad you weren't too tired for that," she murmured in a voice that was as effective as a siren's lure.

So was he. But now he had to do something to get rid of the cloud the kiss had put in his mind. It took some doing to focus on something other than Olivia.

"I need to go through your mother's journals," he said, and he watched as that shifted her back to reality.

No gusting breath or flushed face for her now. Just a resigned nod. "Barrett copied everything that was in the envelope Bernice gave him," she said. "I can look through that while you're on the journals."

It seemed like a good way to divide the work. Then, if neither of them hit on anything new, they could trade stashes. Leo also needed to make time to get warrants to go through the financials for all of their suspects. With the eyewitness account of the vehicle that'd been at Olivia's, that might be enough to convince a judge to let him take a look at bank accounts to see if anyone had recently paid for a hitman or two.

Leo picked up the bag with the laptops and files he'd brought from the sheriff's office. "We can set up in the room next to the nursery," he suggested. "That way, we can keep an eye on Cameron."

Olivia readily agreed and didn't say a word about a bed being in there. That made her a wise woman since there was no need to add any more sexual fuel to this attraction.

Leo took the bag upstairs to the smaller of his two guestrooms just as his phone rang. It was Barrett again, and Leo nearly groaned. He'd spoken to his brother only about ten minutes ago, so something must have come up.

"This time I have good news," Barrett said the moment Leo answered.

"I'm definitely ready to hear some." Since Olivia was, too, Leo put the call on speaker.

"The psychiatrist is going to certify Milton competent to stand trial," his brother explained.

Leo certainly hadn't been expecting that. Everything they'd learned about Milton had pegged him as having mental issues. Apparently though, Milton did understand the judicial process and the charges that'd be levered against him.

"You're charging him with attempted murder of a police officer?" Leo asked.

"I am. I just told him this, and after he got past the shock, Milton said he wants to talk. He wants to tell us all about the person who's trying to kill you."

OLIVIA DIDN'T BOTHER to groan or huff. Yes, it was good news that Milton finally realized he was in scalding hot water and would likely spend the rest of his miserable life in jail.

But she felt another ploy coming on.

Another attempt to get Leo and her out into the open, maybe so one of Milton's cohorts could try to murder them.

Apparently, Leo felt the same way because he huffed and muttered something profane. "I'm not taking Olivia back to the sheriff's office," he insisted. "It's getting dark, and I don't want her outside."

"I agree," Barrett said as fast as Leo had objected. "No need for it. When Milton insisted on talking to the two of you, I told him he'd have to do that with a video call. I can have that set up in just a couple of minutes if you want to hear what he has to say."

"Oh, we want to hear," Leo assured him. "And who knows, this time Milton might stop playing games long enough to give us some real info. Has he asked for a plea deal?" he added.

"Of course. That was one of the first things out of his mouth. I told him that I'd consider a deal if he actually gave us anything we could use to convict the person who hired him."

Good. Because Olivia didn't want Milton to walk unless they had his boss in custody. It twisted at her to think that the boss might be her father. Still, if he'd done these horrible things, then she wouldn't want him anywhere but behind bars.

"I'll call you after I have everything set up," Barrett said right before he clicked off.

Leo put aside his phone so he could set up one of the laptops that he apparently intended to use for the video call. While he was doing that, Olivia took a moment to go check on Cameron. He was splashing in the tub in the nursery bathroom, and she gave him a quick kiss.

"Is everything okay?" Izzie asked her.

Olivia nodded. "There might be a break in the case."

And Olivia hoped that wasn't all wishful thinking. Still, she held on to the hope that they'd soon have the name of the person responsible for terrorizing them. Then they could all deal with the fallout. Even if it wasn't her father who'd done this, it was someone she knew. Someone he'd trusted.

When Olivia made it back to the guest room, Leo already had the laptop booted up and she could see the camera feed of the interview room on the screen. The room was empty, but that changed almost immediately as Barrett ushered in Milton. Barrett had kept the man cuffed. A good thing, as far as Olivia was concerned. She didn't want Milton using this as a chance to try to escape.

"This is being recorded," Barrett told Milton. "And I've already read you your rights. I need you to say on record that you understand those rights and that you're waiving your right to an attorney."

"Yeah, I understand all that stuff. Are Leo and Olivia listening?" Milton immediately asked.

"We are," Leo said. "You'd better not be wasting our time."

"I'm not. I swear I'm not." Milton looked straight into the camera. "But I need a deal. I need immunity."

"You're not getting a free ride," Barrett assured him. "I've already told you the only deal you're getting is that I'll put in a good word for you with the DA if you give us your boss. That's it, Milton. That's the best you'll get from me."

Milton shook his head, muttered something Olivia didn't catch. *Great.* He was going to clam up again, or so Olivia thought. But the man's gaze zoomed to Barrett.

"You've got to swear to me that you'll work your butt off to get me a lighter sentence. Swear it," Milton repeated.

Barrett gave him a flat look. "You tried to kill my brother, and because you withheld information, it resulted in another attack, one where Olivia and my nephew could have been hurt. Added to that, there are two people dead. Working my butt off for you isn't high on my priority list. But," Barrett quickly added, "help me arrest the person behind the attacks, and I'll spell out to the DA that you're just a lackey."

Olivia thought that maybe Milton would be insulted with the term "lackey," but it seemed to make him relax a bit. Maybe because he thought being a hired gun would give him a lighter sentence than the person who'd hired him. She didn't think it would, though, and was pretty sure that accessory to murder, even after the fact, would carry the same penalty as murder itself.

"Okay," Milton said, gathering his breath. "I don't actually know the name of the person who hired me, but I can give you a description. He's in his thirties, is tall and has dark brown hair."

Well, that ruled out Bernice, Rena and her father, but it must have triggered something for Barrett because he paused the interview. He then searched through something on his phone. When he obviously found what he was looking for, he turned the screen in Milton's direction.

"That's him," Milton said right off. "That's the guy who hired me."

Barrett shifted the phone screen so that Olivia and Leo could see, as well. It was Lowell, the dead gunman.

"What?" Milton asked when he noted the frustrated expression on Barrett's face. "That's the guy, I swear."

"He's dead," Barrett provided. "Now, I'm wondering if that's a nice coincidence for you so you can make us think that all of this is tied up in a neat little bow."

"No." Milton seemed adamant and repeated his denial when he looked at the laptop screen where he knew Leo and she were watching him. "He's dead? Who killed him?"

Olivia didn't think it was her imagination that the

news had alarmed Milton. Maybe because he'd known Lowell. Or perhaps because he thought he might next in line to die.

"I had to shoot him," Leo answered. "To stop him from murdering Olivia and me. So, tell me why Lowell had it in for us and would hire you to come at me with a knife?"

"The only thing he said was that I could make a lot of money if I took you out. I swear," Milton repeated, probably because Barrett was looking plenty skeptical.

Olivia was skeptical, as well. Milton would probably tell them anything to save his hide, and he'd withhold info, too, for that very same reason.

"Money?" Leo questioned. "That's why you agreed to kill me?"

Milton groaned and generally looked about as uncomfortable as a man could look. "I'm in trouble. I owe money to the wrong people, and I had to come up with some quick cash."

Leo jumped right on that. "How did you know Lowell? How'd he know you'd be willing to become a killer for hire?"

Milton shrugged. "I figured he worked for the men I owed the money. He just came up to me and asked if I wanted to get out of the hot water I was in. Not many people knew about my debts, so I just assumed he worked for the guys who'd lent me the funds."

"But you didn't find out for yourself?" Leo demanded.

"No. I was desperate. Those guys were going to kill me if I didn't pony up, so I saw the job Lowell offered as sort of self-defense."

That made Olivia sick to her stomach with disgust.

This snake had been willing to end a good man's life to save his own one. And all because of money.

"How much did Lowell pay you?" she snapped. She wanted to add more, to blister him with some backlash from her temper, but that wouldn't help. It might even hurt if it caused Milton to realize how much trouble he was in and clam up.

Milton hesitated, and she could see the battle he was having with himself as to how much to tell them. He maybe thought he should paint himself in the best light possible, but he was well beyond that. There was no "light" that would make him appear to be a decent human being.

"Ten grand," Milton finally said.

Oh, that didn't help with her bubbling temper and disgust. For ten thousand dollars, Milton had been willing to kill Leo, and for her father, that would have been chump change. Maybe for Bernice, too. Olivia didn't know her financial situation but suspected that the woman had saved most of her high salary. Bernice had certainly never taken a vacation, and to the best of Olivia's knowledge, she didn't have any expensive jewelry. Didn't even have her own car. Whenever Bernice needed to leave the estate, she used one of the vehicles.

Like the one that'd been spotted around the same time as Randall's body dump.

Bernice could have been in that vehicle. Then again, her father used the same type of SUV. And if Rena had access to the estate, she could have been behind the wheel of one, too. The keys for the vehicles were kept in the ignitions while they were in the garage.

"And FYI," Milton added a moment later, "I didn't get the full payment. Lowell only gave me three thousand up front and said I'd get the rest when I finished the job. Then he made me do a confession of sorts so that I wouldn't renege on the deal and run with the cash that I had."

"A confession?" Barrett asked, jumping right on that.

Again, Milton hesitated before he explained. "Lowell used a phone to record it. He had me say my name and that I was going to kill Deputy Leo Logan."

Olivia exchanged a glance with Leo. He was probably wondering the same thing she was—whether Lowell had planned to set up Milton to take the fall for Leo and any other attacks. Milton certainly made a perfect fall guy, and as he'd admitted himself, he was desperate.

"From everything we've gathered so far, Lowell was a hired thug, too," Barrett pointed out. "So, who hired him?"

That put some fresh alarm on Milton's face. "I don't know. That's the truth," he added in protest over their groans.

Leo huffed. "If you don't know that, then you're wasting our time," he snapped. "No information, no good word for you with the DA." His tone made it sound as if he was about to end the video session.

"Wait!" Milton pleaded. "I've got something. Something that should be worth more than just a good word with the DA."

"What?" Leo and Barrett asked at the same time, and both had plenty of skepticism in their expression. Olivia was right there with them.

"Lowell gave me a burner cell that he used to call me," Milton went on. "He told me to toss it right before I went after Leo, and I did."

"And how the heck is a burner going to help us?" Barrett fired back. "Lowell's dead, and what does it matter if he called you on it? He was probably using a burner himself."

"Probably," Milton admitted and then flashed an oily smile. "Lowell wasn't the only one who called me on it, though. I got another call, right before I went after Leo."

Suddenly, Olivia was very interested in what the man was saying. Leo, too, and they automatically moved closer to the laptop screen.

"Who called you?" Barrett urged.

The smile stayed on Milton's mouth. "The person didn't say who he or she was. The voice was all muf-fled-like. But the caller said Lowell was having trouble with his phone reception, but that I should go ahead and finish off Leo Logan."

There were indeed plenty of areas with bad recep-tion near her place where the second attacker—Low-ell—had likely gone. Someone had fired shots into her house shortly after Leo had arrived.

"I'm betting that caller was Lowell's boss," Milton insisted.

Barrett stared at him. "Let me guess. You have no idea where you tossed this burner phone."

"Oh, I know, all right. And this really oughta be worth more than just a word with the DA."

Obviously, Milton wanted to use this as a further bar-gaining tool, but Barrett just shook his head. "So far, you've given us little to nothing. Give me something now, or you're going back to your cell."

"All right," Milton said after what was obviously a mental debate with himself. "I figured if I could finish off Leo all quiet-like, then I could go back and get the burner and my own phone, which Lowell said I wasn't to have on me during the attack. So, I hid my cell and the burner in the bushes in the back of the parking lot and covered them with some leaves."

With his restraints rattling, he motioned toward the side of the building where there was indeed a parking lot. One with a row of hedges at the back.

"Go ahead and look," Milton insisted. "You'll see the number of the person who called me on the burner. Then you can listen to the conversation on my phone."

"You recorded it?" Leo asked before Olivia could jump right on that.

Milton's smile widened. "I did with my own phone. Listen to it, and you'll hear the voice of the person who wants you dead."

## Chapter Fourteen

Leo wished he could be in two places at once. He wanted to be at the sheriff's office, helping Barrett look for those two phones Milton had claimed he'd tossed. But Leo couldn't do that at the possible expense of Cameron and Olivia. Just because Lowell was dead and Milton was in restraints, it didn't mean the person who'd hired them hadn't sent another killer after them.

Olivia was pacing across the guest room, so obviously she was on edge, too, while they waited for word from Barrett. They had used some of their waiting time to go into the nursery to say good-night to Cameron. Leo had also brought in some covers for Izzie who'd insisted on using the sleep chair next to Cameron's crib. That was good because Cameron wouldn't be alone, but Leo figured when he and Olivia finally went to bed, they'd be bunking in the nursery, as well.

Leo checked the time and cursed when he realized it was only two minutes later than when he'd last checked. It hadn't been long—less that fifteen minutes—since Milton had told them about the phones, so it wasn't as if Barrett was dragging his feet on this. Plus, it was possible that the phones weren't where Milton had said they were.

Or they might not even exist.

The sigh he heard from Olivia told Leo that she was probably stressing over the same thing.

"Milton would be stupid to lie about this," Leo told her, though it probably wasn't much assurance because Milton clearly wasn't a smart man. Still, Leo could see how a stall tactic would help him.

"He or she," Olivia muttered. She stopped pacing and turned toward him. "That's what Jace said about the person who'd called him with the anonymous tip about Randall's body."

Leo nodded. Yeah, he'd remembered that, and if an indistinguishable muffled voice was all they had, then this wouldn't be much of a lead. Then again, he or Olivia might recognize something. Maybe even some background noise.

"Even if these phones end up ID'ing the killer," Olivia said, "I want Milton in jail. I want him to pay for what he did to you."

Yeah, but more than that, Leo wanted the person who was pulling the strings. Or rather, pulling the trigger. Because that's what this person was—a killer.

Because she looked as if her nerves were worse than his, Leo went to her and pulled her into his arms. He'd stopped trying to talk himself out of doing stuff like this. Plain and simple, he didn't even want to try to keep resisting Olivia.

He could hear the whirl of the AC, feel the cool air spilling on them. Feel the heat of her body, too. And her warm breath hitting against his neck.

Leo gave her another of those cheek kisses, but she didn't exactly melt against him. She was definitely wired, not only by the wait but from the stress of the constant threat of danger. The tension went up a significant notch when his phone rang.

Even though Leo had been anticipating the call, he still bobbled his phone when he yanked it from his jeans. Barrett's name was on the screen, so Leo answered it as fast as he could.

"I found the cells," Barrett said, his voice pouring through the room as Leo put the call on speaker. "They were right where Milton told us they'd be."

Leo released a long breath. "That's a good start. Please tell me he actually recorded his boss giving the order to kill me."

"He did. I've only listened to it once, so all I can tell you is that the voice is indeed muffled. Barely audible, in fact. But I'll send it to you so you can hear it for yourself."

Leo was certain both Barrett and he would be listening to it multiple times. So would the crime lab.

"I expected the caller to be using a burner, too," Barrett continued a moment later. "He or she didn't."

Olivia made a small gasping sound. "You know who made the call?" she blurted.

"No, but I know where the call originated," Barrett corrected. "It came from a landline at your father's estate."

It took Leo a moment to wrap his mind around that, and he didn't like the conclusions he reached. "Lowell gave Milton a burner, but the person who hired them didn't take that simple step to cover his tracks?"

"Yes," Barrett agreed.

It was obvious they thought that maybe this was some kind of stupid scheme meant to make Samuel look guilty.

"It's just like the vehicle," Olivia said. Her forehead

was furrowed, the worry plentiful in her eyes. "Any of the three could have used a landline phone in the house."

Bingo. That could have been intentional or an oversight. After all, maybe the culprit hadn't thought Milton would record the call or ditch the phone so it could so easily be found.

"I'll get a warrant to access the phone lines at the estate," Barrett advised. "After I have the info I need on the calls, I'll question Samuel, Rena and Bernice again in the morning. In the meantime, listen to the call and let me know if you hear anything that I've missed."

A moment later, Leo's phone dinged with the recording Barrett had just sent him. Leo ended the call with his brother so that he and Olivia could listen to it.

"Lowell's got bad phone reception," the caller said. Either Milton hadn't managed to record the "greeting" or there hadn't been one. "Do the job on Leo Logan, and when we have proof it's done, you'll get the rest of your money."

That was it. No flashing neon light of information, and Barrett and Milton had been right about the voice. It was muffled and, to Leo's ear, indistinguishable. Apparently, it was the same for Olivia because she cursed, as well.

Leo hit Replay, listened, and then hit Replay again. On the fourth listen, Olivia sank onto the foot of the bed and shook her head.

"I hear some background noise," she said, "but it only sounds like wind blowing or maybe a ceiling fan."

"Same here," Leo agreed. And if it was indeed wind, it could have been coming from the parking lot of the sheriff's office. In other words, no help whatsoever.

He sank beside her, took her hand and tried to put at least some positive spin on things. "Once Barrett gets the warrant and the phone records from the estate, we might be able to pinpoint which landline was used."

Though he figured there were many extensions off a single line, he thought it best not to remind Olivia of that since she already looked as if she was about to crash and burn. He knew how she felt. He'd clung to the hope that the phones would give them a solid clue. And *that* they had. The call had come from the estate, which meant the killer had been there. That wasn't a surprise, but maybe they could use the phone records and compare them to the alibis or statements of their suspects.

Or they could bluff.

"Barrett's allowed to lie in interview," Leo explained. "He could bring in Rena, Bernice and Samuel, tell them that Milton recorded the order for the hit on me, and the person responsible might break."

*"Might,"* she repeated in a mumble.

Even though it hadn't helped with the stress the other times he'd done it, Leo pulled her into his arms again.

"I wish Barrett could arrest them all," she added.

Yeah, too bad he couldn't do it. But even that might not end the danger because there could already be other hired guns out there, waiting for their shot. When Olivia pulled back and met his gaze, he knew that she was well aware of that scenario, too.

"We should listen to the recording again," she said, not breaking eye contact with him. "We also need to go over my mother's journals. And brainstorm as to why Bernice, Rena or my father wants us dead."

They did indeed need to do all those things. But Leo went for something totally different.

He kissed her.

Again, there was no *melting*. In fact, Olivia went stiff,

and he figured she would put a quick stop to this. After all, kissing wasn't one of the options she'd just spelled out for what they should be doing.

The weariness was still in her eyes. Actually, on every part of her face, and because he had his arms around her, Leo could feel the knotted muscles in her back.

"Bad timing," he said and started to move away from her.

Olivia stopped him by catching the front of his T-shirt. "The timing is awful," she agreed. "Plenty of things are awful. You're not. This isn't."

And this time, she kissed him.

Leo didn't stop her. He wasn't an idiot. This was exactly what he wanted. He could even try to make himself believe that it'd be a great stress reliever. A way for them to forget the hell they'd been going through. Well, forget it for a short time anyway. But this wasn't about stress or forgetting. This kiss was about giving in to the heat that they'd both been fighting for way too long.

She was the one who deepened the kiss, threading her fingers into his hair, bringing him closer to her. Not that Leo needed any such adjustments to get him closer. He had already headed in that direction and made some adjustments of his own so that her breasts landed against his chest.

The kiss continued, but he added some touching to this make-out session. He slipped his hand between them, cupped her breasts and swiped his thumb over her nipple. The silky sound of pleasure Olivia made nearly brought him to his knees. Thankfully, though, it didn't rid him of common sense. He stood, leading her with him to the door so he could lock it. No way did he want Izzie walking in on them.

Even with all the moving around, Olivia didn't miss a beat, and she didn't haul him back to the bed. Instead, she pushed him so that his back landed against the wall and she went in for a kiss that was well past the make-out stage. This was a carnal invitation to sex.

And Leo's body responded.

He went hard as stone, and every part of him urged him to strip off her clothes and take her now, now, now. Leo wanted *now* more than he wanted air in his lungs, but he didn't want to take Olivia in some frantic coupling. It would leave them both sated, that was for sure. However, it would be over way too fast. He didn't want fast. He wanted—no, he *needed*—to hang on to this even if just for the night.

"Your arm," she said out of the blue. "You're hurt."

"I'm not hurting," he told her. That was the truth. He wasn't sure he could feel a mountain of pain right now.

"You're sure?" she pressed.

He took her hand and put it over his erection. "I'm sure."

She smiled. A sly, wicked smile, and kept her hand in place. "I haven't had you in over a year and a half."

She looked at him. Her eyes hot now. The need had replaced the weariness and fatigue. He thought for a second that she was going to tell him they needed to rethink this, that there were reasons why they'd been apart for over a year and a half. That there were reasons, like the investigation, why they should table this and go back to it when Barrett had made an arrest.

"A year and a half is too long," she said.

Her voice was a throaty whisper. Like the rest of her, it tugged and pulled at him until Leo felt the snap. The one that told him he wouldn't be able to draw this out, after all. The *now* was going to win.

So, he took her now. He kissed her, the hunger and need clawing through him. Through her, too. Because she kicked off her shoes and began to tug at his shirt. Leo helped her with that and did the same to hers. Their tops landed on the floor. He unhooked the front clasp of her bra and tossed it down with the other items of clothing. This wouldn't be pretty, but they'd get it done.

Suddenly her hands were on him. On his bare chest. His back. Touching him. Making him crazy. The craziness climbed when she went after the zipper of his jeans. *Now* was winning for her, too, but through all of that, she made sure she didn't touch his wounded arm.

He backed her toward the bed. Kissing her. With skin sliding against skin. Her nipples were too much to resist, so he dipped his head and took one into his mouth. His reward was that she made that silky moan of pleasure again and bucked against him.

They fell onto the bed together.

Leo kept tugging at her nipple and then he kissed his way down her stomach. To her jeans, which he shimmied off her. Her panties came next, and he did even more kissing. Pleasing her. Pleasing himself.

"Don't mention the stretch marks," she muttered.

Because his pulse was throbbing in his ears, it took him a moment to realize what she'd said. Since his mouth was still right there, he kissed the marks, as well.

"If you think they're a turn-off, you're wrong," he told her. Just the opposite. She'd had his child, their son, and the marks were a reminder of that.

Olivia made a sound that let him know that she wasn't quite convinced. Leo would have *convinced* her, too, but she rolled on top of him. Again, she was mindful of his arm.

"I don't want you reopening the cut," she said, levering to straddle him and go after his zipper.

Leo was about to insist that he wasn't concerned about the damn cut, but then she got off his jeans. Got off his boxers. And nearly got him off when her hands skimmed over him.

He gritted his teeth and let her do what she wanted. Apparently some kisses and touching as he'd done. Or maybe she was just trying to drive him insane. She nearly managed it, too, before she finally made her way back up his body and, sliding her hips against his, took him inside her.

Now he had to grit his teeth from the sheer pleasure of the sensations firing through him. Mercy, the woman was good at this.

Olivia stilled, giving them both a moment to catch their breath. She waited until their eyes were locked before she braced her hands on his chest and started to move. She was good at this, too, but there was no way Leo could just lie there and not get involved. He caught her hips, adding some pressure to those thrusts that would soon push them both right over the edge.

His body begged for release while he also tried to hold on. To make this last as long as possible. He was doing a decent job of it when he felt the orgasm ripple through Olivia. She fisted around him, giving him no choice but to give in to the need.

Leo pulled her down to him and followed her.

## Chapter Fifteen

Olivia lay on top of Leo and tried to level her breathing. Tried to shut out the thoughts, too. She succeeded in doing the first but failed big-time with the second. The thoughts came. Both good and bad.

Making love with Leo had been something starved for. It'd been like coming home, Christmas and her birthday all rolled into one.

And that was the problem.

Great sex only made her want him more, and while he certainly seemed able to put their past troubles behind him, they had a very rough road ahead of them. One that might involve her own father's arrest for attempting to murder them. Even if it wasn't Samuel, she and Leo wouldn't have an easy time putting aside everything that'd happen and just move on with their lives.

Besides, Leo might not want to "move on" with her.

He'd certainly not said anything about an ever-after or even a commitment. Of course, they had a commitment because of Cameron, but being with Leo like this made Olivia realize that she wanted more. She wanted the whole package. Leo. Their son. A life together.

Even though the timing was lousy for it, Olivia worked up enough steel to open that "life together" conversation with him. Best not to do that, however, while he was still inside her, so she eased off him, mindful not to touch his arm, and dropped onto the bed so they were side to side. She pulled the edge of the quilt over her and looked at him.

Just as he cursed.

It wasn't a mild oath, either, and she figured it had to be aimed at her. Or rather, their situation. Mercy. Here she was fantasizing about a life with him, and he probably thought this had been a huge mistake.

"No condom," he groaned.

Olivia blinked. Then her eyes went wide when his words sank in. She practically snapped to a sitting position and stared down at him.

"Yeah," Leo said, obviously noting the extreme shock that had to be on her face. He straightened, as well, groaned and cursed some more. "I'm so sorry."

She opened her mouth but wasn't sure what to say. This wasn't something she could just blow off and tell him not to worry about. Still, she could give him a little reassurance about one possible pitfall to not practicing safe sex.

"I'm okay," she said. "I mean I've been tested, and I haven't been with anyone since you."

He turned his head, slowly, his gaze snaring hers. "No one in nearly two years?"

Olivia realized that it sounded as if she was stuck on him and unable to move on to anyone else.

And that was the truth.

However, since it was the truth, she didn't intend to admit it to him, not now when declaring her feelings for him would be the last thing he'd want to hear.

"No one," she verified. "I stay really busy with Cameron. I don't have time for a relationship."

He just continued to stare at her with those stone-gray eyes. Eyes that seemed to see right through her to suss out the lie she'd just told. Yes, she was busy, but she hadn't wanted another man. Hadn't wanted to be with anyone other than Leo and maybe would have been had it not been for her father.

"I haven't been with anyone since you, either," he said.

Olivia was certain her look of shock returned, intensified. She nearly laughed because it seemed a joke that someone who was at hot as Leo would go that long without having a woman. But he was serious.

Cursing again, he rubbed his hand over his face and then groaned. "No condom," he repeated as if to get them back on track with the conversation. Apparently, he didn't want to launch into a discussion of why they'd been living celibate lives. "Any chance you can tell me it's the wrong time of the month?"

No chance whatsoever, and that's why Olivia settled for a shrug. Her cycle hadn't been regular since she'd had Cameron so, as far as she knew, there was no such thing as the wrong time of the month.

"It'll be okay," she insisted though she had absolutely nothing to back it up. Well, nothing except what would certainly sound like lame logic. "We used protection before, and I still got pregnant with Cameron, so maybe that means the odds are in our favor that I won't get pregnant now."

He turned to stare at her again. A flat stare that told her he'd had no trouble figuring out the "lame" part. But the turning and staring put his face very close to hers and, despite this serious concern, Olivia felt a little weak in the knees just looking at him. Here, only minutes had passed since she'd had him and she wanted him all over again.

Olivia leaned in and saw the surprise flash in his eyes before she kissed him. She'd thought he'd resist. After all, they had work to do, and there was that whole part about them literally having had sex just minutes earlier. But he didn't resist. Leo muttered something she didn't catch, slid his hand around the back of her neck and hauled her to him. She laughed, kept kissing him and slid back onto his lap.

The kiss turned instantly hot. Then again, it wasn't possible to kiss Leo and not feel the heat. But this time they didn't get to push it any further. That's because Leo stopped.

"I think I hear something," Leo said, causing her laughter, and the heat, to vanish. "I need to talk to the ranch hand."

He swore when he reached for his phone and it wasn't there. That's because it was in jeans' pocket and all their clothes were scattered on the floor. As soon as they got off the bed and located it in his jeans by the nightstand, Leo made the call.

"Wally," Leo greeted. "Is something wrong?"

Alarmed at Leo's tone, Olivia moved closer to hear, but Leo fixed that by putting the call on speaker so that it'd free up his hands to pull on his jeans.

"Maybe," Wally answered. "There's someone walking up the road toward the house. Or rather, staggering. I can't tell who it is, but it is a woman."

Olivia certainly hadn't been expecting Wally to say that. Her worst fear was that he had been about to tell them he'd spotted a gunman. That's why Olivia had practically been throwing on her clothes so she could hurry to Cameron. But this didn't seem like an immediate threat.

Well, maybe it wasn't.

It quickly occurred to her that it could be some kind of ruse. Something set up so an attacker could get closer to the house.

"Is the woman armed?" Leo asked the hand.

"I don't think so. She's not carrying a purse or anything…hell, she just fell down. Should I go out and check on her?"

Olivia saw the sleek muscle tighten in Leo's jaw and knew he was debating how to handle this. His ranch was miles from town, so he didn't normally get foot traffic out here. However, it could be someone who'd been in a car accident and was looking for help.

"Wait," Wally said a moment later. "She's getting up and looking up at the house. She's coming this way, boss."

"Don't go check on her yourself," Leo instructed. "Send two of the other hands and make sure to tell them to be careful. We have two women who are suspects, so whoever it is, she could be armed and dangerous. Report back to me as soon as you know who she is."

"Will do," Wally assured him.

The moment Leo ended the call, he finished getting dressed and motioned for Olivia to follow him. "Tell Izzie to take Cameron and get in the tub with him. I'm going to the front windows to see if I can spot our visitor."

Olivia hated to alarm Cameron or Izzie, but when she hurried into the nursery, she could see that Cameron was asleep. She relayed Leo's orders and then tried to reassure Izzie that it was simply a precaution.

She prayed that's exactly what it was—a precaution.

Once she'd helped Izzie move Cameron into the bath-room, Olivia rushed back out to find Leo. He was in his office, a room on the second floor at the front of the house. He had a pair of binoculars pressed to his eyes and was looking out the window. She hurried to him, but he motioned for her to stay to the side. That, of course, was so that she wouldn't be in the line of fire. Unlike Leo. He was standing there, his weapon drawn and ready for whatever was about to happen.

"I can't tell if it's Bernice or Rena," he told her. "But two hands are in a truck and heading her way."

Olivia stayed to the side of the window, but peered around the frame, hoping to get a glimpse of what was happening. She did. She saw the headlights of the truck making its way down the road. Several moments later, the truck stopped, and the headlights shone right on the woman.

"It's Bernice," Leo muttered. "She's got blood on her face."

So, maybe the car accident theory was right. Except that wouldn't explain what Bernice was doing out here in the first place.

Olivia continued to watch as both men got out of the truck and walked toward the woman. Bernice fell for-ward, practically collapsing, before one of them caught her. The second man took out his phone and, seconds later, Leo's phone rang. He put the call on speaker and it didn't take long for the ranch hand's voice to pour through the room.

"The woman says her name is Bernice Saylor," the hand explained. "And she says she needs to see you. She claims that that somebody ran her off the road and then tried to kill her."

LEO HAD ALREADY cursed way too much tonight, so he didn't add more. Though this was definitely a situation that called for profanity.

And caution.

His first instinct was to dismiss this as some kind of dangerous ploy for Bernice to get to him, but then Leo thought of Randall. He, too, had said someone had tried to kill him.

That someone had succeeded, too.

Leo didn't want to take the risk that the same thing would happen with Bernice. Especially if the woman was innocent. But he would need to add some layers of security to the help he gave her.

"I'm calling Barrett," Leo told the hand, Carter Johnson. "Stay put until I do that."

He hadn't even had time to end the call with Carter when there was a loud blast and a fireball shot up from the pasture just to the right of where his ranch hands were standing with Bernice. The two men dropped to the ground, pulling Bernice down with them.

"What the hell?" he heard Carter grumble just as Bernice shouted, "She's trying to kill me."

At least that's what Leo thought they'd said before their voices were drowned out by another blast. Then another. All three flare-ups had been in the pastures, too far from the house to do any damage, but his two hands and Bernice could be in immediate danger.

"Check to make sure Bernice isn't armed," Leo instructed Carter when he came back on the line. "If she's not, put her in the truck and drive her to the house, but don't bring her in. Get out of there fast," he added when there was a fourth blast.

"The flames aren't big enough to burn through the

pasture grass," Leo tried to assure Olivia. "But I'll call the fire department anyway."

"I'll do that," Olivia volunteered, taking his phone. "You keep watch."

He didn't turn down her offer because keeping watch was critical right now. Leo doubted that the person who'd set those fires had actually been close enough to light them. No, the fireballs were probably on some kind of timer or device, the way the one in Randall's truck had been. There hadn't been time for Leo to send the hands into the pastures to look for any devices, but clearly there'd been some.

"Tell the fire department to approach with caution, that there could be a sniper in the area," Leo rattled off to her. "And then call Barrett to let him know what's going on. Same rules apply to him," he insisted. "I don't want him caught in the crosshairs of a gunman."

Olivia gave him a nod, a very shaky one, and her hands were trembling a little, but she made the calls. Leo half listened to her relay what he'd told her to say, but he kept his focus on his ranch hands and Bernice. She didn't protest when Carter frisked her. He must not have found any weapons because, seconds after, he all but carried Bernice to the truck and put her inside.

Another fireball shot up. This one was at the end of the drive, and it was different from the others. Those first ones had been blasts, but this was more of a line of fire that created a wall to prevent someone from getting to or from the house. It was as if someone had poured gasoline onto the asphalt and then lit it. Of course, that could have been done with a timer, as well.

And that was also why he had no intention of trusting Bernice.

Olivia was still on the phone with Barrett when the truck started toward the house. The lights slashed through the darkness, and Leo used that light to try to glimpse anyone who might have managed to sneak onto the grounds. He didn't see anyone, but that didn't mean someone wasn't out there. That's why he wanted Izzie to stay put with Cameron until he was certain the place was secure.

"Oh God," he heard Olivia say.

Leo whipped toward her. "What's wrong?" he demanded.

"Barrett was leaving his house and a firebomb went off at the end of his driveway."

Hell. Leo knew that wasn't a coincidence. "Is Della there with him?"

"Yes," Olivia verified, her voice now shaking as much as the rest of her.

"Then tell Barrett to stay put," Leo insisted.

Barrett's fiancée, Della, was pregnant, and Leo didn't want to put her or their baby at risk by Barrett leaving her alone. Della was a deputy sheriff and could likely take care of herself, but the person behind these attacks could try to take Della hostage and use her as leverage. Leo couldn't do that to Della or Barrett.

"See if Daniel can come," Leo told her. "But let him know what he could be up against and tell him that he'll have to use the trails to get here."

Olivia finished her call with Barrett and made the one to Daniel just as Leo watched Carter pull the truck to a stop in front of the house. Not too close, though. And there was a lot of open yard between the vehicle and the house. If Bernice got out and tried to run toward them, there'd be plenty of ranch hands to stop her.

He heard the soft ding on his phone to indicate an incoming call. A moment later Olivia said, "It's Carter." Handing him his phone, she added, "Daniel's coming ASAP."

Leo had no doubts that Daniel would indeed try to get here fast, but he had to wonder if there'd be another fire. Another distraction. Something that would stop backup from getting to the ranch.

"Carter," Leo said when he took the incoming call. "What's going on?"

"The woman wasn't armed," the ranch hand answered. "That's about all I know right now. That, and what she's saying about somebody trying to kill her. But I don't know who set those fires. I didn't see anybody, boss, and I've been keeping watch for hours."

"The fires could have been rigged days ago," Leo explained. In fact, they could have been set even before the one that'd taken out Randall's truck. The bomb squad hadn't gone out into the pastures to look for more devices because they'd concentrated on the house and the outbuildings.

"Put Bernice on the phone," Leo instructed Carter.

It didn't take long for Carter to do that and Leo soon heard Bernice. "Thank you for saving me," the woman blustered, her words running together. "She nearly killed me."

Leo had plenty of questions, but he started with the big one. "Who tried to kill you?"

"Rena." Bernice didn't hesitate, either. "She ran me off the road and then tried to shoot me. I got away from her."

"Rena," he repeated, both skeptical and curious. He didn't doubt that Rena was capable of doing something like this, but he also had no doubt that Bernice could be lying. "Where did all of this happen?"

"Just up the main road, not far from your ranch. I was coming here because of Samuel. He's distraught, and I thought I could talk Olivia into calling him. I guess Rena followed me."

Leo didn't press the point that it was a stupid idea for Bernice to try to convince Olivia to call her father. There were too many other things he needed to know. Obviously, things that Olivia should know, as well, because she was leaning closer to listen to the conversation. Leo didn't want her in front of the window so he switched the call to speaker.

"You're sure it was Rena who ran you off the road?" Leo pressed. "You saw her?"

Now, Bernice paused. "Not exactly. But I saw the logo on the door of the SUV. Rena was at the estate, and she must have taken it."

Maybe. Or it could have been Samuel in the vehicle. The man might have had motive to off his estate manager after what'd gone on between them in the sheriff's office. Then again, maybe Bernice and Samuel had mended fences if she was telling the truth about trying to convince Olivia to speak to him.

But that was a big *if.*

"Stay put in the truck with my ranch hands," Leo told Bernice. "And I mean stay put. I'm going to call Rena to see if I can get her side of this."

"She'll just lie," Bernice insisted. "She'll say I made it all up."

Yeah, she might, but Leo ended the call with Bernice. Since he didn't have Rena's number handy, he worked his way through the dispatcher to have the deputy place the call. During that wait, he also looked at Olivia to make sure she was okay.

She wasn't.

All of this was giving her another slam of fear, and he hated to see it in her eyes. Hated that he wouldn't be able to stop it until he'd worked out this situation with Bernice and now Rena.

"You could wait in the nursery," he suggested. "You could be with Cameron."

She glanced at the doorway. Then back at him. And Olivia shook her head. "No one can get into the nursery without us knowing. The security alarm would go off if someone tried to get into the house."

He nodded and would have tried to give her some kind of assurance that everything would be okay, but the call to Rena finally went through. The phone rang and rang, and just when Leo figured a voice mail recording would kick in, she answered. Or rather, someone did.

"I'm hurt."

It was a woman, and it was possible it was Rena. It was hard to tell, however, because the voice was muffled— a reminder of the other calls that had been mentioned in this investigation.

"Rena?" he asked.

"Yes, it's me. I'm hurt," she repeated.

A muffled voice as well as injuries could be faked, and Leo had no idea if that was the case. "Where are you? What happened?"

"I'm hurt," she repeated. "Help me."

Leo frowned because she hadn't answered either of his questions. He tried again. "I'll help you as soon as you tell me where you are."

Of course, he could try to have the call traced and her

location pinpointed by using the cell towers, but all of that would take time.

There was a long silence before Rena muttered, "I'm in one of your pastures, I think. I think I can see the lights from your house."

Hell. He didn't want her that close, and it really didn't help him pinpoint her location since he had hundreds of acres of pastures. Plus, it was possible that the lights she was seeing weren't from his house but rather one of the outbuildings.

"How'd you get in my pasture?" he snapped.

"Um, I was looking for Samuel." Her breath was pitched and labored.

Well, that seemed to be tonight's trend for the women in Samuel's life. Leo didn't bother to ask her why she thought Samuel would be at his place.

"Use the landline," he instructed Olivia, tipping his head to the phone on his desk. "Call an ambulance and tell the EMTs what Rena just said. But they need to approach with caution."

"Because this could be a trap," Olivia supplied with a nod.

"Not a trap." Rena's voice was even more slurred now than when she'd first answered. In fact, if this was an act, she was doing a damn good job of it.

"The ambulance is on the way," Olivia relayed several moments later.

"You hear that?" Leo asked Rena as he kept watch out the window. Because this entire conversation could be a distraction so that someone could sneak onto the ranch. "An ambulance will be here soon. What are your injuries?"

There were some moans, and it sounded as if she was

moving around. "My head. Everything's spinning around. And I'm bleeding. God, I'm bleeding."

"Tell me what happened," Leo persisted.

"I'm not sure. I was driving and everything started spinning. My head's bleeding. I'm hurt, so I must have wrecked. I wrecked and then I got out and started walking to get help."

"You could have used your phone to call 9-1-1," he pointed out.

"Not thinking straight. So dizzy." There was a thud. It sounded as if Rena had fallen.

Leo wasn't ready to give up. Besides, he needed to keep Rena on the phone until the EMTs arrived and managed to find her. If she was talking, they might be able to hear the sound of her voice. However, he did have to wonder if she'd been drugged—just as Simone had been. But that was something he'd need to figure out later.

"Did you just try to kill Bernice?" Leo demanded. "She said you did."

"Bernice?" she mumbled.

"That's right. Bernice. Did you try to kill her?" he asked.

"No." She muttered some things he couldn't make out. "But I know who tried to kill you."

"Who?" Leo snapped.

Nothing. No moans, no more sounds of Rena moving around.

"Rena?" Leo said. "Say something. Keep talking to me."

Still nothing, and that started a war within him. If Rena was indeed hurt, he needed to get to her to try to save her life. But he couldn't leave Olivia, Cameron and

Izzie. He certainly couldn't leave them long enough to go wandering around his pastures, looking for Rena.

"I need to talk to Bernice," he declared. "Not on the phone. I need to get in her face to see for myself if she knows what's going on."

Olivia touched her fingers to her lips for a moment. Obviously, she was having the same internal battle as he was. Except she had the added concern of not wanting him to get hurt.

"I'll get Carter to move the truck closer to the house so I won't have to cross the yard," Leo explained. "And I'll have him wait inside with you until I'm done with Bernice. You can stay up here but keep away from the windows." He paused, hating to add this last part since he knew it was only going to put more alarm on her face. "There's a gun on the top shelf of the closet." He tipped his head to the door just a few feet away from his desk.

Olivia nodded, and because he figured they both could use it, he gave her a quick kiss. Leo pulled back, looked at her. And then gave her another kiss that wasn't so quick.

"I won't be long," he said and hoped that was true.

Keeping his gun ready, he called Carter while he went downstairs. Leo waited at the front door until the hand had moved the truck right up to the porch. Even then Leo waited until Carter was out and at the door before he disarmed the security system to let the hand in.

"No matter what happens," Leo told him, "protect Olivia, Cameron and Izzie."

"I will, boss," Carter assured him.

Leo dragged in a long breath and, hoping this wasn't a huge mistake, stepped outside and hurried to the truck.

He got in behind the wheel and immediately turned to face Bernice who was in the center with the other hand, Edwin Dade, on the passenger's side.

Bernice did have blood on her face, along with some cuts and scrapes. None looked serious. Being the skeptical cop that he was, Leo decided they could have been self-inflicted.

"Start talking," Leo told Bernice. "You said Rena tried to kill you, and I want details."

"Of course." Bernice took her own deep breath.

But before she could say a word, all hell broke loose and the front end of the truck exploded.

OLIVIA'S HEART WENT to her knees when she heard the blast. This one was much louder than the others, and when she glanced out the window of Leo's office, she saw smoke and flames shoot out from the truck.

Oh God.

Someone had used a firebomb on the truck, and Leo was inside it.

She hurried out of the office, made it halfway down the stairs before she saw the thick black smoke. Not only in the truck now. It was billowing in through the front door where Carter stood. "Go help Leo," she insisted.

Carter had already started in that direction, and Olivia went down the rest of the stairs to look out to see if she could spot Leo. She couldn't. She couldn't even tell how much of the truck was still intact. It could be blown to bits.

Leo could be dead.

The hoarse sob left her throat. Tears stung her eyes. But then so did the smoke and it wasn't long before she started to cough. She had no choice but to close the door because she couldn't breathe. She also couldn't risk the smoke and fire getting to Cameron.

As much as she wanted to see Leo, Olivia knew she had to protect their son. She raced back up the stairs, going straight to the nursery. The fist around her heart loosened a little when she saw that her baby was asleep in Izzie's arms.

"What happened?" Izzie asked.

Olivia couldn't speak. Her throat had clamped shut and her fear for Leo was skyrocketing.

"Just stay put," she managed to tell Izzie. She ran back out, racing into Leo's office so she could get a better look at the truck.

She cursed the smoke that had blanketed the entire front yard and the front of the house, but she could see someone moving around. Carter, she realized when, a moment later, he pulled someone from the truck.

Leo.

Mercy, Leo looked unconscious, or worse, and the hand had to drag him away from the burning truck. She reached for the landline to call an ambulance, only to remember that one was already on the way. So was the fire department. Maybe they would both get here soon. And while she was hoping, she added a plea that the EMTs would be able to get past that fire on the road. It was still blazing, as were the ones in the pasture. But those fires didn't have the thick smoke like the one in the truck.

Olivia continued to keep watch, knowing that she was breaking Leo's order for her to stay away from the windows. She couldn't. She had to see if he was all right; it crushed her to think that she could lose him.

She was in love with him and had been since they'd first become lovers. Olivia knew that now—for all the good it'd do because she might not get a chance to ever tell him.

There was more movement in the smoke, but she lost sight of where Carter had taken Leo. She lost sight of pretty much anything when the smoke billowed up, blocking any view she had from the window.

But Olivia could still hear.

And she heard something that put her body on full alert.

She hadn't seen anyone come into the house, but she was pretty sure she heard footsteps in the foyer. Then the front door closing. She nearly rushed back downstairs to see if it was Leo, but everything inside her warned her that it wasn't.

Someone was in the house.

Someone who could try to kill her and get to Cameron.

Everything froze for a moment. Her feet. Her breath. Maybe even her heart. But nothing stopped the fear that shot like icy fingers up her spine.

She forced herself to stay quiet. To think. And she remembered Leo telling her about the gun. Stepping as softly as she could, she went to his office closet and, moving to her tiptoes, felt around until she found it. She'd had some firearms training—*some*—and prayed that she remembered it. Maybe, just maybe, it wouldn't even be necessary.

With the gun gripped in her hands, Olivia made her way to the office door and looked out. The smoke was still there, thick in the foyer and drifting up the stairs. There were just enough breaks in the drifts for her to see someone walking up the steps toward her.

"Leo?" she blurted.

"No," someone answered. The voice was muffled, but

Olivia had no trouble hearing what was said. "Move, and I start shooting. And I won't be careful about keeping the shots away from your little boy."

# Chapter Sixteen

Leo's lungs were on fire, and he couldn't catch his breath. Worse, he couldn't see squat, but he forced himself to try to clear his head. To think. To remember what the hell had happened to him.

He felt around and realized he was lying on the grass. Maybe his yard. There was smoke everywhere, along with the stench of burning rubber and gasoline. He was coughing, but so was someone else. He soon realized that someone else was Carter. The ranch hand was on his knees next to Leo, and he was trying to bat away the smoke.

Groaning, Leo tried to sit, but he failed on the first try. His head was throbbing, and he was dizzy, but he'd thankfully managed to hang on to his gun.

"The truck blew up," Carter mumbled in between coughs.

It wasn't easy, but Leo picked through the memories in his spinning head and tried to piece things together. Yeah, there had been some kind of explosion. Maybe one of the firebombs. And it'd indeed ripped through the front end of the truck. The airbags had deployed. But that wasn't the reason his head was throbbing.

No.

Leo remembered someone clubbing him.

Who had done that? Bernice maybe? Maybe someone who'd come up from outside the truck? He just didn't know, but he sure as hell was about to figure that out.

*Cameron. Olivia.* Those two names made it through the blistering pain and the dizziness. Olivia and Cameron were inside his house, a house that could be on fire, and he had to get them out.

He cursed, getting to his hands and knees so he could try to lever himself up and stand. Leo finally managed it, with Carter's help, but he wasn't sure he could make it even a step without falling.

"I think Edwin's still in the truck," Carter said, still coughing. "Wally and some of the other hands went running over there, I think. I think," he repeated to let Leo he wasn't sure of that at all. "I need to get Edwin away from the fire."

Damn. Leo hadn't worked his thoughts around to the ranch hand who'd been in the truck with him, but now he looked back at the truck. Or rather, what was left of it. It was about thirty feet away from him, and the front end was definitely on fire. It was those flames that were causing the smothering black smoke.

"Go to Edwin," Leo told Carter. "And if Bernice is still in the truck, get her out, too."

Leo wanted to help, but he had no intention of doing that at Olivia's and Cameron's expense. He needed to get to them, to take them to safety. Heaven knew, though, where that would be right now, but the cruiser was still in the yard. He could get them inside and drive away from the burning truck, away from the house. Maybe then they'd be safe.

Carter hurried in the direction of the truck and disappeared into the curtain of smoke. Leo got moving, too, though each step was an effort. The seconds were just ticking by, and each second was time he needed to rescue Izzie, Olivia and his son.

Leo hadn't even made it to the porch when he heard the footsteps behind him. With his gun aimed as best he could manage, he whirled in that direction. He'd expected to see one of his hands since they'd no doubt be coming to help, but it wasn't.

It was Samuel.

"Don't shoot," the man said, lifting his hands in the air. His breath was gusting and his face was covered with sweat.

"What the hell are you doing here?" Leo snarled, but figured he knew the answer. Samuel was there to try to kill him.

Maybe.

Leo shook his head because that didn't make sense. If Samuel had wanted him dead, he could have shot him in the back. Leo knew with his head injury, he probably wouldn't have even seen it coming.

"I got an anonymous call," Samuel answered. He was coughing, too, and trying to bat the smoke away from his face. "And the caller said Olivia had been taken hostage, that I was to get here as fast as I could. I had to leave my SUV at the end of the road because of the fire, and I ran the rest of the way here."

Leo wished his head would stop throbbing for just a second so he could figure out if that was the truth. Then, he decided it didn't matter. The only thing that mattered right now was Olivia and Cameron, and he didn't have time to interrogate her father. Or to arrest him.

"Wait here," Leo told him. "I'll deal with you when I get back."

Samuel didn't listen. He was right on Leo's heels as he made his way up the porch steps. "Is Olivia inside? Has she really been taken?" Samuel's two questions ran together, and his panic and fear sure sounded genuine.

*Sounded.*

But Leo wasn't about to take that reaction at face value. Too bad he didn't have any cuffs on him that he could use to restrain Samuel, but he did do a quick frisk of the man. Samuel didn't stop him and voluntarily handed Leo the handgun he'd been wearing in a shoulder holster.

"I need to make sure Olivia and Cameron are okay," Samuel said between his coughs. His breathing sounded more labored than Leo's.

Leo didn't waste time arguing with the man. He bolted into the foyer and glanced around. Olivia wasn't there, but someone had tracked dirt onto the floor. Maybe Carter when Leo had sent the hand in to stay with Olivia.

But the feeling in his gut told him it hadn't been Carter, that it'd been someone with bad intentions.

That got Leo moving faster as he headed for the stairs. Again, Samuel was right behind him.

"I didn't know," Samuel said. "I swear I didn't."

While Leo very much wanted to know what the man meant by that, he didn't respond. "Olivia?" he called out.

He listened for her to answer while he drowned out the other noises. The ranch hands in the yard who were apparently trying to put out the truck fire. He could hear water running, so they were likely using the hose. In the distance, he also heard the wail of sirens. Maybe the ambulance and fire department. Maybe Daniel. But what Leo didn't hear was Olivia.

Leo called out her name again and, despite his blurred vision, he hurried up the stairs. There was some smoke here, too, and the lights were off. But Leo could still see the gun on the floor. The gun that Olivia had no doubt taken from his office closet.

And he could see Olivia.

His heart stopped.

There was Olivia in the dark hall. Not alone. Someone was behind her. And that someone had a gun aimed at her head.

Dragging Samuel with him, Leo automatically ducked for cover behind the wall at the top of the stairs, but he glanced out to see if he had a shot to take out Olivia's captor.

He didn't.

The person was using Olivia as a shield. Hell. Olivia could be killed.

"The caller was right," Samuel declared, and he would have darted from cover if Leo hadn't held him back.

Yeah, the caller was right, and later, Leo would figure out if Olivia's captor had made that call and if Samuel was in on this plan. He didn't appear to be. He seemed to be just as shaken as Leo, but Leo didn't trust the man one bit.

"If you do anything stupid," Leo warned Samuel, "I'll kill you. Understand? You're not going to do anything that'll put Olivia or Cameron in any more danger than they already are."

Samuel must have seen that Leo wasn't bluffing, that he would indeed kill him, because the man quit struggling. Groaning, he sank onto the stairs.

"Help her," Samuel said like a plea. "Help her."

That was the plan. Well, as soon as he had a plan, that would be Leo's top priority. For now he had to figure out what was going on. Since Olivia was obviously a hostage, he had to find out what her captor wanted.

"I'm Deputy Leo Logan," he said, identifying himself. And while he was a thousand percent sure it wouldn't work, he added, "Throw down your weapon."

He couldn't be sure, but he thought the person laughed.

"I'm sorry, Leo," Olivia called out, her voice trembling. "I didn't have a choice."

Hearing her caused so many things to hit Leo at once. Fear—yeah, it was there big-time—and a sickening dread that he'd made a huge mistake by going outside to question Bernice. If he hadn't done that, if he'd stayed put, he would have been inside and stopped this.

Leo glanced out just as Olivia opened her mouth as if to say more, but her captor jammed the gun harder against her head. Leo wanted to rip the person apart when he saw the trickle of blood slide down Olivia's cheek.

"I told her if she didn't throw down the gun," the captor said, "that I'd start shooting."

The rage came like a low, dangerous simmer, and Leo had no doubts that it would soon go full-boil. This SOB had just threatened not only Olivia but also Cameron. The nursery was just two doors down from where Olivia was standing.

Leo pushed everything out of his mind—or rather, tried to do that—to focus on the voice. Not a normal speaking voice. This was a mix of gravel and hoarse whisper. Obviously a ploy to disguise who was speaking. And it was working. Leo didn't know if this was a hired thug or one of their two remaining suspects, Rena and Bernice.

"I was afraid one of the bullets would hit Cameron," Olivia said in a mutter. "So I yelled for Izzie to stay put with him."

Yeah, he was right there with her on this. Like Olivia, he would have done whatever it took to stop someone from firing a gun this close to Cameron. Still would. That meant this couldn't come down to a shooting match even if Olivia could get clear enough for Leo to have a shot.

"Who are you?" Leo asked. "What do you want?"

"I'm leaving with Olivia, and you're going to make sure that happens," her captor readily answered. "I need a vehicle."

"That's your plan?" Leo taunted. "To go driving out of here with Olivia?"

"That's my plan that'll work," the person countered. This time the voice was louder, not so much of a whisper, and Leo was almost certain that it was a woman's voice.

"Is that Bernice or Rena talking?" Leo murmured to Samuel.

The man's head snapped up, the shock in his eyes, which meant he hadn't considered it to be either of them. And maybe it wasn't. After all, it could be a female hired gun.

To give Samuel another chance to listen to the captor's voice, Leo went with another question. "I'll get you the vehicle," he said, "but tell me what you want. Is it money?"

However, before Leo got an answer, someone called out from the bottom floor. "Boss? You okay?"

Wally.

Leo had to make a snap decision. He didn't want to put

another person in danger, and that's exactly what would happen if Wally came upstairs. Added to that, it might spook the captor and cause her to start firing.

"Wally, I need a truck brought around to the back of the house," Leo instructed. "Park close to the porch and leave the keys in the ignition."

"Uh, sure. Are you okay?" Wally repeated. Since Wally wasn't an idiot, he knew something was wrong, but hopefully he wouldn't do something to escalate this standoff.

"Tell him to hurry," the captor snapped.

"Hurry," Leo added to Wally and looked back at Olivia. He wished he could do something to ease that terror in her eyes, but the only thing that would make that go away was to get her out of this situation.

"How much money to do you want?" Leo asked the person holding her. "Or are you after some kind of leverage. I'm guessing this is a whole lot more than you wanting me to fix a parking ticket."

"I'll pay whatever you want," Samuel added. "Just name your price."

The person made a strange sound. A snarl dripping with outrage.

"Enough of this!" Olivia's captor spat the words out and before Leo could even react, bashed Olivia on the head.

"Stop!" Leo shouted, trying to take aim. But he didn't have a shot because the captor dragged Olivia back up and put her in a choke hold.

And that's when he saw the face.

Bernice.

THE PAIN SHOT through Olivia, so fast, so strong, that she wouldn't have been able to stay on her feet had her captor not latched onto her. And was now choking her.

Bernice.

She was trying to kill her.

Olivia didn't know why—not yet—but it had to have something to do with her father. Was that why he was there? Olivia had only caught a glimpse of him, but she'd seen him with Leo.

And Leo had been hurt.

There'd been blood on his head and, while he'd looked formidable, he'd also looked a little dazed. Like her. Mercy. Had her father done that to him?

Olivia somehow managed to catch her breath and jab her elbow into Bernice's stomach. The woman grunted in pain but only dug the barrel of the gun in harder on Olivia's head.

She didn't know where Bernice had gotten the weapon since she knew the ranch hands had frisked her before they'd put her in the truck. But, obviously, she'd managed to get her hands on one.

And would without hesitation use it to kill.

Olivia only hoped she found out why this was happening. She didn't want to die without knowing that, and not without knowing that Leo and Cameron would be safe. If necessary, she'd sacrifice herself for them.

But so would Leo.

In fact, he was no doubt trying to figure out how to get her out of this.

Olivia heard Leo's phone ring. It was in his jeans' pocket, but he didn't answer it. Seconds later, it rang again.

"Let's move," Bernice ordered and practically shoved her forward. Something that Bernice didn't need to do. Olivia desperately wanted to put as much distance as she could between Cameron and Bernice's gun. "If the truck's not there waiting for us, then I start putting bullets in you. Is that what you want, Leo? You want your lover to bleed out in front of you?"

"No." Leo stepped out, much too far, and gave Olivia a quick glance before he fastened his gaze on Bernice. "I'd make a better hostage than Olivia," he proclaimed, attempting to bargain. "Nobody will fire at you if you have me."

"I don't want you." There was so much anger and venom in Bernice's voice.

"But you tried to have me killed," Leo fired back. "That's why you hired Milton. You called him from the estate to tell him to go ahead with the attack."

Bernice certainly didn't deny that, and with her grip still tight on Olivia's neck, they moved forward a few more steps. "I wanted Olivia arrested," Bernice spelled out. "I wanted her in jail."

"For Samuel," Leo stated. Unlike Bernice's, his voice was nearly calm now, but there was a dangerous cop's edge to it. Like a rattler ready to strike. "You did all of this for him, didn't you?"

"Did you?" her father asked. He moved out from cover, too. "God, Bernice. Did you do this for me?"

Bernice wasn't so quick to answer this time. "Yes, and you repaid me by getting back together with Rena. I would have done anything for you. *Anything.*" She emphasized the word, sounding more than a little frantic. "And you kept throwing that gold-digging bimbo in my face."

Olivia thought of Rena and wondered if the woman was still alive. Maybe Bernice had taken care of her before she'd come here. Clearly, this was a last-ditch mission to finish what she'd started. A mission that had left two dead. Possibly even more.

"I'll go with you, Bernice," Samuel offered. He stepped even farther out, too far now to dive back to cover if Bernice fired at him. "Leave Olivia, and I'll go with you. We can get out of the country, some place that doesn't have extradition."

Olivia sucked in a breath. Held it. She knew there was no way her father would actually do that. This was a ploy to try to free her, and she welcomed it. Not because she thought it would work, but because he might be able to at least distract Bernice while Leo and she did something.

"Move down the stairs now," Bernice ordered Leo and Samuel. "No stupid tricks, either, or I'll start firing. I know where the nursery is. I heard when the nanny answered Olivia, and that's where I'll aim the shots."

Olivia was close enough now to see the look in Leo's eyes. The rage. She felt the same. How could this witch threaten their son like that? And all because she had wrongly believed that Samuel owed her something. Maybe owed her love. Well, Olivia wasn't going to let Bernice take away the people she loved.

Leo and her father walked backward down the stairs, each of them watching every move that Bernice and she were making. Olivia tried to calculate the best place for her to make a stand—whatever that stand would be, though, she didn't know. Not yet. But if she could just get Bernice out of the house, then it might lessen the risk for Cameron.

It would increase her own risk, though. Because there was no way Bernice would keep her alive once she'd finished using her as a shield.

"Bernice," Samuel tried again. "Please stop this."

"Shut up," she snapped. "Leo, you'd better tell your ranch hands to back off once we're outside."

"Hear that, Wally?" Leo said, and from the corner of her eye, Olivia saw the man in the foyer. He was still armed, but like Leo, he didn't have a safe shot. "Let the other hands know to back off."

With his eyes wide, Wally nodded and took out his phone. "Daniel's at the end of the road," he relayed. "He's walking up now. Said he tried to call you but that you didn't answer your phone."

So that's who had been trying to get in touch with Leo. Good. Daniel was a smart lawman. He might be able to lie in wait and do something to stop Bernice.

The moment Bernice had Olivia on the bottom floor, the woman started moving her through the open living room and into the kitchen. Olivia kept her attention focused on Leo, looking for any signs of what they could do. He seemed steady. Determined. And he was watching every step that Bernice took.

Olivia wished the woman would trip but then rethought that. Bernice's first instinct might be to pull the trigger, and they were literally right below the nursery.

Bernice's hold finally loosened as Olivia felt the woman reach behind her. She heard the rattle of the doorknob as Bernice unlocked the door and used her elbow to push it open.

Olivia immediately felt the rush of the still hot summer air. Air tainted with the stench of smoke. She prayed that the hands had been able to put out the fire so that it couldn't spread to the house.

"The truck's waiting for you," Leo said.

Because Bernice quickly regained her choke hold, Olivia couldn't see the truck, but she could hear the engine running. Could also hear some muffled conversation, no doubt from the hands.

Bernice's arms were already tense, the muscles knotted to the point where it had to be painful. Olivia hoped she was in pain anyway. Hoped that her pain would get a whole lot worse before this was over. Olivia wanted the woman to pay for all the misery she'd caused.

Muttering obscenities, Bernice stepped onto the porch and immediately shifted Olivia to the side. No doubt so that she could check out the truck while keeping an eye on Leo and Samuel.

"Bernice, if you do this, I'll kill you," her father said. He was practically shoulder to shoulder with Leo as they slowly made their way to the porch. Leo still had hold of his gun, and her father's hands were balled into fists.

Olivia felt Bernice's muscles tighten even more. "No, you won't kill me," Bernice snapped like a challenge. "Because I'll kill you first."

Bernice shifted the gun, obviously trying to aim it at her father. Leo brought up his weapon, too, and in that split second, Olivia knew she had to do something to stop Bernice from killing them both.

With the adrenaline slamming through her, Olivia threw her weight against Bernice, ramming her body into the woman's. It worked. Bernice started to fall backward.

But she took Olivia with her.

Olivia's head bashed against the porch floor and the two of them tumbled down the steps together.

Just as Bernice pulled the trigger.

# Chapter Seventeen

Leo shouted for Bernice to stop, but he knew it wouldn't do any good. Nor could he get to Olivia in time. He was running toward the women as they fell.

And as the shot blasted through the air.

He refused to think that the shot had hit Olivia. Refused to believe that she could be hurt or dead.

Bernice was definitely alive, though. Despite the fall, the woman tried to aim her gun at him. Leo did something about that. He kicked it out of her hand. The gun went flying and he didn't bother to look where it landed. He gave Bernice a kick, too, right in her face, and the woman wailed, falling back into the yard.

Leo kept his eye on Bernice, but he took hold of Olivia's arm and pulled her back onto the porch. That was a risk, since moving her could aggravate her injuries, but he needed to get her away from Bernice.

He cursed when he saw the blood on Olivia's face. Blood on her shirt, too, and she was moaning in pain. Maybe from a gunshot wound, or maybe just from the wounds she'd gotten in the fall.

"Check on Cameron," Leo called out to no one in particular, but he knew one of his hands would do that.

After all, the shot Bernice had fired could have gone into the nursery.

"Help Olivia," Leo added to Samuel as he readied himself to ease her out of his arms so he could jump down in the yard and deal with Bernice.

But Samuel beat him to it.

Samuel rushed past him, barreling down the steps and snatching up Bernice's gun. He dropped to his knees and in the same motion grabbed on to the woman's hair, dragging her head off the ground.

He put the gun to the center of Bernice's forehead.

"Any last words before I kill you?" Samuel asked. Of course, there was emotion in his voice.

The wrong kind of emotion.

Not anger or fear from what had just happened. This was an icy-cold hatred that Leo knew could cause the man to commit murder. And that's exactly what it would be if he pulled the trigger now and shot an unarmed woman. Leo couldn't let her life end like this.

"Samuel," Leo said, keeping his tone as calm as he could manage. "We need to help Olivia. We have to make sure Cameron is okay."

"Any last words before I kill you?" Samuel repeated, shouting the words at Bernice.

The woman's face was covered with blood, and her nose was likely broken, but she still managed to look defiant. "I loved you," Bernice told him. "And you betrayed me. Go ahead. Kill me. Then, you'll have to live with that for the rest of your life."

A life Samuel might spend behind bars if he actually pulled the trigger. Leo didn't care much for the man, but he didn't want things to end like this.

"Dad…" Olivia murmured, her soft voice carrying

over the sound of the truck engine and Samuel's ragged breaths. "Let Leo arrest her. Bernice will spend every day she's got left in a cage."

A hoarse sob broke from Samuel's throat, but he kept the gun in place. "I believe Bernice killed your mother. I think she gave Simone those drugs that made her wreck the car. She could have killed you."

Bernice certainly didn't deny any of that. Just the opposite. "I did what I needed to do."

And there it was. The confession that Olivia had no doubt waited years to hear.

Keeping watch on Bernice and Samuel, Leo slipped his arm around Olivia and helped her get to her feet. She practically sagged against him, but considering everything that'd happened, she was a lot steadier than he'd thought she would be.

"I stopped Simone from divorcing you and taking your daughter," Bernice told Samuel. There was the same cold rage in her voice now that had been in Samuel's. "I would have done the same to stop Olivia from taking Cameron from you."

So, that was her motive. It turned Leo's blood to ice to think that Bernice had nearly gotten away with it.

Leo spotted Daniel peering around corner of the house, but motioned for his brother to stay back. With Samuel still armed, Leo didn't want him getting spooked and shooting Bernice.

"Dad, you need to put down your gun," Olivia tried again. "We don't want any more shots fired. It could scare Cameron."

Leo finally saw something he wanted to see. Samuel pulled back the gun. It was still aimed at Bernice, but was no longer pressed to her forehead.

"I want her dead," Samuel said, his shoulders shaking with his sobs. "I want her to pay."

"And she will," Leo assured him. Since he wasn't sure Olivia could stay standing without his support, he motioned for Daniel to move in. "My brother will take Bernice into custody. She'll be charged with murder, murder for hire and a whole bunch of other charges. Olivia was right about her spending the rest of her life in a cage."

"As if I care," Bernice snarled, still challenging Samuel with her fierce stare. "Go ahead and kill me." She smiled, a sick smile given the blood trickling out of her mouth.

"Bernice wants to die by your hand," Olivia told her father. "That way, she can keep on punishing you because you'll have to come to terms with what's gone on here. She wants you to suffer. Make her suffer instead."

That finally seemed to get through to Samuel. He leaned away from Bernice and sat back on the ground. Daniel moved in closer, reached down and took the gun from Samuel's hand.

"You were supposed to kill me!" Bernice shouted, darting glances around the yard. "It wasn't supposed to end like this."

Daniel ignored her shouts, hauled Bernice up and slapped a pair of plastic cuffs on her wrists.

Leo didn't want to give the woman another moment of his attention, nor did he want to keep Olivia outside. He turned to lead Olivia back inside so they could check on Cameron. And so he could see how bad her injuries were. However, before he could do that, Wally came hurrying out.

"Cameron and the nanny are fine," Wally said. "Not a scratch on them."

This time Leo thought Olivia sagged from relief as she went into his arms and buried her face against Leo's neck. "He's okay. Our baby's okay."

Yeah, and Leo felt a mountain of relief of his own. Bernice hadn't done her worst. She hadn't managed to hurt their son.

"I would have killed her had she hurt Cameron," Samuel said, looking up at them. He moved closer and sank onto the bottom porch step. He looked exhausted and beaten down. Like a man who'd lost way too much and might not recover from those losses.

Considering their past, Leo was surprised that he felt any sympathy for Samuel. But he did. It had to be hard coming to terms with the fact that he'd been living under the same roof with his wife's killer.

"I told Izzie to stay put until you got up there," Wally said, breaking the silence. "Didn't figure you'd want Cameron out here. Also didn't figure you'd want him to see Olivia and you like this, all covered with blood."

They were, indeed, covered with blood, and Wally was right. Leo didn't want Cameron anywhere near Bernice.

Leo pulled back and took a moment to examine Olivia. There was a gash on her head that needed tending, and from what he could tell, that's where most of the blood had come from. Still, she'd need to go the hospital.

"The truck fire's out," Wally told them a moment later, giving Leo yet more good news. Wally tipped his head to Bernice. "You want me to help Daniel get her out of here?"

Leo definitely wanted that. "Yeah. Bring the cruiser to the backyard and see if Carter or one of the other hands can go through every inch of the house to make sure it's secure. And call for an ambulance," Leo added.

"It's already here," Daniel supplied. "Well, it's nearby anyway. The fire department's putting out the flames on the road, and the ambulance can get up here then. We might need two ambulances, though. Edwin's hurt. So is Rena. I found her trying to crawl through the pasture to get to the road."

Leo certainly hadn't forgotten about Rena, but she wasn't a high priority for him now. Obviously, though, she was for Samuel.

"How bad is she hurt?" he asked.

Daniel shrugged and kept his hand clamped around Bernice's arm. "Not sure. But I don't think she has a lot of injuries. She seemed drugged to me."

"That bimbo was supposed to die in a car crash like Simone," Bernice snarled.

So that's what had happened to Rena. It would add another count of attempted murder to the charges that would be filed against Bernice.

"The idiot I hired to steal the journals from Olivia's house was going to doctor them," Bernice added, "to make it look as if Simone was afraid Rena would kill her."

It wouldn't have worked since Olivia had made copies of the journal pages, but Bernice obviously hadn't known that. That also meant burning down Olivia's house had been all for nothing.

Bernice glanced around the yard again, putting Leo on alert. He eased Olivia behind him and readied his gun in case there was about to be another attack.

"I think she's looking for her hired thug," Daniel said, his voice as calm as a lake. "When I was walking up the road, and before I spotted Rena, I caught some guy hiding in a ditch. According to his driver's license, his name is Frank Sutton. I cuffed him, and a couple of the hands are guarding him until I can get back down there."

Bernice made a sound of outrage and tried to ram her body into Daniel's. Daniel just slung her around and yanked back her arms.

"Guess Bernice isn't too happy about losing the last of her lackeys," Daniel commented.

"You're sure he's the last one?" Olivia asked.

"Yeah," Daniel confirmed. "Sutton was pretty chatty and got even chattier when I mentioned that the first to make a full confession would be the one to get a lighter sentence. I didn't bother to tell him that the lighter sentence would just be taking the death penalty off the table, so the guy prattled on. He claims that Bernice hired him to attach a firebomb to underside of the truck when the hands drove down to check on her."

Leo hadn't spotted anyone doing that, but it would have been possible. The guy could have used the ditch for cover and sneaked out of it when the hands had been talking to Bernice.

In the distance, Leo finally heard the ambulance sirens coming closer. It wouldn't be long before they arrived and he could get Olivia the medical help she needed.

Carter and another ranch hand came out from the side of the house, heading straight to Daniel in case he needed help with Bernice, but Leo thought his brother had it under control. Better yet, Leo no longer had that feeling in his gut that something was wrong. For the first time since this all began, he thought the danger might finally be over.

"You took a risk putting a firebomb in the truck and having it go off while you were in it," Leo pointed out to Bernice just as Wally pulled the cruiser into the backyard.

Bernice clammed up. Probably because she didn't want to fill in any blanks for them. But apparently her lackey had already done that.

"According to our chatty *friend*, Frank Sutton, the fire-bomb didn't have much juice," Daniel explained. "Just enough to mess up the front of the truck and create a distraction."

A distraction that Bernice had used to her advantage. It'd helped, too, that she'd known it was coming and had been ready to bash Edwin and Leo.

"How'd Bernice get in the house?" Olivia asked.

Again, it wasn't Bernice who answered but Carter, just as Daniel and the ranch hand stuffed Bernice into the back seat of the cruiser.

"Edwin told me that Bernice grabbed his gun," Carter explained, "and she bashed both him and you on the head when the airbags deployed."

Leo hadn't needed to be told about the head bashing part. He had a knot on his temple, and it was throbbing badly. Still, he'd been lucky that his injuries hadn't been a whole lot worse.

"How's Edwin?" Leo asked Carter.

"Fine. He might need a couple of stitches. You might need some, too," Carter added, giving Leo the once-over. "You want me to ride with your brother to the sheriff's office?"

"Sure." Though Leo figured with Bernice cuffed, she wasn't much of a threat. Still, it wouldn't hurt to have a little overkill, considering the woman was a murderer.

"One more thing," Leo said before Daniel could get behind the wheel of the cruiser. "Did Sutton mention who killed Randall?"

Daniel huffed. "He volunteered that it was Bernice,

that she'd tried to rile up Randall to get him to kill you, but then he figured out what she'd done. He says Bernice killed Randall and got him to dispose of the body. He claims it was Bernice's idea to use a Sycamore Grove SUV because she intended to set up Rena."

Leo gave that some thought. "You think Sutton is the one who killed him?" he proposed.

"That'd be my guess," Daniel answered.

Leo nearly added for Daniel to push getting that info during interrogations, but knew his brother would do that without the reminder. Besides, even if Bernice hadn't been the one to pull the trigger that'd killed Randall, she'd still go down for his murder.

"Come on," Leo said, slipping his arm around Olivia again. "Let me take you to the front to the ambulance."

She stopped, held her ground and stared up at him. "I don't want to go to the hospital. *Please*. I don't want to leave Cameron."

It wasn't the *please* that got to him. It was the look on her face. Not pain or panic. Just a mountain of concern for her child.

"All right," he agreed. "We'll have the EMTs check you, but if they say you should be in the hospital, then you will be." He kissed her to try to soften the order he'd given her. "I'm not going to risk losing you."

"You shouldn't risk losing her," he heard someone say. "Olivia loves you."

Leo was surprised those words had come from Samuel. Sighing, her father got to his feet, walked closer to them and gave Leo a pat on the arm. It felt awkward coming from Samuel, but it was a helluva lot better than the verbal jabs he'd given Leo in the past.

"I'm sorry," Samuel said, his gaze moving to Olivia.

"I swear, before tonight, I didn't know it was Bernice who'd killed your mother."

She hesitated as if, Leo presumed, trying to gauge if that were true. She must have decided it was because she nodded.

"If I could fix things between us, I would," Samuel added and then turned to walk away.

"Wait," Olivia said, causing him to stop in his tracks. "Why do you think I'm in love with Leo?"

Leo tensed because he sure as hell didn't want to hear Olivia say that her father had it all wrong, that it wasn't true.

"Because you are," Samuel simply said. "And he's in love with you."

Obviously, that stunned both Olivia and him into silence because neither confirmed nor denied it. They just stood there, waiting for Samuel to leave. He did. Not through the house, though. Instead, he went in the direction of the front yard. Hopefully, one of the EMTs would check him out, as well.

"I want to hate him," Olivia muttered. There were tears shimmering in her eyes when she turned back to him. "But right now, I'm just so tired of the hate. I'm ready for that being-in-love part."

That sounded...well, hopeful, and despite his throbbing head, Leo found himself smiling. And kissing her. He'd intended it to be a quick reassurance, but it turned into something longer. Deeper. And hotter. The kind of kiss that could land them in bed—if they hadn't been so banged up, that is.

"You're in love with me," he said when they finally broke for air. "And if you're not, then—"

"I'm in love with you," Olivia verified.

Smiling, and then wincing because the smile must have caused her face to hurt, she kissed him. And, yeah, it was one of those long, deep hot ones that made Leo forget all about such things as pain and injuries.

"If you're not in love with me," she said after she'd just rocked his world with a third kiss, "then—"

He stopped her with a fourth kiss. "I'm in love with you," he assured her.

Leo used the fifth kiss to show her just how much.

\* \* \* \* \*

# CONARD COUNTY: CHRISTMAS BODYGUARD

**RACHEL LEE**

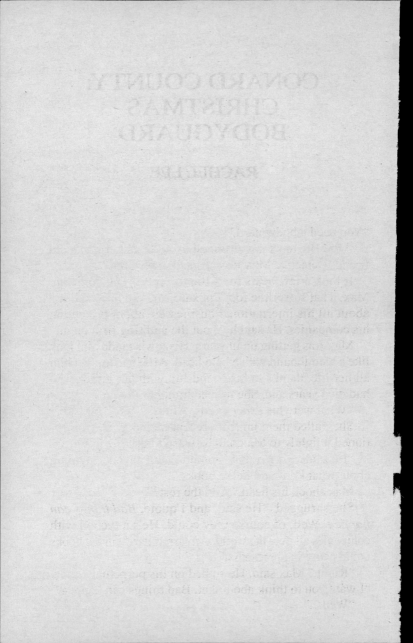

# Chapter One

"You need a bodyguard."

Allie Burton's jaw dropped as soon as her dad's old friend, Detective Max Roles, spoke the words.

It took a few beats for Allie to reply. "Oh, come on, Max. That's over the top. I'm sure Mr. Ellis was talking about all his international businesses, about protecting his companies. He said he'd put the auditing firm on it."

Max was getting up in years. His jowls made him look like a bloodhound with a bald head. Allie had known him all her life, thanks to his friendship with her father, who had died years ago. She trusted him, but this?

"What were his *exact* words, Allie?"

She pulled them up from recent memory. She'd mentioned it lightly to Max, but he wasn't taking it lightly.

"He said, *exactly*, that I shouldn't tell anyone anything about what I'd found in the books."

Max shook his head. "And the rest?"

She shrugged. "He said, and I quote, *Bad things can happen*. Well, of course they could. He's a tycoon with companies all over the world. Any irregularity in the books could cause big problems."

"Right," Max said. He sipped on his perpetual coffee. "I want you to think about that. Bad things can happen."

"Well…"

"Don't 'well' me. Just listen."

Allie frowned. "I guess you're one of the people I shouldn't have told about this. I thought you'd laugh and wouldn't tell anyone."

"I won't tell anyone except the bodyguard you're going to hire."

"Damn, Max. How am I supposed to afford that anyway?"

Max shook his head again. "Your grandfather left you a pile, didn't he?"

Allie rolled her eyes. "And I'm supposed to waste it on this?"

"It's not wasted if it saves your life," Max said sharply. "Now will you just listen, or are you going to be like my damn dog who only listens when he feels like it?"

Allie could have smirked at the thought of Max's stubborn mastiff, a dog bigger than Max, but she resisted the urge. Folding her hands primly in her lap, she gave in. "I'm listening."

"About damn time." Max reached for his cigarettes, a habit Allie often tried to get him to break. She pointedly waved smoke away.

"Cut it out," he said mildly. "You won't get cancer from half an hour."

She sighed. "Just tell me what you think I need to know."

"Gladly. Or unhappily. You've been on the inside of Jasper Ellis's business. You know he's like an octopus with a whole lot of tentacles."

"He's successful. So what?"

Max leaned forward. "I have nothing against the man's success. One of the things I can tell you is we've been investigating him for years, and we've never found a thing we could hang on him. He's good at covering evidence.

Hell, he's better than good. The government could take lessons from him. Not that his methods would be legal."

"Investigating him for what?"

Max blew a cloud. "For the unexplained disappearances and supposed suicides of a number of his employees."

Allie felt a chill run down her spine. She could tell that Max wasn't joking. Her own dismissal of the situation began to feel naïve. "You're kidding," she murmured.

"I wish I was. Here's the thing. At first it could be dismissed. But then the numbers really caught our attention and we started looking into it. Nothing traces directly back to Ellis except he's at the top of the pyramid. Or the head on the octopus, to round out my original analogy. You may remember I fought against you going to work for him."

Allie did. Max had strenuously argued with her, something he never did. He was doing it right now. That worried her as much as what he was saying because Max believed it.

He was not a man given to conspiracy theories. A hardnosed detective, he stuck to the facts. He seemed to have some facts right now.

"Allie, the cops can't protect you. We wouldn't have justification since his threat was so indirect. But you tweaked the tiger's tail, evidently with something that he needs to hide. Jasper Ellis is not a man to cross."

Allie's voice was growing thin. "I only told him so he could fix it. So there'd be no trouble for him or his businesses."

"Does he care? You have knowledge that could harm him. He takes care of those threats. Somehow."

Forgetting the perfect posture her aunt had drilled into her, Allie slumped back in the chair. "Really, Max?"

"Really. So I'm going to call that bodyguard. I've known him for years since he was still in the Marines. I trust him with your life. And you're not leaving my house before he gets here."

"God, Max!"

"Just go make yourself a cup of whatever. Or have some orange juice. But you are *not* going anywhere."

He punctuated those words like bullet shots. Truly shaken, Allie rose to get that orange juice. Could this possibly be true? But she trusted Max. Completely. He'd been like an uncle to her for most of her life. If Max said it, it was true.

As she passed through the short hallway, she saw her reflection in the full-length mirror. Max's wife had placed it there years ago, before she had passed from a stray gunshot.

Allie paused, staring at her reflection, wondering who that woman in there was. She felt so changed that she shouldn't look the same. Neat dark blue business slack suit, a blue striped button-down shirt, collar open. Her ash-blond hair in a fluffed loose short cut because she didn't feel like fussing with it. A trim every couple of weeks solved that problem.

A bodyguard? The thought sent a tendril of ice creeping along her spine. Seriously?

Before she continued along the hall, Max called to her. "Get that frozen key lime pie out, will you? Never met anybody who didn't like it. Hale will be here in about an hour and it takes that long to thaw."

The juxtaposition of a threat and a key lime pie seemed absurd. Except she couldn't smile at it or laugh about it. Her face had grown as frozen as her spine. "Sure," she called back, glad that her voice didn't shake while everything inside her felt as if an earthquake had begun.

She pulled the pie from its box and left it covered on the counter to thaw. Then, deciding she couldn't possibly swallow orange juice, she returned to the small living room with empty hands.

She asked, "You really think I'm in danger?" The war inside her still had not quit.

"Jasper Ellis is not a man I'd want to screw with."

"But if I don't tell anyone…"

Max repeated himself slowly, firmly. "You have dangerous knowledge. He only wants you to keep your mouth shut until he can deal with you."

Allie's world was tilting off its axis. She vaguely wondered if life would ever appear the same again. If life would ever *be* the same again. A whole new reality bore down on her and she hated it.

Her wonderful Max was about to entertain a bodyguard with pie. Seriously?

"For heaven's sake, Max…" *For heaven's sake what? Fix my world for me?*

"I know," he said. "It's a shock. Kinda like the first murder scene a cop goes to. Nothing's ever the same again."

Max fell silent, lighting another cigarette. This time Allie didn't make a show of waving away the smoke. What harm could it do her if her life was truly threatened?

"God," she muttered. "I can't believe this." But she did. Max's words had pierced her like an arrow. An internal ache began, twisting her stomach painfully.

"Just listen to Hale," Max said presently. "He's tuned in. He'll know."

Allie could only stare at him. Belief still warred with the conviction that this was impossible. "Mr. Ellis could fix the problem I found."

"He could. But consider that the man has been under constant IRS audit and they still haven't nailed him. You might well have found the irregularity that could blow the whole thing open."

She hadn't considered that. She could scarcely imagine the back taxes and penalties that might ensue. It would damage the share price, costing him additional wealth. Or worse.

"God," she whispered again.

Max let her ruminate in silence.

She could just get up and walk out of here now. Continue at work tomorrow as if nothing had happened. Except it had. Max was right about that.

The protection guy arrived a bit earlier than projected. When Max opened the door, the first thing Allie noticed was his height. Wearing a loose windbreaker and jeans, he didn't appear muscular, but that probably wasn't necessary for what he did.

At least he didn't appear muscular until he greeted Max, stepped inside and twisted to look at Allie. As the windbreaker moved, it outlined wide shoulders and powerful arms. In shape.

First impressions and all that. Okay, he was intimidating and trying to conceal it. His face was as impassive as rock, some of it hidden behind a scraggly beard. His hair was long and shaggy, nearly inky. Eye color indeterminate in the inside lighting although it, too, appeared dark. In all, not very reputable in appearance.

Max made the introductions. "Alicia Burton, Hale Scribner. Take a seat, Hale. Allie's run into a problem with Jasper Ellis."

Both of Hale's eyebrows lifted as he settled onto an edge of the couch, the only place remaining with Max in his favorite, battered recliner. He splayed his denim-clad legs and rested his elbows on them. Allie already perched on a gooseneck chair. All the upholstery was dark in color. It probably concealed a lot of spills from over the years.

Hale spoke, his voice deep and carrying something like darkness. "Jasper Ellis, huh? How much trouble?"

Max replied. "He said bad things can happen."

Now the great stone face darkened. "Not good."

"Which is what I keep trying to get Allie to believe. I can understand why she's finding it so difficult."

Hale nodded, a sharp movement of his head. "Jasper Ellis is bad news. Very bad news."

The chill dripped down Allie's spine again. "You both really think he'd kill me?"

Hale answered, his voice calm and steady. "Absolutely. You wouldn't be the first."

Allie gave up. She put her head in her hand. "God, Max."

"She's not going to help. Ellis sold his soul a long time ago."

Allie had always liked the way Max referred to God as *she*. Turned out that was okay in their Catholic religion. She'd checked the first time he'd used the gender. But that didn't help at all.

Hale remained silent. Allie looked at him again, finding nothing reassuring in his nearly immovable face.

She spoke. "So what do you do? Keep an eye on me in my apartment?"

"No."

The single word was unilluminating. "What, then?" she demanded.

"You're going to leave that apartment. I'd need a whole phalanx of guards to protect you, and there'd still be a way to get to you. Even the best group is permeable."

Allie's insides tightened again, enhancing the ache that was already there. "Then what?"

Max spoke. "How about we have some key lime pie, then discuss this in more detail."

Max was not to be deterred. He disappeared into the kitchen and returned with three white pie plates, each decorated with a fork and a wedge of pie. He passed them around.

"Eat," he said. "Food always helps."

Allie doubted anything would help, but she obediently took a small mouthful of pie. Hale was not so delicate. Clearly he was a man who enjoyed his food.

Allie still waited for answers.

At last Hale set aside his plate on the end table and wiped his fingers and mouth with a napkin. Finally he settled his attention on Allie.

"We're going on the run."

Now her stomach dropped and her brain sought a way to deny what he was suggesting. "Isn't that overkill? Run how far?"

"As far as it takes until I can find Ellis's goons. Until I can be sure you're safe."

"Oh, come on," Allie retorted, feeling stubbornness rise in her. "That's not necessary."

"It is if you want to be alive in a week."

Allie could no longer contain her growing anxiety. Her stomach twisted until she wanted to vomit. Her breath came raggedly, fast.

"Put your head down," Max said amiably. "If that doesn't work I'll get you a paper bag."

Why did she have the feeling that he wasn't as distressed by this as she was, then realized, *because Max*. He never let anything disturb him too much. Maybe to help her calm down.

At last she was able to lift her head, her breathing stabilizing even if her stomach didn't.

"I don't understand all of this," she said weakly. "I don't. He didn't threaten me."

Hale spoke. "He did. I've heard enough indirect threats to recognize one. I also know enough about Ellis. Max isn't exaggerating. We go on the run."

A nice dark hole sounded good right then. A cave. A storm drain. She wasn't feeling picky.

"What good will that do?"

Hale answered. "It'll keep you out of the line of fire until I can take care of the threat."

"How can you do that if you're running with me?"

"I have contacts."

As if that explained anything. Maybe it did. She was having trouble wrapping her mind around all this. She wanted more in the way of explanations, but suspected she wasn't going to get it. She looked at Max.

"Do it, Allie," he said. "I love you. Just do it for me."

That was a plea she couldn't ignore. Again she looked at Hale. "How do we do this?"

"First we go to your bank and withdraw enough cash to cover my retainer and our expenses. Cash can't be traced."

Her stomach lurched. "And then?"

"I'm taking you back to your apartment. I'll give you a couple of duffels, easier to manage than suitcases. You'll pack for a time in rough areas. Like you're going camping. None of those business suits."

Her stomach rolled again. If Max thought this was good, safe, she would do it. "After that?"

"Then we're getting the hell out of this city. First night out you're going to dye your hair. Then we move again."

"Oh, God," she whispered. Appalled. A nightmare was descending.

Hale rose. "Don't call your friends. Don't tell them you'll be away. Leave no hint of our plans." He looked at the impressive black watch on his wrist. "We go to the bank first. They'll still be open. Apartment next. Then we leave. Together."

He gave her one last look. "Ellis probably thinks he has a few days. You went to work today, right?"

She nodded.

"Then he probably thinks you don't suspect anything yet. We'll get going because tomorrow morning he'll know you've slipped the noose." He paused. "Wait here. I have some friends I need to speak with."

HALE MET HIS best buddy at a small out-of-the-way coffee shop. Stu Dembrowski had fought beside him and worked beside him since Afghanistan. They'd each saved the other's life, and a deep trust had grown between them. More trust than Hale could usually muster.

"Jasper Ellis," he said to Stu.

"Oh, man, you're not going up against *him*!"

"I need to. And what I need from you and the rest of the crew is tracking devices. Get them on as many cars from Ellis's local security team as you can. If necessary, follow some of them on the road until you get an opportunity to tag them. Then I'm going to call in frequently for position reports."

Stu nodded. "And you'll be where?"

"Driving all over like a maniac. Can do?"

"Will do," Stu answered firmly. "Just remember, those transmitters don't work everywhere. There'll be some gaps."

"I can still get enough information to put it together."

Stu nodded and rose. "We'll get to work."

Hale waited five minutes before leaving the coffee shop. Then he followed a circuitous route back to Max and Alicia Burton.

There wasn't any time to waste.

## Chapter Two

Hale followed Allie to the bank as he'd said he would. The huge sum he wanted her to withdraw made her catch her breath.

"You'll have to sign some kind of papers for the IRS," he warned her. "Just do it."

She did this while he waited outside with a black duffel for her. She practically had to swear to the bank officer that she knew what she was doing. Then she signed all the paperwork, and twenty minutes later walked out with a very large bank bag containing small denominations of an unbelievable sum of money.

Hale stepped into the outer lobby and opened the duffel. She dropped the heavy bank bag in it.

"Now to your apartment."

Allie drove her car, her hands shaking, and hoped she didn't have an accident. Well, that was one way to kill her.

She made it into the parking garage. Hale was right behind in his massive black Suburban, pulling into a guest slot. As promised, he carried several duffel bags as he followed her into the elevator.

For the first time she wondered if he was armed. If so, it wasn't showing under his windbreaker.

Rather rudely, she thought, he supervised her packing. She wasn't overloaded with jeans or sweatshirts or heavy jackets. Or anything really. She mostly limited herself to summery weekend hikes with friends. Some lazing-around clothes.

"Bring just a few days of underwear," he told her. "We can pick up other clothes for you along the way."

With the untraceable cash, she supposed. Maybe the best thing to do would be to pretend she was starring in a suspense movie. For now. Just pretend and get this part over.

"Leave your cell phone behind," he ordered. "It can be tracked and there's no way to prevent it even if you turn it off. Every cell tower we pass will ping you."

Leave her phone? It would be like cutting off her arm. She wasted a few minutes and he waited while she deleted apps such as her bank.

"My friends will notice I'm gone."

He answered. "I'm sure they will, but you don't want to draw them into this mess. I'll arrange for you to call them in a few days."

Hale carried her bags and threw them in the back of the Suburban. He waved her into the passenger seat, then they were driving away. Away from her life as she knew it.

Sickened again, all she could do was look out the darkly tinted windows at the passing familiarity of her neighborhood. Then she closed her eyes, trying not to care anymore.

Hale never spoke a word.

ALLIE MUST HAVE fallen asleep, amazingly enough, because when she next looked out at the world, night had fallen and they had driven into the spreading suburbs. Traffic on the highway had lightened from its usual rush-hour crunch. Hale drove near the top of the speed limit.

"We'll stop when we get out of this mess and get something to eat," he said, speaking for the first time since they left. "You must be getting hungry by now."

"I don't know if I'll ever want to eat again."

"Think of it as survival."

Allie apparently needed to think in those terms now. Horrifying. "Do we have to travel like this?"

"Trust me to know my job."

No conversation. She got it. Well, no entertainment there. "Radio?"

"Lady, I ripped off everything on this truck that could be traced by anyone. No friendly voice giving me directions or asking me what kind of music or who I want to call."

She figured she would come to hate this man before long. "So nothing?"

"I didn't even leave the radio. Taking no chances. You never know what technology can do these days. Maybe along the way we'll find some CDs you like."

Like she was going to be shopping for CDs during this awful trek. She smothered a sigh, fearing it might be audible over the quietly purring engine. "It's almost Christmas," she remarked irrelevantly.

"I heard."

End of subject. Allie wasn't accustomed to sitting around with nothing to do. If friends didn't come over or call, she had music, she had books, she had cooking. Now she had nothing except this taciturn man who obviously wasn't going to provide much in the way of distraction.

*Max, what did you get me into?*

Several hours later, when houses and people had dissipated to almost nothing, he pulled over at a gas station with a diner beside it. Oh, man, the best food in the world, she thought sarcastically. Fat and more fat. Overcooked veggies that might have come out of a can.

"Stay in the car while I gas up," Hale told her. "Then we'll find you a bathroom and food."

The bathroom would probably be awful. She gave up her internal struggle. Whatever else happened, she was here for now.

To her amazement, Hale didn't follow her into the bathroom, and the bathroom sparkled. Somebody cared. The tables and booths were clean, too, and the menu made a stab at catering to urban tastes.

"Eat more than a salad," Hale ordered her. "We may not see food again until tomorrow."

Planning ahead, she thought, but for once she didn't get stubborn. What was the point? She heeded him. Besides, this gave her an opportunity to eat foods she liked but normally avoided because they weren't healthful.

A hamburger and fries with a side of salad. When was the last time she'd eaten fries and a burger? And this proved to be good food. Tasty. She decided to enjoy her excuse.

Hale ate in silence. Surprise. Not. He had two burgers, a double portion of fries and some onion rings.

He apparently felt this diner with its short-order cook and two waitresses would keep her safe enough for twenty minutes while he took his own bathroom break. Then he threw cash on the table, and insisted she head for the locked SUV. He followed at a distance, probably keeping an eye out.

Once they were on the road again, she spoke. "I bet you don't come cheap."

"Not since I was in the Marines. Worried about my retainer?"

"Just curious."

"You ought to be. Twenty grand."

Ouch. "You definitely aren't cheap."

"For this you don't want cheap."

He had a point. "Max seemed awfully sure about you. He didn't call anyone else."

"Max and I go back a ways. I've done jobs for him before."

Allie wondered what kind of jobs but figured he wouldn't tell her. Nor should he, she guessed. She'd want her own privacy.

She tried to settle more comfortably into her seat and resign herself to this road trip continuing for a while.

As HALE WATCHED his Suburban eat up miles of highway, some of it winding away from major arteries and into narrower roads through small towns, he decided Allie Burton might be a handful.

He felt nearly constant resistance in her, even when she didn't argue or protest. Eventually some of that was going to burst out of her. Not everyone could be like his previous protectees, terrified and willing to do anything.

Maybe the seriousness of this threat hadn't really sunk in yet. He'd find out, he supposed.

He needed to find a pharmacy or retail store to get her the hair dye. Her ash-blond hair was striking, striking enough to be noticed.

But Jasper Ellis. The idea that Allie was in trouble with that man seriously worried Hale. He knew Ellis's reputation, knew how concerned the police were, and knew from his web of contacts that the body count was getting high.

Now, for the first time, he had someone to protect from Ellis. He didn't think it was going to be easy. Hale had a small business, relying a lot on friends who knew how to glean intelligence. He didn't begin to have Ellis's resources. Not even remotely.

But he also knew his own capabilities.

First he had to get Allie far enough away, surreptitiously enough, that she'd be somewhat protected from whomever Ellis sent after her. Then he could deal with *that* threat and maybe gather information that would help the cops get Ellis. There was no other way to keep Allie Burton safe long-term.

This was an unusual case for him. Most people he protected suffered from a single personal threat. Allie was a whole new ball game.

And he didn't doubt that at some point in this flight she was going to dig her heels in. He just hoped it didn't come too soon.

That first night he booked them into an out-of-the-way seedy motel. Not what she was accustomed to, he was certain.

He had phony IDs and checked them in himself, paying in cash. Allie glumly watched the entire process. Her money, being used for this.

"Retail store or pharmacy nearby?" Hale asked the clerk when he received the keys.

"Up the road about half a mile. Small grocery, good enough. Has nearly everything we need around here."

Hale hoped that included hair dye. He expected a struggle from Allie over that. He was not to be disappointed.

But first he insisted she remain in the locked car while he went in to find the dye. Trying to avoid notice, he added a few bottles of water and some small snack items to his purchase. The kinds of things most travelers might buy.

When he climbed back into his car, he sensed annoyance once again. Well, he'd be pretty annoyed himself at having everything taken out of his hands.

Small talk had never been his thing. Since he'd never practiced it, he didn't know how to make it. Less said the better.

But Allie must feel like a lump on the seat beside him. He spared some thought on figuring out what he might say but was soon relieved of the necessity by the return to the motel.

He left all the bags in the car, taking only the hair dye. They wouldn't be here for long, anyway.

He could hardly wait to hear her reaction, first to the dye, then to the news they'd be moving again tonight.

As he expected, she looked at the box of dye he handed her and said, "No way."

"You have distinctive hair."

"I *like* it."

He reached into his well of patience. "I understand why. It's very pretty. It also makes you easier to recognize. You'll have to resign yourself to this."

Her response was a mulish look, but after a minute she headed to the bathroom. "Are you immovable?" she demanded over her shoulder.

"When it's best. If you need help with that stuff, let me know."

LIKE ALLIE WANTED his hands all over her head. No way. She pulled out the contents of the box, angry enough to tear it a bit, then scanned the directions.

If she needed his help? Did he take her for an idiot? She looked one last time in the mirror, then started the job. Max had recommended him. She must have reminded herself several times as she destroyed her hair.

The woman who looked back at her no longer looked like Allie. All that dark brown hair… She grabbed another towel to dry it off with quick, impatient movements. No comb. Then she looked at the stained towels. Screw it.

When she walked back to the other room, doing her best to finger comb her fluffy cut, Hale said, "Much better."

"I beg to differ."

He nodded. "You would. Let's go."

Her jaw dropped for the second time that day. "Go where?"

"Get on the road."

She felt her face settle into stubborn lines. "Why the hell? You checked us in for the night."

"And we were in this town too long. I went into that grocery. Time to kick the dust off our heels."

"Oh, for Pete's sake. Hale, you're out of your mind."

"I know my job. Let's go."

She studied the immovable monolith that was Hale Scribner and tried to tell herself he knew what he was doing. He was right, it was his job. That didn't mean she had to like it.

"Damn," was all she said and headed for the door. "After this is over, I'm going to find a way to get even with you."

He didn't answer. She no longer expected it. Although he'd already explained why they had to move on, they hadn't been here that long and it seemed unlikely to her that anyone would notice them.

He was paranoid, she thought grimly as she climbed into his SUV. Paranoid as hell.

But that seemed to be part of his job, too.

# Chapter Three

Miles of country road fell away behind them. Wiggling like a snake, this way and that, Hale was always keeping an eye out for a tail. Nothing yet.

They had until morning to get as far away as possible. As soon as Ellis or one of his minions realized Allie hadn't come to work and wasn't answering her phone, the hunt would begin—if it hadn't already.

Hale said nothing as Allie fell asleep beside him. She must be exhausted after such a stressful day, but when she awoke she was bound to pepper him with questions. Rightfully so, since the only reason she feared Ellis was because of Max.

God help her if she hadn't had such a good friend.

The eastern sky had just begun to lighten with a hazy red when Allie stirred.

"Dang," she muttered sleepily, "I don't think I can take another minute in this seat. I ache all over."

"I'm not surprised. Hang in there for a bit longer. There's a rest area a few miles ahead, amazingly enough considering we're on a back road."

She stirred again and sat up higher, looking around them. "Where are we?"

"In the middle of nowhere."

"Well, that sounds inviting." Her answer was sarcastic.

In a way, he agreed with her. Other than the fact that they were getting into the mountains of Northern California, which were beautiful. Ahead, Mount Shasta's perennial snowcap burned with the sun's early glow. At least the glaciers hadn't melted, not completely. Rolling land surrounded them.

"*Why* are we here?"

"How well do you know Jasper Ellis?"

She sighed. "He seems like a nice enough man. Not at all threatening."

"He wouldn't." Hale paused, turning them onto a different road, this one heading east. "He wouldn't have made it this far if anyone thought he was a villain."

A minute of silence from her. "I guess so. But why are you and Max both so certain he's dangerous?"

Hale pondered how best to answer that question, given that there was no evidence. He put words together because sometimes he couldn't choose reticence.

"Because," he said slowly, "too many people who work for him have disappeared or died by suicide. More than can be explained by statistical averages." He figured she'd understand that because she was an accountant. She worked with numbers all the time.

Naturally she had an answer. "But statistics can only show correlation unless the numbers are high enough."

"The numbers are high enough that the police have been investigating for years."

That hushed her, but not for very long. "How can anyone be certain Ellis is behind it?"

"As tight a grip as he keeps? Because no one would dare do any of this without his approval. Too much risk."

Then, after a few minutes, Allie asked, "What are we doing?"

"Ellis will figure out you've taken a runner shortly after

you haven't come to work. When they can't call you to find out what's wrong."

"That still doesn't explain this."

"Actually it does. I need to get you as far away as I can before he sends someone out to find you. I have to make us untraceable." Unless someone had managed to put a tracker on his car. He couldn't imagine how, though, as fast as they'd moved. He'd check soon anyway. For now he didn't mind the possibility because it might reassure Ellis's men that they could find Allie. Might make them slower.

"So that's why we're in the middle of nowhere."

"Exactly." Mount Shasta's glow was becoming brighter, whiter.

"I couldn't have remained in the city?"

He paused, turning them another way. "Funny thing about cities. They seem anonymous but you'd probably be surprised to learn how many people you've met, people who would recognize you, at least from a photo. Everyone from restaurant waiters to places you go regularly, like a jogging trail or a park. Where you shop. Where you go to a doctor or dentist. That's why the witness protection plan moves people hundreds of miles away."

Silence claimed her again briefly. "I need a bathroom."

"A few more miles unless you want the side of the road."

Apparently not, because she didn't speak again. At last he found the rest area. It was small, probably not very well-kept, but nature's call and all that.

He felt they were safe enough to allow her to go by herself. A vending machine offered a selection of canned drinks and junk food. It would have to do for now.

When she emerged, he asked her what she wanted. "It'll be a while before I can get us a meal."

She nodded, her fight gone for now. It would come back. "This looks awful except for the canned cranberry juice."

"Pick something anyway. You need food before you're up to arguing with me again."

She sent a startled glance his way, then smiled faintly before choosing some chips and a candy bar. He made sure to get her several cans of cranberry juice. She'd want them later, if not now.

He wondered if she had any idea how very pretty she was. How memorable. Probably. Most attractive women did. He allowed her nearly ten minutes to walk around and stretch. He did the same, keeping a weather eye out for any car that slowed down as it passed.

Then the road again.

"I need a shower."

"Today, I promise. I could use one, too, before you're hanging out the car window to avoid smelling me."

That at least got a small laugh out of her.

ALLIE SETTLED BACK into the rhythm of the road, not at all happy about any of this. The seat beneath her felt more comfortable than it had upon awakening, but that was small by comparison with this insane trip.

It was like being kidnapped, she thought. She didn't even know where she was. Max had put the kibosh on those fears, however. Max wanted this, and Hale appeared to know what he was doing.

At least he'd explained, although not nearly enough. She was still having trouble believing that Jasper Ellis could be the evil they said he was.

But thinking back over the nearly two years she had worked for the man, she had to admit she'd heard whispers. She'd always dismissed them because rumors were so unreliable and often fanciful.

Maybe not. In the brightening land of Northern California, with Mount Shasta as a guidepost, she at least had some vague idea of their location. Extremely vague. If she were to leap out of the car and try to run, she'd only get lost before she found a phone to call for help.

What if Max and Hale were right?

The man beside her offered only a minimal explanation. Too quiet by half. Her only link to her old life. Her only promise of a safer one.

How the hell was he supposed to find someone sent out to look for her, to put the threat to bed?

But he'd said that was the intention, although she couldn't imagine him managing that. Not if they were hiding as well as he thought.

God, this had turned into a nightmare without any end that she could see. Nor was the taciturn man beside her helping by his decision to say little. It would help if she knew at least a bit about him, but all she knew so far was that he'd been a Marine.

A double helping of frustration for her. She was not accustomed to ceding personal control over her life to someone else. She preferred to make her own decisions. She was also aware that she could be very stubborn about that.

But this time there was Max. She kept coming back to him. He'd managed to unnerve her.

Thus she was riding into the unknown with a monolith of silence. Carved in stone, he seemed.

The restaurant he'd promised turned up two hours later. It advertised "down-home" cooking. She imagined congealed fat.

"Not what you're used to," Hale remarked. "But a good breakfast."

"Have you eaten everywhere on the continent?"

"Hardly."

When? Why? How? She didn't bother to ask, knowing by now that he'd probably ignore her. She zipped her lips and waited for her answers, at least about the food. Soon she was going to demand some answers. She'd hired the man after all, and she deserved to be some kind of partner in this insanity.

But her life seemed to depend on Hale now. It wouldn't be wise to annoy him too much. At least not yet.

After an onion-and-pepper omelet, cooked by a grill man who was amazing to watch, she felt a whole lot better. She even got to put the marmalade on her own toast, which came without butter at her request. One small victory for independence.

Hale ate a huge breakfast in comparison. Another thing about him that didn't surprise her. Hidden beneath that jacket was a lot of man. He must be ripped.

Eventually they left the diner. This time he didn't allow her to walk around outside. Protecting their secrecy, she supposed. This trip would become tiresome very quickly.

The day had grown overcast, giving her no real sense of the countryside. All she knew was that Mount Shasta had begun to disappear behind them. Then, even that was gone. They headed mostly east now, she guessed. The alternative was driving into the Pacific Ocean.

She loved that ocean, especially north in Oregon. Rugged cliffs standing guard over water that was rough and wave-tossed most of the time. She especially loved those high cliffs. Continental plates colliding. The extreme power of nature visible to the world.

She occasionally indulged a fantasy of living in a house high above the water with a view over the cliffs. Not possible anymore. Oregon protected the coastline, and almost all habitation existed on the shore below. Once fishing villages, she supposed they were now mostly owned by the wealthy who seemed to be determined to take over every beautiful space on the planet.

She would have enjoyed a drive along that coastline, a lot more than this doglegging trail into the hinterlands. Hours later they'd put away another three or four hundred miles. Then relief appeared in the form of a gas station.

She headed for the bathroom and when she emerged she saw Hale talking on a telephone. She waited until he finished talking indecipherably in what seemed like a coded message.

"What is that?" she asked, annoyed because he hadn't let her bring her own phone.

He held up a finger, quieting her.

Allic bit her lip and waited. Then he walked over to a huge truck with a business name on the sides and rear. It appeared to be headed in a different direction. What the heck?

She watched as he stuck the phone inside a gap in the truck's rear end, then signaled her to get into the car. When they were rolling away, he gave her chilling news.

"My contacts say that Ellis is already trying to find you."

She bit her lip, absorbing the shock. Maybe Ellis was indeed the man they claimed him to be.

A dozen miles later, she could repress her exasperation no longer. "You wouldn't let me bring my phone. Was that a burner of some kind?"

"Not exactly."

She waited for more information and when it didn't come, she spoke impatiently. "Damn it, Hale. What's not exactly a burner phone?"

He didn't answer immediately. She suspected that he kept telling her only what he felt she needed to know. That irritated her. After all, she was riding passenger on some quest she didn't fully understand.

"Burner phones," he said finally, "aren't exactly burners the way you see them in movies."

"Why not?"

"Because every burner has to be in touch with the service that was paid for and that also provides the location. How else would they know when you exceed your hours? How else would they know when to cut off the service?"

A good point. She looked out the window again, then felt she hadn't been told enough. "What's different about yours?"

He offered a heavy sigh. "Time for some education. I have a whole box of them in the back. A metal box that keeps them from ever being pinged. I bought them all months ago and kept them in there with the batteries removed. After a while the service pings less frequently, then finally not at all, assuming the phone has been lost. They don't bother to cut off the hours then, either."

"I never thought about any of this."

"Why should you?"

"But once you use them…"

"I only use each phone once. Not enough to get any real attention from their algorithms. Then I get rid of it."

"On the back of a truck?" She was growing more astonished by the moment.

"Yes. In case it gets pinged somehow, it'll be pinged moving in the wrong direction. As simple as that."

Now she had plenty to think about. All this secrecy. All this covert activity. All of it to protect her.

Fear began to fill her again. She wanted to be sick.

"I need to pull over," she said, her mouth salivating, her body growing hot.

"Bathroom?"

"I wish."

Her stomach had begun to heave just as he found a

place to pull his vehicle to the side of the road. She heard the door lock release when she opened the door. The grass wasn't close enough, but gravel was. At last it stopped.

A rag appeared in front of her face. "It's okay. Just wipe off, then I'm going to give you a swig of water to rinse your mouth. No more than that."

It had to be enough. A lot now was going to have to be enough.

Then they returned to their journey to nowhere.

## Chapter Four

Three nights later, the rebellion Hale had been waiting for happened.

He said, "I'm going to an outfitter to get you some more clothes."

Her expression grew stubborn. "Why can't I go with you?"

"For reasons that should be obvious by now. If that hunter has managed to get closer somehow, I don't want him to be able to follow closely with your photo. I told you that. Just give me your sizes."

"You know everything," she said querulously. "I should at least be able to pick out what I wear."

"Not this time."

"Damn it, Hale, we've stayed in a different town in a different motel every single night. We arrive well after dark and leave in the morning before dawn. I doubt even a bloodhound could find us."

He provided a stoic answer. "Of course not. A dog can't track a car indefinitely."

"So why can't I choose my own clothes?"

His face remained expressionless, but she still felt him studying her as if she were a complex problem. Maybe she was. At least he didn't speak patiently this time, as if to a child.

He was facing her and spoke quietly. "Allie, you'd pick out clothes you like."

"Damn straight."

"That's part of the problem. I don't want you to look anything like you used to. Styles, colors, whatever."

"Oh, God, this is insane. What about the place you buy the clothes? They're not going to notice that a man is buying women's clothes in the wrong size for him?"

"I have a wife," he said flatly, then exited the room, locking the door behind him.

Allie sat down, everything inside her annoyed beyond words, with her unavoidable fear making it worse. She wanted this to end *now*.

He had a wife? She found that hard to believe. Who'd want a silent man like him? Who'd let him run on these long trips without explanation? A woman far more compliant than she, obviously.

Hale returned an hour later, tossing several large bags on the bed. "Change," he ordered. "Everything you brought with you is going into a trash bin farther along the road."

"That's illegal, to use someone else's bin!"

"Most of what I do is illegal. Get used to it. Change, now."

"But…"

"We're leaving as soon as you do."

Again? Wearily she went to do as he demanded. He was right. The clothes he had found for her were nothing she would have chosen for herself. All dull colors. All downscale.

The woman in the mirror had become even more unrecognizable.

When she stepped out, her old clothes wadded in her hand, she found a transformed Hale. His black windbreaker had given way to an army-green jacket with many pockets. While it was open, she saw he wore a double shoulder holster. It didn't shock her. Her father had often worn one when he was in plain clothes on the job. But now she knew why Hale had never removed that windbreaker.

His jeans were the same as before, but his black boots had been replaced by desert boots. Military.

But the biggest transformation was his hair. The shaggy locks were gone, neat now although still a bit long.

"Where'd you get your hair cut?" she demanded.

"I pulled out the extensions. There's a warm jacket in your bags. You might need it. Anything you don't want now I'm throwing in the trunk."

"And my duffels will be empty?"

"Believe it."

Oh, she believed it. Thank God that while her hiking clothes carried famous brand names, they weren't the most expensive items in her wardrobe, not by a long shot. "Just don't throw out my underwear."

"I won't. No one can see it."

Except him, with his hands all over it. Looking at him, she accepted that she wasn't going to win this battle.

Taking his advice, she found the jacket in the bag. A drab match for his. She also discovered a flannel night-gown.

"Oh, for heaven's sake!" As if anyone but him would see her in it. She thought wistfully of the satiny gowns she preferred, even the occasional peignoir. Of the Egyptian-cotton robe for warmth.

No point. Things could all be replaced eventually.

If this nightmare ever ended. Her fear had been slowly subsiding with each day on the road. She was growing so weary of this.

But then fear bit her again, hard. The reality of what was happening with her clothes had just become *real*. The reality of this hardened man sleeping on a floor, giving her no solitude except in a windowless bathroom. It was all *real*.

Max and Hale took the threat seriously. She needed to, as well. Except she hated every moment of this flight.

STUBBORNNESS HAD BEEN replaced by sadness on Allie's face. Hale noticed it before they returned to his car. Noticed it in the inkiness of a night brightened only by a few pale streetlights.

He helped her into her seat this time and received no objection. That was a bad sign indeed. He didn't know what he could possibly do about it.

Pallid streetlights soon gave way to the pitch-black of the road, punctuated only by his headlamps. No other vehicles traveled this way, and Hale allowed himself to relax a bit.

Then the moon started rising to the east, in its quarter phase, yet strong enough to splash the world in blue light. Before long, a wind picked up, tossing the silvery leaves on the trees like ocean waves. A storm was brewing.

The one thing he missed was being able to check the weather on his watch. A watch that had been gutted to its most basic functions. A tool he'd been able to rely on over many years, now merely a possible threat.

Hale didn't like this flight any more than the woman beside him did. He was a man used to confronting danger head-on in one way or another. But this was the career he'd chosen, using his skills to protect the lives of others. It was never glamorous. The only real thanks he got was knowing he'd saved a life.

Even the life of a person he didn't admire at all. Not even a lowlife deserved to be killed. Leaving the law to deal with those clients was better by far.

This one was certainly different. This one was genuinely an innocent. She'd done absolutely nothing to deserve this.

And now she had reached sorrow or despair. He had no way to know which, but either troubled him greatly. Her life had been changed by trying to be a good person. She would never see the world through the same eyes again. The man who initiated this needed to spend the rest of his days in jail, stripped of the power he worshipped and the money he loved.

And, damn it, he was going to find a way to ensure that. To ensure that Allie didn't need to live the rest of her life in fear.

But how? The question haunted him.

ALLIE HAD DOZED but now she woke to the suffocating cocoon of darkness. She'd slept her way through so much of this trip that she wondered if she'd ever be able to sleep through the night again.

A bolt of lightning ripped the sky, blinding in its brilliance. So fast it offered little illumination.

"A storm," she murmured pointlessly.

"I was hoping we'd outrun it, but maybe not."

"Not likely, given that you're driving to every point of the compass and a few that I'm sure don't exist." Her tone was tart. She was shocked to hear him laugh quietly. So he had some emotions after all.

"You know," she said, "it would be nice if we talked about something. Like who you are."

He was slow to respond. "I am *not* an open book. A nerd friend of mine has removed me from every possible database. I have to be private to do this job."

She hadn't even thought about that. Pondering for a few minutes, she then asked, "Can you erase *me*?"

"Not if you ever want a piece of your life back. I doubt you'd want to be nobody."

He had a point.

A couple of minutes later he spoke again. "I promised you could call your friends. One friend. She can let the others know you're alive. But it has to be a circumspect conversation. I'll tell you how."

Of course he would. Even directing her conversations with friends now. But given all he was doing to make them untraceable, she understood. Hated it but understood.

Eventually the storm clouds lightened enough to reveal low-hanging cumulus. Lightning expressed the rage of the heavens ever more frequently. Then a drowning downpour began, locking them into an even smaller cocoon. Silvery drizzles of rain poured everywhere until Hale turned on front and back wipers.

Even those weren't much help.

"Hale?"

"Yeah?"

"Do you have any idea where we're going? An end point?"

Once again that delay before he answered. "I'm doing my best to prevent you from going to hell."

The calm way he spoke was as scary as his words.

Allie subsided into her seat, watching the storm darken the growing day.

MIDMORNING BROUGHT ANOTHER roadside diner. Allie sighed. "I think I'm going to have the measure of every grill man between home and the Rockies."

"You could know a worse bunch of people."

Which she apparently already did.

She waited in the car without being told to as Hale filled

the gas tank. Then, once again, they did the unexpected and drove away without sampling the diner's menu.

He probably thought he was reassuring her as he said, "I believe there's another small town ahead. We'll find a place there for lunch."

"Do you carry a detailed map in your head?"

"It helps if I open one every night."

"I never saw you do that."

"Not everything I do has to be visible."

Far from it, Allie thought. Inscrutable and now invisible. Or maybe the other way around, since he'd erased himself from every database.

She tried to imagine what it would be like to erase her entire past, to walk forward in life with all those years consigned to a void.

"Do you ever want to be a normal guy?" she asked.

"I never have been. But what's normal anyway? Only what someone else thinks it is."

She turned that around in her mind as more miles slipped away. Hale might be right. How did she make herself feel normal? By fitting in with a group, by feeling she belonged and was like them. Was that everyone's normal?

Her "lunch bunch," as she and her friends liked to call themselves. A group of women diverse in their backgrounds but most working for Ellis. Some they had known since college. A band of women on similar wavelengths with similar interests. But that's what helped build bonds, wasn't it?

They reached a small town that looked hospitable despite a sky that promised vengeance.

"There's a café here," Hale said. "You might be able to get a meal more to your liking."

He pulled a U-turn around a median that had clearly been constructed to enhance the town's appearance. It left barely enough room on either side to allow parallel parking. He wheeled into a space with the ease of a pro. Allie couldn't remember the last time she had done that. Diagonal parking was the best.

"There it is," he said, pointing.

The rain had lightened to a sprinkle. Allie climbed out of the car feeling every cramped and stiffened muscle from all the time spent driving. She wondered if the kinks might become permanent.

She also felt awkward in her new clothes. Like a misfit. She must present a dumpy picture, unlike her usually smartly dressed self.

But then she realized from glancing at people around her that she didn't look out of place. Not here. The town seemed to be populated by folks who worked at physically demanding jobs, the kinds of jobs that kept them in old clothes. Perhaps kept them unable to afford anything fancier.

Inside, the café was decorated in red gingham curtains and matching tablecloths beneath plastic protectors. The vinyl seats echoed the red. The menu picked up on the theme.

A pleasingly plump young waitress brought them menus with a smile and asked if they wanted coffee.

"A gallon might do for me," Hale answered, looking at Allie. "You?"

"Coffee will be fine."

An insulated carafe accompanied by blue ceramic mugs along with a saucer of small cups of half-and-half. Allie didn't take much time to scan the menu. A turkey club sandwich? With actual lettuce and tomato? Heaven. Plus her side of salad so she could feel like she wasn't persistently poisoning herself.

For the first time it occurred to her that she might need

some adjustments to her thinking. About food in particular. Only now did she realize that she had grown picky. Maybe even snobbish about food and clothes. The idea didn't make her feel any better about herself.

"I was lucky in my childhood," she offered. She didn't want silence, especially while sharing a meal.

Hale picked up the baton and ran with it. "How so?"

"My dad was a cop, a close friend of Max's. Mom taught elementary school. They loved me and I never doubted it. Not many people can say that from what I've seen."

"No, they can't." He revealed nothing by tone or expression.

"My life crashed down around me the day my dad stopped to help a motorist with a broken-down car. A pickup never saw them, and to this day I can't imagine why flashing lights didn't catch his attention. Anyway, the pickup hit the back of Dad's vehicle with my dad right in the middle between the patrol car and the disabled car."

"God."

"*She* had nothing to do with it," she replied, echoing Max. "But my dad, do you know what his last act was? To shove the driver of the disabled vehicle to the side of the road just before the truck hit. With his last breath, my dad saved a man's life."

"Remarkable man."

"I think so. I've always tried to live up to him but I'm pretty sure I haven't succeeded."

She stared at the remains of her sandwich, her appetite lost. Why had she brought that up at this time?

Then she looked out the window at people passing on the street and she knew. They were the people her dad would have identified with. Not with the woman she'd become.

"Can I take this with me?" she asked.

"Sure. And more if you want." Hale was eating a double portion of fries and a juicy-looking roast beef sandwich. "It may be a while before we stop again."

She expelled a slow breath between her lips. "Of course it will. How was your childhood?"

"I didn't have one." End of subject.

Did he mean that for real or was that just his answer to protect his secrecy? But something about him suddenly struck to her core. It was the truth. Whatever lay in his past, especially his childhood, was better forgotten. It must have been dreadful.

THEIR NEXT STOP came at dusk in a busy truck stop. Multiple large eighteen-wheelers grumbled in side-by-side slots. The sun hadn't appeared all day, and now the air felt pregnant with ozone.

Hale handed her one of his phones. "Keep it short. Don't give them a hint of where you are or what you're doing."

She spoke drily. "Basically tell them that I'm alive and not to worry."

"No more than that. One call, so pick wisely. Like I said, you don't want to pull them into this mess."

No, she didn't. She imagined goons trying to get her location out of her friends, and the image wasn't pretty. "It's not as if I know where I am."

The problem was, she discovered, that because of the convenience of modern phones, she hadn't memorized phone numbers. "Ah, crap," she muttered, and ransacked her brain. At last Shawna's number emerged from the scramble, and she tried it.

She was relieved to get Shawna's voice mail, which exonerated her from explaining anything. "Shawna, I just want to let you know I'm alive and I'm fine. Tell you all about it later." She hoped. Then she let go of the brief link to her friend and watched Hale shove it into the back of a truck. Some poor driver was going to carry the thing for hundreds of miles now.

Hale made a call from yet another burner. He kept his voice too low for her to hear much over the growling engines all around her.

When at last he disconnected and pulled the battery and SIM out, he looked at her. "Ellis has definitely put his security team on finding you. Let's eat, then get the hell out of Dodge."

"For real?" Ellis's security team really was looking for her? A rivulet of ice dribbled down her neck. She couldn't help darting her gaze around as if some horror was about to emerge from the deepening shadows around these trucks.

If Ellis was using his security apparatus to find her, then there was no question of what was going on. Her last, small doubt washed away.

But before they departed, Hale got down on the ground and ran a piece of equipment beneath the vehicle. Ten minutes later, he emerged with a small black box. He tossed it in the nearby trash bin.

"What was that?"

"A transmitter. Time to ditch it."

"You knew it was there?"

He shook his head, but she couldn't tell if that was a negative.

ALLIE WAS GROWING used to the rhythm of her new life. Food twice a day whenever Hale felt they could stop. She had to eat or get carryout to avoid hunger.

The truck-stop diner was busy, full of boisterous men who seemed glad of company and glad to be out of their truck cabs. She envied them.

The menu offered a cornucopia of hearty foods. Allie

shut down the last of her guilt and helped herself without regard to all the dietary habits she'd learned. It was, she admitted, more like the cooking she'd grown up with.

Pea soup, always her favorite. A ham and Swiss on a crusty roll. Even a piece of pie. Well, she could spend hours in the gym whenever this flight was over. Then she squashed such thoughts and decided to be glad that she could fill her stomach and ease her hunger. She even felt okay about walking out with a paper bag holding a few pastries. Nights could be long.

They didn't dawdle. Hale gave her the chance to stretch her legs for maybe ten minutes, and he seemed as glad to move around himself.

Then it was off into the deepening night with a sleazy motel somewhere ahead.

"They can't have followed me this fast," Allie said. Was she trying to reassure herself?

"You're making a mistake," Hale answered.

"How?"

"You're forgetting that Ellis's team can reach out almost anywhere in the world. That's why we're not stopping. That's why we won't stop until I can get a bead on the threat and hopefully shrink it."

Maybe the most unnerving thing was that she was beginning to believe in this crazy world she'd fallen into.

Her life no longer sounded like a bad movie script. It had *become* one.

HALE SENSED THE shift in Allie's reaction to the threat marching toward her. It hadn't been easy for her.

But why should it have been? She'd apparently grown up in a happy family with a father who went out to round up bad guys every day and probably never spoke of what he saw or had to do. Her mother had likely come home from teaching with a cute or charming story many days. Even her father's death had been an accident, not murder.

How could Allie have known about the evil beneath her bright world? How could she have suspected there were shadows in which *real* monsters lurked?

Her innocence was shattering right before his eyes and he had to let the destruction continue in order to protect her. Most of his clients had possessed a more realistic view of the dangers, but not Allie. She evidently had been protected her entire life.

He could have hated himself right then but resisted the urge. He had to allow this. It was part of his job. It was part of keeping Allie safe. But it was still ugly to behold.

Hale had learned from his earliest days that life could be painful, hideous, even horrific. In the end, he had come to believe that he could trust only himself.

Maybe that was why he had joined the military, where faith in your unit was demanded, where you had to have your comrade's back. Or maybe the biggest reason was to grow strong, to face fear, to never doubt his abilities again.

But war had changed his entire direction. He'd made up his mind to spend his life helping people. His first attempt, by joining a security company, had crashed and burned. So he had started his own *personal* protection business. Taking care of individuals instead of being hired out as a mercenary.

Now he was racing across the countryside with a woman who didn't deserve to be tangled in this hell.

At least his men had been able to plant tracers on most of Ellis's men, providing him with more information so he could help Allie better.

He might even be helping strangers, in the case of Ellis. A perk.

It would sure make Max's life better. He doubted that

Allie had any idea that Max had been heading up the investigation of Ellis for years now except for the brief bit he'd told her. Max would probably dance on air with his mastiff if he could get Ellis.

Hale decided to break the silence even if it went against his grain. To distract Allie. "That dog of Max's is something else."

He sensed Allie stir beside him.

"Yeah," she answered. "I sometimes think Harvey is at least twice his size."

"And obedient only when he chooses to be. Damn smart dog."

"Smart how?"

"He's in charge."

That pulled a small laugh from her. "I think Max knows it."

"He doesn't care. He dotes on that pooch."

When Allie didn't reply, he thought he'd reached a conversational dead end. He was good at that. He tried again.

"I bet you didn't know that mastiffs were used as draft animals in the First World War."

Another laugh escaped her. "Come on."

"I'm being serious. They pulled munitions carts. I wonder about that."

"Using dogs that way?"

"Nah," he replied. "Using mastiffs. They're famous for sitting down and refusing to budge when they feel tired. Read about one guy who swore he takes a wheelbarrow with him on long walks with his dog in case the animal decides he's had enough."

"Oh, Lord. I've never seen Harvey do that."

"Probably because Max learned that lesson long ago. Maybe they take short enough walks together."

"Well, Harvey is stubborn. I can easily see him just plopping his butt down."

"I enjoy watching the two of them together. Max *really* dotes."

"Dogs are easy to dote on." There was a smile in her voice.

"You have one?"

"Not since high school."

And that seemed to be the end of conversation. Again. Well, he'd kept that running longer than he usually did. Not that he cared. Shooting the breeze had never appealed to him.

But he sharply felt Allie's need for more than staring out a car window. Well, he got it. He'd rather be doing something else, too. He'd have preferred to hike this trip.

Unfortunately, he could think of nothing more to talk about.

Fifty miles later, it was Allie who spoke. "Why do you do this, Hale?"

"Someone has to."

"But people can hire all kinds of security around their homes and so on."

"That might be enough for some. It's not good enough for some."

"Why not?"

"Sometimes it's best to trust only one person. Less chance for loose lips and bribery."

"I didn't think of that," she admitted. "But this must be as boring for you as it is for me."

"Not quite. I have to stay on high alert."

"Watching everything. I kind of noticed. But that still doesn't explain *why*."

He sighed inwardly, then gave the short answer. Maybe the only one he had. "Because people need protection."

"You're helping people."

He didn't respond to that. He didn't see himself as a caped crusader of any kind. He didn't think he was on a mission of mercy. He just had a set of skills that were useful for protecting people. It was something, anyway.

"You said you were going to get a bead on these people. How?"

He didn't answer her question but diverted. "We'll have a face-to-face when I find one or two. My contacts are working on it."

"Then?"

"I'm going to do some serious interrogation."

ALLIE DIDN'T ASK for details. Ugly images from movies and TV sprang to her mind and she hoped he didn't mean *that* kind of interrogation.

Probably not, she decided. While she had felt the granite within him, she'd also noticed that so far he was a decent man. More decent than many of the men she worked with who seemed to be incapable of talking to her face. But stripping her with their eyes? Some kind of male failing?

But not with this man.

Satisfied, at least as much as she could be, she resettled herself in her seat and dozed. One way of making this endless travel easier.

As she drifted away, she remembered the comic books her parents had bought for her when they faced a long car drive. She wondered if those characters were still around.

IT MAY HAVE been hours later. Allie had no idea because she'd slept a bit, but Hale at last pulled into another motel. It looked about as appetizing as the previous ones.

A bedroom, a bathroom. This one with double beds and coverlets as outdated as the rest of the place. She stifled a sigh and let him carry in whatever he chose. Life had slipped from her hands into his. For the moment, she'd let it be.

"In the morning," he remarked, "I'll get us some more clothes. You especially."

"But that's wasteful. We have clothes."

"We're not going to stop at a coin laundry to spend two hours."

Well, that made sense. She sat on the edge of the bed, watching him drop two duffels. His and hers. They ought to be labeled, like towels.

"Then I'm going to need more underwear," she informed him. "I guess you can say your wife is sick."

All he replied was to ask her what sizes. And there went the last of her lacy garments. Oh, well.

He showered first since she insisted. That was something *she* could control and she had begun to feel mulish again. Maybe she wouldn't shower at all. A day skipped would hardly make her smell bad.

While he occupied the bathroom, she changed into that flannel nightgown. It proved to be soft and warm and she decided she liked it. Then she crawled into bed beneath the questionable coverlet onto sheets that felt and smelled clean. A plus.

Her mistake was in not turning her back to the bathroom door. When Hale emerged, he wore only a towel around his narrow hips. With the only light coming from the bathroom behind him, she could see only his general outline and a bit of his muscling across his chest and in his arms.

She snapped her eyes closed immediately. Too much. Too good. Honed muscles, not for show, and likely a washboard belly. Boy, she had friends who agonized in gyms trying to get those abs. But they seemed of a piece with the rest of the man.

Yeah, she wished she could open her eyes again and just stare, but Hale didn't invite that. He was a focused man, trained for action, certainly not for riding around in a car day and night.

Rustling suggested he pulled on some pants. Then she heard his breathing speed up a bit, and she at last opened her eyes.

He was on the floor at the foot of the bed doing push-ups. Then deep knee bends, then thrusts, then sit-ups, then some other exercises she couldn't name.

Heck, she ought to do that, too. Before she calcified in the shape of a car seat. But not now. Not in her nightgown.

Just about the time she heard him slide into the next bed, she drifted off. She hadn't had nightmares in many years, but she had them that night.

THEY CHECKED OUT of the motel well before dawn. Allie's sleep had been restless and she didn't hesitate to yawn openly, however impolite. The silvery moon from the start of their trip had vanished. New moon, she decided, although she rarely paid attention to the moon.

This was a lousy time of year to travel, she thought. Winter was blowing in everywhere. They had begun to see patches of snow, and the air was turning colder. This morning she could see her breath.

"What's on the menu today?" she asked irritably.

"Some beautiful mountains. Enjoy them."

That sounded more like an order than a suggestion. She snapped on her seat belt. What was the choice? She needed to find one soon, before she erupted like Vesuvius.

They had their usual truck-stop breakfast, no better or

worse than those that had come before. It was still dark when they began rolling again.

The ground rose steadily, then she saw the first flakes of snow. "Couldn't you have taken us by a southern route?"

"More people."

Well, that answered her. Maybe. "If this snow gets heavier, it's going to be hard to drive." Especially for a Southern California girl who'd seen it only in the Sierras. She'd never had to drive in it, though.

"I've done it before."

She supposed that was meant to be reassuring. It wasn't. Very little about this trek was reassuring.

As the snow thickened, the roads remained clear for a while. Their climb continued. Then she saw a sign that at last told her where she was:

*Nez Perce Reservation.*

"We're in Idaho!"

"So it would appear."

She thought over the days of travel, which at the rate they were going probably should have carried them most of the way to the East Coast. It also gave her a good idea how winding a route Hale had chosen. Avoiding large towns, sticking to out-of-the-way places...

It was a wonder her head hadn't spun. They must have backtracked on different roads more than once.

She would have loved to know how he planned this. Evasion. It was incredible.

She spoke again. "You heard anything from your contacts?" He'd called again last night.

"Yes. Ellis's security seems to have concluded that we headed north."

"How could they have done that?"

"My guys are checking on that. They're keeping an eye out."

His guys. She wondered who made up this invisible web of contacts. How many there were. Did he employ them or just rely on friends? He wouldn't be likely to tell her.

"We'll change our general direction soon," Hale announced.

"Well, that might be warmer."

The falling snow thickened. It began to stick to the pavement. Then at some road or another, he took a right turn, presumably moving them southward. More tiny towns spaced far apart.

At long last, he parked in front of a store, an aging structure that fit the town around it. *Dilapidated* would have been a kind term.

"Clothes," he said. He tossed her a faded green hat that was crushed and wrinkled. It looked like something a fisherman might wear. "Wear that, don't take it off, and keep your head down."

She put it on, wondering why she needed it.

He astonished her. "You're coming in. Just don't choose something that will stand out because I'll take it from your hands."

That sounded like a threat. After all this, however, she was willing to accept his dictum. Standing out would not be a good thing.

Inside, the store was quiet. Hardly another customer. The plump sales lady jumped to help them. A grandmotherly looking woman, she might have owned the store.

"Stocking up for a long hike," Hale said in answer to the woman's question.

"In this weather?" The clerk pretended a shiver. "You're braver than I am."

Hale managed a rusty smile. "Not as bad as jumping naked into a hole in the ice."

The woman laughed, then left them alone to pick out their items.

Inwardly sighing, Allie followed directions. A pair of dully colored flannel shirts, distinguished only by the fact that they tried to appear plaid. More jeans. Socks. And the underwear, plain white briefs.

No taste in this town, she thought. Or maybe taste was unaffordable.

"You come to join the militia?" the clerk asked as she checked them out.

"Could be," was Hale's inscrutable answer.

The woman smiled. "Then you'll be back for camo, unless you want to get it now. We've got plenty in the back."

"We'll wait and see if we're welcome."

"Might be a good idea." She waved them on their way.

At the car, Hale put their bags in the back. Once inside, as they drove away again, Allie could no longer contain herself.

*"Militia?"*

"Idaho collects a lot of survivalists, mostly up north. And some get together in bands."

"Oh, man."

"You must have read about it."

"It seems they don't make the headlines."

"They don't want to."

Another glimpse of a new world, Allie thought. She'd had a general idea that militias existed but she hadn't much thought about where. Here, apparently.

"It was a good cover," Hale said.

Allie turned her head toward him. "You expected that?"

"Not necessarily that we'd be asked, but I was sure that would be the interpretation."

He was always thinking ahead and living in a world

Allie had never met. It seemed Hale could navigate almost anything, and she felt her first glimmer of reluctant respect.

THAT NIGHT, AFTER the usual roadside dinner, they stopped at yet another awful motel. How did Hale find these places?

But this constant running and driving was exhausting her.

"Can't we at least spend an extra night somewhere?" Although what she'd do with the time... Oh, heck. Just avoiding more road miles would have been great.

"No."

If she could have, she might well have shaken him. "I'm paying for your services," she said point-blank. "I ought to have something to say about this!"

"I'm doing what you're paying me to do. You don't have to like it."

Well, that was the end of that argument. If it had indeed been an argument.

He emptied the duffel of all her previous clothes and put the new ones in it. At least he didn't switch out the flannel nightgown. *Something* remained.

"They surely can't find us overnight," she remarked, another stab at disagreement.

He straightened from his own duffel and faced her. "Someone could. It only takes one."

"Sheesh." She shut up. She had a feeling that if she simply refused to get into his car, he wouldn't leave her standing in the middle of nowhere. No, he'd probably pick her up bodily and place her in the seat.

She glowered at him as she sat on the edge of the bed. Tonight there was only one bed, a double. He'd be sleeping on the floor again.

Hale gave her plenty of privacy, but no solitude, a distinction she was learning. It was also one she didn't like.

"How are you going to know when we're safe?" she asked a while later.

"I will."

"Your invisible contacts, I presume."

"No. I'll catch whoever. I'm good at that."

"Is there anything you're not good at?"

"Talking."

She rolled her eyes, then grabbed her nightwear and headed to the bathroom. She wished she'd purchased shower shoes. Blech.

"I'm going to step outside and make another call."

Of course he was. The calls seemed to be coming closer together. Had he learned something that worried him?

She'd never know, she guessed. But maybe that ought to worry *her*.

Oh, hell. What was the point? For once in her life, she had absolutely no control.

OUTSIDE, IN A night so quiet Hale could hear his own breaths, he placed a call to a memorized number.

"Are we having vegetable stew?" he asked.

"Hearty and it makes you hale. A great meal." Stu paused. Then, "I can scarcely believe it, but the host has hired a professional chef."

Hale tensed until his teeth clenched in a rictus. He didn't need an interpreter. *Chef* meant *assassin*. While his eyes never stopped scanning the immediate area, his mind began to spin around possibilities. "Okay."

"Does she have the recipe?" Did Allie possess any written or recorded information?

"Only in her memory. Maybe she should have written it down."

"No use now."

"When is the chef supposed to arrive?"

"No idea. I'm going to check on that. To get the kitchen ready. I hear a few of the sous chefs are on their way."

"Already?" Several security men were on their way, too. Hale paused, then decided to take the risk again. "Why. I'd a thought it would be too soon."

"Ya think?" Stu replied. "I'll check. Maybe I can find the damn chef."

Hale disconnected, yanked the battery from the phone and put the burner on a car with Oregon plates.

An assassin was on the way? Why weren't the security people enough? And how were he and Allie being tracked? Stu had understood the code last night, and now he knew that Hale and Allie were somewhere between Idaho and Wyoming. Because how else could Stu and the others hope to find out how close the threat had come? Or maybe to locate the threat themselves?

Hale had needed to reveal that they were at the border between Wyoming and Idaho only because of the "chef," but he'd chosen his words judiciously. *Why. I'd a.* No one overhearing should have grasped that as a location reference.

He stood outside for a long time, rocking on his heels. This had gone way over the top. Way, way over. Why would Ellis bring a professional killer into this?

Because Allie knew something extremely dangerous, and it didn't matter if it was on paper or a computer flash drive. She had to be permanently silenced. Completely silenced.

Hale swore quietly. It wasn't as if he couldn't deal with a pro. He knew their methods and their mindsets very well. But this tracking thing…

Why were the security guards even out there, given the assassin? Did they know a pro was looking, as well?

Or did they have some inside information they were following, possibly unaware that the pro was tracking *them*?

Inside information. Hale's gut twisted. Had one of his team sold out? Or talked too loosely?

All of a sudden staying here seemed like too much of a risk. Stu knew they were somewhere along the border, but he didn't know which direction they'd take. They had to skedaddle *now*.

But he sure as hell wasn't going to tell Allie about the pro. She didn't need any more worries.

At last he went inside. In the dim light from the bathroom, he saw Allie in bed with the covers drawn up to her chin. He also saw that her eyes were wide-open.

"Get up," he said. "We're leaving now."

"Why? It's too soon."

"Just do it."

"I deserve an explanation!"

"If a gator was nipping at your heels would you argue with me or just jump away?"

She gasped, then threw the covers back. "But you're going to tell me when we get on the road. I've had enough of being kept in the dark!"

He didn't bother to argue. He'd already gathered the clothes they needed to trash into the shopping bags. For just an instant he considered leaving them behind.

No. Now was not a good time to change his habits. Leave no trail.

Except somehow the breadcrumbs were out there. He'd probably spend the next few days racking his brain trying to figure out how he'd gone wrong. Or *who* had gone wrong.

# Chapter Five

Once they were on the road again, Allie didn't press him for an explanation. Instead she fell asleep in the seat beside him.

Which left him entirely too much time to ramble inside his own head. For the first time he considered that silence was not always the best way to handle life.

But considering how many times as a child he'd been swatted or mistreated for opening his mouth, silence had become his friend.

Not this night. He'd have cheerfully gabbed about some of the bars he'd visited or questioned her about her life before Ellis.

Anything but feeling the knife of betrayal turning in his gut. What the hell had gone wrong? Stu would suspect it, too. He'd start guarding information, start looking for one of the guys who was acting unusually.

In the meantime, he had to lower their profile even more. Maybe not give Stu another hint of the course they were taking.

If he'd been inclined to such displays, he might have hammered his fist on the steering wheel.

Before dawn, he saw an unattended dumpster near the road. He pulled over, left the engine running so Allie wouldn't get cold, and pulled the bags out of the back. He emptied them into the bin but kept the bags. Next stop to fling them. No trail, no trace.

Then they took off again. And, of course, Allie woke up.

"Where are we?" she asked drowsily.

"Between here and there, in the middle of nowhere." Or so he had thought. He tweaked the heater to blow more warm air on her. She needed a blanket, he decided. Maybe a neck pillow.

Hell, someone might know *he* was a part of this flight. Yeah, he'd switched license plates in the dead of night while Allie slept, but maybe that hadn't been enough. Maybe putting his plates on a different car had caught the owner's eye and it had been reported.

But so fast? Most people looked at their plates only when they put a new sticker on them.

Or maybe that person had been ticketed.

He smothered a sigh, the hamster wheel of his thoughts driving him nuts. Then came the question from Allie.

"Why did we have to leave so quickly?"

"Because I seem to have left some breadcrumbs behind."

He felt her sit up straighter. "I don't see how that's possible!"

"I'm trying to work it out so it doesn't happen again."

Clearly she wasn't reassured. "Good God, Hale, you've been driving us everywhere but straight. Nobody's got anything they could track. I don't believe this."

It wasn't a choice. He didn't *want* to believe it. He *had* to.

Time passed, then Allie spoke again. "Could there be a transmitter on this car?"

"I swept the thing. I got rid of it."

How it had gotten there was still a mystery. He had left the car in her parking garage while he made her pack up.

Could she have already been under such close watch? It didn't seem likely but it wasn't impossible. He wanted to hammer his fist on the wheel again. She'd gone to work that day. She'd left Max's almost immediately with him. The getaway had been too fast to have been anything but clean.

Hell's bells. There was only one thing left to do. "Next time I see an option, I may buy a new vehicle."

"But that'll involve all kinds of paperwork!"

"Not a street sale. It won't be easy to find a baby this good, though."

"No, it won't. Plus it'll have all kinds of equipment you'll need to yank out."

"Done it before."

She subsided, twisting until she stared out the side window at the ink of the night speeding past them.

The ice between them came from more than the weather outside.

ALLIE CLOSED HER eyes but she wasn't sleeping as the first rosy light of dawn appeared on the passenger side of the car. Heading north again?

Maybe it would have been better to face out this threat in LA. It would at least have been more comfortable.

On the other hand, she didn't think Hale was doing this because it was fun. He had honestly believed he needed to take her away. Now he must be feeling just awful. Or worse, stupid.

But stupid was the last thing she would have accused him of. There were plenty of other epithets she could have applied, but she no longer felt like it.

Now she decided they were *both* in trouble. If these bad guys found her, would they stop with her? Maybe they'd go after Hale, too. She felt ashamed that she hadn't thought earlier that he might be risking his neck, too.

The sky was no longer leaden. A bright day began to be born. As long as they didn't turn the wrong direction right into bad weather, anyway. She could see pregnant clouds over the mountains to her side. Which mountains?

She hardly cared. Alligators nipping at her heels. They must be close for him to have pulled her out of bed before she'd even slept.

"Can you drive faster?" she asked him.

That drew a rare laugh from him. "Sure, so I can spend some time talking to a cop about a speeding ticket. Nailed."

Another thing she hadn't considered. "But you have fake IDs."

"Sure. And stolen plates on the car."

She blinked. "My God."

"Now you know."

She chewed her lip, then had an idea. "What about getting me a fake ID?"

"No."

"No?"

"Lady, I may break some laws, but I'm not going to allow you to. If we ever get you back to a normal life, it's going to be your own. And you're not going to live in fear that someone will catch you out on your ID. That's jail time."

She swallowed hard. This swamp just kept getting deeper. Only remembering Max telling her how other Ellis employees had died or disappeared kept her from calling this whole thing off.

What could Ellis do to her? A lot, evidently.

Glumly, she watched the breaking day, unable to enjoy the beauty of it.

"A new car? Really?"

"Maybe not." As usual he said no more.

HALE FELT LIKE a stinking pile of manure. There was something he hadn't considered, not the least of them a mole in his crew. But a transmitter? He supposed he could figure that one out quickly enough, and without replacing his car.

A detector for RF frequencies occupied a compartment in his trunk. He should have used it again sooner. Well, he'd use it before this day was over. Definitely. Put his mind at rest about one thing.

He was getting as restless as Allie. This perpetual running went against his grain. He preferred action, preferred facing threats head-on.

But this was different. The people he'd protected in the past had limited enemies. Maybe a drug gang. Maybe just one person.

Ellis was a whole different kettle of fish. He exceeded the threat any gang could present. Tentacles everywhere. Eyes everywhere. And methods of keeping any blame far away from him.

He doubted a drug cartel could pose as many dangers. Ellis operated right in the open as a respected businessman. His was no cover story. It was a *clean* story.

Until they could nail him with something. That was the thing. He had to help Max crucify this guy or Allie could never sleep easily again.

But right then, he was learning nothing about the enemy. Instead he was running. He hated this.

"Allie?"

"Yes?"

"Did you take any paper, files or computer flash drives from your office?"

"Good God, no! That would have been stealing. Violation of protected company secrets."

He nodded into the dawning day. "So you have no proof."

"No…" Her voice sounded thin. "None."

"I bet your memory is pretty good, though."

"Well, yes, but I can't prove anything. That's why I can't understand this. I have *nothing.*"

"How's Ellis supposed to be sure of that? And Ellis would know about your relationship with Max."

Allie stirred in her seat restlessly. "Hale? I didn't drag Max into this mess, did I?" Then before he could respond, she murmured, "Oh, Max, what have I done?"

Hale's hands clenched on the steering wheel until his knuckles must have turned white. Beneath his leather gloves, they were hidden.

"Allie."

"What?" she answered gloomily.

"You didn't do a damn thing wrong. You're an accountant. You found an error in the company books. You took it to the boss, who said he'd handle it. *He* was the one who made the veiled threat against you."

"But Max…"

"Trust me, Max knew exactly what he was stepping into. He knows all about Ellis. But what were you supposed to do? Cut off a guy you've known your entire life? Pretend he'd vanished when you didn't even know that you'd been threatened?"

"I guess." Her tone hadn't improved.

"Believe me, not understanding that you'd been threatened, why in the world should you avoid Max?"

"I don't know. Maybe I shouldn't have told him my little story, which I thought was amusing at the time."

Hale relaxed his grip on the steering wheel. "Ellis won't go after Max."

She drew a quick breath. "How can you be sure of that?"

"Because Max is a cop. Max has been investigating Ellis for years. If something happens to him, the rest of the team are going to point their eyes right at Ellis. Worse scrutiny than now. Max should be safe."

He hoped that had helped, but he wasn't sure. It had been pretty thin, his yarn about Max being safe. Allie was no fool. He just hoped she didn't think this one through.

He needed to do more for this woman, to fill her days with something besides endless driving and scenery, which, while it could be beautiful, palled after so long.

But the noose was drawing tighter, and he couldn't afford to slow them down, not yet. Maybe never, at least until he had a real idea how to protect her.

"You ever been married?" he heard himself ask. Where the hell had that come from? He didn't usually ask personal questions.

"No. Not even close."

That surprised him a bit. "Why not close? A woman as pretty as you…"

"That's exactly the problem," she said tartly. "Some guy will have to realize that I'm more than a pair of boobs walking around on top of his version of heaven."

It was a good thing that he didn't have anything in his mouth just then. It would have sprayed all over the windshield.

"Wow," was all that escaped him.

"Well, it's true," she said sourly. "They think I'm an idiot. I'm not. Having sex if I want it would be easy. I don't need any entanglements unless there's real respect."

"You go," he said approvingly. "But I've never met anyone who had your way with a turn of phrase."

"Maybe just not a woman who's so blunt."

That was possible. He'd never lived in a woman's world so he had no idea what had made Allie feel this way. He applauded her opinion nonetheless.

"I gather you decided this from experience?"

"Since I was fifteen or so. Nothing has changed it."

"I guess you met a lot of boors."

"That's a kind description."

Maybe it was. How much did women put up with that he'd never noticed? Probably a lot.

"Men need to corral their eyes and their hands," she added. "But it goes beyond that. I always pay my own way on a date. I learned not to let a guy buy me dinner because then he thinks I owe him something."

"Well, damn," he said. "Just *damn*."

"Where have you been living, Hale?"

"On a different planet."

A tiny laugh escaped her. "I could have guessed that." A rare smile cracked his face.

NEARING MIDDAY, ANOTHER truck stop appeared. Apparently, the country's lifeblood sometimes traveled along roads other than major arteries. Not all of them were big rigs, however. A number of them, large as they were, appeared to be smaller shipments.

Hale pulled something out of a compartment in the back of the car and Allie watched him walk around the vehicle, bending down and occasionally getting on his knees. He looked like a man who'd heard an unusual sound from his undercarriage. Then he lifted the hood.

A man wearing a heavily lined denim jacket walked over to them, pulling his pants up over a sagging belly. "Need some help, friend?"

"I think I got it," Hale said, reaching into the engine. "Been over some rough roads. Thought I might be slipping a tire belt, but not that I can see. This damn alternator cap, though. Sometimes it just goes loose on me, so I tighten it up."

"You might want to use some wire over those tabs," the guy said, and strode away.

"Good idea," Hale called after him. "Thanks."

He slammed the hood shut, then put his equipment in the rear. "Let's go," he said to Allie.

"No lunch?"

"Not here. We just got noticed."

She'd given up sighing and, for now, arguing. He'd presented her too much food for thought that morning, and she was still digesting it.

Once they were on the road, he said, "No transmitter that I could detect."

"Then what could it be?"

Hale didn't answer.

Before long, however, he spied an aging pickup standing alone on a small dirt turnout and pulled up behind it. Allie couldn't see a soul in sight.

"Close your eyes," he said. "Theft is about to occur."

But she couldn't close her eyes. He went to the trunk, then came around front. With what looked like a wrench in his hand, he lifted the hood once again.

No other vehicles passed them. A quiet road in the early afternoon.

Three minutes later, he closed the hood, returned to the rear and threw something inside with a clatter. A minute after that, they were driving again.

"What did you do?"

"If you must know, I just heisted that man's plates. I didn't leave mine behind. In a few more hours I'll do it again. Don't ask any more, Allie. You don't want to be complicit."

"Like I could tell anyone. I doubt it's a major crime anyway."

"Major or minor, you don't need a record."

Their next stop was a drive-through on the edge of another small town. At least this one boasted a grilled chicken sandwich, which appealed to her a lot more than a burger of dubious lineage. Hale tripled her order and added a large soda. He ordered plenty for himself.

They didn't even stop to eat.

"You're driving like someone is right behind us," she remarked, fear causing her heart to skip.

"Not that close. No way. But I don't want to give them a chance."

Then some tired Christmas decorations began to show up on the widely spread houses. Ranches? She had no idea as they turned up into the mountains again. The decorations disappeared.

They pulled in for the night at a small lodge that looked downscale. Probably for cheap skiers, but there wasn't enough snow nearby to draw them.

"Just let me sleep tonight," she told Hale. "Damn it, I need some time when I'm not crunched up like a pretzel. I'd stay two nights but..."

"But I won't let you. Not now."

"Or ever," she muttered, pulling out her nightgown.

HALE WENT OUTSIDE. He'd really screwed up somewhere. Now he wondered if he should even call Stu again. Too soon. If he did, however, he wasn't going to give Stu a clue as to where they were. Not this time. Maybe not for a while.

Once again, he ran his meter under and around the car. Then he found it. Small. Intermittent bursts. Easy to miss.

He yanked it out, then checked for a duplicate. When he was satisfied, he threw the transmitter into the metal box with his phones. The box was a Faraday cage and would allow no electronic transmissions in or out. Maybe he'd need the transmitter later.

In fact, the only good news was that he didn't have a traitor working against them.

Then he went in to tell Allie they were hitting the road again. Because, sure, he just loved to tell her that.

This time she turned into a hornet's nest. "This has got to stop, Hale! I get that you're protecting me, but I can't go on like this indefinitely. I'd be surprised if you can, either."

"I sure as hell don't want to."

"Then find a way we can stop for a little while. Get out of that damned car. Just to take a long walk. Hike up a mountain, build a snowman. *Anything!*"

"It would be too dangerous to stop now. They followed us to this point."

She clenched her jaw. "Some bodyguard you are. Get out so I can dress."

He'd deserved that. Absolutely deserved it. There'd been a hole in his assessment of the situation before they left LA, a great big gaping hole.

He kicked his own butt harder than she ever could.

The only thing that struck him was that, given he'd been carrying a transmitter, the bad guys were too far behind. It was taking them too long.

Why?

Endless night miles fell behind them as he beat his brain to understand exactly what was happening here.

ALLIE WAS ANGRIER than she'd ever been in her life. They'd been driving hither and yon all over the place, stealing license plates, and carrying a *transmitter*?

How the hell had he missed it when he checked earlier? Him and his fancy equipment, his burner phones and a car stripped of everything that might emit a signal. How the hell?

If she hadn't sensed the anger in him, she'd have erupted again. He was mad at himself. Oh, poor baby.

She snorted and tried to wrap her jacket more closely around herself. At night she usually felt a little cold, but this was worse. A frigid night combined with lack of sleep. She wondered if she would ever feel warm again.

Without a word, Hale reached over and turned up the heater.

She didn't bother to thank him.

Hours passed before he spoke again. "I was thinking that perhaps that transmitter was placed before we left LA."

"When?" she asked acidly. "Why would they put it on your car instead of mine?"

"Maybe when I came to your apartment with you. I thought it was too soon for them to be worried. You'd been to work that day after all. No reason to expect you wouldn't return the next day."

"You said that. Well, you're right about that, although apparently not, given what you found. Hell, I came home from work, went over to Max's for an early dinner..." Her voice trailed off.

"Max," she said. "I went to see Max. A detective. Then you came."

"Maybe." How would anyone know why he'd gone there? He tried to keep himself in the shadows at all times. Out of sight and out of mind. Covert in every aspect of his life. Only a handful of people knew what he did for a living.

Maybe that handful was too big.

"Why did you miss that transmitter earlier?"

"It's a burst transmitter. It only sends a signal every so often. I just managed to catch it tonight."

"Lovely." Her tone was acid. "So much for your phones."

The endless night offered a nearly endless opportunity to consider his screwup and how best to handle it. Then Allie asked the most useful questions of all.

"Tell me, Mr. Genius Bodyguard, why they haven't been on top of us already? Why aren't they here now?"

"I'm working on that."

"Work faster," she said testily.

He kind of liked the way she was reacting. Mad at him, justifiably. Furious about the entire situation. No despair, no tears, no quivering terror. Allie was made of some stern stuff.

"I've been thinking about it," he repeated.

"Then think out loud, for Pete's sake. I'm tired of being a pawn on this chessboard. Move me here, move me there, sit down and shut up like a good girl."

He nearly winced. "I've been doing my job. I didn't intend to be…" He searched for the word.

*"Patronizing,"* she said sharply. "You give a fresh meaning to that word."

"Hell." And this time he didn't keep the cuss to himself.

"Exactly."

A few more cusswords jabbed through his brain but he didn't allow them to pass his lips. Talk about what he was thinking? How he was working through this? Man, did that go against his grain.

But maybe it was time to start rubbing his own grain the wrong way.

"They haven't found us because they can't."

She blew a loud sigh. "You just said we've been transmitting our location."

"Let me finish, please."

She settled, but from the corner of his eye he saw the disapproving way she folded her arms.

"First of all," he said, "I told you it's a *burst* transmitter.

It sends a signal every so often. I suspect they didn't think they'd need more than a couple of bursts a day."

"Why not?"

"Because most people drive a straight line, here to there. A couple of those bursts would have told them where we're going. This zigzag route we've been following has prevented that."

For a few beats, she said nothing. "You suspected we could be followed somehow. Or you wouldn't have done this."

"Always expect the worst. Anyway, they probably even thought that when we reached a destination, we'd stay. A few days or more. They'd have us nailed because they'd be right behind us." He paused. "A typical run, they believed. Go hide in another city."

"There's nothing typical about this run," Allie remarked. "Damn."

"We've been confusing them. But they still must have figured out we hit the Pacific Northwest. Maybe they've gotten even closer. That's not good. The transmitter was sending a burst when I found it. They got the location of that lodge."

"Oh, man."

"I also think that in some of the places we've been staying, there was interference with their transmitter. You know, like places where you can't get a cell phone signal. Or even a satellite link. Under thick trees, in the mountains, just to name a few. So there were times they had no idea where we were."

"Then we'd pop up somewhere really weird."

"Yup. Unfortunately nothing is really random, not even me. They've got our general directionality."

"But we're not going anywhere in particular."

"I think it's time we took a drive on a long, straight, fast road. To get away from that lodge. If I missed something, I need to confuse them again. So… It's going to look as if we're headed to Bozeman in Montana. If there's any tracking left that I haven't found, that'll turn their attention that way."

"And then?"

"We're going to turn south into the real middle of nowhere."

"But if they're still tracking somehow?"

"I'm going to stop at a garage along the way. Get this puppy up on a rack and take a good long look."

"And get a new license plate," she said glumly.

"Yup."

## Chapter Six

By the time they stopped for a meal, midday had arrived and the area had begun to look more upscale. Christmas lights were so plentiful here that they delighted Allie. After a high-speed drive along a major artery, she wondered when Hale would turn them again. It couldn't be too much longer.

But her eyes felt as if they were full of sand. The medium-sized restaurant offered a varied menu, a pleasant change from the hearty fare at truck stops.

"Christmas," she remarked as they passed under eaves twinkling with icicle lights. The windows were decorated with lighted wreaths and the season had been taken inside with lights running around the ceilings and a toy train making endless circles on a shelf on the wall. "I wonder if I'll miss it completely."

As they sat at a table, Hale spoke. "You have a lot of happy attachments to the season?"

"Yes, I do. Memories that are great. Even after I lost my parents, my aunt and Max would put on a special celebration for me."

"Nice."

"What about you?"

He didn't answer. They were served plenty of piping coffee and plates full of steak. Allie had chosen a baked potato and broccoli but Hale had gone with his usual home fries with a nod to green beans.

"Christmas?" she prodded again.

He looked away, out the window. "Too much drinking and fighting."

"That's awful!"

He shrugged one shoulder. "It was what it was. I guess I shouldn't have answered."

Why? Allie wondered. Because it revealed too much? This guy was a clam. But she'd been right when she had sensed darkness in his past. Being right, however, didn't make her feel even a bit better. She backed away from personal questions, knowing his privacy was important to him.

After a delicious meal, Allie took quite a bit of hers in a carryout box. Despite the feast-or-famine nature of this trip, she still hadn't made the switch to feasting at every opportunity.

Nor did they linger long. All too soon they were back in the car. The drive through Bozeman was pretty, however, and full of evidence that it had become a tourist destination. Ski slopes carved their way up the sides of mountains. The central city, however, had maintained some of its Western appeal.

Suddenly, on the far edge of town, Hale pulled into a parking place. "Stay here," he said. "Keep the doors locked. I won't be long."

She didn't bother arguing. Despite her earlier doubts, she didn't doubt him now. He was doing his darndest to keep her away from the pursuers, whoever the hell they were.

He was as good as his word, returning less than ten minutes later with a large puffy plastic case and a smaller bag. Once again he threw everything in the back.

"Next the garage."

He was fast there, too. While she watched through the window in the waiting room, in record time Hale got the car up on the pneumatic lift and tires were being changed out while he watched closely. Then he stepped under the vehicle and scanned the entire bottom.

Allie had thought it wasn't allowed for anyone but a mechanic to be under the car, but he must have sweetened the pot somehow.

Half an hour later they were on the road again. He took them four or five exits beyond the populated areas, steered down a ramp and pulled into a rest area.

"Go use the facilities," he suggested. "I'll keep watch out here."

Damn, the place wasn't heated. Not at all. She could have frozen in there.

But a surprise awaited her back at the car. Hale held something in his hands.

"Climb in, Allie."

She slid into the seat, becoming convinced she was going to get pressure sores from it. Then he astonished her.

He unfolded a large burgundy blanket with a Sherpa knit and spread it over her. Next came a neck pillow.

"Hale…"

"It's the least I can do. Get comfy if you can."

It was a whole lot easier now. She settled into warmth and the neck pillow was just right for her.

"Heaven," she said.

"Good."

"What did you mean when you said we're heading for the middle of nowhere?"

"Wyoming cattle country. Almost all of it is grazing land."

She didn't ask why they'd come here if he wanted to go there. She was past that part. In fact, for the first time, she was rooting for this zany drive to continue. That man beside her had piqued her interest. "You didn't find anything more under the car?"

"Not even inside the tires or the rims."

She digested that. "You bought four new tires because of that?"

"Believe it. Although I guess they're *your* tires."

It was only the second time since they'd left that he'd alluded to the fact that this was all on her dime. Even his new tires.

"What are you going to do with them?" she asked wryly. "Try to put them on *my* car? I don't think they'll fit."

"Knock it off my retainer."

Her jaw dropped a bit. Man oh man, had she just insulted him? But she'd agreed to pay all the expenses on this junket and if he felt new tires would help ensure their safety, she wasn't going to cavil.

"Hale, I was just joking."

He didn't answer. Great, she thought. Just great. The stone face was back and not a thing she could do about it.

She scrunched down farther in the soft, warm blanket and finally found a dose of the sleep she'd been needing for a while.

She awoke again when she heard gravel beneath the tires. Night had rejoined them, but so had the twinkly lights of a…what? It didn't look like the usual truck stop. Outside the parking lot was plastered mostly with pickup trucks.

"Where are we?" she asked sleepily.

"A roadhouse. And trust me, you don't want to go in there. Stay snuggled under your blanket while I get some food."

"But the steak I saved."

"That's safely flash-frozen somewhere in the back. Keep the doors locked."

The locks *thunked* as he walked away. Even through closed windows she could hear loud country music wailing, and a few of the men smoking on the porch didn't look any too steady. She felt around with her hand and found that crushed hat Hale had given her back in, well, whatever place. She crammed it on her head and pulled it down. As unnoticeable as she could make herself.

The seedier side of the world, although in fairness this was just a bunch of guys out for a good time.

Fifteen minutes later, Hale returned with a couple of handled paper bags. He unlocked the car, climbed in and put the bags behind his seat before taking to the road again.

He spoke. "Fried chicken. Potato salad. Burgers that *have* to be better than any drive-through."

"Any vegetables?"

"Radishes. They go well with beer, I hear. I hope you like them."

"I love them. One year when my mother was planting a garden she said she'd plant any vegetable I wanted. When I asked for radishes, I think she believed I'd lost my mind. But I ate them. Maybe most of them."

He chuckled quietly. "We'll pull over soon so we can eat before everything grows icicles."

"Where are we, Hale? It seems stupid to keep me in the dark now."

"Wyoming mountains. When I find a place for us to sleep, I'll dig out the atlas and show you."

"Thanks for telling me at least what state I'm in. You want to talk about disorientation? I've always liked to know where I am in relation to what. My place on the map."

"I'm not much different. I should have thought about you."

Well, that was a significant admission from him. "This is all so James Bond."

"Hardly," he said drily. "I don't have those fancy cars that can turn into boats and all that."

"True. But it seems we have our own Mr. Big."

"No kidding."

He took a sharp turn onto a dirt road.

"Um…" she began as the trees closed in around them.

"I know where this comes out. Relax."

What choice did she have?

However, it wasn't long before he pulled over and grabbed the bags from the back seat. "A feast," he said. "Sorta."

She was happy to tuck in. All this cold seemed to be making her hungrier, and the fried chicken was some of the best she'd ever eaten. The potato salad, which she ate with a spork, was pretty good, too. And the radishes were crunchy fresh.

They drank bottles of water and for a long time there was no sound except rustling paper, eating and drinking.

"Who invented the spork?" she asked.

"A mad scientist who probably wanted to save plastic."

That pulled a giggle out of her. "Plastics should have gone extinct by now."

"The world would be a happier place if they did. But imagine putting them in zoos to save them."

A real laugh escaped her then. "What an image."

Hale liked hearing her laugh. Maybe she was coming out of despair and her fury with him.

He still had something to figure out, though. What would their pursuers do now?

BUT STU SEEMED to have a pretty good idea where some of them were. At one point or another, his men, according to their training, had placed at least one transmitter on the security guys or Stu wouldn't have been able to tell Hale they were on his tail. Nothing, however, had been said about the whereabouts of the assassin.

Maybe, like Hale, his guys figured the pro was following the security men. Or waiting for them to settle around a particular area. No reason for the killer to follow them all over the place. Waste of his very expensive time.

None of this made Hale happy.

Yeah, surprise.

He'd thought his web of contacts would be able to trace at least one of the security people to a point where he could make Allie safe enough to go after the guy. To question him. To find out something useful against Ellis.

Instead he was going to be facing a pro, much more dangerous to Allie, and a whole lot harder to find.

But Hale *had* to find him. Pros took one shot. If it didn't succeed, they faded away. Until they found another chance.

Stopping that was more important than getting the security men. He'd have other opportunities to get at them. Not so the assassin. One chance, that's all Hale would get.

Unless he wanted to keep Allie on the run for the rest of her life.

Another day. Another six or seven hundred miles. At this rate they were going to run out of Wyoming. He'd replaced the plates again, this time leaving the most recent ones on the truck he'd vandalized.

No trail. Maybe he was getting too good at it this time. Maybe they'd get so far from their pursuers that they could be forgotten for a while. But that wouldn't allow Allie to return to her old life.

Worse, finding that burst transmitter at the lodge last night had made his gut twist. All the running around and zigzagging had been confusing but perhaps ultimately useless.

Eluding the security men for a while had seemed wise.

The pro changed all of that. This was no longer about a man or two trying to kidnap Allie at a convenient time and bring her under Ellis's control. Not any longer.

He might never see one of those security men now. He might never know when someone came close enough to tip off the pro unless his guys were successfully tracking them.

That night he found an oddly pink motel back off the road, under the shadows of the trees. He installed Allie in the room he rented, then told her to stay locked inside.

She threw a nightshirt at him but didn't complain. Probably too tired to argue right now. He figured he'd be glad when she grew stubborn again. Part of the real Allie.

Hale was starting to feel exhausted, too. He hadn't been able to catch naps while he was driving, unlike Allie.

Instead he gnawed his insides trying to find a way out of this damn conundrum. On the one hand, he might have done this too well. On the other, he'd screwed up.

But it all came down to making Allie safe for the rest of her life.

He paced around outside for a while, filling his lungs with sharply cold air. This motel wasn't brightly lighted, and it boasted no Christmas decorations at all. Hanging on by a slim thread, he thought.

Finally, much as he didn't want to, he got a fresh cell and walked to a clearing where the starry sky was visible. Maybe he'd get a signal. Or not. This motel at least had an ancient satellite dish, so some kind of signal had to get through.

Much to his amazement, after walking around the clearing for a bit, he found a strong enough signal. There must be a tower out there somewhere.

Stu answered on the second ring. Not much coded language this time. He simply asked, "What's up?"

"You know where those sous chefs are?"

"Believe it. I've got D and J watching close. Listen, did something happen last night? The wind-up dolls are walking in circles."

"Yeah, I found their remote control."

"Hell, man." Stu fell silent. "You ditched it?"

"Of course." Although not exactly, but no need to reveal that.

"Frick. Sounds like the Keystone Kops."

"I'm not laughing. Keep D and J on it. Knowing where the dolls are…"

"You're right. Well, they started to walk straighter after a couple of hours. Something or someone started to put them in a row. Should we watch out for stairs?"

"Maybe not yet."

Hale rolled back on his heels, staring up at a sky so full of stars that it looked like twinkling diamonds scattered on black velvet.

"Down then sideways," Hale said after a moment. "Not over the edge yet."

"Why?"

"You'll figure it out."

Then Hale stripped the phone and trashed it. The dolls had started to follow a straight line? He wanted to smash more than that phone.

There was a leak, and he didn't know how to plug it. Hell, it might even be an innocent leak.

But it was dangerous regardless.

ALLIE WOKE TO sunshine in the morning. After all these days with Hale she'd grown accustomed to waking in the dark. Sunlight?

She sat bolt upright and saw him sitting in the room's one rickety chair. "What's wrong?"

"We both needed sleep." He rose and stretched. "Take your shower. I'll be waiting outside when you're ready."

As he stood, she smelled the scents of soap and shampoo. Evidently he'd already showered. How had she slept through that?

Napping in the car wasn't enough, she guessed. A long stretch felt good to her, too, as did a nice hot shower. This place might look like a fleabag, but it got a few things right.

Outside, she found Hale pacing. Again she had the feeling that something was wrong but didn't bother to ask. If she'd learned one thing about Hale it was that he wouldn't tell her anything he didn't want to.

After he collected all their bags from the motel room and dropped off the key, he joined her in the car and opened an atlas.

"Wyoming," he said. "Here."

He stabbed at the map with one finger, but at least it gave her a decent idea of their location. The mountains of western Wyoming, slightly to the south of Yellowstone Park.

"I always wanted to go to Yellowstone," she remarked.

"Maybe once we get this sorted out."

Then he tucked the map beneath his seat and they drove away from the pink motel.

ANOTHER SMALL TOWN, this one boasting Christmas ornaments hanging on their few lamp poles. Wreaths in most storefronts. Somehow the attempt seemed half-hearted.

"Christmas," she said again.

"What's with you and Christmas?"

"It's a beautiful time of year. Lots of good memories. I like gathering with my friends, I like the songs and music. There's magic in the air. I hope I don't have to miss it."

Again, no answer. Then she remembered. "Sorry, I guess you have plenty of reason not to feel the same."

After a bit, he said levelly, "Christmas at my house was a war zone. Christmas was when my mother died."

Allie's heart lurched and pain tightened around her chest. "I'm sorry," she murmured thickly.

"Not your fault. Forget I said it."

Forget he said it? Not likely. The picture he'd just painted was heart-wrenching. Wisely, she didn't attempt to say any more.

But now she had plenty to think about. His Christmases had been laced with violence and fighting? His mother had died at Christmas? She felt there was more to the story than he'd ever tell her, but the images of what he had just revealed to her stuck like thistles.

Of course he didn't feel the magic of the holiday season. How could he? Maybe he even hated it. At best he had to be indifferent.

There was no way to change that. Nothing she could say. But one nugget of determination grew in her. There was no way he was going to deprive her of the holiday if there was something she could say about it. Anything she could do.

Because just as he deserved to keep his own attitude, she deserved not to have her own feelings smashed. She had enough smashed already.

Besides, she was so sick of feeling like his duffel bag.

Grimly closing her eyes, she stopped thinking about their pursuers and tried to envision a Currier and Ives Christmas. Something snowy and beautiful and filled with people she liked. A toast of eggnog or mulled cider. Laughter, smiles. Singing whatever carol she chose.

The funny thing about growing up in Southern California was that her only snowy Christmases had been on postcards. But she wanted one anyway. To stand and look up into a dark sky and watch snowflakes fall gently. To feel that added magic surround her. She had long promised herself that she was going to take a trip one year just for the experience.

Now here she was with snow beginning to accumulate around her and sitting with the original Grinch.

At home, her friends would already be planning. Stringing lights and garlands from their balcony rails. JayZee would have put up her artificial tree. She was always the earliest among them. Maybe she was holding her decorating party soon.

The others would be pulling their trees out of storage, some of them predecorated and lighted. Only Kay insisted on a real tree, clinging to it despite the fire hazard because she loved the pine scent that filled her apartment. Allie admitted that she did, too.

Then, of course, all of them would have to help her get rid of the huge tree. Kay couldn't bear having it up after the new year. That was another fun time. After an evening of celebrating the brand-new year, they'd all stand around looking at Kay's tree, their heads aching, and promising they'd get rid of it in a day or two. Not that Kay wanted it gone on New Year's Day, but with hangovers they had a whole lot of fun indulging in a bit of self-pity plus a whole lot of careful laughter.

Boy, she was getting homesick.

She also resolved not to make a deal about Christmas again. Not when the holiday seemed to have so many bad memories for Hale. Keep his mouth shut or else? His mother had died on Christmas Day?

More than bad enough for anyone. She needed to stop pricking him with her desire to have Christmas. Resolved, she kept her mouth shut as they passed through the occasional small town twinkling with lights as if it promised a wonderful day.

When she *did* speak, it was about their current difficulties. "How are you going to find these guys if they can't track us? You got rid of the transmitter, right?"

"I disabled it in case I need it. But otherwise, I'll know where they are, how close they're coming."

Interesting. "Your friends?"

"Yes."

"But how come you don't have *them* take care of this?"

Once again he remained silent, leaving her to wonder.

BUT HALE KNEW. He just didn't want *her* to know. The only way he could get this assassin off her tail would be to take him out. Permanently. Bringing in his team would only make matters worse.

He knew the type who took jobs like this. Knew that in order to keep getting hired they had to complete every assignment they took, no matter what was required.

He also knew there'd be no way to get information out of the pro. Zip. If the assassin revealed even a single bit of information, then he'd be on another assassin's target list.

It was a hell of an occupation to get into. It also required a soulless killer. Far worse than a sniper in battle who at least had a reason other than money and the thrill of a kill.

He remembered one aging SEAL he'd known, a sniper who'd been active in Vietnam. He'd talked about a great many things that he'd never forgotten, but one was branded in his brain and haunted him constantly. The time the man had taken out a Vietcong general as he sat on a porch with his family.

Some things could never be forgotten, not if you had a soul, a heart, a conscience. The type who was after Allie possessed none of that. Being able to take out a target at a kilometer was the least of it.

Hale also hoped the guy didn't have a spotter to aid his calculations on the shot, which would limit his target range. Or that he couldn't get a clear line of sight, which would force him in closer.

A lot to hope for, although the use of a spotter was highly unlikely. These assassins worked alone, counting on experience, without help with important matters, such as wind drift, air temperature and density, even the movement of the earth over a sufficient distance. Or the movement of the target. No decent sniper fired in a straight line.

So the pro would have to come in reasonably close, which made him a much easier target for Hale. Still, even with a hunting rifle, a sniper could be deadly over two hundred yards.

Nor would there be a red dot on the target the way the movies showed. Laser sights were useless except at very close range, such as with a pistol.

Even so, the red dot, despite movies, wouldn't give the target time to move out of the way. A bullet came fast enough that dodging to one side, or even falling to the knees, wouldn't be fast enough. By the time the dot was sighted, it would be too late. A bullet would already be on its way at supersonic speed.

Hell's bells. Thinking all this over wasn't making Hale feel any better.

Yeah, the sniper would have constraints, but would they be enough?

Hale mulled over the problem as the miles slipped away. He also made a point of avoiding any clear lines of sight. Trees and irregular movements made damn good cover.

Then he noticed that Allie wasn't mentioning Christmas any longer. Damn, had he done that to her?

That ought to remind him to keep his mouth shut.

ALLIE WAS BUSY trying not to think about anything at all. Using every meditative technique she'd ever learned wasn't helping.

Brains just never shut up.

Her thoughts insisted on returning to the friends she missed. To Christmases past. To gifts she had wrapped and that waited in her closet for Christmas Eve. About the gifts she'd bought to donate to children, from the Angel Tree to Toys for Tots.

"Hale," she said, breaking her silence for the first time in hours, "do you know about the Angel Tree?"

"No." No question followed.

She decided to tell him anyway. "The tree is covered with little paper angels. On the back of each is written a gift some child wishes for, along with age and gender."

"Okay."

"Of course, there are the usual. You can't keep a middle schooler from wanting a video game."

Hale snorted. "No kidding."

"But then there are the ones that just break your heart. A four-year-old who wants a jacket. Another little kid who just wants a pair of shoes. Nothing about an expensive athletic shoe, just shoes."

"Hell."

"Yeah. Plenty of kids live in it. Anyway, when I'd come across those I'd put the item in a big holiday bag and then add a large teddy bear, something to make a kid smile."

"Joy."

"I always hoped so." Deciding he wasn't totally opposed to this discussion of the holiday, she continued. "There was a church nearby that had a congregation that was mostly migrants. That was a different kind of shopping expedition. Lots of large bags of rice and beans. Canned goods. School supplies. So much need out there."

He didn't answer immediately. Then he said, "You have a good heart."

"I don't know about that. I'm just *aware*. I've been lucky my entire life. How can I ignore the fact that's not true for everyone?"

"Lots of people seem to get by doing exactly that."

"Unfortunately." She sighed quietly, leaning back onto the neck pillow. "Mostly I just felt I never did enough. Anyway, I have stuff for the Angel Tree and Toys for Tots. I hope one of my friends remembers that and pulls them out of my closet."

"I'm sure they will." So someone else had a key to her apartment? That made him uneasy. Another target for questioning?

God, this black hole just kept getting deeper. He had to finish this soon.

# Chapter Seven

Even for Hale, the days had begun to run together. Endlessly the same.

Until several nights later when he checked in with Stu.

"I don't know what happened, man," Stu said. "But the
dolls seem to have direction. I don't know if they're headed
toward you or what."

Hale felt everything inside him tighten. "Where?" he
asked.

"Better question is how close." Stu waited.

Hale no longer had any intention of sharing his position,
however vaguely. The idea of a traitor among men he had
believed to be his friends was getting stronger. Right then
the feeling was pinging him like a transmitter.

"Stu," he said. Nothing more.

"Yeah. I'm wondering. I'm working on it."

"And the dolls?"

"I heard they were bought by a store near Bozeman."

Hale's stomach knotted so tightly that it felt as if it had
been stabbed. "Not anymore," he said, revealing his concern. "They passed through on their way to another re-
tailer."

Stu swore a long stream. Loudly and vociferously as
only a battle-hardened veteran could do. "I get it. I want

the whole damn collection, and the collector, too. This was supposed to be a present for my godchild."

"Nice to know why they got sold in the first place."

"Can't trust anybody, it seems."

It certainly did. Hale began to run a mental check of his entire network. "I'll think about it."

"You're not the only one."

So the security men had followed them all the way to Bozeman. How? And Stu had no idea where the hit man was. Not yet.

The only way this could get worse would be waking up in the morning with a gun barrel in his face.

Hale dumped another phone on another truck, then took Allie inside for a hot meal. She must be sick of roadside diners and this place claimed to be something more. Breakfast around the clock. Considering the number of vehicles outside, he hoped that was a recommendation.

Inside, the charm oozed but the diners looked happy and chatted like it. He and Allie found their way to a table away from the windows. He might be a fool about his friends, but he wasn't a fool about precautions.

The four-page menu was breakfast end to end. Allie surprised him by ordering pancakes and breakfast sausage. Soon a thermal carafe of coffee sat between them along with bottles of three kinds of syrup.

"Nothing to go with that?" he asked. He expected her to be scouring the pages for veggies of any kind.

"If I'm going to misbehave, I might as well do it up."

For once he smiled. "Enjoy."

"Oh, I intend to."

When the server returned with their order, she added a small cheese-and-potato casserole.

He exceeded her indulgence only by quantity and by the

fact that he preferred ham to breakfast sausage. He also made a private bet with himself that she wouldn't eat half of what she had ordered.

She spoke during their pigout. "I was able to go to college on my dad's insurance. His union helped a bit with it, too. But I felt guilty as sin for doing it."

"I'm sure that's what he hoped you'd do."

"Maybe. But it was like taking blood money."

Oh, for Pete's sake, he thought. Blood money? She didn't understand the term, but he let it slide for now.

"Anyway, despite everything, I enjoyed myself. It was a great time. It was also the first time I realized that my entire future was ahead of me and that I could do anything I chose with it."

"That must have felt heady."

"It did. For a while."

He tilted his head to one side. "But?"

"I made all the usual mistakes. Boyfriends for one. They're a great sidetrack to get on."

"Off the rails?" he asked.

"Easily. I still remember the day I broke up with one of them. I wasn't brokenhearted."

He nodded. "Okay."

"I felt relieved. Totally relieved. As if I were getting my life back."

An interesting reaction, he thought.

"You ever break up with anyone and feel better for it?"

Her question deserved an honest answer, much as he hated revealing himself. He took a moment to eat another mouthful of nicely browned ham before he spoke.

"I think I felt that way most of the time."

Allie raised both brows. "No broken heart?"

"I never let myself get that involved."

ALLIE HAD PLENTY to think about that after they started driving again. Never let himself get that involved?

He was more than a monolith of silence. Apparently he was locked up so deep inside himself that feelings rarely surfaced. What the hell had done that to him?

She expected no answers, not from him. Which gave her reason to speculate. Except that the only thing she really knew about him was that his mother had died on Christmas and that there'd been a lot of fighting. Could that have been enough to shut him down?

Maybe so. Maybe so. But she'd lost both her parents and hadn't closed herself off. She enjoyed all the memories.

Something else was going on.

HALE KEPT WAITING for it. He'd said too much about his relationships with women. She was bound to want to know why. Even he understood that no one would consider it natural. And Allie didn't always hesitate to tread where angels feared to go.

But he hated her questions because they kept drawing bits of himself into the open. Bits he really didn't want to share.

But he couldn't bring himself to lie to her, not directly. Except by omission, because it was necessary, but not to one of her point-blank questions when he couldn't see an honest way around it.

Winter was growing deeper, at least to judge by the amount of snow he was beginning to see alongside the road, from the way snow and ice now blanketed the pavement. Here they were, heading south into what appeared to be the remains of a blizzard.

How very unfortunate. It was slowing him down more than he otherwise would have needed on this curvy road.

But they were making their way through trees, and most roads like this happened for a reason. They tended to be built along tracks that had been used for a long time, not just built for no reason at all. Someone had traveled this way countless times over the years.

Then a house seemed to pop out of nowhere, surrounded by dozens of blue-lighted artificial holiday trees, by clear lights strung around evergreens and along bare branches, by multicolored lights hanging from the edge of the roof. It seemed totally overdecorated for a dwelling so isolated.

Then he glimpsed Allie's face. Her expression had softened, a faint dreamy smile curving her mouth. He slowed down even more, allowing her to drink in the scene. Christmas. She wanted her Christmas.

He could smell a burst of stubbornness coming. The only question was how he would deal with it.

After the house had disappeared into the darkening woods, Allie remarked, "You said you had a wife."

He tried to remember telling her that, then recalled the tossed-off answer to her question. "It was a cover story. You asked how I'd justify buying women's clothes."

"Oh."

Yeah. *Oh.* He'd told her he didn't get involved, so naturally she summoned that from the depths of her memory. And he'd believed that he'd learned to keep his mouth shut. Not tight enough, evidently.

As the darkness deepened even more, he turned them onto an eastbound road. He hoped he'd get a clue from Stu about how closely they were being followed.

Allie spoke again, miles later. "You said your mother died on Christmas."

"So?" He hoped he made the word forbidding enough that she wouldn't pursue the issue.

She either didn't get it or didn't want to get it.

"How did it happen?"

His hands tightened on the steering wheel until they hurt. Then rage hit him and he poured the sewer on her.

"My dad was a drunk. A terrible drunk. He'd beat my mother over nothing. Hell, he beat me, too. We lived in fear, always tiptoeing around. Trying not to get his attention. That didn't work. It didn't help when he'd apologize the next morning. He didn't mean to do it, he said. But he taught me to keep my mouth shut. He didn't want to hear a word from me."

"Oh my God," she murmured.

"A lot of children grow up with that. Nothing unusual." *Let it go, Allie. Just let it go.*

"That doesn't make what you endured any better."

"No." Nothing made it better.

"And your mother?" This time she spoke tentatively.

But he was past caring. Rage still held him in its thrall. He could have told her nothing. He could have refused to answer, but fury pushed him.

"Then, when I was twelve, he beat my mother to death on Christmas Day. I tried to stop him but he hit me so hard I could barely breathe. Then I tried again anyway and he kicked me in the head and broke my jaw. I was afraid he'd kill me. So I didn't move, didn't try again. I cowered in a corner while he beat and kicked my mother to death."

"Oh, Hale…"

"I never saw him again after that. He went to prison. Too late."

"And you?"

"Foster home." He bit off the words and at last she stopped pressing him. Still, she'd brought the memories to the forefront, a place he tried to never let them go. He saw red and probably should have stopped driving. He drove too fast for the road conditions.

Finally he shoved the memories back into the black hole where he tried to keep them. One way or another, they'd played a part in making him the man he was, and that man was trying to save a young woman's life.

This fight had become personal.

ALLIE NOW HAD more to think about than she wanted. A mind filled with images she'd never seen herself, but images she had no trouble filling in.

God, that any kid should be treated that way. That any kid should see his mother beaten to death.

She knew it happened, of course, but she refused to follow such stories in the news. Playing ostrich because it was hard to deal with such things. Because it made her heart hurt.

Now her heart was hurting for the man beside her. Now she knew why he was so silent and she couldn't criticize him for it.

She shouldn't have pressed him like that. She should have practiced some silence herself. But the desire to know Hale better was growing inside her like a force of its own.

As annoyed as she got with him putting her through this endless trip, she didn't hate him. She'd never hated him. He just drove her nuts. Then she'd pierced his brick wall of self-protection. Well, she'd gotten exactly what she deserved, an ugly, angry explanation she'd never be able to erase from her memory. As he probably couldn't.

She wanted to apologize for her trespass but decided that could be dangerous. He'd just remember his father's apologies, apologies that had meant nothing. Apologies that hadn't prevented his mother's death.

She was relieved when he slowed the SUV down. Yeah, she'd been worried about their speed, but not as upset as she was by what he'd revealed. He must be sitting beside her feeling like a raw nerve. Angry with her for pushing him into memory.

Why had he even answered her prying? He could have told hcr it was none of her business. Although she had to admit she probably wouldn't have given up.

People called her stubborn, even Max, but she was more persistent than stubborn. Or so she'd always believed. Persistence had gotten her a long way.

But maybe others were right. Maybe it was cusscdness on her part. Her dad had always said so when faced with it.

What did it matter what she called it? She'd done it, she shouldn't have, and now they both had to live with the results.

It wasn't as if she could change her personality in an instant or two. But maybe that was a lousy excuse. Especially this time.

A while later, she changed tack. "Max is okay, right?"

"Max knows how to take care of himself. Ellis isn't the first bad guy he's had to deal with. He's probably got his whole team on alert."

She hoped so. "I'm worrying more about him than me."

"Ellis makes one wrong move and Max will be all over him like white on rice. Max is just waiting for a chance and Ellis probably knows it. What's more, he doesn't want to stir the hornet's nest that would come from attacking a cop."

"That's a good point." And it was. Several times in her life she'd seen how cops reacted to one of their number being hurt or killed. They wouldn't let go until they had the perp.

"But you and Max said Ellis is too insulated."

"Maybe. But one little mistake…"

He left the statement unfinished. It hung on the air like a threat. Maybe it was.

"You really think you're going to be able to take care of Ellis?"

Hale's response was flat and cold. "Or die trying."

Allie subsided, thinking about the man who was escorting her to safety. She hadn't been wrong when she had decided he was dangerous.

HALE STARTED TO feel awful about dumping on Allie. All his life he'd remained silent about what he'd seen. Even when social services insisted he see a counselor, even though his foster family had tried to get him to open up, he'd never said a word. Not once. Not even when it might have helped.

Instead he'd focused on a career that would force him to face down fear, that would make him physically strong enough to deal with men like his father.

A job that would forever prevent him from cowering in a corner.

At twelve there hadn't been much he could have done to save his mother. They didn't even have a phone so he could call for help. Not that he could have talked after his jaw was broken.

But that wasn't what truly troubled him. He'd hated himself for that cowardice. Even if he couldn't take on the beast who had sired him, it was the cowardice that stuck with him.

The Marines had taught him something useful, however. Everyone felt fear. If you didn't feel fear there was something wrong with you. But you had to face the fear. That was the birth of all bravery. Facing the fear and not giving in to it.

The man he was today never would have let that bastard beat his mother. He wouldn't have been afraid to open his mouth. He wouldn't have lived in terror or allowed his mother to.

No, he'd have decked that SOB as many times as were necessary to drive him from the house. His father would have been the one cowering.

But he still hated that twelve-year-old. He still felt guilty. He couldn't even find forgiveness in his heart for that kid. The boy had failed miserably. Seriously. Horribly.

He'd transformed himself. He worked now to save people. Maybe that helped make up for some of his past. He didn't know. He could only hope.

Hope was a slender thread.

# Chapter Eight

As the middle of the night arrived, while he kept an eye out for a motel, Hale became acutely aware that Allie hadn't spoken in hours.

Huddled in the corner of the passenger seat, she was silent. And he didn't think she was sleeping.

He cleared his throat. Something needed saying. Instead of remaining comfortable in his silence, as he usually did, he began to feel badly.

"I shouldn't have dumped on you."

She stirred at last. "I'm glad you did."

Glad? *Glad?* She was losing her mind, hardly surprising after this journey he'd kept her on. But having been followed at least to Bozeman, he no longer felt even moderately safe only because he believed there was no longer a transmitter on the car.

Not even keeping mostly to roads with tree cover, or roads surrounded by mountains, felt like enough to make Allie safe.

Damn, he had to nail this Ellis guy. Put a stop to his killings. Put a stop to *him.*

He spoke again. "Men like Ellis."

When he didn't continue, she prompted him. That was Allie, never let it go.

"Men like Ellis," he continued. "They shouldn't be able

to sit safely atop their billions twisting the law with their batteries of lawyers. Things that would get an ordinary man convicted of felonies, of frauds, maybe of murder, skate by without a worry."

"I can't disagree with that. But I never saw him that way."

"Almost nobody does. But you remember that kid who couldn't save his mother? Too afraid? Well, Ellis has that kind of grip on too many people in his organization. When he needs to warn them, he does. All without it tracing back to him."

"God, you make him sound like one of those villains on TV or in the movies."

"Yup. And he is. He's not the only one, either. The world is full of men with his resources who never face any real legal threat. Or consequences."

Which left her chewing on thoughts that had nothing to do with his past. That was fine with him, because he didn't want to face any more questions about his childhood. More cowardice? Maybe, but this time he didn't care.

As they reached a large clearing, the moon emerged in a clear-as-crystal sky. Full now, it cast its silvery light on the world below, creating a snow glow that was brighter than the moon itself.

Then he spied a turnout that he suspected had been dug by a plow changing direction. He pulled over, thinking Allie would at least get a chance to stretch. He needed one himself and, cold or not, it would make them both feel better.

"Let's take a breather," he said as he switched off the ignition.

She nearly leaped at the opportunity. She was out of the car before he could come around the front to her side. Her head tipped back as she looked up at the full moon, as she inhaled deep breaths and blew large clouds on each exhalation.

"Take it easy on those deep breaths," he said. "They'll chill you much faster."

She surprised him with a laugh, then spun around with her arms extended. "We should stay here tonight."

"Well, if we had polar sleeping bags, and a tent..."

She laughed again. "I know. We'd be frozen peepsicles before long."

He couldn't resist and laughed with her.

"It's still a lovely thought," she added, lowering her arms and looking around. "Much better than those motel rooms. Are you picking the worst ones or what?"

"Very downscale," he admitted. "People coming through those places are nearly invisible. You'd be surprised how rarely they want me to register."

"Maybe I wouldn't be. As near as I can tell, you have the corner on being covert."

He wished he had, but he didn't disagree. "I think it helps that I pay in cash. I suspect it doesn't get reported as income."

She paused, then said, "I guess a lot of those places are barely hanging on. I wouldn't blame them."

She turned more slowly this time, taking in the entire clearing, the snow-laden branches of the evergreens that encircled it. "It's perfect," she breathed. "Just perfect."

He spied a game trail just beyond the snow that had been mounded by the plow. He pointed it out.

"Do you see it? The game trail?"

She moved forward a little. "Oh, yes! What do you think comes through there? And why? For what?"

"Food mostly, whether they're browsers or carnivores. Maybe there's a water source that hasn't frozen over yet, although I imagine the larger animals, like elk, could break it open, helping out everyone else."

"I like that idea." A smile filled her face, and Hale thought the sight of Allie enjoying something could become addictive. She asked, "Bears are hibernating right now?"

"Sort of."

"What's that mean?"

"They come out of their dens every so often to browse."

"I never knew that!"

Another wave of delight filled her face. "But I bet life is tough right now for most animals."

"Except beavers."

She faced him, her expression disbelieving. "In frozen streams and ponds? How could they be better off?"

"Beavers are the original good neighbors. They spend all their time until winter building their dams and filling them with food. Planning ahead. But then, this will amaze you, other little animals find their ways in. And the beavers let them stay all winter and eat from the food supply."

"Wow." She drew another deep breath of the fresh air. "Imagine if we were all like that. Think we'll see any animals come along here?"

He smiled faintly. "Not likely. They'd want to avoid us. Anyway, the full moon messes up their rhythms."

"How'd you come to learn so much about this?"

"It interests me. I don't spend *all* my time dragging young women all over the place."

"From nowhere to the middle of nowhere."

Hale gestured to the surrounding area. "The middle of nowhere can be a wonderful place."

It wasn't long before he urged her back into the car. He

saw the small shivers she was trying to repress. Time to warm her up.

He was damn glad he'd been able to share those minutes with her.

ALLIE TOOK A while to warm up, even wrapped in the blanket Hale had given her, remembering the clearing with a sense of magic.

She dozed fitfully until the sun rose well in the sky. She stirred, clearing her throat, reaching for one of the bottles of water Hale kept stashed behind the passenger seat. After she downed a half bottle, she asked, "Where was our motel? Did I sleep through it?"

"Time to alter the routine. We'll stop soon and spend a day sleeping instead of a night."

"I can probably do that." She tried and failed to stifle a yawn.

"I'm sure we both can. I'll try to find a place where you can walk around."

"I'd love that. But why always these out-of-the-way places? I mean, there's rarely a town around."

"The more places you're seen, the easier…"

"To identify me from a photo. I remember. But I don't look much like my old self, starting with my hair. You know, I still resent that. My hair was my best feature."

"If you believe that, then you need a new mirror."

She supposed that was meant as a compliment, although given her experience of Hale, she wondered if there were other ways it could be taken. He didn't at all seem like a man who paid compliments. In fact, given that he hardly talked, he probably wouldn't know how to summon one.

With her head turned sideways on her neck pillow, she studied him, wishing he'd get rid of that beard, which was getting too long for her taste. Too long period. He was well on his way to resembling one of those scruffy reality TV stars.

On the other hand. Yeah, on the other hand. Chiseled cheeks, a strong forehead, a thick hairline. When her attention was drawn to his mouth, *she* was drawn to some pretty hot thoughts.

And that body. One glimpse of him wrapped in a towel had remained engraved on her brain. She didn't have to wonder what was under that green jacket or those jeans. Or even under the flannel shirts he usually wore.

Sighing, she turned her head back to look out the window. He might be eye candy, but he was dangerous in so many ways. Trying to get close to him would probably singe off her wings.

Midmorning, just about the time Allie thought she'd throw a hissy if she couldn't escape this car, Hale apparently saw a so-called motel that appealed to him.

Just as he was getting out of the car to get the room, she said, "I should warn you now. If there's anything crawling in that room, I'm going to throw a fit."

"I wouldn't blame you."

"I'm serious, Hale. I don't want to stay here." She felt her chin stick out stubbornly. Naturally, he just ignored her protest.

He'd probably spent some time on the ground with many things that crawled, given his Marine background. She doubted he'd shrink from a roach.

But *she* would. "I've stayed in better places that had a critter problem."

"What made you bring this up? You've never said anything like this before."

She cocked an eye at the building. "There's something about this place."

"At least it's not the Bates Motel."

Which was probably intended to make her laugh, but it failed. She didn't need a Norman Bates to make her scream in the shower.

No, creepy-crawlies could bring her to her knees. She'd once hired an exterminator to take care of one spider. Well, spiders could have more than two hundred babies at a time. She felt as if the insides of her walls were crawling just from seeing that one ugly thing. A *furry* one, for heaven's sake.

The exterminator had agreed with her, probably justifying his charge, but nothing could stir her from her conviction. And nothing could make her comfortable with parts of the insect universe.

But why this motel was the first to give her the willies she didn't know. She hadn't *liked* most of them, but she hadn't thought about bugs.

Maybe this constant flight was driving her mad. For real. But there didn't seem to be a way out of it, not when Max had said she should run, not when Hale kept following his crazy path and talking about pursuers being too close.

Most especially when he'd found a transmitter on the car.

It was still hard to believe anyone wanted her that badly. Hard to believe the error she'd found in Ellis's books couldn't just be fixed by auditors. Just something out of balance. Just a few payouts overlooked. Dealing with a business so complex, things happened.

It should have ended there. She'd reported it, he could fix it. But evidently no one thought Ellis would be content with that.

She must have found the tip of an iceberg of some kind. Or the loose thread on a sweater that should never be pulled.

She might feel a bit better about all of this mess if she had at least known how she'd set it in motion.

She saw Hale come out of the office, but instead of heading directly to the car, he let himself into one of the rooms. He'd never done that before. Did he feel like he might have met Norman Bates after all?

Growing increasingly edgy, she waited for ten minutes until he returned. He knocked on her window and she rolled it down, feeling the blast of frigid air.

"All inspected, Allie. No bugs."

"Thank you," she answered with as much dignity as she could muster, given that she now felt incredibly embarrassed.

"It's okay," he said with a gentleness that totally amazed her. She'd never heard anything approaching that tone from him.

"I shouldn't have made such a big deal out of it." Although her feeling had been strong.

"I said it's okay." He leaned in a little. "People have phobias. They're not a choice. Anyway, I don't think either of us wants to spend all day trying to desensitize you."

"No," she admitted, horrified by the thought.

"It wouldn't work anyway."

Which left her wondering just what he meant. She seemed to do a lot of that with Hale.

But that gentleness in his voice... Dang, she couldn't let that tug at her battered feelings. She couldn't allow herself to be attracted to him. She tried to tell herself that she didn't even like him.

Besides, he worked for her. She didn't want to be guilty of sexual harassment, even inadvertently.

Or did she?

The question brought a small smile to her lips as she trudged her way across snow behind Hale, who carried their duffels.

HALE WONDERED IF Allie had the least idea how she revved his motor as she exercised on the dubious floor. He'd spread out towels for her to keep her from feeling icky, then went to the office and got another stack for their showers.

So he got the full view of her bottom cased in the softer pants he'd bought for her. The sight made him pause on the threshold, then he quickly corralled himself.

Nope, absolutely not. His desires right then hardly qualified as protection. The more so since she was in his charge.

But he enjoyed a savory moment of self-indulgence.

Ah, well. He eased around her and stacked the towels on the bathroom sink. He felt no desire to fuss with hanging them on the rack.

Then he went to the little sink in the bedroom to take advantage of the small coffee maker and one of the two packets of some kind of cheap coffee. At least it smelled good while it brewed.

"Want some?" he asked when she finished her workout. "Or will it keep you awake?"

"It would take a nuclear explosion to keep me awake," she retorted. "Oh, wait, that would only be for a split second."

"Coffee?" he repeated as he smothered a grin.

"Please. After my shower."

When she sat on the edge of the single bed with her hair wrapped in a towel, he brought her coffee.

"They always say those things make four cups," he remarked.

"And it's never more than two."

He took the one creaky chair near the window. "I'm going to make a call in a little while."

"Okay. Getting more information?"

"I hope something useful." If those guys had gotten any

closer, he wanted to know how they'd managed. "Soon I might make use of that last transmitter I found."

She turned a bit on the bed so she could look at him more directly. "What will that do?"

"It'll send some bursts headed a long way from us."

She nodded approvingly. "Good idea. But don't we have to let them get close?"

He didn't want to go there because he could imagine all the ideas she'd throw up at him, every one of which would put her in danger. Then she'd give him hell when he wouldn't cooperate.

"Not yet," he said. "Not until I'm ready."

"When's that going to be? The twelfth of never?"

He didn't respond. What was the point? He had to be sure one of the security guys was close enough that the pro would probably be nearby. He needed to find out when the hunters tapered off to just one or two in the same area. For that he needed Stu.

This situation was beginning to frustrate him beyond belief. He'd had good reasons for taking Allie on the run, but the determined tracking, the hiring of a hit man, more than concerned him.

He'd cherished the faint hope that Ellis would give up when he couldn't find her. That he'd give up when he realized she'd gone too far away to make trouble for him. That all this skipping around would make the task look damn near impossible.

All he'd wanted was to get his hands on one of the security men to interrogate him. The hit man brought everything to a new level.

A much more dangerous level. Even if the security men gave up, the pro wouldn't. Not ever. So the assassin needed the goons Ellis had sent as bloodhounds, because there was no way the hit man would waste his time without leads.

Someone had to be guiding them toward Allie. The question plaguing him was who or what. The growing worry was that he might not know in time that trouble was on them.

He began to consider ways to make Allie safe while he went on a hunt of his own.

Maybe that illegal ID wasn't such a bad idea after all. She needed to be able to rebuild her life, and she wasn't going to do it at home unless he totally demolished the threat.

Allie would lose too much, beginning with her friends. Like going into witness protection, she'd have to cut all ties with everyone and everything in her past.

He couldn't stand the thought of doing that to her. He wouldn't wish that on anyone, except possibly a hardened criminal.

"Heard a funny true story," he said in answer to a silence from her that was beginning to be weighted with despair or anger.

"Yeah?" she asked quietly.

"Yeah. Big-time criminal squealed on the mob. He was put into witness protection but it seemed he couldn't mend his ways. In a new town, a new city, he started running scams."

Now she sounded interested. "Some nerve."

"That's what the local police thought. Five times they arrested him, and five times the Marshals stepped in, demanding the charges be dropped because they'd reveal the guy's identity and he'd be at risk for his life."

"Tell me they got rid of him!"

"Sure did. The fifth time the cops arrested him, they ignored the Marshals' pleas. They not only charged him but shared his identity, old and new, with a reporter. The local paper couldn't resist a scoop like that."

"I should hope not."

He was relieved to see that she was smiling again. "Anyway, the Marshals had to scoop the guy up and move him. And thus the cops cleared the idiot from their town and all local areas."

"That must have been a relief."

"I bet it was. Enough that the chief did an interview with the paper, telling them about all the times the Marshals stepped in."

"Does anyone deserve that much protection?" She shook her head.

"Some do." Then he rose. "I'm going to make that call now."

She shook her head again. "At least this time tell me something about it. I hate living in the dark."

"I'll do what I can." But he wasn't going to promise anything. He knew better than that. Allie would never let him off the hook.

Her stubbornness was returning, too. Of course it was. She was beginning to find her stability in this new way of living.

Trouble was brewing from more than one direction.

STU ANSWERED ON the second ring. Hale came right to the point.

"News?"

"Headed south on Ninety-Five."

Everything in Hale tensed into steel. "Why?" he demanded.

"When did I become a mind reader? This a problem?"

But Hale refused to reveal his whereabouts or that the goons seemed to be following a parallel path. Someone knew too much and he didn't know who. "Odd way for them to turn," he said instead.

"Been thinking about that," Stu replied. "I think the big-city route is being followed. Next is Cheyenne. Unlikely to think you headed east into the Badlands, or something."

So Stu was giving thought to Hale's whereabouts, too. Uneasiness pricked Hale. Stu couldn't be the traitor. Not Stu. For God's sake, he'd saved the man's life.

But there were other guys working this job. Other guys who might have found an incentive to provide info to Ellis's cronies. Other men he'd trusted but who might be thinking hard about where Allie was.

"Cheyenne isn't that big a city," he remarked, then waited for the answer.

"Isn't it the capital?"

"I'm not sure." Providing no real information. "Not that there are a whole lot of people in that general area." For a fact, Wyoming was a huge state, land-wise, but populated by around six hundred thousand people. It made sticking to the boonies so much easier. "Anyway, there are fewer in the Badlands." Stick that in your craw, Stu.

"I would have thought you'd be looking for a busy place by now."

Seeking information. Hale ground his teeth. Not Stu. "How many are you still tracking?"

"Two."

Which meant either that Hale's network had lost the trail of the rest, or that Ellis had called them back as extraneous. Now, why would Ellis think that?

It felt odd to be talking to Stu in the light of day. "I've been on too long," he said, then disconnected. This time he put the phone, battery removed, in his lock box. No poor person was going to carry it all over the hinterlands. Not this time. Something had to be pinging them, and he was beginning to distrust his phones, despite all the precautions he'd taken.

"Well, hell," he announced to the universe. "Just damn it all to hell."

He looked up into the blue overhead, wondering about eyes in the sky. Could Ellis actually be following them by satellite? But if he was, wouldn't his henchmen be closer to Hale and Allie than they were? Or maybe he kept losing track of them because of Hale routing them through trees.

Could the guy actually get that much time on a satellite? Pay for it, yes, but get the time?

Maybe he needed to find an out-of-sight place to spray-paint his vehicle.

Or maybe his skills weren't as sharp as he'd thought.

When he reentered the room, Hale felt like his hands were going to fall off. He should have worn his gloves.

Allie slept soundly in the bed, so he settled quietly on the floor to sleep.

Except that he couldn't. He closed his eyes, but his mind was in hyperdrive, buzzing like angry bees, wondering how best to guard against this new threat, whatever it was. Maybe traveling at night would be best now. Finding a place to go to ground in the daylight.

Unless, of course, Ellis was getting infrared images as well from that possible satellite. Hale's car's engine would show up like a beacon any hour of the day or night.

What if he hadn't been as canny with those phones as he thought? He'd learned the methods from an electronics security expert, but that didn't mean he'd learned everything. Or that phones hadn't somehow changed. Or that algorithms for pinging them hadn't changed.

He rolled on his side, ignoring the concrete under-flooring and the pressure it put on his shoulder. Light still streamed between the curtains, allowing him to see the puffy bundle that Allie had become.

She needed her rest. She needed to be comfortable. She

needed a whole bunch of things he couldn't provide on this road trip from hell.

So far he'd evaded their pursuers, but now they were getting closer. Allie was right, that day needed to come so he could deal with it and set her free.

But she couldn't be in the middle of it. Absolutely not. He'd have to stash her safely somehow. Out here, places to stash her weren't thick on the ground.

He closed his eyes, telling himself to catch a nap. As a soldier he'd learned to sleep whenever and wherever he could.

That was another skill that seemed to be eluding him.

# Chapter Nine

Hale lugged them out of the motel just after twilight. Allie still seemed groggy after her long sleep.

"Food next," he said.

"Yeah, this place is just brimming with restaurants."

Well, she hadn't lost her bite, groggy or not. Once again he smothered a smile. This woman was getting under his skin and he enjoyed her bursts of attitude.

Much more entertaining than most of the people he'd protected. But... She had stopped mentioning Christmas, and he was sure that was his fault. He should never have let the dam break and spill *his* Christmas story.

Well, it was done. He couldn't take it back now.

"I'm sorry I can't take you to better restaurants."

"Oh, for heaven's sake, Hale. We're on the run. I don't have to like it."

"True," he agreed. "One more greasy spoon coming up."

She snorted. Had that sound just escaped her ladylike mouth? "Did you learn anything last night?"

Back to his phone call. What should he tell her and how much? He had to keep her on this road trip, but he didn't want her threatening to stand her ground. That would be one headache too much.

"Well," he said carefully, "they're moving south from Bozeman. Maybe on the way to Cheyenne."

She said nothing for a few beats, then asked, "Are we headed that way?"

"At the moment we're heading west. All good so far."

"But they have to come closer, don't they? You've got to catch them, right?"

Back to this again. His answer was blunt. "Not until I'm ready to stop them."

"Oh, for..." She stopped. "How the heck will you know?"

"I just will. Trust my battle sense."

"I've been trusting you a whole hell of a lot."

"I know you have." *Let it lie, Allie. Just leave it.*

But she didn't. Naturally. "How do they even know what state we're in?"

"I'm working on that. In the meantime, I planted a false clue. We'll see if they react accordingly."

"And somehow that's supposed to get us free of them?"

"Not exactly." But it would sure give him some idea of how they were being tracked. Whether someone in his intelligence network had sold them out. The very thought made his gut twist.

"Seriously, Hale, why not just bring them in right now?"

"Because I choose my own place and time." His tone foreclosed further discussion, and he guessed she heard it.

Funny how her silence could be louder than her words. If she hadn't already, she was going to drive some guy nuts. He wouldn't mind watching.

Then she punctured the ice. "Am I a pain, Hale?"

"Only when you choose to be."

"Such a diplomatic answer," she retorted tartly. "Probably as close to the truth as you get."

"I never lie."

"Only by omission. And there are plenty of those."

He couldn't deny it. He was glad to see a diner ahead.

Stuck out in the middle of nowhere, probably supported by ranchers and hired hands who didn't have the time or the money to head for bright city lights.

The parking lot was only half-plowed, the rest fairly mashed by tires. There was hardly anyone in the lot, however. He'd have preferred the place to be busy, providing more cover. On the other hand, in places like this people tended to be tight-lipped with outsiders.

Inside, the establishment boasted age-roughened plank floors, wood walls covered with beer signs and photos that seemed to be of rodeo stars. The country music that played was of an earlier generation.

The menu was a big painted sign over the lunch counter. Despite the neon beer signs, there was no bar. If you wanted a drink, it had to be beer.

Allie looked around, then moved to a table away from the window.

"You want something to drink? I'd be surprised if there isn't coffee."

"Just water, please."

He went to the counter and got himself a coffee and her glass of water. None of the bottled stuff here.

"Have you had a chance to scan the menu?" he asked.

"Such as it is. Not yet."

He couldn't blame her. There wasn't a whole lot to choose from and he was almost surprised there wasn't some kind of blue plate special. People of extremely moderate means must patronize the place.

Customers began to dribble in with friendly greetings. The early breakfast crowd. They all glanced at the strangers, then ignored them. No real interest in people passing through. A tight-knit community, he bet.

Allie's stomach roiled as she scanned the menu. No greens or veggies of any kind. No amazing short-order cook in sight. Eggs with home fries. Eggs with bacon. Eggs with ham. Stacks of toast or flapjacks.

She *had* to eat something. She was starving. It had been a long time since their last meal, but she wondered if she could hold any of this down. Her stomach was trying to tell her not.

But she couldn't afford to listen. When she spied the biscuits with cream gravy, she decided on them without the gravy. Just a teeny bit of butter she could add herself. Better than white-bread toast.

Hale cocked a brow at her, then went to the counter to order. It wasn't long before the food appeared and he carried plates to the table. Napkins poked out at her from a metal dispenser, flanked by salt and pepper shakers and the inevitable squeeze bottle of ketchup. The flatware was already on the table, wrapped in more paper napkins.

"You sure that's enough for you?" he asked.

"I don't feel much like eating." The biscuits astonished her, however. Amazingly light, not the hockey pucks she'd anticipated.

Hale had his usual large portion. The guy must have a cast-iron stomach. The way he'd been eating on the trip, he must be getting close to a heart attack despite working out and staying in such good shape.

When they finished, Hale paid the bill and they headed out to the car again.

"Funny," Allie said. "I used to dream of seeing this much snow. Now I'm getting sick of it."

"Want your palm trees and jacarandas, huh?"

"Something warm. That's all." Something other than white and dark green and occasional neon signs. This road stop hadn't even bothered with a weary string of Christmas lights.

Soon they'd find another fleabag and spend the day there, evidently. Changing patterns. She wondered if it worked.

Miles later Hale surprised her by pulling into the parking lot of a grocery in a tiny town. "I'll be right back," he said.

Allie should have wanted to go inside for the change of scenery, but something had made her listless, as much as it had killed her appetite. Some part of her must have settled into a cocoon of self-protection. How else was she supposed to deal with this?

Hale returned about fifteen minutes later with a couple of plastic bags. "A cornucopia," he said as he put the bags behind the front seat.

"Of what?"

"We'll be stopping for the day soon. You'll see."

The next fleabag motel looked a lot more reputable than the last one. But maybe her measuring stick had gone nuts, too.

She said nothing to Hale as he carried everything inside.

"New clothes next stop," he said as he placed the plastic bags beside her.

"Sounds good. These are getting overworn."

"I haven't seen a place," he answered.

"Me neither."

Scintillating conversation.

He spoke again as he pulled his jacket off. "Don't want to peek in those bags?"

She looked at them. "Should I?"

"I think so."

When she opened them, she gasped. A pint of fresh strawberries and large bag of seedless grapes. Containers of fruit yogurt. Bananas. Hummus and pita chips.

"I never expected such a good selection, not there," he

remarked. "Anyway, there are plastic utensils at the bottom of the bags. Help yourself."

She raised her gaze. "But why?"

"Because I've fed you enough junk food for a lifetime. So save your arteries and dig in."

The gesture nearly brought tears to her eyes. Such a caring, observant thing to do.

He'd also bought some small paper plates, and she had no trouble loading one. Strawberries and grapes first. Then some yogurt. Oh, Lord, it was heaven.

"Aren't you going to eat?" she asked him before popping a delicious strawberry into her mouth.

"In a few. I want to see you fill up first. I'm going to watch you." He waggled his eyebrows at her. "No picking."

"I couldn't pick at any of this." She smiled. "How did you know?"

"Could be a breakfast consisting only of biscuits without gravy. Or it could be that I don't eat diner food all the time, either. Should have occurred to me sooner."

"You didn't want to stop long most places."

"I wasn't long."

No, he hadn't been, and the yogurt tasted like ambrosia. As did all the fresh fruit. "Please eat," she said as she opened her second yogurt. She had begun to feel full. "I'm almost out of room."

"I suggest the hummus and chips when we wake up later."

"Good idea."

When she finished gorging, feeling contentedly replete for the first time in a while, she lay back on the single bed, fully clothed, and spread her arms. "I'm going into a food coma."

"Go ahead. Enjoy it."

It really wasn't long before she fell into dreams. These were happier dreams than any she'd had since the start of this trek.

HALE WATCHED HER sleep for a while, thinking she looked like an angel, then grabbed another purchase out of the bottom of one of the bags.

An hour later, when he emerged from the bathroom amid steam from his long, hot shower, he was clean-shaven. He always wore a beard, whether short or long, but the times called for looking very different. He supposed Allie would be shocked.

He felt a flicker of amusement over her imagined response. Time to stop looking like Jim Bridger.

WHEN ALLIE WOKE, the early winter night had fallen. Then she saw Hale sitting in the chair by the window, reading the atlas in the light of a lamp.

Was that *Hale*? She rubbed her eyes. "Hale, what happened?"

He looked up from the atlas. "Face met razor. Razor won."

My God, he was handsome. She'd guessed it, but now that she could see his square jaw and get a real look at his mouth, she no longer had to imagine.

"Changing your appearance?" she guessed.

"My best friend wouldn't recognize me right now. Beards are a great way to change your appearance but removing one can have the same effect after a period of time. Are you shocked?"

"I kinda like the way you look now."

He returned to his atlas without replying. Either he didn't care what she thought, which was highly likely, or after his burst of caring last night he was returning to his monolith persona.

She rose, feeling grimy after sleeping in her clothes. "How long before we have to go?"

"Long enough for you to take a shower if you want."

She took him up on it and returned wearing her last fresh change of clothes. She felt remarkably better.

Then even better when she saw he'd broken out the hummus and the pita chips. Plastic knives decorated the paper plates.

"Eat a little," he suggested. "It's going to be a long night."

She didn't doubt it. When Hale got behind the wheel, there was almost no stopping him. He still occupied the lone chair, so she perched on the foot of the bed facing him. He pulled the small table over between them with its passengers of plates and food.

"There's still a bit of fruit left if you want it, and a banana or two."

She smiled, putting some chips and hummus on her plate. "Unless you want them, I'll save them for later."

She was still getting used to his new look. The absence of a beard made him so attractive. Not "pretty" attractive. Not the look of some Hollywood heartthrob, but attractive in a harder way.

And he still struck her as dangerous. Which he probably was, but she hoped never to see that side of him. She hoped they got through this somehow without violence, but the way he'd spoken a few times warned her that it was not going to be that easy, especially from the men who were following them.

It wasn't long before they were on the road again, sunshine bright from a blue sky, sparkling off the snow that seemed to be growing deeper on either side of the road.

She was grateful for the darkly tinted windows or she would have been wishing for sunglasses.

"PUT YOUR HAT ON," Hale said in the late afternoon.

"Why?"

"Shopping for clothes, remember?"

They were driving along what seemed to be the main street of a quaint town with strong hints of its Western and Edwardian past. Called Conard City according to the green-and-white sign at the city limits. Grandiose name for such a small place.

"Charming," Allie murmured as she drank in the Christmas lights hanging from lampposts. The decorated tree in a central square. This place had spared nothing in the way of holiday ornamentation, including the businesses and houses she could see. It was beautiful and magnetic with its bright joy in the season.

Hale pulled over, parking near the front of a store labeled *Freitag's Mercantile*. A mercantile? Who used that term anymore?

Age showed in the darkened green wood that was highlighted by a dark-hued reddish color. A little gold paint here and there.

"Let's go in," Hale said as he switched off the ignition. "We need warmer jackets as well as everything else. Just remember—"

She cut him off. "I know. Don't buy anything I actually like."

"Except possibly candy."

Candy? Where had that come from? But her legs were thrilled to be out of the car and walking again. She still didn't feel stretched out by the time they walked through the big door with paned windows.

Inside quite a few people were wandering around with

the small carts that clothing stores often had. They appeared to be shopping for gifts and were all smiling and looking quite happy.

Allie envied them. Then, with a quiet sigh, she started looking through stacks of folded clothes and putting them in the small cart that Hale pushed for her.

More dull colors when she was more than ready for something brighter. She pulled out a red sweatshirt and, when she heard no critical commentary, she took the matching pants, as well.

Then, to please him, she turned to navy blue.

There was a green sweater she couldn't resist, and its pattern had rows of polar bears and penguins. Ha! When he wasn't looking, she tucked in a pair of seasonal pajamas. Maybe she'd get away with it.

Again no critical commentary. All Hale said was, "Don't forget a warmer jacket."

So along with a couple of pairs of jeans and two flannel shirts, she chose a loden-green jacket that wouldn't go with her sweat suits unless she wanted to look like an ornament herself. What was so bad about that?

More undies, of course. Socks, a couple of bras. Mittens. Basics.

But then Hale drew her over to some boots with high tops.

"The ones with the wool liners are best," he said, "but your choice."

Now she became practical. Meanwhile, as they'd strode the aisles, he'd outfitted himself. Nothing that would stand out, of course, but to her an interesting choice was a white parka and snow pants. Neither the pants nor jacket made a sound when he rubbed the fabric together. The kind of thing a hunter might want.

Her heart nearly stopped. Camouflage for this weather?

With a hand that nearly shook, she pointed. "Should I get white, too?"

He shook his head. "You won't have a need if I have anything to say about it."

So he was planning again. Far from comforting her, it made her more nervous. A lot more nervous. Especially when he picked out a white balaclava.

Oh, man. Ready for winter warfare?

When they were back in the car, piles of handled paper bags behind them, she asked, "Have you learned something?"

"Not yet."

To her surprise, he didn't head out of town, but instead drove west to another one of those motels, right across from a grumbling truck stop. With a diner, of course.

Night had fallen by the time he checked them in and started replacing older clothes with the new ones.

"Hale?" she asked.

"Yeah?"

"I want to go for a walk. I'd like to see some of the decorations." She knew she was pushing him, but she didn't care. This issue was never going to get resolved if they kept moving.

He looked up. "Wait until I can go with you."

Wow. She went to the bathroom and began to change into her red sweat suit, her new boots. Then she went looking for her jacket, sort of puffy enough to be a green Michelin man. She giggled when she saw herself in the mirror.

"Not used to it?" he asked mildly.

"How would I be? I look funny."

She saw him almost smile. "You'll look like most everyone around here right now."

He was ready about twenty minutes later, wearing his new white jacket. "Let's go and see your Christmas lights."

The boots felt odd on her feet, with thick soles and the wool liners, but she adjusted fast enough and he was right about the warmth.

"Why the liners?" she asked as he locked the door behind them. A new blue watch cap pretty much covered her hair.

"So that if you get snow inside your boot, the wool will keep your feet warm. Then the liner can be pulled out and dried reasonably quickly."

"Good idea."

As they walked toward town, he astonished her by taking her hand.

"Hale?"

"We're a couple," he said quietly. "We should look like one."

Oh. A ruse. She only wished it made her feel more comfortable rather than as if an electric tingle ran up her arm.

The closer they drew to the town center, the brighter and more frequent the holiday lights became. Storefronts were decorated with lighted wreaths. Strands of multicolor light swags hung from their fronts. Even the sheriff's office was decked out.

"Oh," she breathed, "this place looks like a Christmas card."

"It sure does."

Then she remembered what he'd told her about Christmas. "I'm sorry. If you want to go back to the motel…"

"I'm fine. Enjoy yourself."

She looked at him, and while his expression was grave, he didn't look as if he were miserable. Although how one could tell with him, she couldn't imagine.

But she took him at his word as they walked along

sidewalks dusted with salt and heard the faint strands of Christmas carols drifting from some businesses and houses.

She paused at the city square and exclaimed with delight, "Oh, look, they're having Christmas carols here at night. But not tonight," she added in disappointment.

"Tomorrow night," he said.

He'd move them on before then. She refused to give in to her disappointment, though. He was letting her take this walk through a town that wore a snowy cloak of Christmas.

But, man, she was getting ready to raise a ruckus about this, and Christmas could give her an excuse.

HALE REMAINED ON alert but he was surprised by the number of people who offered holiday greetings as they passed. Smiling faces.

Who had made this damn town so friendly?

If anyone felt disturbed by the strangers in their midst, they gave no evidence of it. Bustling along with shopping bags and bright smiles on cold-reddened cheeks, they seemed to be anticipating a wonderful event. A happy one.

He imagined excited children counting the days in their homes. Parents trying to sneak parcels and bags past them. Stockings hanging ready and waiting.

The kind of Christmas he'd never known.

They turned a corner and soon came upon a storefront labeled "Conard City Bakery." Mouthwatering smells emanated from it and Hale looked at Allie's delighted face. "Want to go in?"

"Absolutely."

Tonight all restrictions were off. The reality of morning would hit soon enough.

Inside a pretty middle-aged woman greeted them. Tables dotted the floor in front of a display case. Tables covered with real white tablecloths.

"We're not usually open at this time of day," she told them with a smile. "But at this time of year, who could pass up fresh Christmas cookies and hot chocolate?"

Allie looked up at him and he answered her silent plea. "Not us," he said. He looked around the dining area and saw only a few people.

"I'm Melinda," the woman said.

"Alice and Hank," Hale answered. "Nice to meet you."

"Just take a look at the case and decide what kind of cookies you'd like. And we have tea and coffee as well as hot chocolate."

Apart from frosted and sprinkled sugar cookies, there were gingerbread men, pfeffernusse cookies the like of which he hadn't seen since Germany. He chose a few of them himself.

Allie was in a "one of each" mood and soon had a ceramic plate full of them.

"Enjoy," Melinda said. "I have doggie bags if you take more than you want right now."

The hot chocolate was creamy and thick, and as he watched Allie's happy expression, he was moved to share a memory.

"I saw a lot of places like this when I was in Germany."

She looked up from her chocolate. "Like this?"

"Exactly like this. A bakery, with tables and chairs. Seemed like there was one on every street. All I know is that when you wanted to sit down and enjoy a bowl of soup or a hot beverage, they had them. And if you took a table, they never, ever rushed you along. You could stay for hours if you wanted."

"That would be nice."

"It sure was. And some of them had rooms set aside for meetings of various kinds. All welcoming and friendly."

"It sounds so gracious." Her smile had widened.

"Yup. In fact, most of the people I met were gracious. One of the things I liked was that well-behaved dogs were allowed everywhere. A place we stopped for lunch there was a man with a very small dog at the next table over. Naturally, his dog wanted to investigate me."

"Of course." She laughed.

"So the little bugger came over and I reached down to pet him. Which caused the man at the next table to engage in conversation. He was German but with a great command of English. And he was full of jokes. I laughed a lot."

She tried to imagine him laughing, especially a lot. She couldn't quite do it. "It sounds like a great experience."

"It was," he agreed. Then he fell silent again. He'd made his attempt at conversation and it had worked to judge by her expressions and her laugh. Now he was out of words.

"Now I want to go to Germany, too," she remarked.

"Too?"

"Oh, I have a whole list. Scotland. Ireland. France. The list keeps growing. To get a Eurail pass and stay anywhere I want for a few days."

"You will."

Her smile became crooked. "If I survive this."

He had no reply for that. He couldn't be 100 percent certain he'd save her. No one could. Certainly not with a surreptitious hit man on their heels.

Which turned his thoughts in exactly the wrong direction during this brief time when Allie looked happier than she had since the outset of this flight. He felt his face turn expressionless again, the best thing under the circumstances. Since Allie, he'd begun to wonder if he was an open book.

He was definitely talking more than was his custom.

After their relaxed dessert, they walked around a bit more while Allie drank in the sights. The streets had virtually emptied, the people evidently gone to their homes.

Then back to the motel. By this time the diner across the highway had turned on some colorful lights. Even some of the rumbling trucks were lit up with red and green, and others had wreaths over their front grilles.

Everyone was participating.

"Want a meal?" he asked Allie. "Cookies didn't count."

"Calorie-wise they sure did."

He shook his head slightly. She must have seen it.

"But of course," she said, "you must need more than a couple of cookies. Let's go."

He hoped she'd eat something more substantial. He knew three cookies wouldn't be enough for him.

The diner had been bitten by the Christmas bug. Inside carols played, and tables were covered with plastic cloths that had been decorated with poinsettias.

There were more poinsettias on the end of the counter, and a lighted and decorated artificial tree in one corner.

He sighed inwardly. "The First Noel" and "Silent Night" didn't make him a happy camper, although over the years he'd become more immune.

Allie darted a look his way, as if she realized this might be uncomfortable for him. Damn him for ever telling her that story. He refused to let his face twitch a single muscle, even when they studied menus. *Just focus on eating.*

He ordered his goodly portion, this time a burger and fries. He was relieved when Allie discovered enough appetite to ask for a side of breakfast sausage and an English muffin. He was sure, calories notwithstanding, that a few cookies wouldn't get her through the night. Nor would she probably want the selection in her doggie bag later.

They should be on the road already, but he was willing to give her another day. He hadn't heard anything yet to make him wonder if danger could arrive that fast and she clearly needed the break. Hell, he did, too.

She skipped her usual shower. The room was still so chilly, and no matter how much he looked, he couldn't find a thermostat.

Energy savings, he supposed. And maybe this temperature didn't feel all that cold to people who were used to winter.

Whatever, she was in the bathroom just long enough to change into her new set of flannel pajamas. Then, with nothing but a "Good night," she disappeared under the covers.

Which left him to spend the night thinking about the difficulties ahead. He had to find a way to end this soon.

What he didn't expect was the difficulty morning would bring.

# Chapter Ten

Allie had finished dressing, including her parka, cap, mittens and boots. He was almost there himself.

Then she dropped her bomb. "I'm not leaving."

Here we go, he thought. He'd expected her stubbornness to make serious trouble sooner or later. The moment had arrived.

He summoned his most reasonable tone. "Allie, we've got to go. Until I can get those guys in my sights, it's not safe."

"I don't care." Her chin thrust forward, a belligerent expression he liked but would never admit.

"I'm serious," he started. "Your life—"

"I don't have a life anymore. You're not stealing Christmas from me, too."

Stealing Christmas? He didn't want to be compared to the Grinch. Or Ebenezer Scrooge. "Ellis is trying to take your life," he pointed out.

"Well, I'm paying you to protect me. So protect me! If we never stop running, you'll never catch them."

Hale felt as if his head would explode with frustration. She was out the door before he could stop her. He finished tying his final boot and grabbed his jacket as quickly as he could to chase after her, catching her before she quite passed the motel.

"I *am* protecting you."

"From what? All the pleasure and happiness in life? What's the point?"

"Allie..."

"Don't *Allie* me. You know it's true. Just because you're so miserable doesn't mean *I* have to be."

*Ouch.* "Let's go discuss this over breakfast."

"Discuss what? I'm not going anywhere! Besides, I've had it with diners."

"I'm not fond of them myself, truth be told. I saw a café in town. Let's go there."

"It's probably the same. Do people in this part of the country eat anything else?"

"That's not fair," he pointed out calmly. "Let's try the café. It's probably not very busy at this hour."

She stopped walking and faced him. "You're not talking me out of this. Damn it, Hale, you work for *me*. I am sick to death of being dragged around like luggage."

He didn't bother reminding her what his real job was, what she'd hired him to do. Nope, she wouldn't stand for that right now.

When she agreed to the café, he steeled himself for a sea of Christmas music and red-and-green decorations. Probably even a tree. God, this town was taking the season way over the top.

He was right about one thing, however. It was only moderately busy this morning and they were able to get a table away from the windows. He hated windows. Too exposed.

At least the menu wasn't decorated around the edges with poinsettia leaves or little Christmas balls or bells. No decorated tablecloths, just bare plastic tops. And the menu varied from the places they'd been eating.

Despite her mood, Allie didn't resist him over breakfast. She chose a bowl of mixed fruit, which proved to be large enough to assure him she was actually eating. Plenty of coffee, too.

Some knot of worry that had begun to tighten inside him let go. They'd deal with the rest of it later. They *had* to.

For now, she'd have her day. *One* day.

"This is good canned fruit," she remarked. "No sweetened syrup."

Okay, she was unquestionably eating. He relaxed a hair more and ate almost as if he were at a training table. Which he very nearly was. They both worked out in the evenings, but his exercising was far more strenuous. It had to be. He had no idea of the problems he might face and where they might come from.

To borrow the Coast Guard motto: *Semper Paratus.* Always prepared. He tried to be.

After breakfast, served by a surly waitress named Mavis, Allie started her walk around the town. Joy. Not.

But for her it seemed to be. Smiles kept dancing over her face, and she greeted people as they passed by, many of them loaded down with bags.

"Why don't people shop earlier?" he asked.

"I don't know. I always meant to, then faced the last minute. And too often some special item I picked for someone had vanished. You'd think I'd have learned."

Well, that was another grin he couldn't quite hide.

They paused at the courthouse square, with its requisite soldier statue on a podium, and Allie clapped her mittened hands together. "Oh, look! There are packages under the tree now."

Yes, there were. Okay, way over the top. Worse, having her in the open like this was winding him up tight.

She asked, "Why don't they get wet?"

Two couples, hearing her, came over. They looked like a pair of grandparents and their adult children.

"They're just wrapped for looks," the younger woman explained. "Hi, I'm Josie." She introduced the other three as Mary, Jacob and Wesley.

"I'm Alice. And this is my fiancé. I won't give him a name."

A sideways swipe, Hale decided.

The three others laughed.

"The presents are a clever idea," Allie said, pointing to the tree. "So festive."

"It's a placeholder," Wesley said.

Allie's brow knit. "For what?"

"Real presents," Mary chimed in. "On Christmas Eve, around noon, we bring out all the wrapped toys that people have donated."

"For kids who might not have anything under the tree at all," Wesley, the older man, explained. "We've got a tree in the courthouse lobby, and all the names and ages are on paper circles dangling from it. You pick one or two and fulfill the wishes. Sometimes it's so sad, though."

Josie nodded. "It brings you to tears when a four-year-old's Christmas wish is for a new winter jacket."

"Or mittens," Jacob said. "Or shoes or boots. They should be wishing for toys."

"Where I used to live," Allie said, "we had the same thing. It was called the Angel Tree."

"We ought to do that," Mary said, looking at the others.

"How late can you donate gifts?" Allie asked.

Hale smelled a shopping expedition coming.

"Well, right up until the party," Josie answered. "But the closer it gets to Christmas, the more we hope folks will wrap them before they bring them. Oh, and please don't forget to put the little name tags on them." She laughed.

Allie looked at Hale. "I'd like to go in and see the tree."

"I was sure you would," he answered, hoping he sounded more like a loving mate than a tooth-grinding bodyguard.

They said farewell to the nice people and Allie headed straight for the courthouse. At least the steps were salted, he thought irritably. His job didn't involve taking her to the ER with a cracked skull because she fell.

*Bah, humbug,* he thought, then stopped himself. *No Ebenezer Scrooge. Just try to enjoy Allie's enjoyment.* That was better than fury over her stubbornness.

At the tree inside, they met more smiling people—God, did everyone in this town perpetually smile?—and waited patiently while Allie examined green-and-red balls cut out of construction paper. Finally she had six of them and she turned to the other people checking out the tree.

She asked, "Where is the best place to go shopping for the kids?"

"Freitag's Mercantile," two of them answered at once. They laughed.

"Yeah," one of them said. "They're stocked up for kids this time of year and you can find anything. Not all of it is expensive."

Which might well be a consideration for that group, he thought. None of them looked as if they'd bought new jackets or hats in a while.

They were generous anyway. His crabby mood lightened a bit. Some people, he reminded himself, could be truly good.

Allie beelined straight for the Mercantile. Apparently she remembered its location, not that it would have been hard to miss. She paused frequently, however, to drink in one house or another.

He remarked, "They sure go all-out around here." Couldn't she just keep moving?

"I think it's beautiful."

It wasn't just lights strung from eaves and perhaps over shrubs or a fir tree. Nope. Glowing snowmen. Bursts of small lights that looked almost like sparklers along the sidewalks. Santa in his sleigh with reindeer. A yard full of lighted polar bears. And it seemed to him that some of the decorations had been collected over the years. Their ages showed a bit.

Impressive, he admitted. These folks were determined to enjoy this season. As Allie was.

Just until tomorrow.

She certainly had fun picking out gifts at Freitag's. She studied her handful of paper Christmas baubles, then began choosing items. One thing she added, however, were six teddy bears in green costumes and red Santa hats. That surprised him.

"Six?" he asked. "Did some kid want six teddy bears?"

"No, but every child should get a little something special, a gift they didn't even ask for."

Well, that was something else. Then he remembered she'd mentioned it once before.

She also bought a bunch of large gift bags. By the time they departed the store, he'd used quite a wad of her money from his wallet and was loaded down like a pack mule. They headed back to the motel.

Which he honestly didn't mind. It would get her off the street. But Allie was having fun, and somehow the fun was rubbing off on him. Just a bit, he assured himself. But damn, he kept getting these stupid half smiles on his face.

In their room, the booty came out. Space rockets, boxes of LEGO, baby dolls, a pink winter parka that looked impossibly small to his eyes. And into each extra-large bag went not only a teddy bear but also a small, warm blanket he hadn't noticed her buying.

"I'm impressed," he told Allie.

"It's not much."

"That isn't what I meant."

Their eyes met, then she flushed and turned quickly away. "I wanted small candy canes to put in these, but I wasn't sure if I should. What if one of these children has tooth problems?"

"I never would have thought of that. Good on you."

"I don't usually think in those terms," she said, her voice thickening a little. "I mean, I always buy a gift or two for the Angel Tree at home, but I've never had to be in a position where I considered such things. I've been so lucky!"

Until now, he thought. "Are you cold yet?"

"Well, I warmed up in here. But I want to go to the bakery for some hot soup and chocolate."

Out into the danger zone again. God, he hoped she wasn't determined to turn herself into bait before he'd winnowed the pursuers enough.

"There's Christmas caroling in the square tonight," she reminded him as they walked hand in hand toward the bakery.

Of course there was. He sighed, trying not to think about how every minute was increasing the threat level.

ALLIE HEARD THE sigh and wondered if she'd brought back bad memories for him. She'd promised herself she wouldn't do that, but she suspected she had anyway with her insistence on having a bit of Christmas. Still, she was determined.

"I'm sorry," she said. "I guess I've made you miserable."

"No," he answered.

"Are you sure?"

"Well, I'm not in a Scrooge mood."

That brought a laugh out of her. "You can be nice sometimes, Hale."

He didn't reply and she let it go. She'd probably gotten more words out of him in the last two days than he ordinarily spoke in two years. Or so that had been her initial impression.

He probably hated having her out in the open like this, she realized. He'd been doing his best to keep her out of sight except for brief periods.

He hadn't objected, though. Maybe he felt the threat was far enough away for now. Although how he was ever going to catch the bad guys she couldn't imagine. Keeping her away from them didn't allow Hale to get very far from her.

But he seemed confident enough so he must have a plan or be constructing one.

Besides, Max wouldn't have recommended him if he didn't completely trust Hale.

"I miss Max," she announced as they sat at a table with potato soup and their cocoa. "We always spend a lot of time together at the holidays. Max loves them."

Hale nodded. "Does he? I wouldn't know. I'm usually working."

She wondered if that was true or just an excuse to stay away from Max's cheer. "I love his hot cider, and sometimes he makes a fabulous Irish coffee. My friends were spending their time with family on Christmas Eve, but Max always invited a few of his friends from the cop shop. Those guys could really get a party going."

"I don't doubt it. Even in Afghanistan Christmas managed to arrive. Even at the distant forward bases where I was stationed. Invariably someone would pull in some bedraggled plant as a stand-in for a Christmas tree. One time someone cadged some foil and the guys crushed it into balls to make ornaments."

Allie put her chin in her hand and listened, delighting in imagining it.

"Then one year we were able to light one of those silly trees. John Hansford's wife sent him a string of battery-operated lights. Pretty enough, changing through a series of colors. Unfortunately, Hansford's wife didn't send a hundred batteries along with it. We all laughed ourselves sick when we discovered the strand would only operate for about three hours before draining the batteries."

A faint smile played around his mouth, and Allie drank it in. It seemed Christmas hadn't *always* been a bad time for him. Then she watched him shut down again, as if he believed he had said too much.

She felt him pushing constantly against the atmosphere in this town. He didn't want to let it in.

Well, too bad. She wasn't going anywhere. This had to be settled. Even if he exploded.

As the light faded from the sky, a whole new layer appeared. Decorations that hadn't been lit all day sprang to life. More people arrived on the streets carrying bags and boxes. The Mercantile appeared to have a line waiting out front. The bakery had placed some plastic chairs and tables on the sidewalk to handle the overflow.

And Allie was indefatigable in her desire to drink it all in. They'd been outdoors most of the day.

He didn't mind that as a rule. He'd spent years outdoors in less hospitable places. But having Allie out in the crowds stretched his nerves.

But she was having a good time. Everywhere she went, she fell into conversation with people. In no time at all she'd be in the midst of a group of locals laughing along with them.

She had a gift for being the welcome stranger in this place.

He must have seemed like a dour lug standing beside her.

Which was fine by him. He *hated* casual conversation.

Anyway, he stood there holding four of the six bags she had filled, and getting to those courthouse steps might take a long time, given how she kept stopping to talk.

Nor was he going to offer to take the bags inside without her. No way was he going to leave her alone. So he stood there, manufacturing some semblance of a smile while she made friends she wasn't going to see again after tonight.

Then she saw that a crowd was gathering in the middle of the square. "Ooh," she said. "Almost time for caroling. Let's get these bags inside now."

Standing there with those colorful, large bags was making him feel like a Christmas tree himself. He'd be glad to dump them. In the lobby, another group of smiling people were gathering the gifts on a large red tarp. More conversation. At this point Hale would have been glad to see one furious face.

But he never stopped scanning all those cheerful faces, looking for anything that didn't strike him right. Anything, however small. Time to check in with Stu again, he decided. He needed to know where the hunters were now.

But for the moment all he could do was watch and wait.

And endure the carols. Even in his miserable childhood, he hadn't escaped Christmas music. Anytime he went to the stores, he was drenched in it. For some it brought back happy feelings. For him it was just a reminder of bad times.

Allie got into it, though. The group in the center of the square seemed to be a more practiced choir, but they weren't there to sing alone. No, everybody surrounding the square joined in. The rising voices, some clearly out of tune, filled the area with a haunting beauty.

He quit trying to fight it. Would it kill him for just one evening to quit nursing old pains and grudges? He believed they drove him, made him the man he had become, a man who'd improved himself. But he didn't need the memories just then.

Allie, beside him, sang in a beautiful flute-like soprano. Right on key, too. He watched her face between glances around them, so bright and shiny, and hoped she'd never lose that expression.

He was damn well going to do his best to prevent it.

DESPITE LONGING TO share the holidays with her friends, Allie was having a wondrous time. That Christmas postcard she'd always eyed with envy surrounded her now, absorbing her, filling her with the very magic she'd always imagined.

Deep within she knew this was a special moment in time, that soon enough these people would leave behind the beauty for the drudgery of everyday life. But she refused to think of that. Right now the world was full of beautiful music and, when snow began to fall gently, the night couldn't have been any more perfect.

A little over an hour later, the concert ended and people began to drift apart. That somehow seemed perfect, too. Trailing away to warm homes with Christmas trees and maybe excited children.

Several people invited her to their homes for hot cider and cookies, but a glance at Hale's face told her she'd better not. He'd reached his limit with this stuff.

A twinge of guilt struck her and she declined the invitations pleasantly, explaining that she was growing tired after a busy day.

"Maybe tomorrow, then," man replied.

"Maybe," she answered.

As they walked back to the motel, Hale said two things. "We need some hot food. And we're leaving in the morning."

Allie gritted her teeth. She'd found wonder and magic

and he had no good reason to tear her away. Unless he could give her a reason other than that they needed to keep moving. But moving meant he'd never be able to face the threat.

She left that conversation for later, deciding he was right about getting a meal.

The City Café had a line out front, so he said they were going to the truck stop. Okay, then. As long as it was hot and filling.

The truck stop was busy but still had plenty of tables. Allie noticed that Hale steered her away from the windows to a table in the corner. He sat facing outward, scanning the room.

"Do you ever relax?" she asked.

"Not on a job."

That's right, she thought as she ordered up oatmeal, scrambled eggs and coffee. She was just a job to him. Maybe she ought to be grateful he'd given her this one day. Except he hadn't given it to her. She'd taken it for herself.

And she was not leaving unless he had a damn good reason for insisting.

"I wish I could call my friends," she said wistfully. Her thoughts of them were growing ever stronger, especially during this season. "I'm seriously homesick."

"Homesick?"

"Yeah. My stomach feels hollow. I'm missing home. That's not unnatural, but I just can't keep this up forever."

"I'm not planning on that."

She frowned as she finished her oatmeal. "Just how are you going to do that when you won't let these guys get close?"

"I'm working on it."

The wall clamped into place again. She sighed. Every so often he'd peek out from behind it, but only in little bits. Somewhere inside him was undoubtedly a fascinating man, but she'd never know. Not when he kept his guard so high.

Just then a tall man with a burn-scarred cheek limped in. Wearing a brown insulated jacket over a dark brown uniform, he didn't need the badge on his chest to shout *police*. Instead of heading to the counter or a table, he came straight toward them.

"Howdy," he said and pulled a chair over. "I'm Sheriff Gage Dalton. Welcome to our little part of the world."

Allie smiled. "My dad was a cop."

Dalton gave her a crooked smile in return. "Family, then."

Allie was about to reply when Hale took over. "People worried about us?"

"Not much, but strangers around here tend to stand out. You a vet?"

Hale nodded. "Marines."

"You have that cut to your jib. So what brings you our way? We're not exactly on the tourist trail."

This time Allie tensed a bit. Did people think they were dangerous? She hadn't gotten that feeling from anyone so far.

Hale answered. "We're on a long road trip. The state highway led us here and Alice couldn't resist staying. All this Christmas caught her attention."

Dalton smiled crookedly again, as if the burn scar tugged at his mouth. "It'll do that. Still to come, a Christmas parade with Santa, and some reindeer. More caroling. The gift-giving party on Christmas Eve. Oh, and the Mercantile with bare shelves. If you want anything, better buy it quick."

Allie laughed. "Did you miss anything on your list?"

"I did," he said with a nod. "A group of students will wander around the neighborhoods singing carols, too."

Allie's expression became wistful again. "That must be beautiful."

"Very," the sheriff answered. When a waiter came over, he ordered coffee and a serving of mincemeat pie. Then his attention squared on Hale. "You haven't looked very happy today."

So people had been paying attention to them, eyeing them suspiciously even while being friendly. She looked at Hale, sensing the tension in him.

Hale answered the implied question. "Alice will tell you that I'm the original Grinch. Not my thing."

"It isn't for everyone." Dalton thanked the waiter as he placed a cup of coffee and a slice of pie in front of him. "I enjoy watching so many people get into the spirit around here. Like folks everywhere, we have our squabbles and a few feuds. For a while they get forgotten."

"Must make your job easier," Hale answered.

"Hell, yeah. We'll have a few burglaries as people stuff gifts under their trees, but not many. And we probably won't have to break up any brawls until New Year's Eve." He frowned faintly. "But there are domestics. They seem to rise around this time."

Allie watched Hale's face darken. God, what a subject to come up right now.

But Gage, who was getting through his pie with reasonable speed, remarked, "What do you two do?"

"I'm an accountant," Allie answered. "About as boring as people come."

"Nobody's boring," the sheriff answered. "And you?" he asked Hale.

"Private security."

Dalton's brow lifted. "Mercenary?"

Allie caught her breath.

"Not anymore," Hale answered. "Looked around, didn't like it."

"Good for you." Dalton finished his pie and his coffee. "Well, I won't trouble you folks any longer. Consider this your welcome to Conard County. Nice meeting you."

With a nod, he placed a cowboy hat on his head, one with a sheriff's badge embroidered on the front, then waved as he left.

Only then did Allie notice he was fully armed, even with a collapsible baton. This had been official.

"Wow," she whispered. "Who did we set off?"

"It was probably just a good lawman keeping an eye out. I didn't get the sense that he was suspicious."

"I guess not."

But now more questions roiled in her head. Mercenary? Had he been? What had he done?

WELL, THAT HAD been unfortunate, Hale thought as they finished up their meal and headed back across the highway to their motel. Now Allie had a million questions, their profile had gotten higher, and he might have revealed too much. Hell.

They sure weren't invisible even in a crowd.

The urge to get on the road again was itching at the base of his skull and felt like a cold breath down his spine. Damn it, he needed more info. More idea of where to play this game out while protecting Allie. Whenever possible, he preferred to choose his own ground for the fight. So far he'd been running pretty much blind, knowing only that he had to reduce the number of their followers. He hated it.

He needed to call Stu. Tonight.

When they got back to the room, he suggested that Allie climb into her pajamas and get warm in bed.

"You have to sleep on the floor again tonight," she remarked.

"I've slept in far worse places. At least gravel and stones won't be poking my back."

The joy was gone from her face, he noticed. The conversation with the sheriff had bothered her. Well, it had bothered him, too. Quite a welcoming committee. They'd been scoped and now he had to wonder if Dalton would try to check them out somehow. Not that he had much to go on. Except for the stolen plates on Hale's vehicle.

Crap. He needed to change them again soon, but not in this town. Not if Dalton might run plates.

If he did, Hale and Allie were going to hit the road before Allie's head could spin. Bait? She wanted to be bait? He hadn't missed the suggestion in all her comments about letting those goons get closer. Maybe they ought to leave right now.

He stepped out into the night's deepening cold and pulled out one of his phones. Stu answered on the second ring.

All Hale said was, "Well?"

"The dolls have been sold again. Headed back north a bit and now east."

Hale's jaw clenched so tight that his muscles hurt. "What does that tell you?"

"Me? Only that someone said the word *Badlands*."

Stu had said it. Jokingly. Why would he mention it to any of the other guys? But Stu also knew he couldn't push Hale in any particular direction, that Hale was in charge of this little journey. Had he mentioned it not so jokingly to someone else on their team?

"What does that tell you?" Hale asked.

"Not enough yet. I'm seriously thinking I need to get rid of an armadillo. Damn thing is building a burrow under my foundation."

"Fill it in with cement," Hale said. "Keeps 'em from digging more. At least there."

"Good idea."

Hale hung up, convinced now that someone in his tight little group had sold out. Was passing along information in more than one direction. Ellis could sure offer some huge enticements.

On the other hand, his contacts were an ad hoc group, some guys he'd known in the past who occasionally offered their expertise in one area or another. They should be invisible to outsiders.

Should have been, he corrected himself. Unless the traitor had gone looking for an inducement.

He tore the battery out of the phone, along with the SIM, then crossed the highway once more to throw the SIM on one truck and the phone on another. He wasn't ready for the battle yet, not in this town, all involved in seasonal joy.

When he returned to the relative warmth of the motel room, he smelled a recent shower and shampoo. Allie was cuddled up under blankets, sitting up and waiting for him. Damn it would have been nice if she'd been asleep, her questions waiting while he thought through all this mess.

He sat on the chair, pulling off his jacket and balaclava, unlacing his boots.

"Learn anything?" she asked.

"Yeah. I'm not ready to discuss it." It would only scare her more to learn that he thought there was a traitor. As bad as when he might have to tell her that a hired hit man was on her trail.

He had to restrain himself from throwing a boot in rage.

This situation was bad enough without a mole in his midst. He changed to fresh woolly socks and began to make himself a pallet on the floor.

"Hale?"

"Yeah?"

"There's room on this bed if you're tired of playing martyr."

He stopped breathing. What was she suggesting?

"I'm not making a move on you," she said forthrightly. "Just that I hate seeing you sleep on the floor all the time. You can sleep on top of the covers."

He started breathing again. Allie was truly desirable, but not now. He couldn't afford anything that might throw his emotions into high gear. He had to stay clearheaded.

"I'll think about it," he replied. "Thanks."

"Your choice. And I'll save my questions for later. You look like you have enough on your plate."

God, was he becoming transparent?

"It's okay," he said as reassuringly as he could. "I just need to figure out some things."

Well, he told himself, if there was a mole, maybe he could use him. All he had to do was decide how.

# *Chapter Eleven*

As if Hale didn't already have an overloaded plate, Allie dumped more onto it in the morning. He said, "Time to get on the road."

"I'm not leaving."

*Here we go again.* "Oh, hell. We're sticking out like sore thumbs in this town."

"Well, you didn't want to go to ground in a big city. I like it here. I like Christmas. I like the way these people are doing it. Besides, you can't get near these guys if they can't get near me. I am *not* going."

She had a point, wrong-headed though it might be. He said nothing as he pulled on his boots. Thinking about it, he decided that at this point he just needed to stay on high alert. Maybe until Christmas was over. He could do that, surely. Besides, if he just grabbed her and threw her in the car, it would be kidnapping, job or not.

And the enemy was headed in the wrong direction, at least now.

For now.

He needed to figure out how to use this mole to his advantage anyway. He gave up the fight with Allie before it began and prepared himself for another day swamped in heavy-duty cheer.

Treat it like a mission, he told himself. Just another

mission. At least the locals wouldn't be lobbing grenades his way.

"Okay," he said.

She froze in the process of reaching for her own boots. "Really? I'm not trying to make you crazy."

"You do that just by breathing. Prepare yourself for another day in the cold, woman. We'll drink in every drop of your Christmas. And your cussed stubbornness."

"Tough," she answered. "Do your job. On *my* terms."

HER CHRISTMAS. NOT HIS. Allie felt a twinge of guilt, then stopped herself. She was paying for this gig. She ought to have something to say about it.

Besides, she'd blow a gasket if she didn't get some time out of his vehicle. Feeling confined didn't begin to cover it. She needed to be out and about, talking to someone besides the Great Stone Face, whose favorite word appeared to be *No*.

And rough, tough Mr. Bodyguard could just deal with it.

Anyway, it had come to the point where fleeing seemed like a useless option, whether he thought so or not.

In the daylight, Conard City had lost none of its charm. The light snowfall last night had whitened the town's blanket even more, obscuring any signs of dirt or oil that might have come from traffic.

What was even better for Allie was being greeted by name, by people who stopped, despite the frigid weather, to speak with her a bit about whether she was enjoying herself.

"I'm having a wonderful time," she replied. "This town is beautiful."

Several mentioned a hope that she would stay at least through Christmas. "You don't want to miss the gift giving on Christmas Eve."

"No, I don't," she agreed with a smile. She didn't glance at Hale as she said so, because she imagined he must be looking like a steam engine ready to blow its boiler.

She wasn't stupid. She understood his concerns. Surely a few days couldn't cause a problem. But as far as she'd heard from Mr. Silent, the pursuers hadn't come close. Or not close enough.

Where would they go from here, anyway? He was being silent about that, too. Merely speaking of "plans" said nothing at all.

She decided they should have brunch at the City Café, which she had learned was locally known as Maude's Diner.

"That Maude is something else," a woman named Betty told her. "She's owned that diner at least since I was a kid, and I don't think I've ever seen her crack a smile. Her daughter is every bit as abrupt and rude. They're characters around here, the kind everyone loves. The kind people write stories about."

Allie laughed. "I haven't really had a chance to see."

"Oh, you will," Betty assured her. "Wait until she or her daughter start slamming the crockery down in front of you. Maude even sometimes tells you what to eat." Then Betty giggled.

"What?" Allie asked.

"Oh, years ago, when I was maybe five or so, everyone in town started laughing behind their hands. The previous sheriff, Nate Tate, decided he wanted to lose a little weight. When he dropped in for his usual coffee, he stopped ordering pie."

"Sensible," Allie agreed, smiling.

"Well, he tried to be. Maude was having none of it. She'd slam a plate of pie in front of him, he'd protest he was dieting and she'd retort 'We can't have you blowing away.'"

Allie laughed outright. "Oh, no."

"Oh, yes. She may be cranky and rude, but Maude, in her own way, looks out for people. Maybe not always the right way, but she does."

Allie was still smiling as they walked toward the diner. "I love it here," she said.

"Right now," Hale answered.

"Right now is all I have, and I love it."

The diner was busier as the breakfast crowd gave way to the lunch crowd. There were still tables and Hale once again chose one in a back corner.

Allie shed her jacket and picked up a menu. Then she asked, "What have you got against windows? I'd prefer to be able to look out."

When he didn't answer, she raised her gaze. The man was turning to stone again.

"Hale?"

He shook his head sharply, just once. Then he leaned toward her, keeping his voice low. "Windows are exposure. You can't have everything you prefer."

Ice trickled down her spine at his words. He'd brought back the reality of this whole damn thing. But she wasn't going to let him ruin this for her. This might be her last experience of a normal world. No, she couldn't let him take that away.

It also gave her an insight into the way this man was thinking. *Had* to think. That brought her another shiver. The things he must have seen, must have experienced. She couldn't conceive of it.

Yet the results were sitting right across the table from her. Apart from his horrifying childhood, there must have been other things in his life to turn him into a man who chose to be a bodyguard. Who chose to risk his life protecting others. Who would go to any lengths to protect her.

God. She looked down at the menu again and tried to concentrate on eating. No food since last night should have made her ravenous, but her appetite slipped away.

"Eat," he said presently. "Find something. It's cold out there and you'll need the energy to keep you warm."

She couldn't argue and she didn't want to grow cold so early that she'd need to head back to the motel. She settled on ham hash with a side of whole wheat toast. And this time she was treated to the slamming of plates and cups in front of them. She nearly giggled. Glancing at Hale, she caught amusement flicker across his face.

"You want a pot of coffee?" the woman asked. Her name tag said she was Maude, an older version of the woman who'd waited on them before.

"Please," Hale answered.

"Damn straight," the woman nearly growled. "Winter. Folks are always wanting a pot. A body can't keep up."

Nonetheless, five minutes later she returned with an insulated carafe. "Bottomless," she said shortly. Then she stomped away.

"Wow," Allie murmured.

"I guess we've met a character," Hale replied. He picked up the carafe and poured for them both.

"You must hate me," Allie said while they ate.

"I don't hate you."

"Well, you hate Christmas and I'm putting you through this. And I'm arguing with you about moving on."

For a minute or two he didn't answer and just as she had decided that he wouldn't, he spoke.

"I don't hate *Christmas*. It's just that I see all these cheerful smiling faces and I can't help but think it's a kind of brainwashing."

That startled her. "Brainwashing?"

"Sure. Everyone is convinced it's a perfect time of year

and that they all feel happy and the world is a wonderful place."

Her heart thudded. "But?"

"You have no idea how many of them will go home to discover nothing is perfect. Or feel let down after all the tinsel and partying are gone. Peace and joy to men of good will lasts about fifteen minutes."

"God, Hale." Sorrow for him blossomed inside her, making her ache until she wanted to weep for him.

"Sorry," he said with a shrug. "I shouldn't rain on your parade. But I've had a very different experience all my life."

"Hale..." She wanted to tell him that they could go right now. Leave all this behind to save him the grief.

He shook his head. "You shouldn't have asked. And I sure as hell shouldn't have answered. Enjoy the illusion, Allie. You're entitled to it."

Well, that hardly made her feel any better. Her appetite was truly dead now.

He looked at her as he pulled out his wallet to go pay the bill. "You really don't want to know me, Allie. You really don't."

But as she rose to leave with him, she was thinking exactly the opposite.

It was a good day to kick his own butt, Hale thought as they began to walk along the street again. He knew how to keep his mouth shut. He didn't know, however, why Allie kept getting him to talk. He was walking proof that he shouldn't open his mouth.

It took a little while for Allie's spirits to rise again and he was relieved to see them return. Damn, he needed to stop hitting her with the hard truths. If she wanted to wear rose-colored glasses, then who was he to crack them? Or worse, rip them from her.

If he were to be honest with himself, he might be the one living in his own private illusion of life, one that wasn't pretty.

Allie, of course, found an organic food store and popped inside. Next thing he knew, he was carrying bags of bananas and grapes and raisins and even avocados and fresh green beans.

"I wish I could cook here," she remarked. "That butternut squash is so tempting."

He suspected a few other items tempted her as well, given how she lingered over them. She moved on, though, and before they departed, she purchased a small kitchen knife and some plastic spoons.

That fruit cost a fortune but, since it had come from so far away, it had to. He figured they were going to dine vegetarian tonight. Or at least she was.

Her pleasure in the day had fully returned and he promised himself he'd keep his lips sealed so as not to disturb her again. He rather liked her naïveté and wanted her to keep as much of it as possible.

On the main street, he looked up and down it again, measuring lines of sight while she conversed with more people. This town seemed to be taking to Allie. Which, he admitted, would be very easy to do.

Down the street was the high steeple of a church. That was the only thing he could see with a height to concern him.

"Allie?"

"Yes?"

"Would you mind wandering down to the church? I bet they have some beautiful decorations."

She appeared surprised but nodded. "I'd really like that, Hale."

Apparently they'd both given up on phony first names. He took her mittened hand in his, as per his desire to appear to be a couple, and they strolled along unhurriedly.

Dang, this town was a bustle of activity, and, of course, it slowed them down, because at least half the people were in the mood for a friendly chat with Allie.

He stood back a little, keeping a phony smile plastered on his face, but his eyes darted everywhere. No relaxation for him. One moment of inattention could be one moment too many.

When they reached the church, he was proved right about decoration. The manger scene out front particularly caught his attention. It was no stylized plaster or plastic model. No, the parties standing around the churchyard were all dressed in poor, ragged clothing. *Real* clothing. Joseph and Mary weren't dressed any better.

The manger was a crudely crafted feeding trough full of hay. A small, ragged burlap blanket awaited the arrival of the child.

"Kind of brings it home," he remarked.

"Yeah, they weren't well-to-do. A good reminder. I don't miss the Magi, either."

"As I recall they didn't arrive for a couple of years."

"That's my recollection."

There wasn't even a fake angel. He was impressed despite himself.

"Let's go inside," he suggested. He wanted to scope out the bell tower.

Pine needle wreaths, decorated with white doves, hung from the carved double doors. Inside, the quiet of an empty church greeted them, along with lingering incense. Votive candles burned near the altar.

Other than the huge cross hanging behind the altar, there was no decoration. One rose window, made of stained glass, gleamed above the cross, but all the other windows were plain glass.

No ostentation here, unless you counted the ornately carved wooden pews.

"This is awesome," Allie breathed.

"Wander around. I'd like to take a look at the bell tower."

As he turned toward the door that should lead to the tower stairs, he saw the choir loft hanging in the rear. All the important parts, he thought. Also an excellent position for a sniper if his quarry were inside the church.

The lock on the door he sought wasn't much of a lock. He twisted it and it fell open. Narrow, steep, spiraling stairs greeted him. No more than one person at a time, he thought. Bell ringers must be in short supply.

About twenty feet above, he reached the platform where the bell ringers must stand. Two holes in the ceiling, both with ropes hanging from them, assured him he was right.

The room was fully closed in, possibly against the elements. But the entire spire wasn't closed in, nor could it be or the bells might as well not have been there.

Climbing more stairs, he reached the bell tower. It gave him a panoramic view of the town below.

He might have admired it, but all he could see was that he'd discovered a good sniper's perch. And looking straight out, he could see more.

The library appeared to have a dome on it. There were two more churches with spires. A few houses towered over the town, bespeaking wealth, at least in the past. He'd have bet they'd been turned into rooming houses.

In fact, from what he'd seen of this town, he had trouble understanding how it survived. The outlying ranches? Maybe.

When he finished making a mental map of the town's layout, he returned to the nave. Allie was waiting in one of the rear pews, looking contemplative.

She turned her head as she heard his steps. "How were the bells?"

"Well, they weren't sporting spiderwebs or birds' nests."

She laughed quietly.

"Let's go and get a hot drink or something, then you can decide what you want to see next."

"Sounds good."

AFTER HOT CHOCOLATE, Allie decided to leave the downtown for a walk through the residential neighborhoods. On Front Street, they discovered the row of gracious old Victorian houses, with their third stories and even in one case a widow's walk.

Here the decorations changed a bit. Instead of lights dripping from every eave, and lit polar bears and snowmen, they saw draped green garlands with red bows.

"I bet," she said, "there was a time when the wealthy and important people lived here."

"Looks like it," he agreed.

"It has a lot of charm. I like the gingerbread. I like the decoration, too. As if the people on this street all agreed to the garlands."

"I like it, too," Hale agreed. "Less effusive."

Allie laughed quietly. "You *would* feel that way."

They walked a little farther in silence, then Allie screwed up her courage to ask, "What was that about being a mercenary?"

Hale was quiet for a while, and as they turned the corner onto a different street, he spoke.

There were almost no people around here, Allie had noticed. Maybe that was why he finally spoke. No eavesdroppers.

"I joined a private security firm after I left the Marines. I thought I'd be protecting *people*. Instead I learned that this company was hiring its troops out to foreign govern-ments. Engaging in their wars. I left."

"Why?"

"I'm not a killer for hire."

His words chilled her. God, what this man had seen! Then she said, "That's when you became a bodyguard?"

"I formed my own company. Protecting *individuals* is a whole different ball of wax."

It certainly was, she thought as they walked along a street where the sidewalks hadn't been worn bare of snow by crowds of people as they had been closer to the town center.

"I bet you left some good pay behind."

"The best," he replied.

This man was admirable, she decided. Truly admirable. She sighed quietly. Her perspective on life was chang-ing, she realized. Starting with having to run from the threat from her former employer. Continuing with the steps Hale kept taking to keep her concealed. She chafed under his restrictions, but he appeared to know what he was doing.

She just wished she knew more about what was going on. Why he was so alert even here? Had she foiled his plan by insisting they remain for a few days?

In the end he hadn't put up a serious argument, but the more she thought about it, the less she liked being bag-gage. She wanted to *help*.

Again she sighed. He clearly had no intention of letting her. Just follow his orders. Gah! She hated that part, espe-cially when it made no sense to her.

When they reached Main Street again, they turned and headed back toward the town center.

God, she was thirsty for the company of people. She was used to it. The idea that she would spend so much time in the company of one solitary man would have made her laugh.

But if Hale was right, she'd be living exactly this way until he could take care of the threat against her.

But how could he do that? How could he be sure he could do that?

"Hale?"

"Yeah?"

"How are you going to take care of this threat? You haven't said anything."

His jaw tightened. "I'm going to choose my own ground."

She believed that Hale could be an extremely dangerous man when he needed to be.

She was just glad that he was on her side. But she couldn't resist one last poke of the lion. "I still think you need to bait this trap."

HALE NEARLY GROWLED at her, but he'd shot off his mouth again. Damn, how did this woman keep pulling things out of him?

He wasn't proud of those months he'd spent with that so-called security company. The mud had kept rising until he knew that if he wanted to save what was left of his rotten soul, he had to get out.

He hadn't even given notice. He'd walked in one day and told them he was gone and wouldn't be back. Surprisingly, given that he had a contract with them, they didn't argue.

He supposed they figured they were better off without him, without a man who didn't want to do their kind of work. Well, they were. He'd have found a way to sabotage whatever operation they might send him on. He refused to be used that way.

That job had been his own blind spot. He should have had a clue before he signed on.

But lots of people he'd known in the military had signed with those guys and seemed to be quite happy. Men he'd once been proud to know. Men he wasn't proud to know now.

At least he'd rounded up some good buddies who weren't involved in that crap.

Good buddies except for one, it seemed. Because how else could anyone think he and Allie had headed for the Badlands?

A simmering anger burned in him. Betrayal was one of the worst crimes.

# Chapter Twelve

Allie hadn't liked what Hale had said about brainwashing. She might have chosen a different word.

But that didn't make him wrong. If people just carried the Christmas spirit through the rest of the year, the world would be a much better place.

Still, Hale evinced a very dark view of life. Some of what he'd said had told her why. It was sad.

Then he surprised her by speaking again. His routine silence seemed to be dribbling away.

"What about you, Allie? What has your life been like?"

"Happier by far than yours, it would seem."

"Share. You've dragged plenty out of me."

*Dragged?* She'd only asked. He hadn't needed to answer. But she responded anyway.

"I've been very lucky. It's boring."

"Losing your father that way couldn't have been boring. Nor losing your mother. At least I think you have."

"Yes. She died about the time I started college. Fell down the stairs."

"I'm sorry."

"No need." She grew silent.

"What made you decide to become an accountant?"

She laughed. "Now, that's a boring choice, right?"

"I didn't say that. I wouldn't say that. I'm just curious."

She thought about it, wondering how she could answer in a way anyone else could understand. "Well, I like numbers."

"Interesting. But there are a lot of fields that use numbers."

"I wanted *real* numbers. No variation, no range, none of that. Numbers are reliable. They always give accurate answers. They don't change because of the way they're used. A seven is a seven. They're solid. They don't lie."

"Don't lie," he repeated. "But they can."

"Until someone with real knowledge looks at them. Then the errors are exposed. They can't be fudged for long."

More silence as they approached the center of town.

"I guess," he said slowly, "that's how you found something wrong with Ellis's books."

"Numbers don't lie," she repeated. She couldn't imagine how to adequately explain her fascination, her love of numerals.

"Do you think the loss of your parents had something to do with that? Or has someone lied to you?"

"People lie all the time," she replied, waving her hand dismissively. "Human nature, I suppose."

"Seems to be."

She decided to change the subject. She didn't need an amateur psychologist analyzing her. "Can we go to the grocery?"

"We can't cook," he reminded her.

"I can eat those veggies we bought. But you need something more and I *want* something more."

She was not at all surprised when he agreed. People could be utterly predictable in some ways. Like Hale's appetite.

THEY FOUND THE grocery down another side street. The parking lot gave it away. Tucked behind it was an older store, with none of the gleam of newer supermarkets. If this could even be called a supermarket.

Allie wandered the aisles without purchasing anything. Hale watched her, wondering what she was doing. But then she made her decision. "Let's get some sub sandwiches."

He liked that idea.

Allie loaded hers with all the veggies she could. Hale was more sparing, thinking of all the vegetables they had in the motel room. Plus, he ordered two sandwiches. When he compared the difference in how much each of them ate, he didn't know whether to consider himself a pig or her anorectic.

He had a lot more muscle to maintain, though.

"Guess we better get these back to the motel," she said. "Before they become giant icicles."

He had to smile at that. Damn, if he wasn't careful he'd develop laugh lines.

More conversations as they passed through town. Allie had an especially long one with a woman named Kerri and the two of them agreed to meet the next afternoon at the bakery for tea and cookies.

*Tomorrow?* Hale felt as if a noose were tightening.

Then Allie looked at him and said, "I suppose I'll have to bring you along."

Like he was going to let her out of his sight. Oh, he could imagine it, him sitting there like a hulk while two women had a tea party. Everyone was going to start wondering if he was one of those abusive guys who wouldn't let his woman do anything on her own.

That would raise their profile around here even higher. *Damn it, Allie, get real.* Or maybe she *was* being real, by her own lights anyway. He had to admit their flight couldn't have been easy on her. She'd given up everything.

He was sure, however, that she didn't want to give up her life.

Hell.

After leaving their sandwiches at the motel, they went out again. As if Allie needed to soak up every possible moment in Conard City. As if she didn't care if someone shot at her. He was going to have to make her appreciate the risk in this.

As evening began to fall, another gentle snow began to fall, as well. Allie must be getting cold, because he was sure as the devil that *he* was and he was used to this kind of weather. Growing cold had stopped bothering him a long time ago in the mountains of Afghanistan.

"Allie, this much cold exposure could give you frostbite. Or hypothermia bad enough to be hospitalized." It was also keeping her outdoors way too long.

She looked at him, a mulish expression appearing, then fading. "You're not kidding."

"No."

Slowly she nodded and turned back toward that confining, bare-bones room.

When they were back inside, stripping their outerwear, he hunted for a thermostat again. No luck. Then Allie spoke, causing him to freeze.

"You must hate me, Hale."

After a moment he turned around. "I couldn't ever hate you. But why do you think I might?"

"Because I'm being a pain in the butt. You want to keep moving and I'm keeping you stuck here. I want to be a partner in this and you just want me to follow orders."

He shook his head. The working of a woman's mind. Much more consideration than a man would show. "I am perfectly capable of putting you in that vehicle whether you like it or not. Have I done that?"

"But you're miserable. You don't like all this. Worse, you're worrying about me."

He sat on a chair to loosen his boots. "You need the break."

"Right." She sounded a bit sarcastic. "And you think I need to be protected. I guess I do. So why aren't you arguing with me?"

He shouldn't say it, but he did. "Because I like to see you happy."

Now he'd done it. He wondered what flood he'd unleashed. But she dropped the subject, turning instead to the paper plates and the vegetables she'd bought earlier. She sliced everything except the bananas into neat piles and placed it on the rickety bedside table. Then she passed out the sandwiches.

"Eat," she said. "You need it more than I do."

"After all this cold, you probably need it more than you realize."

"Can't argue with that," she said cheerfully.

"At least there's something you can't argue with."

For a while there was blessed silence in the room. No questions, no desire on his part to answer them.

Allie was affecting him and he wasn't at all sure he liked it. Something deep inside him was softening. He couldn't afford that.

The vegetables disappeared almost as fast as their sandwiches. Allie watched him take the last grapes.

"Ha!" she said. "I knew you'd like them."

"I'm not a fast-food freak."

"You're too healthy-looking to be."

He helped her clean up, then left her for a few minutes to take the detritus to the outdoor trash receptacle. There might not be any roaches he could see running around the room, but he didn't want to put out the welcome mat.

When he returned, Allie was in the shower and steam came through a crack in the door. Along with the scents of her shampoo and soap. Scents he liked.

Another curse wafted through his mind and he warned himself to cut it out. Allie could barely tolerate him, and he couldn't risk getting soft.

He wondered if he should call Stu again, then decided against it. Too many breadcrumbs. He wasn't ready to start dropping them.

When Allie emerged from the shower, towel around her head, she was wearing new pajamas she'd bought at Freitag's Mercantile. They had reindeer and Santas on them, of course.

He smothered a smile. Damn, she was something else. Tomorrow she'd probably want to get a decoration for this room. Then he looked down and saw fuzzy slippers in red and green. He hadn't noticed her picking them up.

Nor was this childish, he thought. This was a woman secure enough in herself to give in to a silly urge without apology. There was something to be said for that.

She told him again to share the bed with her. This time he did, on top of the covers. His feet had warned him, despite wool socks, how cold that floor had become.

ALLIE FELT HALE lower himself into the bed. She was drowsy and not at all worried about it. She trusted him. He struck her as a man of honor.

But during the night, she woke to find herself cuddled in his arms. Startled, her eyes flew wide-open. What the heck?

He was snoring gently, his arms were slack. He was sound asleep. And the bedspread still served as a wall.

Her cheeks began to flush as she realized what had probably happened. Growing cold, still sleeping, she had undoubtedly sought his warmth. He was certainly radiating enough heat to warm her face and hands, even her entire body. He smelled good, too, after his shower.

Nor had he reacted to her pajamas. That made her smile because she'd expected a glimmer of disgust. Even a small frown at the silliness. Nope.

Content and warm, she stayed where she was. Let morning bring whatever came. As sleep crept over her again, she thought, *he's damn sexy, too.*

HALE WOKE EARLY in the morning, as was his custom, while Allie still slept. He was astonished to find her curled up against him, horrified to find his arms around her.

What had he done during the night? Tried to hug her?

But he was well and truly stuck. He couldn't slide out of bed now without waking her, and she needed some sleep after the last few days.

Now he had nothing to do with his mind except try to ignore Allie's curves pressed against him while his mind wandered over a situation he'd been pondering enough to bore himself.

A mole in his group, with no way right now to figure out who it was. Yeah, maybe now he could lure the goons and the assassin into a good place for him to take care of them, but he needed Allie safely away. He'd die before he put her in worse danger despite her insistence.

She stirred a bit, slamming his mind right back into the present. Hell, he needed to get out of this bed soon. Besides, she'd probably be horrified if she found herself in this position.

Determined now, he began to ease his arm from beneath her. He achieved success at last and moved to the single chair. Allie still slept.

Well, he was capable of covert movement, he thought

sourly. This woman was crashing a lot of his beliefs about himself, however. He didn't know if he appreciated that.

God knew at what point she might decide they had a relationship.

He just shook his head and waited for her to rouse from slumber. The way she'd been going since they arrived here, she probably needed a lot more sleep.

He was beginning to long for breakfast, though. The crazy idea of leaving her here asleep and running across the way for a couple of takeouts began to dance through his mind. *Crazy* was the word for it. He wasn't going to leave her on her own until he had a truly safe place to stash her. This room wasn't it.

Needing to move, he rose and pulled on his double shoulder holster. Allie knew he had it but she'd always looked away as if she didn't approve. Or as if it reminded her they weren't playing a game. Or maybe it reminded her of her father, or Max.

Loaded, with a couple of spare clips in his pockets, he resumed his wait. Patience. He had practiced patience for many years. Why did it seem so difficult right now?

At last Allie stirred, stretching, yawning and sitting up. She gave him a hazy smile. "We're still alive?"

A dig. He accepted it. "If this is heaven, I'd rather check for another lodging."

That widened her smile. "It's so warm under these covers I don't want to get up."

But he needed her to. His stomach chose that moment to growl loudly.

Allie laughed. "I'm getting up. Must feed the lion."

She disappeared into the bathroom for a few minutes, then emerged to start quickly putting on her outerwear. "The truck stop?"

"Easiest place."

"Okay." Then she flashed him a look from the corner of her eye. "Quickest, too."

Damn, she was going to make him laugh.

AFTER ALL THE vegetables she'd stuffed in last night, Allie wasn't dismayed by the diner's menu. This morning, more trucks than ever grumbled in the parking lot and plenty of male and female truckers occupied tables. Some were available, however, and Hale once again chose seating that was away from the windows.

She wondered if he'd ever break that habit. Unlikely.

This morning she ordered fried eggs, bacon and toast. The little cups of marmalade tempted her, too.

Hale spoke after placing his own large order. "Looks like I've dragged you down to my own level of dietary misbehavior."

She smiled. "As you reminded me, it's cold out there. Besides, I filled myself with vegetables and fruit last night."

After breakfast and coffee arrived and they began eating, Hale asked, "What are your plans for today?"

"The bakery with Kerri. I'm looking forward to that. Otherwise..." She shrugged. "I'll play it by ear."

That answer had to annoy him. He was a man used to planning. Play it by ear? Did he ever do that? Or maybe he was doing that all the time, and that's what made him such a good bodyguard. After all, he was pretty much letting her have her way by staying in Conard City.

He'd hate it, but she wished she knew more about what was running around inside his head.

Then she remembered last night and how good it had felt to be curled up with him that way. It went beyond her desire for warmth. She hoped she hadn't betrayed anything else. Dang, her cheeks were flushing again. She looked down at her plate as if it were the most fascinating thing in the world.

Maybe it was. She couldn't remember the last time she'd eaten bacon so perfectly cooked.

After he'd made a good dent on his breakfast, he asked, "What are you going to do this afternoon other than meet that woman for coffee and cookies?"

"Wing it," she said again. "I love all the nice people around here. It's almost like a Christmas postcard."

"It is one."

She could almost hear the thought that must be in his mind when she said that, though his face betrayed nothing as usual. He was probably thinking that Christmas postcards were ephemeral, a thin piece of paper that could be easily torn.

A sorry way to look at life.

She wished she knew something, anything, that could make him feel cheerier. Ah, well. No chance of that, she supposed.

"What about the library?" she suggested. "Maybe I can find a book about local history."

That caused him to arch a brow. "Won't that slow you down?"

She grinned at that one. "We'll see."

SEVERAL HOURS LATER, after Allie had popped into a few shops, she looked around. Conard City *was* small, leaving little for her to explore now. Well, there was the parade tonight, but there was little else on her menu of choices for the day.

But she still refused to leave. She could, however, feel Hale growing tenser, as if he were increasingly unhappy about them lingering. Maybe he was right, but she wasn't ready to get back in that car again and drive endlessly to nowhere.

"Tomorrow is Christmas Eve," she remarked. "The children's party and gift giving. I'm looking forward to that."

There, she'd staked her claim on tomorrow, as well. If he erupted, she'd weather the storm and plant her feet more firmly.

The threat of Ellis and his minions seemed to be fading away, growing more distant. At least in her own mind. She judged Hale didn't agree. Regardless, this had to come to an end soon.

But Ellis could have given up, she reasoned. If Hale knew much about what was happening, he hadn't told her anything, which was frustrating.

"Hale? How far can we run?"

"As far as it takes."

"But how is that going to fix anything?" Not the first time she had asked.

He faced her. The street here was quiet, almost empty. Maybe most people had finished their shopping and were now at home preparing all kinds of delights for tomorrow and Christmas, for their families. Excited kids, smiling parents, flour dusting the air as cookies and pies filled the house with delicious aromas.

She felt both wistful and envious.

"Hale?" she repeated.

He was still looking at her, as if deciding what to say, how much to tell her. Then, "We're losing some of the pursuers. Ellis's goons have dropped to a smaller number. The remainder won't quit, unfortunately, but there are fewer to deal with."

"I guess that's good."

"Considering I don't have an army, yes. That's why I've been keeping us on the move."

So something had been accomplished by all that driving. "Have they gotten closer to us?"

"Yes."

"But how?"

"When all this is over, I sure as hell am going to find out how."

She watched his jaw tighten, his eyes harden. A dangerous man indeed.

THE ENTIRE POINT of this flight had not only been to get Allie out of the immediate line of fire. It had been for him to get a bead on the pursuers so *he* could turn the tables and go after *them*.

Diminishing the number of goons had been important to his plan. Reduce their number to three or four and he could take them all out. Even better, he could question them until they squealed on Ellis.

The reduction of their numbers had at first seemed to indicate that Ellis thought he had time. That he believed Allie hadn't gone to the authorities with her knowledge and maybe proof. That he could take care of her at his leisure.

The hired assassin had been a monkey wrench in the works. Now the diminishing number of Ellis's security people probably meant that Ellis was sure they'd find Allie. That they were growing closer to their quarry.

They'd sure been drawing closer, albeit still behind as far as he knew. He needed more adequate information about them. He wondered how to pry it out of Stu. A longer phone call would ping a tower multiple times, putting a great big X on the map, making it more dangerous when the goons were coming closer. God knew what resources Ellis had within the various phone companies.

But maybe it was time to cut line. Pull them into a trap of some kind sooner, as Allie kept insisting. He could take care of the goons but the hit man was something else. Not only would he be a sniper so he could shoot safely from a distance, but he'd also be experienced in covering his tracks before and after.

Whichever way the attack came, Allie was walking around this town like a sitting duck and didn't give a damn.

He decided it was time to call Stu again, and this time to hell with the opaque language. The threat was looming over them now, and he couldn't afford to care about eavesdroppers.

Given the way they'd been followed, he had no doubt they were drawing closer. The time was fast approaching.

He looked at Allie. "I need you to do something for me."

"What?"

"Go to the bakery and stay there until I come back. And don't sit in front of a window, okay?"

Her face paled even though her cheeks were reddened by cold. "Did something happen?"

He shook his head. "Not yet. I need to do a little scouting, and I need to know you're safe indoors with a lot of people, okay? And mind me about that window."

She nodded, her cheer deflating. "I can do that."

"Promise me, Allie."

"I promise."

"I'll walk you to the bakery before I go."

But his gaze kept straying to that church tower, looking for something, anything.

Nothing.

ALLIE MANAGED TO salvage her mood by the time Kerri arrived, escorted by a beautiful white dog with a gray face mask, like a husky. But he didn't appear to be a full husky.

"Oh, he's beautiful," she said to Kerri. Then she saw the "service dog" embroidered into his vest. "A service dog?"

Kerri nodded. "A lifesaver. You want anything from the counter? My treat."

Allie decided on a Danish and a refill on her coffee. Kerri returned with a plate full of various pastries and two coffees.

"I love this time of year," Kerri remarked. "Melinda's rarely open after noon because she's sold out."

Her dog sat beside her, watching her with adoring eyes.

"What's his name?" Allie asked.

"Snowy. Well, actually it's Snowball, but I've always called him Snowy. He doesn't seem to mind." She smiled at Allie. "Help yourself to anything. I sure can't eat it all myself. What brings you and your fiancé to this out-of-the-way place?"

"A winter holiday," Allie answered, wondering if she was about to be grilled. "We decided to meander around. I'm glad we meandered here."

Kerri grinned. "Me, too."

Placing a piece of Danish on a paper napkin, Allie broke some off. "I'm an accountant. What do you do?"

Kerri sighed. "I used to be a cop. Well, I guess I still am, of sorts."

"Used to be?"

"I got shot in the head. Epilepsy. Hence Snowy. He warns me of seizures so I don't get into trouble."

"I'm so sorry."

"I was for a while, too. I loved being a cop. But things turned around once I got here. I came to teach criminal law at the junior college. One thing led to another and I'm working as a victim counselor for the sheriff. Made me feel better." Then her eyes twinkled. "And I met my husband. Very cool."

"I should say so!"

"He's a cop, too." Kerri laughed outright. "Guess it gets into the blood in more ways than one."

"Any kids?"

Kerri spoke, a little subdued. "I'm not sure. I mean, I get these spells when I'm absolutely not aware of anything around me. How could I safely take care of a kid?"

Allie didn't know how to reply to that. It was so sad, but she didn't want to say so. Kerri appeared to be the kind of woman who'd just keep picking herself up somehow. "You're brave," she offered.

Kerri shook her head. "I'm a survivor."

"That doesn't mean you're not brave."

Kerri smiled. "Keep it up. I could get used to this."

Allie laughed.

HALE SCOUTED OUTSIDE TOWN, knowing he was probably wasting his time but needing to do so for his own peace of mind. He brought out his infrared binoculars and paused every so often to survey the wide-open expanses that surrounded the town. Not a lot of cover.

But looking through the goggles for heat signatures, he wondered if he'd see anything that looked like human passage. There were sure a lot of animals out there. Heat signatures wouldn't last long in this cold, however.

The roads into and out of town were pretty bright, though. Lots of traffic keeping them warm.

Well, that wasn't going to tell him anything. No suspiciously parked cars, either. He reckoned the assassin wouldn't arrive on foot. He needed to blend in only briefly in town, and he'd need a nearby escape vehicle. Maybe not out here, however. Parked somewhere in town, most likely.

Disgusted with his feeling of helplessness, Hale headed back into town. How the hell would this killer stick out anyway? He'd noticed that a lot of locals packed guns on their hips, and some carried hunting rifles slung over their shoulders. Hell, probably nobody would have blinked if they'd seen his twin pack.

No gun restrictions in Wyoming. Shades of the Wild West.

Hale found parking right in front of the bakery. A few people were leaving and he stood aside to let them pass, answering their smiles and greetings with a nod of his head.

Inside he saw Allie with her new friend Kerri. They seemed to be having a whale of a good time, with laughter flowing frequently.

He hated to rain on the parade but he couldn't hulk in a corner and ignore his supposed fiancée. Nope. Talk about raising a lot of gossip.

He unzipped his jacket and strode to the women, easing his way around other tables. When he reached Allie and Kerri, he did the obvious thing: he bent down and brushed a kiss on Allie's lips. The zing that zapped through him startled him. Her eyes widened.

"How you doing, darlin'?"

"We're having a wonderful time," Kerri said. "Pull up a chair and join us, Hale."

Hale could have winced. Not only had Allie revealed her own first name, but she'd apparently revealed Hale's. *X marks the spot*, he thought grimly. Don't ever assign this woman to a covert mission.

He didn't want to pull that chair over, however. First, he didn't want to talk aimlessly. Second, he was certain he'd be gently questioned about his job or whatever. What was he going to say? A lie or the truth? He hated lies.

Saving him, Kerri looked at her cell phone. "Oh my gosh, I've been having so much fun I lost track of time. We've got this faculty thing at the school tonight. I need to get ready."

The two women hugged as Kerri departed. Hale looked at Allie. "Want anything else?"

Allie was still smiling. "No thanks. Kerri kind of over-whelmed me with pastries."

He nodded and rose. "Let's go, then. I need to make a stop."

"Where?"

"You'll see."

She shook her head a little but pulled on her jacket and zipped up. Then they walked around the corner to the door of the sheriff's office.

She stopped. "Hale?"

"Yeah?"

"Has something happened?"

He shook his head. "I just want to check something out, that's all. Nothing wrong."

She didn't look as if she believed him but followed him inside. When he asked for Sheriff Dalton, he was given directions to a back office.

But first Hale looked at Allie. "Please wait here."

"But I want to know…"

"There's nothing to know. I want to describe some of the situation. Just in case. Okay?"

She nodded slowly and sat in one of the visitors' chairs, looking angry. He couldn't blame her. Then he marched down the hall.

Gage Dalton sat behind his desk wearing a dark brown winter-weight uniform. He nodded and waved Hale to a chair.

"So what's the real story?" Dalton asked before Hale could say much more than hello.

"Real story?"

"Odd couple suddenly shows up in my town claiming to be tourists on holiday and the man looks like trouble on the hoof. What's more, the two of you don't look romantic with each other. You didn't just stumble here. Or maybe you did but you've got some reason for moving around that has nothing to do with tourism."

Hale gave Dalton props. The guy didn't miss a thing.

"Well, that's what I wanted to talk with you about."

Dalton nodded. "I'm all ears."

Hale hesitated. He had plenty of good reasons for letting the sheriff know the outline, but how much detail should he provide? He began to speak, knowing there'd be questions, and not at all sure he should answer them.

"I'm not Allie's fiancé," he started. "I'm her bodyguard."

Gage Dalton sat up a little straighter, wincing as he did so. "What is she? Some kind of heiress?"

Hale shook his head. "She's an ordinary woman, an accountant who ran afoul of a very dangerous businessman as she was doing his books."

Dalton frowned. "How dangerous? Powerful?"

"Tentacles everywhere. A history of making employees disappear. Cops have been after him for years but can't get enough evidence. Anyway, Allie found something, reported it to him so he could get it fixed, and he told her *Bad things can happen.*"

Gage nodded slowly. "A veiled threat?"

"Her friend, a detective that's been working this case for years, believed it was. He made her hire me and get her out of the way."

Now Gage leaned back, swiveling his chair to one side. He thought for a few minutes. "So you've got her on the run?"

"Temporarily. If she weren't so damn stubborn, we'd have been back on the road almost as soon as we got here. But she wants her Christmas, and she loves it here." He didn't mention her desire to stay here because she wanted to tighten her own noose.

"That's understandable."

"Well, I haven't dragged her out of here yet."

At that, Gage snorted. "Iron-willed."

"To say the least."

"I'm married to a woman like that. My Emma. Powerful and strong. It's made her a survivor. Okay, what more?"

Again, Hale hesitated. He wasn't accustomed to sharing a lot of detail about his operations, but he sensed in Gage Dalton a potential ally. One who probably wasn't going to like it at all when he learned the kind of threat Hale might be drawing to his jurisdiction.

"Okay," Hale said finally. "On the QT. Maybe you've heard of Jasper Ellis?"

"Some bad stuff, nothing proved."

Hale nodded. "There are several of Jasper Ellis's security goons tracking us. Worse, it appears that hard on *their* heels is a hit man Ellis hired."

Gage's face hardened when Hale spoke of a hit man. He asked, "The pro is following the goons?"

"That's my assumption, yes."

"How are they tracking you?"

Hale frowned deeply. "I suspect I have a mole in my team."

Gage swore fluently and forcefully.

"My sentiments exactly," Hale replied.

"Fire away." Gage sighed and swiveled to face him again. "You got a plan?"

"I'm trying to figure out how to draw these guys out without endangering Allie. Once I decide, I'll take them out. With interrogation, of course."

"I don't need to hear that." But one corner of Gage's

mouth lifted. "I've done a little interrogation in my life. Former DEA," he added by way of explanation.

Hale nodded acknowledgment. "Anyway, I'm hoping nothing will happen while we're here. Last I heard, the goons weren't *that* close. But that's no guarantee."

Now Gage leaned forward. "You deal with it when you have to. Even here. No, I don't want the threat in my county but I also don't believe a young woman should be on the run forever when she's done nothing wrong. Trouble is, we've got a lot of fresh faces around here because of the holidays. It's not like I can pick out strangers for you."

Then Gage's eyes crinkled a bit. "You're the first legit bodyguard I've ever met. Something new under the sun."

"I don't feel new. I feel old." Hale stood. "I'll keep you posted if there's something you need to know."

"Appreciate it. And if you need any help, give me a holler." Then he added, "Got someone I can contact to verify all this?"

Hale pulled out his wallet and fished out Max's card, passing it to Gage. "Check us out with him. Careful what you say."

"I have some practice with elliptical speech."

Then Hale walked back out into the front room, where Allie was the picture of annoyance. Another small smile escaped him. Damn, that woman was a double helping of something else.

"What's going on?" Allie demanded after they stepped out into the cold again.

"Nothing you don't know." With the exception of the hired gun.

"Then why speak to the sheriff?"

Hale looked at her. "Because if hell starts raining down in this town, I want him to know we're the good guys, okay?"

She fell silent and he escorted her to the grocery, whether she wanted it or not. He kept her hand tucked firmly in his.

"Why do we want the grocery?"

"Because you're going to find something you actually *want* to eat while we warm up enough to survive tonight's festivities."

That relaxed her a bit. Probably because he wasn't threatening to put her in the car again.

One of the worst things about this, Hale thought, was having to drag this woman all over the West and keep her as cooped up as a kidnapping victim. How much difference was there really? Only that he was trying to save her life.

He wasn't sure she appreciated it much.

ALLIE FUMED ALL the way to the grocery store. She was sick of being led around like a dog on a leash. So maybe she didn't know all the ins and outs of protecting herself, but she deserved to know what was going on, deserved better explanations. She deserved to feel more like a partner in this rather than a carry-on bag. Hell, she needed an active role, not a passive one.

"Why can't we just eat at the diner?" she demanded before they entered the store.

"Like you're a fan of diners. Load up, woman. It's going to be cold tonight while you watch the parade."

"Quit talking to me like I'm an idiot. Don't I get to choose anything?"

"So choose. Diner? Grocery?"

She could have hated him just then. Plus, she wasn't even a bit hungry and now she had to decide what to eat later?

Well, that left the damn grocery and he probably knew it. No way was she ready to order at the café or truck stop.

Most everything in a grocery needed cooking, though. That left her wandering in front of the deli counter, trying to decide which prepared foods would please her later. Preferably foods that wouldn't freeze beyond hope by the time they walked back to the motel.

She sure didn't want to load up on chips and canned beans.

The sushi looked as if it had come from somewhere else, but she picked up a package of twelve pieces. A savory chicken salad in a large container. Potato salad. Bread to make a sandwich on with the chicken salad. Then she spied smoked salmon and added that, along with some packaged bagels and cream cheese. She topped it off with some fresh broccoli and a hunk of smoked Gouda.

In all, more than enough to feed her tonight, for a midnight snack, and for breakfast. Probably enough to feed Mr. Granite, too, but she didn't have a problem when he doubled some of her choices and added a few of his own, such as cold cuts. She only wished she could make more than a couple of cups of coffee in the room. She muttered that aloud.

Hale surprised her then. He chose a cheap twelve-cup coffee maker, a container of coffee grounds and a dozen packets of dried soup. He even thought of foam cups.

Good idea, she thought acidly as she watched him. All of it was followed by paper and plastic to eat with.

Getting by must be his stock-in-trade.

She didn't feel much happier as they trudged back to the motel. Much as she loved this beautiful Christmas setting, she had to admit she was growing tired of the constant cold. A blazing fire sounded good. Even a gas fire.

No such comforts in the motel room, though. However, shortly after she stripped her outerwear, she heard the new coffeepot start to burble and the aroma of fresh coffee joined it.

Allie threw her jacket on the foot of the bed, then lay back on it. The mattress felt good and allowing her body to stretch out felt even better. She closed her eyes, then the memory of Hale's brief kiss at the bakery raced through her. Part of their role-play, she told herself. But her body didn't want to believe it.

Sighing, she rolled to her side and watched him. Best view in town, she thought with an inward giggle. He'd dumped his jacket but not his double shoulder holster. Sort of iconic, she thought. Out of a movie. Even the beard he'd been letting slowly grow back. Who was that actor who always had a two-day beard? Probably dozens of them.

Whatever, it looked good on Hale.

In fact, as much as he irritated her, Allie felt a strong and growing attraction to him. She must be losing her mind.

Stockholm syndrome, she told herself, but didn't believe it. She was *not* his captive, though she sometimes felt like it.

Sheesh. If he ever succeeded in removing the threat to her, he'd disappear back into the void of his secret world. Did she want to be left pining for the impossible?

She sighed. As if she could control her feelings.

Hale looked at her the instant she sighed. "What's wrong? I'm driving you crazy?"

"You need to ask?" She saw a furtive smile touch his mouth. He was becoming less stony as time passed. That might be even more dangerous than the man she had originally met.

The *zap* she felt when their eyes locked ran through her entire body. She closed them at once, shielding herself.

As if she could. Long-ignored desires fluttered hotly inside her, making her core pound in time to her heartbeat.

An overwhelming wish that he'd come over and begin seducing her wouldn't leave her alone. A chicken's response, she argued with herself. Putting herself at the mercy of Hale's decision. She ought to have more gumption than that.

Except she didn't need his rejection right now. On top of the way her life had been torn apart, she didn't know if she could handle it. Strong as she'd been trying to be, stubborn as she'd insisted when she could, she felt as if the remains of her life might shatter.

But of course he wouldn't approach her. If nothing else, he'd believe it to be a violation of trust. If there was one thing she was sure about, it was that Hale was an honorable man.

The yearning still thrummed in her anyway. She had to hope Hale hadn't read it on her face in those few moments. Had to hope she hadn't embarrassed herself.

But she was still a young woman with healthy needs and while she didn't give in to them often, this time the need was almost overwhelming.

God, he was sexy. Sexier than any man should be. Yet he let no one close. No one. Even the few times he'd opened up to her, while they gave her a snapshot of his internal life, he didn't reveal much. Didn't she have to know a man better than this?

Her body didn't think so.

Then she felt the edge of the bed dip beside her. Startled, she opened her eyes again and found Hale sitting beside her.

"Allie? There are a million reasons I shouldn't touch you."

"Yeah," she said a bit sharply. "Naturally. Hale Scribner, the man who won't let anyone close. God forbid a mere woman should penetrate your armor."

"Hell, you're not a *mere* woman. I've told you things I've never told anyone else."

"So. Just save your precious isolation and go away."

Quite to the contrary, he leaned over her, caught her chin gently in his hand and turned her face upward so he could kiss her. No light brushing, but a strong, determined kiss.

"Allie," he breathed, "I want you. I want all your fire, all your stubbornness, all your fear and bravery. You take my breath away."

She wanted a snappy comeback, but it wasn't there. Instead her arm, as if it had a mind of its own, reached up to wrap around his powerful shoulders.

"Are you sure?" he asked against her lips, his breath a warm whisper.

"Yes." A quiet reply.

"Then I'd better get rid of this holster."

And more than that, she thought, her mind hazy through her deepening desire. But by the time he did that, he'd have plenty of opportunity to change his mind. She tried to steel herself.

Except he didn't change his mind. He not only got rid of his double holster, but he got rid of every stitch of clothing until he stood in all his naked magnificence in the golden light of the room's only lamp.

Just as she'd seen him come out of the shower that night, only now without a towel. Every one of those toned muscles was dangerous, but she didn't care. He'd taken care of her this long, he would continue to.

"I'm going to make you cold," he said quietly, then started removing all her clothes. Carefully. Pausing to take time to brush over her nipples, her waist, then the secret between her legs.

Cold? She felt like a flaming torch. She wanted no delay. She needed culmination. To feel him deep inside her, filling an empty space that demanded it. Needed it.

But he continued to take his time until even her socks were gone. Then he kissed the arch of each foot, moving upward to kiss her inner thighs, to drop kisses on her belly. When he reached her breasts, he licked them and sucked on her nipples.

He was driving her out of her mind.

She clutched for his shoulders, trying to drag him closer. She wanted his weight on top of her, surrounding her.

Then he answered her wish, cloaking her in the heat from his body, capturing her face between his hands.

"You're perfect," he murmured. "Absolutely perfect. Beautiful. More beautiful because of how drowsy you look right now."

She was more interested in the rigidity of his staff pressing against her belly and her private parts. So stiff, so ready, so large, like the rest of him. More thrills ran through her, and never had she felt so worshipped.

He moved against her, tantalizing her, not yet entering her as if he wanted to drive her to insanity first. She was coming close.

"Hale," she murmured huskily. "Hale, please…"

He answered her plea, entering her slowly. Gently. With each deepening of his penetration she felt herself expanding, the most delicious sensation ever.

Then he was all the way in and he reached down between them, rubbing the nub of her need even as he began to move.

She felt as if she were caught on a welder's arc, so hot, so needy.

But before long his movements sped up and she felt as if she were riding a whirlwind of hunger. Higher and higher until satisfaction claimed her in a thunderclap of ecstasy.

He wasn't far behind. With one final thrust, he shuddered and reached his own pinnacle.

She drifted down like a feather on a gentle breeze.

HALE PULLED THE bedspread over them and cuddled her in a warm cocoon. His hand ran up and down her side, almost like petting.

"I'll have to go back on duty soon," he offered quietly.

"I know." This departure from the norm might have been risky. At least he would think so.

"I'd like to stay right here with you all night," he answered huskily. "But I can't. We're already running enough of a risk staying in one spot for so long."

"Then why haven't you dragged me away?"

"Because you're stubborn. Because I want you to have your Christmas."

His answer pierced her heart with warmth. He'd cared enough about that to run a risk. Maybe a huge risk. Would he never stop surprising her?

"Still want to go to that parade?" he asked her as he finished dressing.

"No," she answered, surprising herself. "I'd like to sit here with you and eat our grocery stash. What I'd really like, if we can, is to go see the Christmas party for the kids tomorrow."

He hesitated before answering. "I need to make a call first, find out how we stand. Okay?"

"It had better be good," she answered saucily.

This time a genuine smile crossed his face. He headed out the door.

She rolled around in the covers for a few minutes, then put on her flannel nightgown. It was becoming her favorite.

Surprising her, Hale stuck his head in the door. "I need to take a short walk. Keep the door locked."

"How short a walk?"

"Fifteen, maybe twenty minutes, okay?"

"But why?"

"I'll tell you when I get back."

She guessed she had to be satisfied with that.

Besides, it would give her time to hug herself and enjoy the afterglow he'd left in her. Her mind ran over his each and every touch as if trying to etch the entire experience permanently in her mind.

Man, sex had never been so good.

# Chapter Thirteen

Outside in the frigid air, Hale retrieved another of his phones. He had a good supply of them but the pile was still shrinking. Without inserting the battery, he stuffed it into one of his inside pockets.

After he closed the tailgate, he checked the packed snow that currently obscured most of the license plate. Good enough. Considering the weather they'd been having around here, it wouldn't even look suspicious.

Then he set out on a hike toward the center of town. He dipped into the Mercantile, spent a few minutes and some of his own money, then came out with a small bag tucked in his pocket. The parade was moving down the street with plenty of noise, so he sought a quieter place to make the phone call.

"Stu."

"Yeah," came the familiar voice. "My cats got out and are now heading west. At least it looks like. You sure you don't have some catnip?"

"I don't believe so."

"Then check again, good buddy. I don't know where that catnip is, but the change in direction…"

Hale understood completely. Someone had picked up on something somewhere. For all he knew they were following a map of stolen license plates. Which shouldn't bring them directly here. And he knew for sure he hadn't revealed his current location to Stu.

The fact that Stu didn't have his location made him doubt he had a leak in his team. Then what?

He tossed the dead phone and chip on trucks headed in different directions, then crossed the highway to the motel.

He didn't enter immediately, however. He had some mulling to do and Allie's presence wouldn't make it any easier.

How closely were they being followed? So far he'd say not. But they were being *successfully* followed. Damn it, *how?*

Could his use of those pay-per-use phones really be tracked? Could a single ping on a tower be getting noticed?

Given Ellis's resources, he wouldn't be surprised. That meant they could be pinged here. He could have turned the air blue with curses but he didn't want to draw any attention.

He should get Allie out of here right away. Except he wasn't sure staying was a problem and he wasn't sure if his phones were the problem and Allie had made her position clear. She wasn't going to move without a damn good reason, especially since she didn't like being *baggage*. She was impatient with the whole idea that he could catch these guys without exposing her.

One more day, he told himself. He could keep her safe until after the Christmas party and then they were going to hit the road again.

One more day. He could do it. He didn't want to take the happiness from her any sooner than he must.

One more day, he promised himself yet again. He'd just have to stay on extraordinarily high alert. No different from Afghanistan.

Although Allie had locked the door from the inside, he

was able to use his key to open it. Another security breach he ought to consider dealing with.

Much to his amazement, when he entered he discovered she'd laid out all their food on paper plates for dinner.

"Five-star service," he remarked as he shed his jacket.

"Well, I had to do something to fill the time. Dig in. I'm going to." She promptly proved it by popping a piece of cheese in her mouth. "It's pretty good, too, although I'm a little afraid of the sushi. I'm sure it wasn't made here."

"Honestly, I'm surprised you found any at all." He paused, then added, "You didn't miss much of a parade. Santa riding a sled on the back of a pickup truck with a couple of mechanical reindeer. Oh, and Santa was tossing candy canes to the kids. The most I can say about it was that the Christmas music piped over speakers was deafening."

Allie laughed. "Charming. But you're right, I'm not sorry I missed it."

"Oh, yeah, don't forget the police car leading the front and the fire truck bringing up the rear. Dang horns were like to make my ears scream."

They ate in silence for a while, even the sushi, which they decided was edible if not great.

But then Allie had to bring it up again. "What did your friend say?"

Well, he didn't have an honest answer to that, so he tried to find a hedge that wouldn't be lying. "They're still looking. No pinpoint yet."

"That's a good thing, right?"

"Yeah." As long as he was getting the full information. The skin on the back of his neck began crawling again.

Something was seriously wrong. But he'd have to face these guys sooner rather than later because Allie couldn't spend the rest of her life on the run. She'd made that very clear, including running an incredible risk by planting herself here. But he wanted it to happen at the place of his own time and choosing, with Allie safe whether she liked it or not.

He needed better info. More than the general direction they were heading. Stu was giving him the best information he could, or so it seemed, yet the noose appeared to be tightening anyway.

Hell. There'd been times in Afghanistan when he'd wanted to crawl out of his own skin because the air had been filled with threats he couldn't see.

This was one of those times. Bad enough to have those goons on Allie's tail, but a paid assassin? What the hell had Allie discovered? Could she even explain it to him in a way he'd understand? Not that he needed to. All that mattered was the danger to her.

Maybe it was time to call Max and see if his web was tingling at all. Except he didn't want to call Max and possibly draw him into this mess. Max's phone might even be tapped, hence his warning to the sheriff.

All he could say at this point was that taking Allie on the run had reduced the number of pursuers to a manageable group. It wouldn't matter, though, if he couldn't corral them and put an end to this chase.

He cleaned up the detritus of their supper, hauling the trash out to the bin at the end of the hotel. His eyes were never still, scanning for any movement, anything out of place. If those goons were in the truck parking lot, however, he'd never be able to pick them out.

Not unless they acted oddly. He watched for a few, then got his butt back to Allie. At least if anyone tried to break in he could stuff her under the bed and take out the threat.

It should only be so easy.

The goons probably didn't have murder on their agenda.

That would be more people than Ellis would want to know his plans.

But the pro seriously worried Hale. Nothing would stop him even if he had to chase Allie to the ends of the earth.

Allie spoke. "You're getting uneasy." Then wistfully she said, "I guess you don't want to stay for the kids' party tomorrow."

He looked into her hopeful face and hated what he was doing to her. "It's at noon, right?"

She nodded.

"Then we'll go afterward." A few hours. He doubted they'd make much of a difference now. If he drew the danger into this town, so be it. He'd scoped the place enough to know where the risks lay.

But he was settling into his mission mindset, the one that had kept him alive in the most threatening situations. Now he needed it for Allie.

Because he was long past caring what happened to him.

ALLIE WAS DISAPPOINTED when Hale didn't come to bed with her. She so longed for a repeat of last night.

But she'd also come to know him well enough to realize he was getting wound as tight as a spring.

She closed her eyes, dealing with her own selfishness. Becoming difficult, wanting her Christmas. All of it was causing him serious strain. He hadn't dragged her all over the place, driving her for miles through one small town to another because he *wanted* to. He'd probably enjoyed it no more than she had.

But he was devoted to protecting her and she was making it so much more difficult by demanding to be part of what he was doing. God, she wasn't one to stand by, especially when she thought her own pigheadedness was the only way they would ever deal with this.

But why hadn't he just insisted that she get in the car? Why hadn't he physically dragged her to get on their way? Why had he let her set herself up? Did he privately agree that hers was the only way to get at the pursuers? Didn't sound like Hale to her.

She could only conclude that he'd judged the threat to be far enough away to make it possible to stay for a few days.

But whatever his judgment had been, she wasn't immune to realizing he was turning into honed steel again.

# Chapter Fourteen

In the wee hours, while Allie slept the deep sleep of the innocent, Hale reached a point where he could barely stand it anymore. He'd pushed this mess to the breaking point and his internal alerts had begun to sound like a Klaxon.

Allie's demand that she take an active role in this didn't help his mood any. He damn well had to find out more about their pursuers.

Stepping outside, just beyond the door, he pulled out another of his phones and stared up at the starry sky. The morning would arrive brilliant with sunlight. That might help.

Then, stepping away from the door, he called Stu again. Stu sounded a bit sleepy.

"What the hell?" Hale demanded.

"I was hoping you'd call," Stu said. "Damn phones you're using, I can't call *you*."

"News?"

"Two more cats have changed direction, leaving only two together. You *must* have catnip."

"I'd like to find it. Lay it on."

"Would you recognize any meaning for two horseshoes tipped on their sides in the same direction?"

Hale didn't have to think. Conard City. Or Conard County. Either one was bad enough. His heart beat more heavily, but more slowly. The adrenaline was just beginning to course through him. "Why do you ask?"

Stu paused a minute. "You know how I told you I was thinking my house is haunted? Nobody's been around to move my decorations. So, I got a ghost and he's been banging around since last evening and tipping my horseshoes. Know an exorcist I can get fast? Like immediately?"

Hale didn't answer. He and Allie had been pinged somehow. Okay, then. And the ghost had to be Casper, only a few hours east of here. He closed his eyes tightly before speaking again.

"Sprinkle some holy water," he said finally. "I'll let you know about the exorcist if I can find one."

He ripped the phone apart, knowing it was now a useless safety measure. How the hell were they being tracked?

Only one thought occurred to him. He opened the tailgate and looked inside his box of phones. At the very bottom he found one that contained both SIM card and battery.

He wasn't stupid enough to have done that. Someone had gotten into his phones. He picked up the one he had just used and called Stu again.

"Yeah?" Stu answered.

"Somebody screwed with one of the phones. Find him."

Then he disconnected, threw the phone on the ground and ground it beneath his heel.

The game was on. Except that it was no game.

And now he had to tell Allie the whole sorry story.

He made a pot of coffee and used the smaller motel pot to boil water for the packaged soup. Then he woke Allie as gently as he could.

She stirred slowly from a deep sleep. As soon as she sat up, still groggy, he put a foam cup of chicken soup in her hands.

"What's happening?" she asked.

"A whole helluva lot. Swallow that soup. We need to talk."

That seemed to wake her instantly. She set the soup on a bedside table and pulled the bedspread up to wrap around herself. "Shoot."

"I told you I was trying to lose as many of Ellis's security people as I could."

She nodded, reaching for the soup. "Yeah. Because you're not an army."

"Well, they've been cut to two."

She reached for the cup and sipped the soup slowly. He was sure it wasn't too hot because that little pot didn't keep the water hot for long. "That's good news, right?"

"To a point."

She wrapped both hands around the cup, sipping more. "What's going on, Hale? Just finally tell me the truth about what you're doing. Tell me the real dimensions of this threat that has you so worried. I'm tired of being kept in the dark, and tired of being treated as if I can't deal with anything."

She'd been trying one way or another to make that clear to him since her initial shock and disbelief had worn off. He'd watched her impatience grow until she had finally dug in her heels and said she was tired of being treated like luggage.

He hadn't meant to make her feel that way, but his focus had been entirely on keeping her safe. He should have listened better.

"I wish you didn't feel that way," he said.

"I'm a woman. I'm *used* to being treated that way. I've never liked it."

Ah, hell, now he was a misogynist? "I don't think

women are stupid or are little girls. I've fought beside enough of your sex to know better."

She smiled with satisfaction, then drained the last of her soup. "So treat me like one of those women you fought beside. Fill me in on the mission."

But how to find the right words? He had to choose, starting with the smallest parts. Then would come the paid killer, and she wasn't going to like that part at all.

"Okay, we're down to two goons on our tail."

"Manageable for you, I'd bet."

"Most definitely. More soup?" He needed the pause to choose his words carefully.

"Why do I have the feeling this is going to be a cold morning? Since we're filling me with hot liquids, bring me some coffee and get yourself some. It can wait that long or you'd have already thrown me over your shoulder and jammed me in the car."

He kept his lips zipped while he made her more soup, then poured coffee for each of them. So she'd imagined him doing the caveman thing. "I won't say I haven't thought about it."

She snickered. "I would never have dreamed."

He felt a corner of his mouth twitch in response as he ferried cups to the bedside table. No, hang on to his iciness. Don't let himself soften.

She helped herself to the coffee first, blowing on it gently. "Spill," she said.

No escaping it any longer. He wasn't looking forward to reading her reaction on her face. He'd become fond of the cheerful woman she'd turned into in this town.

"Okay. Two goons. Minimal threat. We winnowed them out good, Allie."

"Well, you did most of it."

"And you came along for the ride."

She looked down and smiled. "Being generous there, Mr. Tough Guy. Better take it easy."

But none of this was going to be easy. None. He sighed.

"All right. They're headed here. Directly here, according to my source. They left Casper just a little while ago, and they evidently know where we are. My source sure figured it out somehow."

She looked at him, reflecting dismay. "How? How do they know? I saw all the precautions you took."

"Honest to God, I really don't know for certain. What I *do* know is that my team managed to get tracers on all their vehicles. I've been watching their numbers fall away, but maybe that means they found a way to keep tabs on us and didn't need as many goons."

"But how?"

He shook his head. "I found a phone in my stash that was still hooked into the network. Somebody must have done that."

"A betrayer?"

"I'm worried about that. But I'm also sure that might not explain it."

She asked for another cup of coffee. "Then I have to put myself in plain sight. I'm sure they won't grab me from the town square."

"Probably not." Now came the difficult part. Now he *had* to tell her. He steeled himself against her probable reaction.

"So here's the thing," he said after a delay to drink coffee. "The thing I haven't told you. The thing that's kept us moving so fast. Those goons by themselves weren't a big enough threat."

He heard her draw a sharp breath. She quickly put aside her coffee and wrapped her hands together. "What is?" she asked quietly.

He fired the words like bullets. "A professional hit man."

Her face paled until it was almost white. The reaction he had feared. Probably to be followed by sheer terror.

She sat frozen for a minute, maybe longer. Finally she shook herself and whispered, "He'd go that far?"

"Ellis is a dangerous man. Max and I have emphasized that enough."

"But why a professional?"

"Because he'll never talk. Because he'll vanish into the woodwork the minute his job is complete." Hale drew a deep breath of his own. "And he *will not quit* until he finishes the job."

"Oh my God…" The words barely emerged from her throat.

"This *is* the rest of your life, Allie, unless I stop him."

She nodded jerkily, still pale. She twisted her hands but he could still see them shaking. He could do nothing to prevent it, nothing to reassure her. And there was more to come.

She looked at him, searching his face. "You always looked hard, Hale, but not as hard as you do right now."

"Mission face," he answered, although that was probably an understatement given the feelings for her that he was burying in a crypt inside his soul.

She drank more coffee. He waited as if for the guillotine. He wouldn't blame her if she erupted like a volcano, or melted into hopeless, frightened tears.

She held out her cup. "Give me a few minutes, please."

Well, that was a calm response. So far. He poured them both more coffee and returned to waiting. She had to absorb this, but a time clock had begun to tick in his head.

She spoke, her voice steady. "A sniper?"

"I think so. Trying to get up close and personal would just get messy."

"God, a sniper." A shudder ran through her. "I thought that happened only in movies."

"I wish."

She drank some more coffee. "They're deadly. Always accurate."

"Usually."

Her eyes had grown hollow. "Usually?"

"Depends. This one is at a disadvantage. No spotter to calculate a trajectory for him. So he'll have to move in closer."

She nodded. "How close?"

"The range of a decent deer rifle."

"That's still a long way."

"It changes my calculations," he said flatly. "He's got only a few lines of sight in this town. And he sure as hell can't shoot much over a hundred yards around here, which narrows the area I have to watch considerably."

"So maybe if I just keep moving…"

Now the rest of the bad news. "Unlike in the movies, you can't move faster than a bullet. No one can."

Her hand shook once, then she finished the coffee and put the cup down with a quiet thump. "That's it, then. I have to be visible or he'll never take a shot at me. He'll just keep coming."

He'd been fearing this from the outset. Trying to scramble together a way to avoid exposing her. But he couldn't just wander around out there hoping to spy a guy who'd probably blend in like one blade of grass in a lawn. That was another thing these snipers were good at: being invisible in their surroundings.

He spewed a few good cuss words. "I'm messing up my job. I've been trying to think of a way to avoid this, to get the sniper without exposing you, but we couldn't get him painted."

"Painted?"

"We don't know where he is. We couldn't get a bead on him. He's out there somewhere is all we know."

She pursed her lips. "Wouldn't he be with the goons?"

"I figure he's following them. They don't know about him."

"Why not?"

"Because Ellis wouldn't want them to know. The more people who know, the more people he has to get rid of. They probably think they've been sent to convince you to keep your mouth shut. Maybe to offer you a lot of money to walk away. But Ellis wants more than a deal."

"I guess so." She frowned thoughtfully. "So how do we handle this? I need to be in the open, and you can't get to him if you don't know where he is."

"You're absolute sure about doing this? Think about it, Allie."

She nodded. "I'm sure. My dad wouldn't have run."

Well, that settled it, he decided grimly.

"I've scoped the town. I know his likely spots. I'll keep an eye on them. But before it gets light, you're going to come with me to the sheriff's office. You won't like wearing body armor."

Now she looked astonished. "Body armor?"

"You better believe it. I'm not going to have you out there walking around like an oblivious deer. The armor will be heavy, but it'll protect you against anything a hunting rifle can shoot."

WELL, THAT WAS some comfort, she thought. Her insides twisted but she wasn't going to quit. Hell no. She'd been arguing that she wanted to be a partner in this, and now was her chance.

"I can take you out of here," he offered as they donned their clothing.

"No." She wasn't surprised he'd offered, but she'd had enough. Maybe all this was making her suicidal or something, but it had to stop. At any risk.

Her spine had stiffened to the point that it felt rigid. All of her was tightened up, but it was now or never, as they said.

Hale drove them to the sheriff's office. It was still dark, but dawn was beginning to gray the eastern horizon.

"Is he already out there?" she asked.

"Most likely, if the goons are convinced you're here then the shooter has been informed by his employer. Which means he's already found a hiding place. But he won't shoot until the light is good enough and you're in the right place."

"Can't we search for him?"

"Not enough time now. I'd have to look too many places. So I'll keep an eye peeled for any unusual movement at any elevation, the higher the better for his purposes."

"There are a lot of upper-story windows out there," she remarked as a shiver ran through her.

No kidding, he thought as he rolled them into a parking space. "Don't stop, just head for the sheriff's door."

He watched her dart inside, then headed for his bank of phones. No point in the usual precautions now. He called Stu again.

"Yo."

"Stu. We're getting ready to take on the problem. What I need from you is a paint job. Keep an eye on the cats. I'll call."

"You got it."

Then Hale stuffed the phone in his pocket and headed inside. To his surprise, Gage was already there.

"You get up early," Hale remarked.

"I'm addicted. Actually, most of my nights are disturbed. Old injury. No point in bothering Emma with my pacing around the house."

Hale nodded. The sheriff had already installed Allie in a chair.

"Don't drink the coffee here," Gage said. "Battery acid. All those bottles of antacid are there for a reason."

"I take the warning."

"Fill me in," Gage said, leaning back against the edge of a desk. A couple of deputies manned other desks and were trying not to look too interested.

"I have reason to believe the pro may already be in town. He probably hid himself overnight."

Gage nodded. "Great. Okay. What do you need me to do?"

"Give Allie some body armor. She's going to be standing in the square being a target."

"Damn! You want me to send some uniforms out to look around?"

Hale shook his head. "Anything changes, he'll skedaddle faster than a cat. Then we gotta look again."

Gage turned to Allie. "You up with this?"

"Now or later," she answered steadily. "I'm choosing my ground."

Damn, she was one hell of a woman. Courageous. Hale tipped her the slightest smile.

Gage spoke again to Hale. "You want armor, too?"

"No. It'd slow me down."

"I'm sure I have some gear that will fit Allie," Gage said as he headed down the hall. "This is some Christmas Eve."

ALLIE NEEDED HELP with the armor. Hale knew the ins and outs. The main thing she noticed was the weight. Heavy stuff. Hanging from her shoulders. Riding up her neck like the world's worst turtleneck. As if that wasn't enough, the sheriff handed over some arm protection and thigh protection.

"Gotta protect those arteries." Dalton walked around as Hale helped her into her jacket. "It has a hood. Good."

Then he went to a locker and handed Hale a dark helmet. "This should fit under her hood."

"God," Allie said when they'd finished dumping weight on her. "My knees are going to hate me."

Hale shrugged. "Sit in the snow if you need to. Or on a bench. At this point…"

"What I *can* do," Gage said, "is make sure some of my folks are wandering in the park with her. If we all keep moving, it might take him longer to sight on her."

Hale nodded. "Good idea. I wasn't going to ask that anyone take a risk."

"You didn't ask. Give me a few and we're going to have some apparently ordinary citizens walking around the square, not too far from Allie. Maybe in a friendly group around her."

"At least I'm warm now," Allie remarked. Then she dropped onto the nearest chair.

Allie knew now the weight and discomfort of this body armor, and she felt the greatest admiration for anyone who could wear it and function. They probably trained with it, but still.

It was also hot, particularly under her outer clothing. Well, she sure wasn't going to get cold this morning.

Hale stopped her before they exited. "Allie, swear to me you're sure about this. It's flying in the face of everything I do."

"You know, Hale, if this is the kind of danger you protect people from, you deserve a lot more than I'm paying you. I'm sure. I'm done. This is no life."

She was determined, but also afraid. Even with the armor. *Nobody can outrun a bullet.* Dear God.

People were already gathering in the square, in a conversational knot. They greeted her like a friend and drew her in with them. Hale came along but his eyes never held still. He had drawn down his balaclava, becoming white from head to ankle. Blending with the snow.

Allie kept looking at him. He hadn't said it, but he'd be a target, too. The thought of never seeing him again scared her more than getting killed herself.

She was pleased to see that Kerri was there with her dog. A couple of the others she recognized from her conversations around town. They were all cops?

But now they were dressed in regular winter clothing. Were they wearing armor, too? She hoped so. She didn't want anyone else getting hurt because of her.

One of the men, tall and lean, spoke to Hale. "I'm Seth Hardin. Retired SEAL. You need anything from me, let me know."

"Thanks. I gotta stroll around. Keep your eye out for any unusual movement from above. Oh, and I may need your help chasing a couple of cats. Need to bring them in."

"Will do."

Hale eased away from the group, sure that the sniper would have to wait until the crowd spread out a bit. Breathing room. But not much.

He tried to look as if he were just wandering while he kept scanning elevations from second story up. Higher if the pro was farther away.

He hoped the balaclava made him unrecognizable if the pro knew who he was. Which had become more likely than not.

ALLIE'S NERVES STRETCHED tighter and she wondered if they would snap. Standing here with these brave people wasn't making her feel any braver.

The guy had to take his shot before he disappeared again. Had to. And Hale had to take him down.

She spoke. "I'm going to step away briefly. He's got to be able to start aiming."

Six faces eyed her with concern. Then the one called Seth nodded. "But don't move too far away. Don't make it too easy on him."

"I won't. Can't you tell I'm scared as the devil?"

Seth smiled. "You're hiding it pretty well. Welcome to the reality of courage."

"Meaning?"

"Courage isn't being unafraid. It's doing the dangerous thing *despite* the fear."

"I'd guess you'd know. All of you." She drew a deep breath. "Here I go."

Just a few steps, she assured herself. She doubted she could do any more than that in this damn armor anyway.

HALE COULD HAVE exploded when he saw what Allie was doing. He didn't know whether to admire her or get furious. Didn't matter. Right then he was filling with enough adrenaline that he was nearly past feeling anything at all.

He performed another quick scan, then saw a small, brief flash of light from the bell tower on the church. The rifle scope had caught just enough light to reflect it. Careless.

But it was the carelessness he needed. Adrenaline took over completely and he started running, unzipping and pulling a pistol from his left holster. Less than two hundred yards. A walk in the park. Seeing him, the sniper might already be packing up.

Reaching the church, Hale wrenched open the door and, still running, he headed for the spiral staircase. His own breaths sounded loud in his ears. Then he heard a gunshot from above. The sniper had picked out his target from the group.

Allie. God, Allie. His vision turned red with rage. Nothing could stop him now.

*Get him. Get him.* The words pounded as hard as his heart.

He tore open the door to the staircase and began running upward because there was no point in trying to be quiet. The guy had already taken his shot. He wouldn't be able to use his rifle on these narrow winding steps, walled on either side.

The hit man was now on the run but with nowhere to go. Because of the narrow stairway, the guy was probably waiting above in the bell ringers room, ready to shoot whoever was coming.

Hale knew one thing. If he opened the door above from the hinge side, the creep wouldn't be able to see him immediately. It should give Hale just enough time to get off the first shots.

IN THE SQUARE, Allie felt a punch in her chest. The pro had fired and the armor had protected her. She felt her knees start to shake. Would he fire again? Maybe she *should* collapse, pretending to be shot. Her throat clogged with terror as she waited for the next bullet.

PISTOL AT THE READY, Hale encountered the man in the bell ringers room, just as he'd anticipated. The man had his own pistol in his hand. At this point, the guy apparently didn't care about leaving tracks.

Hale didn't hesitate. He fired six shots in rapid succession. Center mass. The guy stumbled and fell, the pistol falling from his grip. The amount of blood that began pouring down the stairs told him the man was dead or would be in less than a minute.

He considered another shot to be sure, then waited. At last he was certain. Eliminated.

Allie heard the shots, amplified by the bell tower, and now did collapse onto the snow. She was immediately surrounded.

"Hale," she whispered. "Hale."

"I'm going," Seth said. Then he raced off in the same direction.

HALE STOOD AT the foot of the stairs, phone in hand, when Seth reached him. "Arrest me for murder. Later."

"Forget about it, man. What now?"

"Making a call. There are two goons out there and my contact better know exactly where."

"Yo," Stu answered the phone immediately.

"The exorcist is gone. Now give me the acolytes. You painted them?"

"Bright red. Ready?"

Hale looked at Seth. "I'm going to repeat some coordinates."

Seth nodded and took out his own satellite phone. "Shoot."

A few minutes later, he and Seth headed out in vehicles in slightly different directions. Hale didn't waste time checking on Allie or reassuring her. It was enough that he saw her and she saw him.

And he still *had* to collect the two security guards.

# Chapter Fifteen

An hour later, stripped of body armor and surrounded by her group of friends in the sheriff's office, friends who had risked their lives for her, she drank coffee that a deputy had brought from Maude's.

Hot, foamy, a perfect latte. Except she could hardly taste it. It was over, or almost so. She felt as if she might dissolve with relief. But she kept shaking. A reaction perhaps.

Hale must be okay, she reasoned. She'd seen him run with Seth to the vehicles out front. Both of them spun tires as they sped away.

They must be after the goons Hale had spoken about. The ones he wanted to question. The last bit. If they revealed enough, Ellis would be taken down. That should be enough to make her safe.

If she could ever feel safe again.

At last, Hale and Seth Hardin came through the door with two zip-cuffed men. Dalton was awaiting them.

Gage asked Hale, "You want to question them now or later?"

"Can you hold them for me? The questioning might take a while and I want to feed Allie, then take her to our room so she can unwind."

Gage nodded. "I can hold them, alright. Got two miserable jail cells upstairs. Maybe we'll start with stalking. I'm sure I'll be able to add more crimes. It appears six people saw someone shoot at Allie, so forget any charges against you. We'll find more."

"Like one of those goons taking a shot at Hale," Seth Hardin said. "Stupid move."

Hale squatted in front of Allie. "Let's go to Maude's. Or you can wait in the car while I get takeout. Either way, after all that adrenaline, we both need to eat."

Allie's only desire was to fall into his arms. The room sounded more inviting, but he was right about food. Especially for him.

"Takeout," was all she said.

"I GOT YOU a salad and a club sandwich," Hale said coaxingly. "Please try something, Allie. You have no idea how much energy you burned up this morning. I don't want you to get sick."

"In a minute," she answered. Her voice trembled and she sat on the edge of the bed without even pulling off her outerwear. "I'll be okay in a minute."

"I know you will. You're tough."

Then he sat down beside her and put his arm around her shoulders. He reached for the zipper on her jacket and pulled it down. "You're going to be hot soon. Let's get you out of some of this."

She didn't resist, even helped by standing up and tugging herself. At last she was in jeans, a sweatshirt and her socks, then sat on the bed again.

Hale rose, stripping his own jacket and snow pants, as well as his double holster.

"Look," he said, "I got us some lattes. Let's drink them before they get cold."

She accepted one, and realized she was coming back from the brink of the breakdown. Steadily returning to normal. "That was harrowing," she said, her voice stronger. "God, a movie has nothing on that."

"Not when it's real," he agreed. "Not when you're the one standing out there knowing you're a target."

"I was more worried about you," she told him flatly. "I was all covered up with armor and helped by friends. You were out there chasing a madman all by yourself."

"Nothing I haven't done before."

Her gaze finally lifted to his. "I know it isn't. How you could do it repeatedly is beyond me."

"Youth and belief in one's immortality."

At last she felt a smile begin on her lips. "That wasn't your excuse today." But she let the subject go as he insisted on bringing out the container with the club sandwich in it.

"Did your man find the traitor?"

"Yeah, he did. He told me when I called after taking down the goon. Guy's name is Dan. And he's been the reason our intelligence was so spotty."

"God, you must feel so betrayed."

He did, but Stu would handle that. Right then, Hale had more pressing concerns.

"Eat just a little," he said, placing the open container on the bedside table. Then he turned, reaching for the jacket he'd thrown over the chair, and pulled out a small crumpled paper bag. He returned to sit beside her.

"I know it isn't Christmas yet," he said huskily. "And I'm not in the habit of doing this, so call me awkward. But I bought you a Christmas present."

She gave a weak laugh, then took the bag from him. Opening it, she found a small black velvet box. Her breath caught. "Hale?"

"No big deal," he said. "The Mercantile isn't exactly overloaded with good stuff. But I thought you'd like this."

She took the box in both hands, then opened it slowly.

Again her breath caught. Inside was a silver butterfly, a small delicate one, on a silver chain. "It's beautiful," she breathed.

"The real thing, too. Not rhinestones."

"It wouldn't matter," she said honestly. "What a fabulous necklace! You're a surprising man, Hale Scribner."

"Yeah, I know I'm not the type, but I can learn."

Putting the velvet box aside, she twisted and threw her arms around him. "Thank you! Thank you!"

Somewhere between her first thank-you and her second, they wound up lying on the bed, face-to-face, tightly embracing.

"Your sandwich will get stale."

"Hang the sandwich," she answered, pulling him closer for a deep kiss. "I want you more."

## *Epilogue*

Two days later, days of wondrous lovemaking as far as Allie was concerned, Hale was content that he'd pried all the information he could from the two goons. He'd passed it all along to Max, promising the Conard County Sheriff's Department would be transferring them. Max sounded like he was over the moon, at least as much as a hard-boiled detective could be.

Allie spoke with Max for a while, even telling him about the armor and being shot at, but she concluded with the highest praise for Hale.

He felt embarrassed.

Then Max said, "Don't come back yet. I need to make sure this end is wrapped up tightly enough to protect Allie. And Allie? Do me a favor and don't get stubborn. Ellis doesn't quit easily."

Allie looked at Hale after she disconnected. "My life is still at risk? For heaven's sake!"

"Only briefly," he promised her. "We've got enough to take him down along with any cooperating henchmen. Once that's done, anyone remaining will be too afraid to continue this hunt. They'll see the cost."

"I hope you're right."

"I'm always right."

That pulled a laugh from her. "You're something else, Hale Scribner."

"I never lied to you. Anyway, I wouldn't mind a week or two here in your Christmas wonderland. It'll give us time to know each other better."

She pursed her lips. "Why would we want to do that, Mr. Tight Lips?"

It was his turn to smile. "How many names do you have for me?"

"Quite a few. Most of this trip I've had nothing better to do than think them up. You still haven't answered my question."

"Because," he answered slowly, as if to be sure she heard every word, "despite all my attempts to remain detached, I haven't succeeded. You're a fascinating, charming, stubborn thorn in my side. And oddly enough, Ms. Amazing, I think I'm slipping into love with you."

Allie caught her breath, her eyes widening. When she recovered her breath, she said, "Make it a fast slide, Hale. Because I'm already in love with you."

He hugged her close, as if he wanted never to let go. "Trust me, it's not going to take long. I'm mostly there. Now, want to take a walk through this over-Christmased place?"

She beamed. "I'll go anywhere with you."

"Almost," he corrected, then kissed her deeply.

"A new life," she murmured against his lips. "I think I'm going to like it."

\* \* \* \* \*

# COMING SOON!

We really hope you enjoyed reading this book.
If you're looking for more romance, be sure to
head to the shops when new books are
available on

# Thursday 1st December

To see which titles are coming soon, please visit

**millsandboon.co.uk/nextmonth**

# LET'S TALK
## *Romance*

For exclusive extracts, competitions
and special offers, find us online:

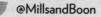 facebook.com/millsandboon

@MillsandBoon

@MillsandBoonUK

**Get in touch on 01413 063232**

For all the latest titles coming soon, visit
**millsandboon.co.uk/nextmonth**

# JOIN US ON SOCIAL MEDIA!

Stay up to date with our latest releases, author news and gossip, special offers and discounts, and all the behind-the-scenes action from Mills & Boon...

 millsandboon

 millsandboonuk

millsandboon

*It might just be true love...*

# MILLS & BOON

## *Desire*

Indulge in secrets and scandal, intense drama and plenty of sizzling hot action with powerful and passionate heroes who have it all: wealth, status, good looks…everything but the right woman.